My Mother's Daughter

For Dee –
I hope you enjoy
My Mother's Daughter
Betty

Rebecca Thaddeus

Rebecca Thaddeus

11 – 14 – 18

 Plain View Press   http://plainviewpress.net
1101 W. 34th Street, STE 404, Austin, TX 78705

Contents

My Mother's Daughter

Rebecca Thaddeus

ISBN: 978-1-63210-037-5
Library of Congress Control Number: 2018962419

Cover Art
Background image: *Mississippi River and Natchez under the Hill, as seen from the Bluffs, Natchez, Miss.*, Pub by T.N. Henderson, vintage postcard
Magnolia photo and Girl photo courtesy of pixabay.com creative commons
Cover Design by Pam Knight

Also by Rebecca Thaddeus
One Amber Bead

We Find Healing In Existing Reality

Plain View Press is a 40-year-old issue-based literary publishing house. Our books result from artistic collaboration between writers, artists, and editors. Over the years we have become a far-flung community of humane and highly creative activists whose energies bring humanitarian enlightenment and hope to individuals and communities grappling with the major issues of our time—peace, justice, the environment, education and gender.

*for the people of Natchez,
whose kindness and willingness to share
their city and its history were the inspiration
for My Mother's Daughter*

Part I—Eugenia—1789

Chapter One

The Mississippi River had cradled the boat carrying Eugenia Meier in its gentle swells all morning. The sun was hot, but not nearly as brutally stifling as it would be in an hour. Despite the bonnet she had fastened snugly under her chin, she would soon need to retreat to the lower deck of the keelboat to escape its strongest rays. Mama had warned her many times to guard her dove-white complexion from the sun so she would look her best on the blessed day when she would meet "her dearly beloved," the man God had chosen to be her spouse.

Eugenia hated to leave her spot on the bow of the keelboat where she could watch the world pass slowly by. Below deck would be steaming in the afternoon heat and humidity, and even lying very still on the cot in her tiny passenger's den would not save her from its intensity. Besides, she wanted to observe the changes in the riverbanks, where flatlands and cane fields were beginning to replace the heavy forest she had observed for so many days. Captain Kerry, the steersman of the keel, had told her that cultivated fields were a sure sign they were nearing Natchez, and she would know her new home by its high bluffs to the east, higher, he asserted, than any they had already encountered on the river.

She anticipated the end of her journey with both excitement and terror, not knowing whether she was escaping an increasingly intolerable situation or advancing foolishly into a worse one. Papa had begged her to reconsider her decision, to not let her quick temper and impetuousness be her guide. But she had been stubborn, another frailty of character she knew she needed to control, and she had said words she felt she could never take back.

"Nia, you still up here? Shan't you be gettin' out o' the sun?"

"Yes, Mrs. Monroe, very soon." Harriet Monroe, the only other female passenger on this trip, had, in some respects, stepped in for Nia's mother. But Nia was grateful for her presence; Papa would never have let her board the keelboat if there had not been at least one other woman making the journey. Mrs. Monroe was traveling all the way to New Orleans, a distance beyond Natchez, which made her an acceptable chaperone for Nia's entire journey.

"And what've you seen onshore this fine mornin', m'dear?"

"Mostly buffalo." The first sight of these massive creatures had entranced Nia. She'd seen cows and bulls during trips to the farmland outside of Philadelphia, but those farm animals hadn't the fearsome presence these beasts displayed. And their numbers: when she spotted a herd grazing on a patch of flat land or drinking from shallow river banks, she often hadn't nearly enough time to even begin to count them.

"And some deer," Nia continued. "A whole deer family, with Mama and Papa Deer guarding their three fawns as they splashed in the water. Just like little children."

"Ah seen that as well, even back home." Home for Mrs. Monroe was Kentucky. The wife and helpmate of a merchant who took household goods down the Mississippi to New Orleans several times a year, she had made this trip many times before. Her weathered complexion and gray hair, interspersed with signs of the sandy brown it had once been, seemed to Nia a testament to the hard life Mrs. Monroe had lived. The battered straw hat, men's boots and sack-like skirt she wore had even made Nia wonder, upon first sight of Mrs. Monroe, whether she was a woman or a man. It wasn't until Nia had heard her voice, its melodic tones and gentle lilt countering the harshness of her appearance, that Nia knew she was speaking with another woman.

"Ah 'magine animals like to have their fun, too," Mrs. Monroe smiled.

"No bears yet," Nia added, a bit of hope sounding in her voice.

"Oh, they's out there all right. They kin be kinda shy. You'll see one soon enough—jes hope it ain't one o' them times you don' wanna see one."

Mrs. Monroe had shared with Nia more than enough stories about what she would find in her new home. Alligators capable of grabbing small children and devouring them in one bite. Wild hogs with bodies as long as a grown man's height. And bears. Bears, she assured Nia, could tear down doors and enter homes. Nia, who shuddered at the sight of a mouse scurrying across the floor or a bat zig-zagging its way above her head, had not considered the fauna she would need to deal with in the Mississippi Territory.

"I did see two of the big birds with the long beaks flying downstream," she continued, hoping to turn the conversation toward more benevolent creatures.

"Blue or white?" Mrs. Monroe asked.

"Blue."

"Then them's herons. The smaller white ones is egrets."

Nia was, as always, amazed by Mrs. Monroe's knowledge of all things on the river, realizing that she, herself, would have a great deal to learn. Mama would doubt her daughter could learn anything worth knowing from a woman whose grammar she would consider contemptible, would even forbid her daughter from having any conversation with such a woman. But when Mrs. Monroe suggested again that she retire below, Nia acquiesced without any objection.

Getting up from the trunk that held all her belongings and now served as her chair, Nia waved at Davey, the youngest of the four oarsmen who skillfully directed the vessel on its journey. The Mississippi was a difficult passage—even she could see that. It meandered its way south, sometimes circling to almost the same spot it had traversed as many as twenty miles earlier. And the current varied constantly. This morning's passage was as gentle as a sailboat ride down the Schuylkill River; yesterday's had been a torrent of frightening eddies and whirlpools.

Her first sight of the keelboat moored peacefully in the busy Pittsburgh harbor had filled her with confidence. Almost eighty feet long, its rough sawn timbers looked sturdy enough to withstand an Atlantic crossing. It comprised three levels: the lowest section, which was mostly below the water level, was both the longest and deepest of the three and held the passengers' quarters as well as storage for supplies and cargo. A second level was set back about a quarter of the length of the boat, providing an open deck in the front where passengers could sit in good weather. This level was manned by the oarsmen and was topped by a much smaller platform from which the steersman could observe the river from a greater height. Passengers entered their quarters from the open space between the lowest level's deck and the second level.

The passage along the Ohio River had been relatively peaceful, with vistas of stately pine and hardwood forests visible on both banks. When the keelboat put in at a small French trading post at the junction of the two rivers and she realized she had actually arrived at the Mississippi River—the river that would mark the western border of her new home—her exhilaration was almost more than she could handle.

But nothing could have been more terrifying than their entrance into the Mississippi, which was the watery equivalent of a mountain range with cavernous valleys. Their small craft had bounced and bobbled in the violent current like a feather caught in a breeze. She'd feared her journey would end before it had hardly begun. The oarsmen had later assured her that what she had experienced was normal—they'd taken the boat safely through the perilous passage many times before. She trusted them, certainly a great deal more than she trusted her own wisdom in even beginning this journey. She worried that what lay at the end of her trip might be even more daunting.

Nia blamed her mother for pushing her into the perilous journey down the Mississippi River. She sometimes feared she acted impetuously, even foolishly. Still, she had made her decision, and she vowed to live by it. After all, she was a grown woman now, almost sixteen years old.

She was coursing down the Mississippi to meet the man who would be her guiding light, her master, the father of her children—her future husband.

Chapter Two

Papa was kind. Every man wanted a son, of course: a boy to follow in his footsteps and to carry his name into the future. And Papa had had two: Nicholas, who had never taken even one breath at birth, and Samuel, who had died of the consumption before reaching six years. Papa visited their graves frequently, never missing one of their birthdays or saint's days or any holiday the family celebrated.

But despite this burden of grief, Papa cherished his three girls, referring to them as his princesses. While Nia appreciated her father's praise, she grudgingly conceded her older sister Abigail's appearance was more princess-like than her own. She would have gladly traded her own straight, honey-blonde locks for Abby's crown of soft, sunny curls. And although she was often told her sapphire-colored eyes were her best feature, Nia wished she had been blessed with Abby's cornflower blue. She consoled herself by realizing she did not have to deal with her younger sister Emilia's bright red locks and freckles, but wished she could duplicate Mellie's endearing, saucy smile.

At other times, Papa would call his daughters his constellation. "There you are," he would say, pointing up at the sky on the summer evenings they'd spend sprawled on an old quilt in a public park to escape the heat of their small apartment. "Those three beautiful stars, with Vega at the crest. Those are my girls."

"And which of us is Vega?" Abby would always ask, tugging at his sleeve. As the oldest, she believed she should be considered first in all things, or at least that was Nia's opinion of her.

"Why, the one who loves Papa the most," he had always answered.

"Me! Me! Me!" Mellie and Nia would chime in unison, climbing on his lap. "I love Papa the most!" Papa would smile, hugging his daughters while kissing the tops of their heads. Yes, Papa was kind.

But Mama: that was another story. Mama seemed to wear every ache and pain, every disappointment, every slight, as a badge of honor. She was certain that the butcher saved for her only the worst cuts of meat, the pastor prayed less for her than for any of his other parishioners, and Mrs. Schultz, their next-door neighbor, spoke unkindly of her behind her back. She seemed to see her girls, or at least her younger daughters, as a burden and a trial, as small monsters who needed constant remonstrance and painful reminders to head them toward the path to civility.

Other women, like Mrs. Schultz, displayed their creativity in the wonderful repasts they made for their families, or, like Mrs. DeVille, the pastor's wife, in the beautiful quilts and dresses she crafted for the parish's many baptisms. But Mama's creativity was displayed in the punishments she designed for her daughters: in the pinches that were always delivered in the areas of their bodies where they would cause the most pain, or in such practices as requiring, for the most minor infractions of her many rules, an hour of gazing, arms held straight out at their sides, at the picture of Jesus displayed prominently over the dining room sideboard.

Many nights Nia and Mellie, who were supposed to be asleep, would lift the attic's trap door just a bit and cram together to listen to their parents' discussions. "Ah, Dorothea, don't you think you were a bit hard on our Nia this evening?" Papa would suggest. "You know her stomach is sensitive, and she was able to finish most of her dinner. Was the punishment really necessary?"

"It is your fault Nia is so ungrateful for what's been given to her. When I think of the times I went to bed without any dinner when I was her age—not because of any naughtiness on my part, you understand, but because there was no dinner to be had at our house that evening. Nia and Mellie should realize how very lucky they are. You spoil them, Nicholas. And I wouldn't have to be so hard on them if you were not so lenient yourself."

"But Dorothea, an hour of kneeling on rice. It must have been very painful: her poor knees were terribly pock-marked. And not finishing dinner hardly merits..."

"You do not understand! It is not about dinner. The girl is insolent and disobedient, and acts this way only to show her disdain for the rules of this household. Do you think you know more about the wickedness of young girls than I?"

At this point Papa would return to his copy of the *New England Courant*, choosing the path of least resistance. Yes, Papa was kind. And Mama was quite a different story.

Still, there were times when Nia appreciated her mother's parental attitude and understood why Mama acted the way she did. Nia understood, more than either of her sisters, how much their mother resented her lot in life. Mama was, after all, the daughter of a man who had made his mark in the community. Grandfather Samuel had begun his life as an itinerant salesman of household goods: thus the evenings when his family had gone without dinner. But through hard work and imagination, he had improved his station to become a successful merchant. Mama's later childhood had been filled with dances, shopping trips and summers at the family's lake cottage.

She had met Papa at a formal society ball. He was the handsome son of a wealthy banker, Nicholas Meier, and had always enjoyed the life of privilege and leisure to which she had just recently become accustomed. She had been delighted to be courted by such an outstanding beau. They married just months before Grandfather Nicholas' fortune collapsed when his bank suffered financial ruin during a recession. His subsequent suicide had robbed his children and grandchildren of any further advancement in society.

Papa had seemed to adapt to their lower station more gracefully than had Mama. His father-in-law had offered him a place as a salesman in his apothecary, but not wanting to become too beholden to his wife's family, he had secured a job as a minor administrator for the postal service. He worked very hard in this position, but it did not provide for Mama the place in society she believed she deserved, even though she had experienced its benefits for a relatively short time. It was no wonder that Mama was so disappointed in the direction her life had taken.

Chapter Three

"Wait until Mama hears. Nia, you're in trouble now!"

Nia looked at Mellie with scorn. Why was the child always such a trial, loving nothing better than being the bearer of bad news? Why did Mama insist she share the attic with a twelve-year old: after all, a spare room had become available in the apartment once Abby had married and moved into her husband's family home. Mama had told Nia she would have to earn the right to a room of her own, but Nia knew Abby had been the recipient of her own room when she was only ten. Surely Abby had done nothing remarkable enough by that young age to have earned such a prize.

"What are you talking about, Mellie? I haven't done anything wrong." Eugenia turned back to continue the task her sister had interrupted—giving her long hair its daily hundred strokes. Others had told her that her eyes, the clear blue of the sapphire in the one ring Mama had been able to keep, were her best feature. But she disagreed. She felt her honey-blonde hair was her best, and perhaps only, claim to beauty, and was determined to keep it looking beautiful.

"You did too. Benjamin saw you."

Mellie's best friend Benjamin—another little brat. But one with a very observant nature. This *could* mean trouble. "What did Benjamin see, or think he saw?" she asked, her brushing becoming harder while her voice suggested only the mildest interest in what her sister had to say.

"Oh, you'll know soon enough."

This *was* enough. Eugenia wanted nothing more than to wring her sister's scrawny little neck. Instead, turning quickly, she grabbed one of Mellie's pigtails and twisted it as hard as she could, ignoring the squeals coming out of the girl's piggish little mouth. "Tell me, you little monster, or I'll twist this pigtail right off your head."

"The swimming hole! Benjamin saw you at the swimming hole!"

17

This definitely meant trouble. Nia had been warned many times to avoid the swimming hole: Mama thought it unseemly for a fifteen-year-old girl to indulge in such activities. After all, Abby had abandoned such forms of childish entertainment by the time she was ten. But perhaps it wasn't too late to avoid another of her mother's tirades. Benjamin could generally be bribed. "Did Benjamin tell anyone else?" she asked, giving her sister's pigtail another, harder twist.

"I don't know," Mellie cried, frantically slapping at her sister, who expertly fended off the younger girl's desperate efforts. "Please stop. You're hurting me!"

"I'll hurt you more if Mama finds out about this," she warned, finally releasing Mellie with a quick push. "Drat! Why must I put up with you?"

"You cussed!" Mellie charged, moving quickly to the other side of the room as she rubbed the section of her scalp that had received the most damage.

"'Drat' isn't a cuss," Eugenia insisted. "'Damnation' is, and I'll make your life a course of endless damnation if Mama ever finds out that..."

"Eugenia Felicity Meier, come down here this very minute!" From the tone of her mother's voice, Nia knew she was doomed. She could imagine Mama standing at the landing of the back staircase, wooden spoon in hand, ready to administer the first of what was certain to be a sequence of admonishments.

"You'll pay for this!" she snarled at Mellie. "You already told!"

"I did not!" Mellie's stance, swaying slightly side to side, feet wide apart, hands behind her back, a wide grin on her face, convinced Eugenia she was right and infuriated her almost beyond bearing. But there was no way to retaliate right now.

Opening the bedroom door, she called out in as sweet a voice as she could muster, "Yes, Mama. I'm coming down right now."

Later that evening, banished to the attic until Papa came home, she fumed about the unfairness of her life. Abby was clearly Mama's favorite, even more so now, as she had married very well and was soon to make Mama a grandmother. Mellie, as the baby of the family, was allowed far more license than she herself had ever been given.

Nia hated almost everything about her life: the crowded apartment, the rules of ladylike behavior that Mama, despite their lowered station in society, expected her to follow, the praise Mama heaped upon her older sister and the indulgence she saw in the treatment of her younger sister.

But this evening she hated herself even more, once she saw the sadness in Papa's tired eyes as his head appeared in the trap door opening. When she saw him holding the paddle her mother used to beat the parlor carpet, she sincerely hoped she hadn't pushed too hard this time.

"Ah, Nia, Nia. What am I going to do with you?" he asked, seating himself next to her on the small bed she shared with Mellie.

"Papa, I didn't do anything wrong."

"Swimming? With the boys? At your age?"

"It was so hot, Papa. I was only in the water for a minute or two, and only stepped in up to my ankles," she lied, hoping the magnitude of her crime had not been fully explained to her mother. This version of the story was far from the truth, as she had hidden behind a tree to remove her homespun gown and bodice and had entered the water in only her shift. She had thoroughly enjoyed the coolness of the pond's water, wading in all the way up to her neck, and had left it with scarcely enough time to get home before dinner. "I'll never do it again," she promised, wiping tears from her eyes.

"You told your mother that you hadn't been anywhere near the pond and admitted it only once you knew you were caught. Surely by now you know that lying to your mother never works." The sadness in Papa's voice made Nia wonder whether he had learned through personal experience about her mother's ability to ferret out the truth.

"But Mama's so mean to me. She hates me. She never wants me to have any fun."

"She does not hate you. She is only trying to do what is best for you girls, even if it does not always seem that way. Some day you will be a mother yourself, and then you'll understand," he explained. "And your mother's lot in life has not been easy. Nia, you're almost a grown woman and will be leaving this house some day to make your own home. Can't you work harder to make your mother happy in the time you have left here?"

"I will, Papa. I promise," she answered, hoping his prediction about a coming change in her life would happen soon. She then looked warily at him as she realized the lecture was over.

"You know your mama sent me up here to punish you," he said gravely.

"I know. But I'm too old to be spanked like a little girl."

"I know that, but your mother doesn't. And you know she will expect to hear some noise from you."

Eugenia's small smile showed her relief. She and her father were to become co-conspirators once again. "You know I can do that, Papa," she answered as her father raised his hand to deliver the first of several blows to the quilt Grandmother Meier had made so many years earlier.

Nia had thought the "punishment" she received from Papa would end her mother's anger, but that was not to be the case. Somehow the incident of the swimming hole had brought their shared antagonism to the fore, with every snide criticism delivered by her mother matched by an angry glare from Nia that made her smoldering resentment all too apparent. She wondered if her mother lost sleep thinking of new tasks for her to do. Yesterday it had been wood for the kitchen. Mama had insisted Nia put down the novel she was reading, a Hannah Foster romance about life in a boarding school that was just beginning to become interesting, and bring in a pile from the woodshed.

"But Mama, that's Zeke's job." Zeke was the boy her mother hired to do some of the heavier household tasks.

"Now it is your job. Zeke has plenty to do here. It's time you start earning your keep."

Nia had spent most of the afternoon bringing in the heavy pieces of wood one by one, tossing each piece loudly into the wood bin before stomping back out to the yard, slamming the door behind her. She practically destroyed her favorite shirtwaist before thinking to put on an apron.

During Nia's fuming demonstration, her mother sat at the table darning stockings without a word or a glance at her daughter. Nia soon learned that weeding the garden, beating the carpets, and sweeping the sidewalk had become her new responsibilities as well.

Perhaps the worst blow was her mother's forbidding her to see friends or to attend any of the social functions she normally enjoyed. Mama always had an excuse: she needed Nia to run an errand, or to stay home with Mellie, or to assist her with some "urgent" task. She constantly berated Nia for her many, many failings, chief of which was her inability to find a beau. But how, Nia wondered, would she find such a person if she was constantly carding wool with her mother or running off to post a letter?

The only respite Nia had was the occasional visitor to their home. It was during an afternoon visit from her Aunt Eulalie and Cousin Clementine that she received the information that was soon to change her life.

She had never enjoyed Clementine's company, finding her cousin's bookishness and religious fervor almost unbearable. But this day loneliness and boredom had caused her to welcome Clem enthusiastically, inviting her up to the attic for an intimate chat after their tea. Clem, who loved gossip, told her about a girl at church who had been engaged to marry a Mr. Phineas Campbell, a wealthy plantation owner from the Mississippi Territory, but had reneged at the last minute. Nia didn't really know where Mississippi was, except that it was a southern territory far from Philadelphia. She asked how Clem's friend had met the gentleman.

"Oh, she never met him. Their engagement was arranged through letters."

"How romantic!" Nia responded enthusiastically. Her thoughts drifted back to the last afternoon she had spent in her grandfather Samuel's library, before her mother had clipped her wings. On the pretext of needing to review some of Paul's later epistles in the family Bible, she had instead searched out Grandfather's *Complete Shakespeare* and reread *Romeo and Juliet*, a play her parents would never have permitted her to read. She'd memorized her favorite lines from the play:

I love thee, I love but thee,
With a love that shall not die,
Till the sun grows cold,
And the stars grow old.

Perhaps Clem's friend had been won through words as romantic Shakespeare's.

"I think it is rather foolish," Clem replied, with a grimace so sour that it looked to Nia as though her cousin had just bitten into a spoiled turnip.

"But it's such a daring thing to do. And the name—Mississippi—wouldn't you want to know how a place with such a name would look?" Nia imagined warm, sandy beaches like the one she had seen the time her father, having legal business in Baltimore, had taken the whole family along for a short holiday. "It must certainly be more interesting than Philadelphia! Surely anyone would want to live there—or at least see it."

"Every wise woman builds her house; but the foolish plucks it down with her hands," said Clem.

"What?"

"*Proverbs.*"

Oh, that insufferable Clementine," Nia thought. "I really do not see what that Bible verse has to do with me."

"Be careful what you pluck," admonished Clem with a condescending grin that made Nia want to slap her.

As soon as Aunt Eulalie and Clem had departed, Nia hazarded to tell her mother about the long-distance engagement, but wasn't too surprised when she received a cutting response: "Hah! What a silly thing to do! Is that all you and your cousin have to talk about? " But it wasn't long before Mama's scathing criticism turned directly on Nia.

"Perhaps *you* should look into this, Dear," she said several days later. "You are not getting any younger: I was already married by the time I was your age. A proposal by mail might be your only hope of finding a beau!" This was accompanied by the contemptuous grin that was becoming far too familiar.

"Perhaps I shall!" she responded haughtily. She wondered why her mother so often criticized her in this way. Was she really so ugly that no one would ever want her as his wife? She knew she was not the family beauty: that would be Abby, with her pale blonde curls, heart-shaped face, and cornflower-blue eyes. It was no wonder Abby had easily attracted many beaus, finally settling on Benjamin Tyler, the son of one of the most prominent bankers in Philadelphia. They had married on the day Abby turned seventeen.

And Mellie, of course, as the youngest, was cute. The reddish tint in her pigtails and the freckles that sprinkled her nose did nothing to mar her attractiveness, particularly when she flashed her saucy smile.

But Nia liked to think that, although she didn't have the radiant beauty of her older sister or the bonny good looks of her younger, some day some wonderful young man would appreciate the quiet comeliness of her own face and form. Why couldn't her mother see that in her?

"Anything would be better than living here with you," she finally blurted out.

"'How sharper than a serpent's tooth is an ungrateful child.'" Nia had heard her mother quote this scripture passage frequently during the last couple of months. "Go up to your room immediately. Your father will hear about your insolence when he comes home."

But Nia had had enough. She responded by storming out the kitchen door into the street, determined to never enter their home again.

Chapter Four

"Looky there, Miss!" Davey McCoy was gesturing toward a point just above the bluff on the east side of the river.

"An egret?" Nia asked.

"No, Ma'am. That un's a ibis."

"How can you tell?" Nia was beginning to believe she'd never master the names of the many strange plants, birds, and animals she had seen on this trip, so many, and so different, than she'd known in Pennsylvania.

"Ibis is white like egrets, and they's both about the same size. But the diff'rence is in the beak. It's curved. Egrets got straight beaks." Davey, as had become customary during his late afternoon break, was visiting Nia for a few minutes before descending to the lower deck. Nia had learned that like the other five oarsmen, he worked four four-hour shifts every day, with two four-hour breaks for such things as eating and sleeping.

The keelboat would continue its journey downstream every moment of daylight, as well as during nights when it traversed areas of the river that were straight and serene. On these nights the lanterns, which were required by all night travelers, delighted Nia, who thought they looked like fairy lights bobbing merrily along the river's wide expanse. The oarsmen, of course, preferred nights when the river's course was too challenging and the boat had to put in on shore, or the rare occasions when the boat put in to make deliveries and purchase needed supplies at one of trading posts that appeared only infrequently. These few breaks from their routine were the only occasions when they were able to get any sustained rest.

"Gonna start seein' gators pretty soon now, Ma'am. That oughta' be purty excitin'."

Nia smiled at the boy, for a boy was what he certainly was. Davey, another "proud Kaintuck" like Mrs. Monroe, shared her sandy brown hair and weathered complexion to the extent that they could have been taken for mother and son. He was only fifteen, but the muscles on his upper arms, quite unusual on a boy with a body so slim, attested to the almost two years he had already served as an oarsman. Nia wondered how he managed such a difficult job at such a young age.

"It must be hard to take this boat upstream," she suggested. "I can't imagine how that could be done."

"Yes'm. 'Tis terrible work. But I only done it the one time. Mos' cap'ns break up the keel an' sell it fer lumber in N'Orleans, then take the Trace back up. That's what Cap'n Kerry's gonna do this trip."

"The Trace?"

"Oh, yes, Ma'am. You don' know 'bout the Trace? 'Tis a real wonder." Davey began to peer closely into the woods on the flat western shore.

"Then tell me about it," she said, a bit impatiently. Davey commonly stopped talking during the most interesting points of their conversations. She attributed this to the fact that he had little experience in social communication. He'd never attended school, had never learned to read or write. His whole education had been on the river. But the river was something he knew very, very well.

"The Trace's a pathway goin' all the way from Natchez to Nashborough. 'Twas a Injun path fer hun'erds of years, they say, an' a path fer buffalo and other animals too. Now folks mos'ly run their wares downstream in keelboats or flatboats—farm produce and tools an' such. Also pots 'n pans and other goods fer folks' homes, like we're doin' now. Then they use the Trace to go back home."

"Is the Trace a paved road?"

"Oh, no Ma'am. 'Tis sand and gravel at some parts, grass in t'others. Natchez is mos'ly sand and swamp-like, so's the pathway's wor' down so far 'tis almos' like a tunnel, what with trees growin' all the way across over the top. 'Tis somethin' to see, all right."

Nia could hardly imagine such a wonder.

"Bes' thing is in the summer," he continued. "All that shade makes it a sight cooler in the Trace. Folks go there to 'scape that Natchez heat. But Ma'am, if'n you don' mind my askin', what brings a lady like yourself to Natchez? 'Tis a place a great deal less civilized than whar you're comin' from."

Something in Davey's tone of voice made Nia wonder how long he had been waiting to ask that question. She wondered whether she should be insulted by the intimacy it suggested. No man in any parlor in Philadelphia would have been so forward as to ask a lady something so personal.

Then again, she wasn't in a parlor in Philadelphia—far from it. And she'd come to see Davey as a sweet young boy who would never do anything to insult her. She reminded herself she would have to adjust her ideas about what was socially acceptable to fit into the strange society she was about to enter. "Well, Davey, I'm going to Natchez to get married," she finally responded.

"Good fer you, Ma'am. I figgered a lady as purty as yerself might be marryin' someone soon. Didja know yer intended in Philadelphia?"

An even more intimate question. But she'd opened herself to such questioning by answering him the first time.

"No," she responded. "I haven't actually met Mr. Campbell, my fiancé. We've communicated only in letters." She lied, telling him that Mr. Campbell was a distant relative of her father's who had written to ask if he knew of a woman who might consent to move to Natchez to become his wife. Responding to the surprised look on Davey's face, she assured him this was becoming quite common; she'd heard that two other young women of her acquaintance had done the same thing. Some women were even heading south based solely on advertisements they'd responded to in local newspapers. "Mr. Campbell owns a plantation," she quickly added, hoping to forestall any further questions from him.

"Why, Ma'am, that's a purty plucky thing yer doin'! It shows a lotta gumption!"

Yet again, Nia wondered whether she should be insulted by Davey's words. But she sensed a lot of admiration in the boy's tone. And she had to admit that on her most hopeful days she too had considered her recent actions to be "purty plucky," to use Davey's terminology. "Pluck," after all, was not a vice.

But on other, darker days when the journey seemed endless and the riverbanks too isolated for human habitation, she had wondered if she'd be better off just jumping right into the rushing waters. She'd tried to stop those thoughts the minute she had them. After all, she could return to Philadelphia. But could she stand having to apologize to her mother, admit she was at fault, and once again live under her mother's roof?

Almost any fate would be better.

Chapter Five

Natchez was near. She could feel it in the stultifying heat, heavy with humidity, which blanketed the keelboat every morning. She could see it in the river banks: in the enchanting cypress forests draped with ribbons of Spanish moss, or in fields of sugar cane stretching for miles into the horizon. She could see it in the occasional alligator sunning itself onshore, and feel it in the swarms of mosquitoes that plagued her every evening, sending her flying below deck for some relief.

She could sense it in the crew, whose laughter, singing and giddy silliness signaled the end of a long journey. Mostly she could feel it in herself, in the mixed phases of exhilaration and trepidation she felt every time she thought of what she had done, and in the homesickness she had never, during her last few weeks in Philadelphia, believed she would suffer. She missed her father, of course, and at times her sisters. Abby's high airs and sense of superiority were only slightly less annoying than Mellie's childish antics. But still, they had at times enjoyed each others' company, playing at make-believe together or sharing the kinds of secrets and dreams only young girls have.

She remembered she was soon to become an aunt. Of course, Abby would write her once the baby was born: she would find out then whether she was aunt to a niece or a nephew. But she would likely not see the baby for a very long time.

At times she even missed her mother. She'd never expected that. Of course she'd had to return home after their argument, soon realizing there was no place else for her to go. Her mother continued to criticize her at every opportunity, calling her selfish, lazy and disobedient. Nia believed if she ever again heard Mama's favorite Bible verse about the serpent's tooth she would surely lose her mind. Her father tried to make peace between the two of them and assure Nia that she was loved. But she had become impervious to anything she heard from either of her parents, as though she were living in a universe apart from theirs.

She did manage a surreptitious trip to Clementine's home to obtain Mr. Campbell's address and then agonized for days composing the letter she finally sent him. His response resembled a legal contract more than anything she had ever read in Shakespeare. But she accepted his proposal, looking forward to springing the news of her engagement on her mother, hoping perhaps that Mama would suffer pangs of guilt and remorse and beg her to stay with promises of kinder behavior toward her. But more than anything she dreaded telling her father, knowing how much her desire to leave would hurt him.

Her mother's response was chilling. "Do whatever you please," she had said, stomping out of the room with a toss of her head. This, of course, did nothing to make Nia change her mind.

Her father's arguments and pleas did make her doubt the wisdom of her decision. "Nia, you cannot be serious about this. You know nothing about this man, or even the place where you would be living." He begged her not to let pride and stubbornness stand in the way of making peace with her mother, reminding her once again that in a short time she might have her own household, here in Philadelphia, near her family. But it was not enough to alter the course of action she'd initiated.

Papa had continued to make his case during their long stagecoach ride from Philadelphia to Pittsburgh, where she was to quit land travel and take passage on a flatboat sailing west on the Ohio River. From there she would board a keelboat on the Mississippi. She came close to changing her mind on the dock in Pittsburgh; seeing her father's tear-streaked face was almost more than she could bear. He had suddenly appeared much older—his beard and hair far more gray, his shoulders more stooped—than he had looked only weeks earlier. The realization that this parting might be the last time she would ever see him tore at her heart.

But board the flatboat she did.

"One more bend in the river, Ma'am, an' yer gonna be seein' yer new home," Davey informed her, his obvious excitement at the conclusion of this trip almost equaling her own. "I'd best get back to my post 'afore it's time to dock."

The previous night's sunset had been the most magnificent she'd ever seen, with a blazing scarlet sun over the west bank, at this point bare of any trees, turning the water a blood red, then amber, then, finally a deep, midnight blue. The air was so dense she wished she could sleep on the upper deck to catch the occasional bit of breeze. And this morning was beautiful. Hot of course: after all, it was the Mississippi Territory in August. But blessedly, the humidity had lessened, and everything on the water and on the banks looked fresh and crisp. Even the Spanish moss looked less menacing than it had the first time she had glimpsed it.

As they entered the bend in the river, Nia craned her neck, looking for the town that was soon to be her new home. She saw the point where the bluff first began to rise: a sheer, pale wall of sand, interspersed with the occasional scraggy brush or tree, gradually, and then suddenly, rising to a great height. Then, abruptly, it appeared: Natchez-Under-the-Hill, nestled at the base of the steepest, most majestic bluff Nia had seen on this trip.

Only a few cabins dotted the wide bank extending into the river, with a few more interspersed on sections of flat land visible on various levels of the bluff. Although she couldn't see a road, she assumed there must be one: she saw the outline of a swiftly moving wagon at about the center height of the bluff tilting downward in what looked to be a treacherous angle.

The river was wide at this point, and to the west the cultivated land past the sandy shore was flat with an occasional small shack almost hidden in the fields. Nia realized these must belong to the plantations that supported the Natchez economy.

"What d'you think o' yer new home?" asked Mrs. Monroe as she emerged from the lower deck.

Nia didn't quite know how to respond. "It's... it's... well, not what I expected."

"Ye've only seen a part o' it. Most o' the town's upward on top o' the bluff. Are ye lookin' for'ard to meetin' yer Mr. Campbell?"

All Nia could manage as a response to Mrs. Monroe's question was a shrug. Mrs. Monroe's smile, surely meant to comfort Nia in her distress, told her that her friend understood her feelings perfectly.

But her first sight of Natchez had given Nia no reason for enthusiasm. It looked so small, so backward and rustic compared to Philadelphia. She determined to overcome her feelings: after all, she had not yet seen most of the town. Besides, she needed to see to her baggage. Already the oarsmen were expertly steering the craft toward a weathered pier, while the steersman stood at the bow signaling directions and Davey and the other off-duty oarsman were pulling up barrels and boxes from the lower deck.

As they approached the pier, Nia carefully scrutinized the four men standing there, wondering which of them might be Mr. Campbell. Certainly not the old fellow in the tattered buckskin who leaned heavily on a gnarled wooden cane, spitting tobacco juice into the water. Or the boy in the straw hat who looked only a year or two older than Davey. *He must be one of the other two,* she surmised, hoping that he was the tall, handsome young man in the black breeches and tan cutaway coat that perfectly matched his fashionable waistcoat. That gentleman looked like the epitome of the successful plantation owner.

Of course, it could be the older man in the dark breeches, waistcoat and white shirt. This man's tousled reddish hair and round spectacles made him look more like a storekeeper or clerk—but then again, she was making judgments based on Philadelphia standards. And no Philadelphia standards could have explained the two young women standing on the pier, whose garishly painted lips and eyelids, brightly colored gowns cut low at the bosom, and hair a vivid blonde shade Nia had never before encountered, made her wonder what, exactly, they were seeking from the boat. Perhaps their high-pitched laughter as they waved coquettishly to the oarsmen was explanation enough.

"D'ye see yer' Mr. Campbell?" Davey asked, wheeling a barrel toward the gangway.

"I don't really know."

"Well, did'yer get a description o' him with any o' them letters?"

Nia felt uncomfortable telling Davey that there had been only two letters—the first with his proposal and the second containing the passage for her journey. He had neglected to give her any explicit description of himself.

"Don' worry, Ma'am. Ah'll ask the gen'lemen which o' 'em is Mr. Phineas Campbell soon as we're docked," Davey offered. Within a few minutes, a sharp bump told Nia the boat had made contact with the pier—her journey was over.

Chapter Six

Davey, true to his word, jumped onto the pier and began questioning the men standing there the moment the steersman completed mooring the keel. He soon began leading the young man in the tan coat toward the gangway. Nia, sighing with relief, summoned what she hoped was her most attractive, most confident smile and pinched the sides of her skirt to execute a graceful curtsey. *Should I speak first?* she wondered, then decided to defer to Mr. Campbell—no reason to appear too forward from the very beginning.

"Miss Eugenie, this here's Mr. Boone," Davey blurted out, saving Nia the embarrassment of a too-friendly greeting. It could not stop her deflated look as she quickly scanned the men remaining on the dock. "Mr. Campbell ain't any o' them other three," Davey quickly continued, seeing the concerned look on Nia's face, "but Mr. Boone here might be able to help."

Introductions were terse. Mr. Boone told her that he did not know a Phineas Campbell, but added, pointing to the log cabin closest to the pier, that a Mr. Finn Campbell was, at that moment, present at the Kings' Tavern. He offered to take her there. Not knowing what else to do, she accepted his offer and, after sharing a quick good-bye with Davey, who did not seem at all pleased with the whole situation, followed Mr. Boone to the tavern. She had to admit that she, too, wasn't very pleased. Why wasn't her fiancé there at the dock to greet her? Why did she need to go looking for him?

"After you," Mr. Boone offered, opening the door, which released the sound of a piano playing some loud, raucous tune accompanied by much chatter and hearty laughter.

"Thank you, Mr. Boone, but I'll just wait here," she responded, retreating to a wicker chair on the long covered porch which extended beyond the length of the building itself. "Would you please ask Mr. Campbell to meet me here?"

Retrieving a handkerchief from her pocket the moment Mr. Boone disappeared through the door and into the din, she carefully patted her eyelids and pinched her cheeks, then began practically shredding the daintily embroidered cloth to bits. When he'd not returned after a few minutes, she started looking around, darting a quick glance at the tavern door every few seconds.

The tavern was a simple two-story log cabin perched above a high stone base that gave her a good view of the few other buildings in this part of town, which were situated at various elevations on the cliff and were all built in the same style and materials. As she had guessed while still on the keelboat, Natchez-Under-the-Hill was built along the length of its single dirt road which followed the curve of the river bank before rising precipitously up the bluff.

Despite its humble appearance, this part of Natchez was a flurry of activity. Wagons, horsemen, and pedestrians bustled about the pier. The only women to be seen were the two she had noticed earlier, their bright red and purple gowns standing out among the men's standard brown and black garb, who were now walking arm-in-arm with Davey and another of the oarsmen. Nia wondered how people could move about so energetically in the intense heat, which had already drenched her heavy linen gown with perspiration.

Finally the tavern door opened and a man, perhaps twenty-five years old, stepped onto the porch and immediately headed toward her. He was tall, surely over six feet, and dressed in buckskin trousers, a full white shirt with sleeves ruffled at the wrists, and a fringed vest, all of which accentuated his slim but muscular build. His hair, straight and black, was worn long and gathered at the nape of his neck with a thin strip of rawhide. His complexion, darker than she had expected of a Scotsman, had a slight bronze tint which suited him well. Deep-set, almost black eyes, a prominent, straight nose, and full lips parted in a friendly smile made him, she believed, the most handsome man she had ever seen.

He extended a hand to her in greeting. "You must be Miss Eugenia," he smiled.

"Mr. Campbell?" she questioned, sincerely hoping that this young man was the one she had come all this way to meet.

"Please call me Finn," he responded, taking her hand in his. "Everyone does. Was your passage down the Mississippi enjoyable?" Bowing slightly, he pressed her hand warmly in both of his, and although his grip was light, she could feel his strength. *Finn*, she mused, thinking he had welcomed her with a singularly informal greeting considering the circumstances. But she liked the informality. In fact, she liked everything she had seen of him and heard from him so far.

"Yes, quite enjoyable, thank you," she said, favoring him with her best smile and immediately forgiving him for any neglect he had shown by not meeting her at the pier. After all, a young man who was already a successful planter must have a great deal to do: he had probably been engaged in an important business transaction. Even in Philadelphia, business was frequently transacted in public houses.

"Let's see about your baggage." There was so much to see on their short walk to the pier: the weathered buildings of Natchez; the bluff towering mightily above the town, the Mississippi, peaceful this morning, sunlight glittering wherever it hit a small swell or wave. But all Nia wished to look at this morning was the young man by her side.

As they rounded the curve leading to the top of the bluff with her one trunk carefully secured in the bed of the buckboard, Nia wondered how the horse was ever going to make it up the steep grade. Already the mare, whose name Finn had told her was Nelly, had slowed her gait, and Nia could hear her wheezing heavily as she pulled against her harness. Finn, handing Nia the reins with a polite "Can you handle this, Ma'am?" jumped down from the seat and, grabbing the mare's harness, began to guide her steadily forward.

"Shall I jump down, too?" Nia asked.

"No, Ma'am. You stay on board. Nelly can handle this. She's already done it dozens of times."

"You're very good with her."

"Thank you. I handle all the horses on the farm. You just sit tight and don't worry. We'll be safely at the top of the bluff in just a few minutes."

Nia wondered for a moment why he had not hired someone to look after his horses, but looking at Finn's bounding energy and obvious skill in handling the mare, she surmised this was a task he had undertaken for his own pleasure. She liked that about him: successful men in Philadelphia frequently considered themselves too important to take on any form of physical labor. Besides, she enjoyed watching Finn as he worked, enjoyed seeing his long, purposeful stride and the subtle motion of muscle beneath his shirt and vest.

Relaxing in her seat as much as the bumpy road would allow, Nia had the opportunity to take in the beauty that surrounded her. Already she could see the roof of every one of the buildings in town, their chimneys standing idle in the summer heat. Below them was the road—Silver Street, Finn had informed her. The people walking it appearing more and more as tiny, doll-like figures the higher the wagon rose onto the bluff. Across the river the land was flat and green, and she could count only three small buildings among the cane fields.

The river, of course, was the most magnificent sight of all, its wide expanse stretching far off into the horizon, its royal blue waters sparkling in the morning sun. If she craned her neck to her right she could see two keelboats, both smaller than the one she had left only hours earlier, turning the bend on their way to the town. Natchez did seem to be a busy place.

As they crested the bluff, Nia could finally see the remainder, and by far the larger part of Natchez. They first entered a wide, beautifully maintained plaza extending along the river almost as far as she could see. Near the precipice of the bluff, benches set under a row of shade trees offered an outstanding view of the river far below.

To her left she could see the town proper, its streets laid out in a grid pattern surrounding a church and its spacious plaza. The houses, most of which were of brick construction, were large and beautifully set in gardens surrounded by intricately designed wrought iron fences. These gardens were landscaped with trees and brightly colored floral arrangements. Nia was stunned at the difference between the Natchez she had first seen under the bluff and this lush, prosperous area.

"What is that up ahead?" she asked, pointing at a cluster of buildings, far in the distance at the highest point of the bluff, as their buckboard slowly made its way through the plaza.

"That's Fort Panmure, or at least that's what the British called it. Some folks still call it Fort Rosalie from when Natchez was owned by the French. The Spanish don't use it much—they're building a new fort in Vicksburg."

"Natchez belongs to the Spanish?"

"Well, Ma'am, we keep hearin' that a treaty was signed that makes Natchez belong to the United States, but the Spanish are still here, so we don't rightly know who we belong to."

"Doesn't this bother people?" Nia asked. Philadelphia had been a hotbed of political thought and action as long as she had lived there, and particularly more so once the revolutionists had defeated the British. Papa had spent many evenings in their parlor arguing with his friends about the direction the new country should take.

"Well, Ma'am, people here are too busy makin' a living and holdin' off the Indians. Besides, folks in Natchez come from all over—French, Spanish, English, Dutch, Scots. They all have different loyalties."

By this time they were traveling up Front Street, and Nia was awed at the splendor of the homes, actually mansions, surroundeding her. Excited at the thought that soon Finn might be stopping at one of these wondrous buildings, telling her this was to be her new home, she contemplated which it might be. Perhaps the red brick mansion with four stately white pillars and a wide second floor balcony, its stone walkway framed by two massive black trees whose tangled limbs met each other to form a grand canopy. The limbs of these trees reminded her of a swarming mass of water moccasins she had seen off the side of the keelboat during her trip.

Or it might be the home where only the full covered porch could be seen, the rest of the house being hidden behind huge trees dripping Spanish moss almost down to the manicured lawn. Or the two-story, all-white mansion, its lack of ornate landscaping probably designed to showcase the matching curved staircases leading from the front balcony to the first floor porch.

Front Street itself was lined by a chain of trees with curiously mottled trunks, their branches abounding with masses of large, fragrant pink and purple blossoms. Many homes also held single specimens or small groupings of these trees within their fenced yards.

"What kind of trees are these, Finn?" she asked, pointing to a tree that was particularly well-laden with bright pink blooms. "We don't have them in Philadelphia."

"The ones with the flowers? Those are crepe myrtles," he answered. "Pretty, ain't they?"

"And the others? The tall ones with the twiney limbs?"

"Oh, Ma'am, those are live oaks. You're gonna see plenty of them here. And the big ones, like those over there with the Spanish moss all over them, are cypress."

Nia was impressed by his knowledge. She was impressed by his skill at navigating the wagon through the narrow streets of the town. In fact, she was impressed by everything she had seen of Natchez, and of Finn Campbell, so far. Bending forward slightly, she peeked at him past the wide brim of her bonnet and said with a smile, "Finn, please call me Nia."

"Well, thank you, Ma'am—I mean Nia. Seems only right, seeing as we're gonna be family, so to speak."

Nia tried to stifle a laugh. *So to speak?* These Southerners certainly had a quaint way of using the English language. But she found it charming. Her smile broadened when she saw him smiling at her as well.

They were soon leaving the city and heading into a flatland meadow; Nia could see a deeply forested area ahead. As impressive as Natchez was, it appeared to be very small, consisting of only five or six streets each at right angles to or parallel to the river. As it became apparent they were heading directly toward the forest, Nia thought she might have been mistaken; perhaps the town continued beyond this large stand of trees. "Are we very far from the plantation?" she asked.

"About ten miles," he answered.

"Natchez is that big a city?" she asked.

"Oh, no," he laughed. "We already seen all there is of Natchez. The plantation's about halfway between Natchez and Rocky Springs.

"Rocky Springs?"

"Yep. Rocky Springs is a stopping place for travelers. The Springs is real pretty, with water falling from where the creek runs over a wide, flat rock into a deeper basin below. Folks like to water their horses and refresh themselves a bit at the springs."

"But how do we get to the plantation?" she asked, gazing at the expanse of forest looming ever larger the closer they came to it. She couldn't imagine navigating a buckboard through the density of this forest.

"On the Trace, Ma'am... I mean Nia. If you look real close a bit to the right... yep, that way," he explained, watching her bend forward and peer in the direction he was pointing, "you can just see that little space opening up. That's the Trace."

"Oh yes, the Trace. Davey was telling me all about that."

"Davey? Who's Davey?"

"Just one of the oarsmen on the keelboat."

"Better be careful who you talk to, Nia," he warned, looking at her closely. "There's some mighty bad men hereabouts."

"Oh, Davey was just a boy," she laughed. "He was entirely harmless."

"Well, you never do know." The memory of Davey walking arm-in-arm with one of Natchez's fancy women suddenly flashed before her. Perhaps Finn was right. But what most interested her was Finn's reaction. Was he jealous? She had never before experienced a man's jealousy as it pertained to her. She soon decided that, on the whole, she rather enjoyed the thought that, so early in their engagement, her fiancé was already seeing her as his, and his alone.

They rode on silently until they reached the forest's edge. Only then did she see the opening, the Trace, before them. Soon the wagon was enveloped by trees, not only on either side, where tree trunks stood sentinel in a dense blur of brown and green, but also in a lush canopy of green leaves above them. She felt the temperature drop immediately.

"This is amazing," she said. "It's like entering a tunnel."

"Well, a mighty long one. But it's not all tunnel—some of the Trace is grasslands and some swamp. It goes all the way to Fort Nashborough, or I guess they're calling it Nashville these days." Finn recounted the story of the Trace much as Davey had told it, but actually seeing it made its long history come alive for Nia. She could imagine thousands of animals using the path, perhaps being chased by bands of Indians on horseback. And Kaintucks like Davey making their way back home. "If you think this looks like a tunnel, wait a bit and you'll be in an even deeper one."

Nia noticed then that the farther they went, the deeper the groove in which the path was laid became. Soon the path was two feet, then four, then at least five feet deeper than the forest floor. Now instead of trees she saw veritable walls of sandy soil on either side of the wagon. Tree roots could be seen trailing down along the sand bank, and the lower portions of the trees' trunks could be viewed only by looking up.

The temperature became even cooler and sounds became more and more faint the farther they drove. Eventually, the Trace was so quiet and still that Nia could imagine that she and Finn were the only souls left on earth.

"I could never imagine..." But Nia was at a loss for words, a situation in which she had previously found herself only rarely.

"Yep, the Trace is a mighty fine sight to see. But it ain't for the fearful. There's lots of dangerous folks using the Trace every day."

"Indians?"

"Well, yes. Indians. But robbers and murderers of all kinds. There's folks on the Trace who'd just as soon kill a person as look at him. But don't you worry, Nia," he added, perhaps in response to the stricken look on her face. "I'm a good shot, and I got a mighty fine firearm back there in the wagon."

Nia beamed at Finn, wondering whether it would be too forward to wrap her arm around his. She already saw him as her protector, and was excited about the thought of beginning their life together: building a home, starting a family.

Besides," he added, "I promised Pa I'd take good care of you."

"Pa?"

"Yep. Pa couldn't come to town today. But I told him not to worry—that I'd be sure his new bride got home safely."

Chapter Seven

It took Finn perhaps fifteen minutes to realize his pleasant dialogue with Nia had become a monologue. During this time he had chatted on about the farm, telling her his father owned several hundred acres with twenty slaves, a small herd of cattle, six horses, some pigs, and a passel of chickens. They raised most of their own vegetables and hunted for much of their meat: there were plenty of deer and turkeys in the forest, and the flatlands were full of buffalo. There was also plenty of seafood to be had: bass, perch and carp in the streams and lakes and blue crab along the shores.

He informed her that most of the property was planted in sugar cane, but Pa was thinking about turning some of the land over to tobacco or cotton. Raising cotton was becoming more lucrative now that steam power could be used to manufacture fabric. Folks also talked about what else steam might power: some even thought that one day steam-powered boats would make their way up and down the Mississippi, but he could not believe it was really ever going to happen. "So what do you think, Nia? Ever gonna be steam boats on the Mississippi? It would sure make the trip to Nashville easier."

After waiting about thirty seconds for her response, he looked closely at her face. "Are you all right?" he asked. "You look a little peaked."

"Oh, no. I'm fine," she quickly answered. "Just a little tired from the heat." Lost in the dense fog of her own thoughts, she had stopped listening to Finn's soliloquy several minutes earlier. *Pa. How old would Pa be?* she wondered. *Finn might be, oh, maybe twenty-five? That would make "Pa" forty-five, maybe fifty? Close to my father's age, anyway.*

"Probably the heat," he agreed. "Miss Hetty's lived on the farm for over five years, and she still gets the vapors when it gets too hot."

"Miss Hetty?" The tapping against her temples that had begun five minutes earlier was now becoming the beating of a drum. Soon she'd have a blinding headache.

"Yep. Pa's sister. She moved here from Baltimore after their parents died. Been a maiden lady all her life. She's in charge of the house—works with the kitchen help and all. Things got a lot more orderly once she got here."

"Oh." So, Nia pondered, *I won't even be in charge of my own home. I'll have to deal with an "orderly" old maid who's been in charge for five years.* She wished she could ask Finn to turn the wagon around and take her back to Natchez. Maybe the keelboat was still there. But then what? Go on to New Orleans? To do what? Become a fancy lady herself? That such a thought had entered her mind, even for a moment, was startling.

She considered a bit more seriously the possibility of joining the keelboat crew to New Orleans, then finding someone to take her up the Trace to Nashville and making her way, somehow, back to Pennsylvania. But upon further consideration she realized leaving was impossible, at least until she had seen the plantation and met the real Phineas Campbell. Perhaps he wouldn't be pleased with her and would offer to pay to send her back home. "How much longer will it be before we get there?" she finally asked.

"A couple of hours. We'll get there around supper time. Miss Hetty said she'd make catfish for dinner, kind of like a celebration. She ain't a great cook, but I've known worse."

Celebration. Nia felt anything but celebratory at this moment. They were currently traveling in a swampy area of tall grasses and cypress trees dripping with ominous-appearing Spanish moss. Nia could imagine its spindly tendrils reaching out for her, smothering her in a moist, fetid, lethal embrace. She almost wished it would.

"Nia, wake up. We're nearly there."

Thank God. It was only a dream. But before she could respond to the voice that she thought for just a moment was her father's, she opened her eyes and realized she was still in the buckboard, now jolting along a narrow path through a forest of tall, thick grasses reaching at least ten feet high.

"Is this grassland?" she asked, straightening out in the seat and rubbing her eyes. Her headache had receded, at least to some small extent. She could not believe she had been able to sleep on the rocking, bucking wagon.

"Nope. Cane fields. You can tell we're getting pretty close to harvest—the stalks are brown almost to the top of the stacks." Nia now realized what surrounded them was actually an arrangement of tight rows of single plants, their sandy colored stalks topped by about two feet of wide blades of a glossy green. "These are Pa's cane fields," he added. "You'll be able to see the plantation once we make that bend up ahead."

Taking a deep breath, Nia straightened her bonnet and tried to press out the wrinkles in her skirt with the palms of her hands. No sense looking slovenly for her first meeting with Phineas Campbell, even if at this moment she thought she might want nothing more from him than passage back to Pennsylvania. Still, her sense of adventure had been rekindled, if just a bit, by her nap; she resolved to be at least open-minded about the situation she had placed herself in, to not give up until she had given the Mississippi Territory, and Phineas Campbell, a chance. Turning her head away from Finn's view, she pinched her cheeks to bring out a bit of color.

"There!" he said, sounding triumphant as they rounded the bend.

Nia had to admit what she saw in the distance looked promising. A wide, neatly cropped field lay in a shallow valley nearly circled by cane fields, with only a small patch of forested area to the right.

Several massive cypress trees, their lower branches reaching outward just a few feet from the ground, dotted the field. They, too, were garnished with the ubiquitous Spanish moss.

She could count six buildings, all cabins constructed of wide wooden slabs of the same weathered gray, all connected by a winding gravel path. The two cabins farthest from her, those closest to the cane fields, had covered front porches, their roofs supported by planks of similarly weathered wood. Nia thought those might be the slave quarters, although there were no people to be seen.

They seemed to be heading toward the largest building, which was situated on the highest elevation of the valley. Three sets of stone steps led to its wide roofed porch. This building, though constructed of the same gray weathered slabs, was mounted on short stumps that lifted it perhaps a foot above the ground. It sported two chimneys as well as a massive, blooming crepe myrtle to its right. Nia thought it might be Finn's home. Or even better, she hoped it might belong to Aunt Hetty.

To Nia, the whole scene resembled the perfect portrait of pastoral charm she'd admired in a watercolor painting that hung in her parents' bedroom. It looked peaceful. Serene. Even welcoming. "Where are the workers?" she asked, unable as yet to say the word "slaves" out loud.

There were slaves in Pennsylvania, of course, but most people in her home state were proud they were the first in the country to take steps to abolish slavery. A law passed in 1780 had prohibited bringing more slaves into the state and required annual registration of all slaves. Slave owners who refused to comply were forced to free their slaves, and all children born in Pennsylvania after 1780, whether black or white, were to be considered free.

"Working in the fields," Finn answered.

"In this heat?"

Finn barely stifled a laugh but did not respond to Nia's question, making her wonder how he could have so little concern for the workers. Her parents, both strong abolitionists, exalted in knowing that once the current generation of slaves had passed away, Pennsylvania would be free of the curse of slavery. One of her father's strongest arguments against her leaving, and one that had at one point almost changed her mind, was that in the Mississippi Territory she would be living within the scope of this evil system. But she had convinced herself the people of the Mississippi Territory would surely realize they, too, needed to abandon slavery as well. She hoped that would happen soon.

Thoughts of the evil of slavery left her mind as Finn pulled Nelly up at the stairs leading to the building. "Well, here we are," he said. Nia, craning her neck, wondered why they were stopping here and where the mansion might be. Perhaps, she thought, it might be behind that patch of forest to her right, or it might still be some distance away, although she did not see any other road leading either toward the forest or in a different direction.

But as soon as Finn jumped down from the seat and began loosening the straps securing her trunk, she understood. This squat, gray building was her new home.

Chapter Eight

"You can leave that trunk right there." Nia's first thought upon seeing Miss Hetty was that she hoped the woman was Phineas Campbell's much older sister. Tall and scarecrow thin, Hetty was dressed in a severe, shapeless black gown, many years out-of-date, covered almost entirely by a faded and frayed bib apron. Small wisps of gray hair protruded under her starched white cap. No adornment of any sort accompanied this somber outfit, although the grimace on her face was itself a fitting accompaniment.

"Yes, Ma'am," Finn responded, pushing the trunk toward the entrance to the cabin, then tipping his head in a small salute to Nia as he turned and quickly started walking back down the stairs.

"Finn, I..." Nia responded to his turned back, wondering why he had not introduced her to his aunt, who had not greeted him at all. She had hoped he would remain for a while to help smooth her way with his family.

"Never mind him, Child," the woman insisted. "Here, help me with this trunk." Together they pushed it over the threshold leading into what was, Nia thought, meant to be the parlor. This was a small room of mortared wooden planks containing a large horsehair sofa, a rough-hewn pine table and two spindle chairs. Its redeeming features were a large stone fireplace and a planked wooden floor covered for the most part by the largest bearskin rug Nia had ever seen. "Leave the trunk right there," she continued. "We can get Leander to move it later."

"Miss Hetty... " she began, but was quickly interrupted.

"Oh, you can call me Aunt Hetty, Eugenia, seeing as how we're going to be related." This offer was accompanied by a strained smile that suggested Aunt Hetty expected nothing favorable from their new relationship. Nia thought she preferred the woman's earlier grim demeanor, which at least looked more genuine.

"Thank you, Aunt Hetty. Is Mr. Campbell here?"

"He'll be here later this evening. He's at an auction in Mount Locust— looking to buy a new field hand and a house slave. Can't say that I know why he needs more house help—I been handling the household for over five years. But I imagine he figures you'll need someone, what with the wedding coming up and all." Hetty did not seem to notice the way Nia cringed at the word "wedding." "Well, come on in and take off your bonnet and sit down," she continued with a shrug. "You must be thirsty from the trip." With this Hetty exited the room from a back door, which Nia surmised must lead to a separate room behind the main house that served as the kitchen.

She took the opportunity to look more carefully around her. The most noticeable thing about the room was its complete lack of any adornment whatsoever. No pictures graced the walls. No knickknacks decorated the table or fireplace mantel. No bit of bright fabric in the form of curtains, seat cushions, or a tablecloth brought any color into the room. Apparently Aunt Hetty was consistent in her sense of style: her home decoration mirrored her choice of apparel.

Soon Hetty returned with a chipped pottery cup full of water, which Nia was pleased to find was both cool and sweet. She drank it greedily. "'Tis a pity you had to come all the way from Natchez with that filthy halfbreed," Hetty remarked, taking the cup from Nia but not offering her another drink, "but it couldn't be helped. I can't believe that Phineas would even let him in the house before I came."

"Do you mean Finn?" Nia was completely taken aback by Hetty's remark about her nephew.

"Well, of course. He's the one that brought you, isn't he?"

"I must be mistaken," Nia responded, "but I thought he was Mr. Campbell's son."

"Well, yes," Hetty harrumphed. "He is that. But don't hold that against Phineas. When he came here there were no white women in Natchez . A man's got his needs, you know."

Nia blushed. No one in Philadelphia would have spoken so openly about this subject, at least not with someone who was not an intimate friend. "So, Finn's mother was an Indian," she finally responded, realizing this explained his rugged looks and bronze skin.

"Yes. And a real piece of work she was. Claimed she was Indian royalty—imagine that! She was nothing but a dirty little slattern who caught my brother's eye. She hightailed it out of here when Finn was just a boy. Went to live with her own people, I heard, at least what's left of them."

"What's left of them?"

"She was a Natchez—the tribe that lived here before the region got civilized. The French wiped most of them out over sixty years ago after those heathens massacred their French colony. There's still a few Natchez left in these parts, but don't worry. They're pretty quiet these days. They keep to themselves outside of town and don't cause any trouble with the settlers, except maybe when one of their men gets drunk and causes a fuss in town."

"So Finn lives with his mother?"

"No, Phineas keeps him on the property pretty much. Finn's good with the horses and sometimes oversees the slaves when they're in the fields. You won't need to have anything to do with him. Like I said, he's not even allowed in the house now that I'm here. But don't worry. Even though my brother lets that savage call him Pa, it's not like he's Phineas' real son and heir—that'll be your boy, once he's born."

Nia had managed to retreat to her room after another hour spent in Aunt Hetty's presence. She had hoped to nap; anything would be better than dealing with the whirlwind of thoughts cluttering her mind, making focused thinking impossible.

She had learned more from Aunt Hetty during that hour. That, for modesty's sake and to forestall gossip, Phineas would be staying nights at a neighboring plantation during the time of their engagement. That he planned a very short engagement. That she had been brought here to perform two duties: to establish a tone of propriety in their household, and to provide an heir as soon as possible.

She also found she had a great deal to learn about working with black servants. Hetty had called Leander, an elderly black man whose days in the cane fields were over and who now worked mostly in the house and its adjoining gardens, to move her trunk into the bedroom. Although his advanced age obviously made the task difficult for him, Aunt Hetty admonished her sternly when she tried to help.

"You leave that be, Child. That's Leander's job to do."

"But he's gasping..."

"Hush now. If you're going to live here, you're going to have to learn our ways. Slaves will try to get out of work any way they can by pretending to be sick or hurt. Right, Leander?"

"Yes, Ma'am," he had responded with a quick nod. "Miss Hetty is sho' right."

Now Nia sat on a straw-filled mattress in a room only large enough to hold the pine log bed, a small dresser and a chamber pot. This was the room she would be expected to share with her husband.

Her husband. Phineas Campbell. He was expected home at any time. She knew she should be preparing to meet him—changing her clothing, washing her face, fixing her hair. But she felt rooted to this simple bed covered by a patchwork quilt of many faded colors that was so artlessly constructed that she was certain it was the handiwork of Aunt Hetty.

She thought of Finn, and of her attraction to him. He was part Indian. Was it wrong for her to feel the way she had felt about him, even though she had known nothing of his Indian mother when she first caught sight of him? Was this a sign of some flaw in her character? She wished she could discuss this with another woman—but certainly not with Aunt Hetty. Would this be something she could have discussed with Clementine? No, that would have been even worse; Clem would have spouted some biblical verse that would have condemned her to perdition. With her mother? Heavens, no.

With Abby? Perhaps. Abby was a married woman, maybe already a mother. Abby could tell her so much she needed to know: about men, about being attracted to men, about marriage. She herself knew little about marriage beyond what she had observed in her own family. She knew nothing about what it took to make a child appear. She wished she had spoken about married life to her older sister during the time between accepting Phineas' proposal and leaving home. But there was no time to worry about this now. She needed to get ready to meet Phineas Campbell, or at least as ready as she could be under the circumstances.

But one thing was certain. In the future, she needed to avoid Finn as much as possible.

The staccato rap on the door, followed by Hetty's shrill "Mr. Campbell is here," ended Nia's reverie.

"Just a minute, please." Her fingers trembling, Nia quickly pushed any stray tendrils of hair behind the rim of her ruffled and beribboned hair comb. She mourned the lack of a mirror in the room, but knew her best dress, a pale lavender brocade with three-quarter length sleeves and a white ruffled neckline, suited her well. Its bodice, secured just below her bosom by a thin band of fabric, accentuated the slenderness of her waistline. She had been pleased to find the hair comb, of a similar style and color as her dress, on her last expedition to the milliners in Philadelphia.

She wished she'd had time for a leisurely bath, but had to settle for a quick splash from the basin of tepid water Hetty had brought her. With a final pinching of her cheeks, a final smoothing of her skirt, and a deep breath, she opened the door and stepped into the salon. The late afternoon sun shone through the open doorway, where Phineas Campbell stood, one hand braced on the door frame, looking out. At the sound of her rustling skirt he turned and, taking three steps toward her, reached for her hand. "Miss Meier?" he asked, taking her hand and, bowing at the waist, lightly kissing it. "Or may I call you Eugenia?"

Nia's first thought was that Phineas Campbell was a bit of a dandy. He was short, perhaps only two or three inches taller than herself, and a bit portly, although no one would call him stout. He was dressed in tan breeches buttoned just below the knee topped by a bright white shirt with a high frilled cravat. His jacket was bottle green with black lapels and buttons. Most surprisingly, he sported rose-colored stockings above his buckled black shoes. She rather liked the idea of the rose color.

She guessed him to be between forty and fifty years old, and probably a bit closer to fifty. His facial coloring was florid, his clean-shaven, pink cheeks topped by eyes of a milky blue. She could not tell the color of his hair, as he wore a white wig that curled down to his shoulders. But both his eyebrows and lashes showed signs of gray. Curtseying, she responded, "Of course, Mr. Campbell."

"Phineas, if you please. Would you care to sit? My dear Hetty is bringing us some refreshments."

Still holding her hand, he led her to the sofa and waited to sit next to her until she had finished fussing with her full skirt. "I hope your trip was pleasant. It's a long journey from Philadelphia to Natchez."

"Well, yes. I must say it was quite an adventure." Nia was pleased with this conversational opening; she could tell him a number of interesting things about her journey while using the opportunity to begin to form an opinion of the man. "I..."

"But you're here now, and I welcome you to Three Ponds Farm," he interrupted. "Ah, here's our Hetty." Taking a tray holding two cups of a pale brown liquid and two scones, he placed it on the table. "Please join us," he said to his sister, who then took a place on one of the spindle chairs.

"Thank you. I..." Nia began.

"My dear, I fear that our visit must be a short one. I have an appointment I need to attend. I'm certain Hetty will be able to see to your needs until I return tomorrow." With this he handed her a cup and a scone. "We'll have many opportunities to get to know one another during the next two weeks."

"Two weeks?" she questioned, fearing to hear any answer he might give about the significance of "two weeks."

"Yes, Dear. We are fortunate a traveling Presbyterian minister is expected in Natchez within the next two weeks. We can schedule the wedding during the time he is here."

Nia almost choked on the bite of scone she had just taken—whether it was from the brittleness of the pastry or the shock of Phineas' last statement, she could not tell. She quickly took a sip from the cup, finding it contained a tea so sweet she nearly gagged.

"But Mr. Campbell..."

"Phineas."

"Yes, Phineas. Two weeks seems hardly enough time to..."

"For an engagement? Yes, of course you are right. And under other circumstances, I would enjoy nothing more than a much longer time for us to get to know each other."

"Yes. A longer time would definitely..."

"But Eugenia, this is Natchez, not Philadelphia. You're now in the frontier, where we must take advantage of any opportunities that come our way. It may be months before another preacher finds his way here."

Damnation! thought Nia, *will this man never allow me to complete a sentence?* "But I need more time," she pleaded. "I don't even have a suitable dress for..."

"The one you're wearing is lovely, my dear," he flattered, "but you'll be pleased to know your future husband is a man who thinks of all necessities. Hetty, fetch that parcel I asked you to put away last week."

While Hetty scurried to the door of the one room Nia had not yet seen, the room she assumed was Hetty's bedroom, Phineas talked about the weather and its effect on the cane crop. He expected a bountiful harvest this year, and planned to use his profits to add some needed space to their home. This topic caught Nia's interest. But before he could specify what, exactly, his plans were, Hetty came back into the room struggling with a large package wrapped in brown paper, which she laid at Nia's feet.

"Open it," he demanded with a twinkle in his eye. "I believe you will like it."

Nia struggled with the twine that held the bundle together but finally tore apart the packaging to reveal yards of a rich, cream-colored fabric. Running her hand across the cloth, she found it luxuriously smooth and wondered if it might actually be silk. In a separate paper-covered parcel she found many yards of trim embroidered in a rose pattern and a packet of lace, both in a light caramel color that contrasted beautifully with the fabric.

"This is lovely," she said. "But what is ..."

"Your wedding dress!" Phineas answered, clapping his hands merrily. "I ordered it all the way from France."

"Thank you. I don't quite know what to say."

"You do know how to sew, don't you?"

Nia's jaw dropped. She did sew, of course. Mama had taught her how to hem handkerchiefs for her father and make small repairs on Mellie's clothing. But a wedding dress! In two weeks! Was the man insane? She slowly shook her head, considering how she could respond to his question. "I... do...I mean, I can... but..."

This time it was Hetty who interrupted her. "Now, Phineas. Quit torturing the child. Show her your other surprise."

"Hetty, Hetty, Hetty. You never let me have my fun." With this he smiled conspiratorially at Nia, although she could not imagine the reason for his smile. Finally, clapping his hands twice, Phineas called out, "Maggie! Girl! Come in now."

With this the back door opened and a young woman, probably, Nia imagined, around her own age, bounded in. Dressed in a pale green skirt topped by a long jacket in a bright, multi-colored floral pattern, she flashed Nia a broad, friendly smile.

"Meet your new lady's maid," Phineas stated with a flourish of his arm. "Eugenia, this is Maggie."

"Pleased to meet you," the young woman said with a spirited curtsey. The brogue confirmed what Nia had already suspected based on the girl's porcelain skin, rosy cheeks, sparkling dark eyes, and thick, nearly black curls escaping from her starched white cap. *Irish.*

"Now, Phineas," Hetty insisted with a scowl. "Not only a lady's maid. You said the girl would help with the cooking and cleaning, too."

"Yes, of course," Phineas responded to his sister. "You ladies will have to share Maggie. But she's a good, hard worker, aren't you, Girl?"

"Yessir."

"And she can sew, too, correct?"

"Yessir. With the best o' them."

Eugenia couldn't have suppressed the grin that lit her face even if she wanted to. She felt as though a prayer had been answered. Something in Maggie's smile and the twinkle in her eye told Nia this young woman would become less of a servant than a companion, a confidante, and a friend.

Chapter Nine

"Ouch!"

"Well, stand still, Miss, if you don't want to get pinched."

"I was just reaching for..."

"And I was just getting this bit o' lace pinned just right on the neckline."

"All right, Maggie," Nia conceded. "I'll be as still as a statue." The gown Maggie was fashioning for her was the most beautiful garment she had ever seen. A full skirt dropped gracefully from the gown's high waistline, and the deep scooped neckline accentuated the delicate bone structure of her clavicle. The gown's short puffed sleeves were trimmed with lace. Enough fabric would be left to construct a full train falling from her shoulders, and even without the rose-patterned embroidered trim, the dress was lovely. The added trim would make it truly stunning.

Nia had learned Maggie was not a slave, but an indentured servant who would earn her freedom in five years. Maggie had been born in a fishing village in the County of Cork, the eighth child in her family. Harsh economic times had forced her father to sign articles of indenture for not only his youngest daughter, but for two of her brothers as well.

But Maggie, whose cheerful and optimistic nature was apparent to anyone who spent even fifteen minutes with her, spoke of her indenture as an opportunity. She was convinced that once her indenture was complete, with ambition and hard work she would find a grand place in this grand new land. A young woman of many talents, she was a fine seamstress and a good cook, a wonder with children, and a soprano with a voice so pure it would melt any heart.

Even now, with a mouth full of pins, she was humming a haunting melody Nia had heard from her many times. "That tune," Nia asked, "is it popular in Ireland?"

"'Tis 'Slane,'" she answered. "A very old song. 'Tis about when St. Patrick brought the Easter fire to Ireland."

"You must miss Ireland very much," Nia responded, considering for a moment those things she herself missed from Philadelphia. Paved roads. Cool summer evenings. Surprisingly, her sisters.

"Yes, Miss, I do. 'Tis lovely there. I miss the green. The green of Ireland is like nothing you see here. So fresh and hearty, even the hills themselves seem alive. But Miss," she said, obviously catching a hint of sadness in Nia's eyes, "'tis a beautiful place here as well, and you will soon be its mistress. Will you be walking with Mr. Campbell this afternoon?"

"No. Mr. Campbell has business in Natchez." Nia had tried unsuccessfully to ferret out the nature of Phineas' business during yesterday afternoon's walk. He had hinted broadly that he would be shopping for something special, and his sly smile suggested to her this something special was for her. It couldn't be an engagement ring: he had already gifted her with his late mother's ring. She lifted her hand to take one more look at the gold band that held a marquise-shaped sapphire sparkling amidst four tiny diamonds.

"Now, Miss," complained Maggie, "put your hand down. If you don't quit moving like that I'll never get this neckline done." Nia complied without a word.

She had actually enjoyed the long walks she had taken with Phineas over the past week. The property was both extensive and beautiful, ranging from deep pine forests reminiscent of those in Pennsylvania to low-lying marshes and swamps, the likes of which she could never have imagined. During their walks the swamps seemed more like an enchanted fairyland than like the menacing wasteland they had appeared to be when she was on the keelboat.

Phineas had already shown Nia two of the ponds that gave the property its name. She found them very different from the clear blue ponds, situated in granite pits and perfect for swimming, to which she was accustomed. The ponds she saw here were shallow and filled with vegetation ranging from ragged cordgrass to the tall, straight trees with swollen bases suitably named pond cypress.

The first pond he had shown her was filled with fragrant water lilies, their numerous cream-colored petals surrounding vividly yellow centers. Seeing the trunk of a fallen cypress jutting out from the shore amidst a multitude of these blooms, she quickly stepped onto it, hoping to pick a bouquet to take home. "Phineas," she said, "take my hand so I may venture out further to pick some of these beauties to grace our table."

"Be happy to, Lass," he laughed, "but they dinna call this Gator Pond for nothing!"

Nia almost tumbled into the water in her haste to get safely on shore, wondering how anything at all in this territory was truly safe when even the most gorgeous blooms held mortal danger. Phineas, grabbing her hand and pulling her back to safety, told her the property's third pond was in an open area where no alligators had ever been known to visit, but he would have to show her that pond some other day as it was several miles distant from the house. This amazed her: no one in Pennsylvania, she imagined, could actually own that much land.

The next day Phineas had suggested they pack a luncheon and ride to see it, but she had to defer. "I've never ridden on a horse," she told him. "Only in wagons and buggies."

"Well, Lass, that's something we'll have to correct as soon as possible. You need to learn how to ride if you're going to live here. I'll talk to Finn— he can give you some lessons after the wedding." Nia had not responded to that suggestion.

She enjoyed their walks most when Phineas spoke of renovating the house. He'd already hired an architect whose work was well known in the area, and he had traveled all the way to New Orleans to purchase slaves who were skilled in carpentry and plaster work. His plans included a second floor to accommodate a bedroom and a nursery and the addition of a balcony above the porch. He also wanted a dining room extension on the first floor to the west of the parlor.

Other plans included smaller improvements: oil lamps to replace the candles that were currently the only form of illumination in the house, carpet for the new rooms he would be building, and a piano-forte in the salon. He told her he looked forward to the day when he would first hear Nia play, although she insisted she was not a particularly accomplished pianist. She highly approved of all his plans, thinking that someday soon the house would become the stately mansion she had imagined.

"Now, turn around," Maggie commanded. "Yes, stop right there."

"Are we almost done for today?"

"Are you getting tired, Miss?"

Nia was perhaps a little bored, but she certainly could not be tired. She had done very little in the way of work in the past week. She had no chores to do: her meals were prepared, her clothing was attended to, and Leander and Sara were responsible for all the household chores. Her days were spent reading from the small library Hetty had acquired over time, walking with Phineas, trying different hair styles, and of course, enduring hours of fittings with Maggie. She was becoming accustomed to this leisurely lifestyle and rather enjoyed it. Her pleasure was marred by only one real concern: her wedding night. She wished she knew something more about what happened in the bedroom between a husband and wife.

She wondered if Maggie might be a good source of information. They had developed a bond over the past week that was, if not friendship, at least something beyond the usual relationship between mistress and servant. In their hours together they had shared stories about their families and their experiences. And although Maggie was only two years older, something in her saucy attitude seemed to suggest she had already had a lifetime's worth of experience. Turning toward Maggie, she haltingly began to ask "Have you ever..."

"Oh, Miss. You're moving again. Won't you..."

"Maggie," Nia interrupted, "have you ever kissed a boy?"

Maggie stopped her work to look closely at Nia, obviously giving some thought to how she should answer this question. Finally she replied with a small smile. "Well, Miss, the boys of County Cork are devilish handsome, don't you know."

"So you have kissed a boy!" Nia triumphantly exclaimed. "Did you like it?"

Maggie laughed. "Well, that would depend."

"On what?"

"On the boy. Or the man," Maggie quickly corrected, responding more specifically to the concern Nia had obviously been expressing, but had not exactly formed into a question. "But Miss," she continued, "'tis a natural thing, you know. 'Tis how every one of us got here on God's Earth—and every animal too, when you think of it."

"A natural thing? I don't know about that." Nia, her eyes fixed on the floor, slowly shook her head back forth. Other than the sounds of unusual grunts and an occasional bit of laughter she had heard coming from her parents' bedroom on rare occasions, she had no idea what they did there other than sleep.

"Well, Miss, that may be because you didn't grow up in a one-room shanty with a passel of sisters and brothers. A person learns a great deal about life that way," she said with a short laugh. But the look of genuine concern on Nia's face and the tears starting to form in the corner of her eyes were enough to make Maggie change her tone. "There, there, Miss. Don't worry. You'll be all right," she said, daring to give Nia a gentle embrace. "Mr. Campbell is a fine man." Nia, sniffing away her tears, nodded and did her best to smile. "He'll help you along. Men seem to be born knowing about these things. And you're going to be a beautiful bride. Now please, turn around so I can measure you for your train. How long do you want it? We've plenty of fabric left. Maybe even enough to fashion a wedding quilt."

"I'll leave that up to you, Maggie," Nia responded, wiping any trace of tears from her eyes.

"Yes, Miss. I think perhaps a long train. And rounded at the bottom, don't you know, like a beautiful puddle behind you."

"That would be lovely." They worked in silence for a few minutes before Nia broached a suggestion she had been thinking of for the past few days. "Maggie?"

"Yes, Miss?"

"Do you think you could call me Nia?"

"Ah," Maggie responded with a small smile, "I'm not sure Mr. Campbell and Miss Hetty would approve of that."

"Probably not. But you could call me Nia when there are just the two of us, couldn't you?"

"I'd be honored to do that," Maggie responded solemnly. "Now, Nia," she said, emphasizing the "Nia" only slightly, "please turn around so I can measure you for the train."

Nia smiled. She felt certain she had found a friend.

Chapter Ten

Nia wondered how an early evening in September could be so confoundedly hot. Sweat dripped from every inch of her body, and even her brain felt drenched in a mugginess that made it difficult to think. Even the pages of her novel were too damp to turn.

When she had lived in Philadelphia, she had thought a life of leisure would be immensely enjoyable, but was now actually finding it quite difficult. Most brides, she imagined, were very busy in the weeks just before their weddings, but this was certainly not the case for her. Phineas was responsible for inviting the guests; after all, she knew no one in Natchez other than those in the household. She felt a pang of regret when remembering no member of her family would be there on her wedding day, but it could not be helped. Some day she might see members of her family again, but that would certainly not happen for a while. She would have to depend on letters to maintain any relationship with her family.

Aunt Hetty was handling the wedding arrangements—or at least commandeering those who were doing the actual work. Hetty kept Leander and his wife Sara busy day and night cleaning every inch of the house and scouring every plate, platter, and pot. Toby and Leville, two of the younger slaves, had been taken from field duty to whitewash the house and plant beds of trumpet honeysuckle, mallow, and blue sage beside the walkway. Finn had found several bigleaf magnolia bushes to grace the walkway leading to the porch entrance. Their shiny green leaves and many showy white flowers would add a bit of elegance to the newly whitewashed façade.

Whenever Nia had asked to help with the arrangements, Aunt Hetty had either told her her help wasn't necessary or had assigned her only small tasks such as hemming frayed napkins. Today Hetty had traveled to Natchez to shop for whatever food items could not be raised or grown on the plantation, and Nia, despite no great desire to spend time with the woman, had practically begged to accompany her. But Hetty had refused. "Now, Dear, I'm sure you have much to do here," she had said.

"Besides, Samuel and I are taking the buckboard. There is no room for an extra person." *An extra person?* She was insulted. After all, was she not the bride? Was she to have no say whatsoever in her own wedding? But she'd already learned that Hetty was intractable; complaining or cajoling would be fruitless.

Nia would have been happy to spend the day with Maggie, but she did not wish to bother her. Maggie was very busy sewing yards of lace on her wedding dress and train as well as completing various items for her trousseau. Maggie would not have turned her away, but Nia knew taking her friend from her work would be selfish; Maggie would only have to work much harder the next few days.

"I'll go for a walk," she finally decided, and was quite surprised to realize she had said the words aloud. When had she started verbalizing her thoughts? "It's this confounded heat," she said, and then, "Oh dear, I've done it again!"

Grabbing her straw sunhat, she hastened out the door and was surprised to hear sounds of laughter and singing coming from the slave quarters. Though she'd been living at the plantation for over a week, she had not yet visited that part of the property. Although Phineas had not explicitly forbidden her to go there, something in the way he reacted whenever she asked about the slave quarters made her think he wanted her to avoid them. But Phineas was in New Orleans. Hetty was in Natchez. Maggie was busy. She had not seen Finn for days. She was an adult and would soon be mistress of the plantation. She turned in the direction of the laughter and singing.

A very short walk led her to a compound of several weathered shacks surrounding an immense live oak, its serpentine branches extending at least thirty feet on either side of its trunk. Several kerchiefed women sat on benches and tree stumps placed below the branches of this behemoth, and numerous children were scattered on the ground below them. All were busily pounding, some with rocks, some with hammers, some with strange-looking wooden contraptions, on hundreds of black balls lying on the ground, and all were singing or chatting with one another as they worked.

"Hallo!" she called from a short distance away. Immediately the singing and chatting stopped, and all looked her way. "I was wondering what you were doing," Nia said, coming closer.

"Workin', Miss," said a woman, looking up at Nia. Her gnarled hands and snow-white hair made Nia believe she was the oldest of the group. The woman immediately bent back over the long wooden implement she held upright on the ground, then pushed hard on an extension of the tool, causing a loud cracking sound.

"I can see that," responded Nia with a smile. "But what, *exactly*, are you doing?"

The women, seemingly perplexed, glanced quickly at each other, but a young, handsome boy with a broad smile responded. "We be crackin' nuts, Miss!" With this he held out a rough black ball approximately two inches wide. Taking it into her hand, Nia felt it to be very light and saw it was was not completely circular; a small knob protruded from the top.

"Dese be black walnuts, Miss," offered a tall, slim woman with deep-set eyes and a honeyed voice. "Dey be fo' yo' weddin' cake." With this Nia noticed hundreds of the nuts lying on the ground, waiting to be cracked.

"Oh, well, thank you," she said, wondering if it was correct to thank a slave. "I see everyone is very busy."

"Yes, Miss, dey be real hard to crack. But de chillen' take dis as a game. Dey like to race each other—see who can crack de mos'."

"May I try?" Nia asked. The children went back to their game, most using stone against stone to crack the nuts. But the women, looking warily toward each other, seemed not to know how to respond. Finally, the elderly woman who had first spoken to Nia rose from her bench and reached out for the nut Nia held.

"Heah," she said, placing the nut in a long, grooved piece of wood holding a narrower piece in its shaft. At the bottom of the shaft was a heavy metal attachment on which she placed the nut, holding it with its knob facing upward. With a quick push on the narrower wooden section, she cracked the nut into two pieces. "You gotta crack it raht on dis li'l bump," she said as she demonstrated. "Now it go to de lit'lest chillen' to crack mo' so's to get de meat outta de shell."

Nia did not succeed in cracking a nut until her fifth try; they were certainly more difficult to maneuver and to crack than they appeared. The shy smiles from the women surrounding her had been encouraging enough to make her continue her efforts.

"How about one of these green ones?" she asked, reaching toward a bucket containing nuts partially covered with a mossy green scum.

"No!" shouted the women and some of the children in unison, startling her. Nia wondered what she could possibly have done wrong.

"Don't touch 'em, Miss," quickly warned the young woman who had first spoken to her. "Dey gonna dye yo' fingahs so brown you nevah gonna git it off befo' yo' weddin' day." With this, she suddenly placed her hand over her mouth, casting her eyes to the ground.

Nia, confused at why the young woman looked so frightened, asked her name. "Eleanora," she answered. "Ah's mighty sorry ah shouted at you, Miss."

"Thank you, Eleanora. That was information I needed to know," Nia responded. "May I try another nut?" The second and third nuts were no easier to crack than the first, but by her fourth try, she felt she was learning. As she was handing her fifth successfully broken nut to Jonas, the boy who had first spoken to her and who she soon learned was Eleanora's son, she heard a familiar voice call her name.

"Nia," croaked Hetty. "Would you please come back to the house with me? Now, please!"

Something in the tone she heard in Hetty's voice, combined with Hetty's absolute silence as they walked back to the house, made Nia realize she had committed yet another faux pas. But this time, at least, she was quite certain she knew what it was.

Chapter Eleven

October 2, 1790

Dearest Mama, Papa and Mellie,

I am a wife!

I know this must seem very sudden to you, particularly since this is the first written communication you have received from me since I left almost three months ago. But Mr. Campbell is a very busy man as well as a man who believes in propriety, and he did not wish to squander an opportunity to marry while a traveling minister was in Natchez. Things are very different here in the Mississippi Territory. It is not exactly a wilderness, but some of the things we take for granted in Philadelphia are not readily available here.

My wedding was three days ago. Mr. Campbell was resplendent in his clan kilt: I do not believe I have ever seen a man in such an elaborate outfit before. I fancy the dress made for me by my ladies' maid, Maggie, also showed me to my best advantage. Mr. Campbell's servants had been busy for days readying the plantation house and preparing food for the event, and our guests included some of the most distinguished members of the Natchez community, including Mr. Andrew Jackson, who is the planning commissioner of the town, Mr. LeFlore, who operates a boat shuttle, Mr. Willing and Mr. Blommart, very successful merchants, and Mr. Ellis and Mr. Dunbar, whose estates are among the most handsome in the territory. Some of their family members were able to attend as well.

I have much to tell you. My trip down the Mississippi River was harrowing at times, but always interesting. The Mississippi Territory itself is a place of beauty and mystery, with swamplands and vegetation unlike anything I could have imagined. Mr. Campbell and I have spent a great deal of time walking on his land, which he has named Three Ponds Farm, but I will be taking horseback riding lessons very soon so I can see the full range of the large property of which I have become mistress.

As Mr. Campbell is very busy with the fall harvest, he has not yet planned a wedding trip. But we hope to soon travel to New Orleans. My husband (so strange to be writing those words) is adding a major addition to the house, and we will need to purchase furniture, carpeting and other things for it. He has even promised me a piano-forte! While Natchez is a town that grows day by day, no establishments there carry materials of the quality Mr. Campbell will be seeking. I certainly look forward to our trip south.

I miss you all. I imagine Abby has already had her baby, and that you are proud grandparents and auntie! Did she have a boy or a girl, and are they doing well? Please send my love and best wishes to Abby, Benjamin, and their new little blessing from above.

I hope you receive this letter. Mr. Campbell will be sending it with the next merchant who will be taking some of his fall crop to Nashville. There it can be posted to you. Please write me very soon to let me know what is happening at home.

Know that I am very happy, and that I made the correct choice in coming here to marry Mr. Campbell. I remain your devoted daughter and sister,

Nia

Nia sealed her letter with a sigh, then wiped the sweat from her face. Mississippi was still unbearably hot in October, a time when Philadelphians were looking forward to color changes in the trees and cooler temperatures. No trees would change color here: the climate was too hot to allow that trick of nature to occur.

She thought back to her wedding, just three days earlier. She had had to stifle a laugh when she first saw Phineas in his wedding attire, having never seen a man in a kilt before. The Campbell tartan was beautiful, with a pattern of bright green bands contrasting sharply with dark blue squares. His sporran and belt were crafted of umber-colored leather, and his short black jacket, cap and hose were loomed in fine wool. Another man might have looked handsome in such regalia, but this outfit only accentuated the girth of Phineas' waist and the shape of his calves, which reminded Nia of certain local varieties of summer squash.

Phineas' knobby knees bore a striking resemblance to small skulls. His cap could not hide the band of bald skin appearing above a fringe of gray hair. Nia, who had never before seen Phineas without his white wig, was surprised to learn her new husband was quite bald.

They had married outside under the limbs of the largest live oak on the property: the house was much too small for the number of people, mostly men, many dressed in buckskin, who attended the ceremony, or for the slaves who stood silently in an area far apart from the invited guests and who disappeared into their quarters immediately after the ceremony.

Food was plentiful. Venison grilled over an open fire and hogs roasted in a pit provided the meat. Yams, okra and collard greens were served, and Aunt Hetty had several puddings as well as an immense pound cake and several black walnut cakes prepared for the great event. Whiskey was plentiful as well, and after dinner the men, including the minister, drank and played cards late into the evening. The two wives and three children who attended had been dispatched to their homes early in the afternoon under the watchful care of their household slaves.

Once the women and children had left, Nia spent hours alone in the bedroom, first pacing the floor, then sitting on the bed shredding the embroidery on a handkerchief to bits, then repeating those motions again and again. More than once, she reopened the package containing the wedding gift Phineas had given her, which she considered both strange and unexpected: a flintlock pistol. She had to admire the beauty of the weapon, with its intricate lattice pattern carved into a curved walnut butt, and was surprised at its weight. But a pistol? She had never expected to own such a thing.

Phineas had made a great show of presenting her the gift, which she opened to a fanfare of approving applause. "Don't you like it?" he had asked, perhaps responding to the confused look on her face.

"Why, yes. It's beautiful." Her response was met with hearty laughter from the group. "I... I never owned a pistol before."

"Ah, Lass, you had no need of one before. But you live in dangerous country now, and I won't always be here to watch over you. Here," he continued, taking the gun from her hand, "hold it like this." With these words he had gently positioned her fingers correctly around the pistol's butt and helped her squeeze the trigger. She cringed but was very relieved when no shot came forth. "No shot yet, Dear, but I'll be giving you a lesson or two later this week. We mustn't tarry about this."

She appreciated his concern for her safety, but the gift only intensified her own worries about the remoteness of her surroundings. Still, other women survived the wilds of the Mississippi Territory. She reminded herself she had summoned up the courage to begin this adventure in the first place. At this moment she wished she could resurrect that courage.

As she waited for Phineas to come to the bedroom, her thoughts vacillated between wanting him to appear and fearing he soon would. She still wore her wedding dress and wondered whether she was expected to wait for him to appear before undressing. A gentle knock at the door startled her enough to cause her heart to beat so rapidly she could manage only a weakly whispered "Come in."

"Maggie!" she breathed with relief as the door opened. "It's only you."

"'Tis me, here to help you get ready. The last of the guests are soon to leave, and I'm certain Mr. Campbell will be here shortly. Oh, Miss, are those tears I see? We can't have that." Maggie rushed to give Nia a quick embrace, then turned her around and began quickly undoing the elaborate chignon she had spent an hour constructing earlier in the day. "Here, give me your brush. We need to see your beautiful tresses flowing. There," she said, turning Nia to face her and brushing some of her honey-colored curls, already showing lightened highlights from exposure to the sun, forward to cascade gently around her shoulders. "Much better!"

"Do I remain...?"

"In your dress? No, probably not. I'm afraid Mr. Campbell is in no condition to undo all the lacing. Turn around again, Dear, and let me do that. And where is that new shift Mr. Campbell brought you from New Orleans?"

Maggie helped her out of her dress and into her shift, a lovely garment in an ivory-colored silk embroidered at the neckline with tiny pink roses. She then suggested Nia recline bolstered by several pillows. Maggie spent several minutes posing Nia in various positions to determine which would be most flattering, finally suggesting she lie on her side, casually propped a bit on one elbow, her head reclining on a pillow placed against the headboard. Finally, she partially covered Nia with the quilt she had found the time to fashion from remnants of the wedding fabric and other scraps stored in a trunk in the main room. "There," she said, tucking the quilt loosely around Nia's hips. "You look like an empress."

"Thank you," Nia said with the utmost sincerity. "Do you have to leave now?"

"Yes, Dear. But I brought a little something else for you." With this Maggie reached into a pocket of her skirt to remove a small metal flask. "Here. Take a drink of this. 'Twill seem a bit sharp at first."

"Maggie, is it. .?"

"Just a wee bit o' whiskey. And don't you fuss with me about taking it."

"But I never..."

"Yes, I figured as much. But now's the time to learn. So hurry up and drink it."

Nia's quick shudder and the grimace that overtook her face with her first small sip of the liquor made Maggie struggle to stifle a laugh. But with Maggie's encouragement, Nia finished the contents of the small flask and was soon amazed at the pleasant warmth that began to infuse her whole body.

"There, now. I'll be going," said Maggie, giving Nia a quick peck on the cheek before quietly leaving the room.

Within just a few minutes, a much sharper, louder knock on the door told Nia her transformation from bride to wife was about to begin.

Nia awoke to bright sunlight streaming through the bedroom's one small window. Stretching her arms out fully to her sides, she noticed immediately that Phineas was no longer in their narrow bed. A gentle knock on the door told her the first face she would see that day would be Maggie's.

"Come in," she called.

"Top o' the morning to you, Mrs. Campbell," Maggie greeted her with a smile. "Or perhaps middle o' the morning, I should say."

"Where is. . ?"

"Mr. Campbell? He has business in Natchez and needed to leave early. He'll be home later tonight. How are you?"

"Fine," Nia answered, although the burning she felt between her legs caused her to wince when she tried to get out of bed.

"Stay still for a while," Maggie suggested. "I'm heating up some water for a hot soak. You'll feel better after that." Once again, Nia was grateful for the kindness Maggie always showed her. Maggie seemed to instinctively know what she needed in any situation. And her advice was priceless. Nia's performing of her wifely duty had been uncomfortable, to say the least, but she had survived it, just as Maggie had assured her she would.

"Ach, where are the sheets?" Maggie asked, rustling the wedding quilt. Nia had a vague memory of Aunt Hetty visiting the room very early in the morning and gently pulling them out from under her. "Aunt Hetty..." she began.

"Oh, of course," interrupted Maggie. "Leave it to that old biddy to want to check. I imagine she was satisfied with what she found."

Although Nia was somewhat interested in pursuing the meaning behind Maggie's comment, she was more interested in the thought that had first entered her mind when she had awakened. "So," she said, "the baby will arrive in less than a year. Is that correct?"

"Which baby, Nia?"

"The one..." she began shyly, "the one we started last night. I've decided, Maggie, to have only the one child. Do you think Mr. Campbell will mind? If it is a son, I would think not."

Maggie's raised eyebrows and deep sigh told Nia that once again, she had said something which illustrated her pitiful ignorance. "Nia," Maggie began, "there *could* be a child, but 'tis not likely, not the first time."

"The first time?" Nia questioned. Would she be expected to go through last night's actions once again? The thought almost made her ill. Last night had been humiliating and painful. Why would any woman want to do this again?

"There, there, Nia," Maggie comforted, sitting on the bed and holding her close. "Don't worry too much about last night. The first time is always hard. And Mr. Campbell, though he is a very good man, perhaps celebrated with a wee bit too much whiskey last night. Tonight will be much better, I assure you."

"Tonight?" Nia shuddered. Would she have to experience that horror again so soon, and many other nights as well? Unthinkable! Dismissing Maggie, she crawled back into her bed and, covering her head with the quilt, wished herself anywhere other than this god-forsaken room in this god-forsaken land that was now her home.

Nia's second night as a wife was only marginally better than the first, and the third only slightly better than the second. The fact that Phineas Campbell would be gone on business for several days was the only thing that had given her the courage to write the glowing letter which did little to express her true feelings to her parents. Even now, with all her disappointments, she was not ready to admit to them she had been wrong, she had been foolish, and she would like nothing better than to return to that once-hated attic room she had shared with her sister.

She feared there was something terribly wrong with her. After all, her parents had shared a married life and a marital bed for almost twenty-five years: those muffled grunts and muted laughs, as well as the appearance of three daughters, were proof they enjoyed what she had been taught to think of as a wifely duty. Her sister Abby seemed to be happily married. And what about those fancy women she had seen at the dock in Natchez? Apparently, they enjoyed what happened between men and women enough to actually seek out partners.

And Phineas Campbell was not a bad man. She often found his company pleasant. She had even found her first shooting lesson, taken on the morning of the third day of their marriage, quite pleasurable. They had walked to an open field where he had set up a series of bottles on the top rung of a fence. She tensed up at first when he, standing behind her with his body aligned closely with hers, had guided her fingers with his own as she took her first shots. But then she felt a true sense of pride when, with his help, she had hit her first target, and even more pride the first time she actually hit a target on her own.

"That's the way, Lass," he had said. "I believe you'll be a mighty fine markswoman someday."

"Thank you," she said, happy to be handing the firearm back to him.

"No, no," he responded. "We've only begun. You must practice, practice, practice. Here's more shot for you."

She had hoped the lesson was over, but was certain Phineas would not allow her to leave just yet. She endured another hour of practice before, taking the pistol from her, he laughed. "That's enough, Lassie," he said. "If you get any better with that pistol, I'd be afraid to ever anger you! We dinna want that!"

On the ride home, she already knew something was missing, but could not determine what, exactly, that something was, or whether it was the result of some failing in herself or in her husband. Realizing her marriage had just begun and she had a great deal to learn, she resolved to do everything she could to make this marriage a success. After all, she couldn't see any alternative.

Chapter Twelve

"Wat dat word mean, Mizz Campbell?"

"What word, Jonas?"

"Mer-zee-fool."

"As in 'Blessed are the merciful, for they shall obtain mercy?'"

"Yes'm. Dat word."

"Merciful means being kind, or forgiving." Nia was astounded at how little education had been provided for the plantation's children. When she found they'd had no schooling, not even any religious instruction, she had asked Phineas if she could begin giving them lessons.

"Teach no reading," he had demanded. "We don't need our darkies reading some of those damned abolitionist tracts."

She wanted to inform him she had grown up reading such tracts, but decided instead to remind herself of the words which had sustained her over the past two months: *This is Mississippi, not Pennsylvania. Things are different here. I must learn to adjust, but also to help them to understand the superior nature of our ways.* "All right then, Dear," she said smoothly. "But how about religion? Wouldn't you agree religious instruction would be beneficial?"

He had finally agreed to allow the children one hour every Sunday morning for religious instruction. This pleased her, particularly because she had very little else to do. Aunt Hetty maintained her firm control over the household, and the slaves, who she still liked to think of as "servants," did all the work. She had been visited by two of the women in the community and had learned home visits were a standard occupation for plantation wives. But she had found little in common with either of them. That she had not received an invitation to visit their homes made her believe the feeling was mutual.

She had set up her "school" on the grass in an open space about half way between the house and the slave quarters. After the second week of instruction Nia, noticing some of the children's parents surreptitiously sitting nearby under trees or behind shrubs, had invited them to attend as well. Now her "classroom" regularly included not only the plantation's eight children, but also most of the adult slaves.

"Merciful?" Jonas asked. "Wat dat?"

Nia smiled. Jonas was one of the brighter children, and one of the most animated. His chestnut-colored skin and dark amber eyes set him apart almost as much as his willingness to ask questions and provide answers to hers. "Well," she expounded, "let's say somebody hit you. If you were merciful, you wouldn't hit them back."

"You mean someone like Massa or Massa Finn?"

"Well, yes, of course. But anyone. Let's say Samuel there hit you," she illustrated, pointing at the smaller boy sitting next to Jonas. She had noticed during their first session that they were friends. "What would you do?"

"Hit 'im back!"

"Not if you were merciful. If you were, you would forgive him. Just like Jesus did on the cross. He forgave all those terrible men who crucified him. He wants us to do the same." Nia could tell by the look on Jonas' face and the muffled giggles of some of the other children that she would have to think of some other way to help them understand this particular lesson. She continued. "Jesus said 'Whosoever shall smite thee on the right cheek, turn to him the other also.'"

"Wat be smite?" Nia was not surprised the voice was Jonas' once again.

"Smite means 'hit.' Jesus said if someone hits you on one cheek, you should turn your head so he can hit you on the other cheek. Jonas!" she said sharply, seeing him raise his hand toward Samuel, "Don't you dare try it!" With a sigh, she realized she needed to choose her biblical tracts much more carefully in the future. It would take time for children who'd had no instruction in the Bible to begin to understand its message. She decided to begin preparing them for Christmas the following week. Everyone could understand the joy of birth, and she knew the stories of the Magi and angels would interest them.

"That's enough for today, children," she said, closing the old Campbell family Bible Phineas had searched for hours to find for her. With these words the children, released from their study, scattered noisily to enjoy the rest of the half-day respite Sundays provided from their normal work.

"Eleanora?" she summoned the young woman she had learned was Jonas' mother. All the servants seemed shy and timid in her presence, as though they feared her, but Eleanora seemed particularly so. Based on the few glimpses Nia had seen of the young woman's face, she appeared to be quite pretty, but Eleanora generally averted her eyes in Nia's presence, studiously examining the ground as though she had dropped something valuable that needed to be found immediately.

"Yes'm?" she answered in a voice so low Nia could scarcely hear her.

"I would like to speak to you about your boy, Jonas."

"He do sum'pin bad, Mizz?"

"No, no—nothing bad. He is just very active and inquisitive."

"Yes'm," Eleanora responded, her head dropping even further onto her chest. "Massa favor de boy. I don' know why."

"Well, I'm not surprised," Nia responded to Eleanora's rather unusual statement. "Jonas does seem to be a bright young man. Your daughter, too, listens very carefully to the Bible lessons. Rachel, isn't it?"

"Yes'm."

"Rachel was a very important character in the Bible. The children will learn about her early next year. Did you know Rachel was Mr. Campbell's mother's name?"

"No, Ma'am." This time Eleanora's response was so soft Nia had to guess at what she had said. And the young woman was obviously in distress; her shoulders shivered as though she were cold, which was not likely in the ninety degree heat. Nia, believing the young woman's stress must be caused by being singled out, tried to put her at her ease.

"Eleanora, I wished only to compliment you on your children, and to tell you I believe they will excel in our Bible class. You may go now." The young woman nodded her head and, turning quickly, hurried back to the slave quarters.

Nia, walking toward the house to check on preparations for the coming meal, once again wondered at the oddity of the master-slave relationship. Every attempt she made at conversation seemed to be a misstep. She was concerned only for their welfare, but their mistrust and actual fear of her were obvious. This was not something she could discuss with Phineas or Hetty: they would only laugh at what they saw as her foolish northern ways.

As she neared the front door, she couldn't help but pause to admire the progress already made toward its renovation. Although nothing had been done on the inside, Simon and Horace, the slaves Phineas had procured especially for this project, had already done an excellent job of roughing the walls and roof of the second floor. Nia could already tell the covered balcony would be a great success; she looked forward to long afternoons reading on its wide expanse. The addition to the first floor, which almost doubled its previous space, was being constructed in the back of the house by several slaves who were required to put in extra time after their day in the fields.

The thought of all the new space delighted Nia, who could see that the house would begin to rival some of the beautiful mansions she had seen in Natchez. She spent hours imagining what kinds of gardens would show the house to its best advantage: the ancient live oaks, of course, could form the basic structure of the gardens, while the addition of magnolias and crepe myrtle would add more needed height to the plantings. She admired the bush palmetto and swamp roses Phineas had pointed out to her on their walks, and could easily have some of those shrubs transplanted. And wildflowers abounded on the property. Arranged properly and supplemented with some rose varieties that could bear the southern heat, they could be become the basis for beautiful formal beds.

She had already staked out an area for a large orchard far behind the house where a few peach and black walnut trees already grew. And Hetty's small vegetable garden would never do: the household would need a much larger and more varied assortment of berries and vegetables than were currently being grown.

The renovation, however, had given rise to her first real quarrel with Phineas, if it could actually be called that. The old kitchen, which was separate from the rest of the building, had been torn down to make way for the new space. Phineas' plan was to rebuild the kitchen as it had been— separate from the house. Every kitchen Nia had ever seen in Philadelphia had been a part of the house: she believed this would be a much better arrangement for the expansion, allowing easier access, and had shared her idea with Phineas.

"The kitchen? Part of the house? Not how it's done here," he had responded gruffly.

"But don't you see, Dear, it would make the kitchen so much more accessible."

"Accessible! Who would want to go into the kitchen?"

"Why, I don't know. I might..." Nia hazarded. Phineas' normally florid face was becoming flushed, and his voice had become louder with each response.

"Don't be a fool, Lassie. Open your eyes! The kitchen is for slaves. Have ye learned nothing in the time ye've been here? "

"But I was only..."

"Keep your mind on your own business, Woman, and dinna tell me how to do mine."

"I. . I'm sorry. I was just suggesting..." But Nia was apologizing to her husband's back. He had stomped away and was now loudly berating Rufus, one of the field workers who had been assigned extra work on the house, about leveling a wooden plank that was being hammered in place. Nia determined that, although it would be difficult, she would never again offer suggestions on the expansion, particularly on those days when Phineas would return from Natchez or Rocky Springs smelling as strongly of whiskey as he had that day.

Still, her new home would soon rival many of those she had seen in town. And she truly enjoyed teaching Bible classes with the plantation's children. Phineas was responsible for both of those good things. Nia knew every marriage was a combination of good and bad: all married couples had quarrels and disagreements. She was still learning how to be a wife and was determined to try her best to please the man she had married.

As she entered the house a delightfully savory smell reminded her it was almost time to eat. "Mmmm, what are we having for dinner?" she asked Hetty, who was busy netting lace on a collar. "I can smell it all the way from the kitchen to this room." Nia marveled at the thought that here doors could be kept open even as winter approached. Philadelphians would already be brushing their winter coats and hats to prepare them for the coming cold.

"Sara's preparing one of the turkeys Finn shot yesterday," responded Hetty. "How was your Bible class today?"

"It went well. The children have a great deal to learn."

"Well, do not challenge them too much. You know they do not have the same kind of intelligence we do. They are much more simple-minded."

Nia thought to challenge Hetty's statement by mentioning that the children had not had the same learning opportunities well-to-do white children in the South had experienced from birth, but realized her argument would land on deaf ears. Still, she wished to let Hetty know her work with the children was already showing some promising results. "Jonas and Rachel seem to be quite bright," she countered.

"Well, what do you expect?" Hetty was once again giving Nia the look that suggested Hetty believed she, too, was hopelessly slow-witted.

"Eleanora said that Phineas favors Jonas," she continued. "Has he given the boy some extra instruction?" Nia could only assume by Hetty's response that Phineas, too, had noticed Jonas' aptitude. Perhaps he was grooming the boy for a position as a house servant.

"Well, perhaps a little," Hetty began. "He has spent some time with him, and with the girl, too. He's almost spoilt them two, making them think they're better than the others. But..." she added, looking shrewdly at Nia, "you do understand why, don't you?"

Nia tried mightily to stop her eyes from reflexively rolling upward. Why couldn't the woman just explain things to her without constantly sounding like a frustrated schoolmarm? Shrugging her shoulders, she shook her head with a frustrated "No."

Hetty, sighing deeply and screwing her face in the smirk Nia was beginning to loathe, placed her netting in her lap. "Buying slaves is very expensive. And as I told you before, men have their needs. Are you capable of understanding what I am trying to tell you, or do I have to embarrass us both by being much more specific?"

Nia was aghast. *First Finn,* she thought, *and now Jonas and Rachel. And doesn't Eleanora have a husband—one of the field hands? And even naming the girl after his own mother!* Phineas Campbell obviously was not the upstanding, righteous man he pretended to be.

She wondered why he needed a wife in the first place, but realized she already knew. He wanted to establish himself as a man of means—as the plantation master he had always wanted to be. For this he needed a wife, as well as a son and heir. That was the only reason he had brought her here.

Well, she resolved, she could certainly become the wife he needed. Few actually married for love: that was just a silly romantic idea. Her marriage, like many others, was primarily a business transaction. And like any other business transaction, it was the responsibility of both parties to make sure they benefitted.

Without another word to Hetty, she turned and, with a stiff back and a head held high, strode to the bedroom, slamming the door behind her.

Chapter Thirteen

"Ooh, this is lovely," Maggie exclaimed, rubbing a swatch of emerald green silk between her fingers. "I can hardly wait to work on it." Nia and Maggie were delving into the many bolts of fabric Leville, the son of Sara and Leander, had just finished carrying into the house.

"It's for a new ballgown. Here," Nia said, rummaging through a rucksack she had brought back from New Orleans, finally retrieving a sketch from among the paraphernalia she had stuffed into the sack. "A dressmaker drew this for me. Do you think you can copy it?"

Maggie's eyes sparkled upon viewing the sketch. It showed a stylish gown with a squared-off neckline, full sleeves, and V-shaped waistline. But the most amazing feature of the dress was its skirt of many intricate layers of flounced panels over a wide, pleated hem. "'Twill be a challenge, but I'll do my best. What about this pale blue linen?" she asked, fingering another bolt of fabric. "What is it for?"

"A simple summer gown," Nia answered. "Something suitable for the racetrack."

"Oh my! Are you and Mr. Campbell planning another trip to New Orleans? Or will it be Nashville this time?"

"Neither. Mr. Campbell has joined a group of men who are building a racetrack near St. Catherine's Creek. He would like to get involved in racing. He spoke to a breeder in New Orleans about a horse. And women will be allowed to attend the races."

"Won't that be fun!" Maggie gushed. "Imagine! A racetrack in Natchez!" They spent the next few minutes admiring several bolts of luxurious velvet. "Winter gowns?" Maggie asked.

"No. Draperies. Crimson for the parlor," Nia proclaimed, "and this royal blue for the bedroom." She described at great length the new rosewood furniture that would be shipped from Philadelphia within the next two months, and how the colors would work in her decorating scheme. She had been delighted to learn that Spanish officials in New Orleans and merchants in Philadelphia had worked together to open trading routes along the Atlantic Ocean. This would give her the opportunity to purchase household items that reminded her of home.

She envisioned Three Ponds Farm as a beautiful union of Philadelphia craftsmanship and Southern charm and was excited at the possibility of someday travelling home by schooner to visit her family as well as perhaps being able to one day entertain them at her home. Wouldn't Mama be surprised at how much she had risen in the world! Suddenly the Mississippi Territory no longer seemed devoid of all the benefits of civilization.

"And what is this I hear about your making the acquaintance of a new gentleman?" Nia asked, sharply arching one eyebrow. But the smile on her face negated the effect of the disapproving eyebrow.

"Ach, you must have been talking to Miss Hetty. Does she approve?"

"Not at all," responded Nia with a laugh. "But she did say he was handsome."

"Aye, that he is," Maggie agreed, filling in further details about Jacques LeBeau, a young French fur trapper travelling down the Trace who had talked Finn into trading a day's work for overnight shelter, a common practice in the territory. "You know the French. Light skin, dark hair, and a devilishly handsome mustache. We did walk out two or three times, but nothing more, no matter what Miss Hetty says. I'm a good girl, don't you know?"

"I do know that," laughed Nia. But she'd already learned from Hetty that LeBeau had stayed a week before heading to New Orleans, and Maggie soon admitted he had promised to visit her on his way back. Further questioning led to Maggie's description of him as being a kind man, very ambitious and very pleasant company. She confessed that his promise to visit her had been sealed with a kiss.

"I know I'm indentured to Mr. Campbell for a good many more years," Maggie continued with a small sigh. "I don't plan on any great romances until then." But Nia knew indentures could be purchased and that if LeBeau was successful in New Orleans, some day soon she might lose her servant and friend.

"Here," Nia said, pulling a bolt of sprightly floral-patterned calico in French blue out of the pile. Nia knew Maggie favored colorful floral patterns. "This is a present for you. Make yourself a pretty new dress for when your young man next comes calling."

As Maggie left the room, she expressed her gratitude as well as her eagerness to begin making patterns for the dresses she would be sewing. Nia smiled broadly—broadly enough, she hoped, to cover the fact that her smile was forced. *How simple Maggie is,* she thought, *to be so excited about sewing dresses. Poor little thing! She's really is nothing more than a child.*

But she soon realized she was being unfairly critical of Maggie, who had in the past few months become her best friend, the woman she could trust completely and with whom she could share secrets. She knew Maggie was completely devoted to her, and without Maggie her only real feminine companionship would have to come from Hetty, a horrible thought. She wondered what emotion had brought those unkind thoughts about Maggie to mind. On reflection, she was surprised and disappointed in herself to realize it was envy.

"This here's Belle," said Finn, leading a beautiful sorrel filly toward her. "Don't be afraid of her. She's gentle."

"Oh, dear," uttered Nia, almost under her breath. She'd had very little experience with horses: this close, Belle looked like a veritable giant of a beast. "I believed I would be using a sidesaddle," she said nervously. Nia had occasionally seen women in Philadelphia riding horses, but had never seen one riding astride.

"Not here," Finn asserted. "It wouldn't be safe. There's too much uneven land, too many marshy areas. No real roads. You have better control with a regular saddle. Pa insisted I teach you on one."

"Very well then," Nia reluctantly agreed as she offered the horse the carrot Maggie had given her as a bribe. Belle was to be her horse, and she wanted to start their relationship on a friendly footing. She had put off this lesson as long as possible, finally agreeing when Phineas had informed her he would not allow her to leave the property until she learned to ride. If she ever wished to see Natchez again, or any place other than Three Ponds Farm, she would have to overcome her fear.

Maggie had tried to sweeten Nia's feelings about the endeavor by sewing her a stylish riding habit in black serge. Combined with the black riding hat and boots Phineas had insisted she buy in New Orleans, Nia was bolstered by the knowledge that she looked stunning in her new outfit. When she had awakened to a beautiful spring morning she made up her mind: she would begin her lessons.

"Ready?" Finn asked, handing her the reins and then crouching next to Belle with his fingers locked firmly together to give her a foothold up. From where she was standing, the height of Belle's back looked mountainous, but with one hand firmly on Finn's shoulder, Nia gamely placed her booted foot into his hands and, at the count of three, boosted herself onto the horse.

Belle shied just a bit, causing Nia some concern. But soon the horse settled in, giving her the opportunity to look at familiar surroundings from a higher perspective. She had never realized how different the world would appear an additional four feet above the ground. She felt more secure in the saddle than she had expected she would.

Finn gave her some preliminary lessons on how to direct Belle with the reins and soon, under his careful watch, she was walking the horse in large circles in the open field. Belle was easy to lead—the mare had been trained to turn at the slightest motion of the reins and to stop on command. Before long Finn was showing Nia how to take the horse to a canter, and within minutes the speed of this gait gave her a feeling of freedom she had never felt before. With this freedom came a sense of power at knowing she was controlling this powerful animal, much larger, heavier, and stronger than herself, with just the slightest movement of her arms, wrists and thighs.

It seemed as though she had been cantering for only a few minutes when Finn signaled her back with a wave of his hand: her first lesson was coming to an end. She competently directed Belle back to where Finn waited for her, then handed him the reins and began to dismount.

"Good job, Nia," he congratulated her, placing his hands around her waist to help her off her mount. She had not expected that. Nor had she expected the slight shiver she felt as her body slid down against his, or her giddiness as she noted the strength of his arms and chest and the scent of the outdoors—of woods and horses and late spring breezes—emanating from his body.

"You're going to be quite the horsewoman," he said. "You took to it well."

Nia blushed at the praise. "I enjoyed it," she said, realizing it was more than the lesson that she had enjoyed.

"Will you be ready for another lesson next week?"

"Do I have to wait so long?" she complained. She felt she would be ready for another lesson tomorrow, or perhaps even in the next hour.

"You were on Belle for over an hour," he said with a laugh. "You're going to be pretty sore tomorrow." But seeing the disappointment on her face, Finn assured her he would be ready to continue her lessons whenever she let him know she was ready. "Based on what I saw today," he said, "you'll be galloping the next time."

"Hallo!" a booming voice came from across the field. Nia looked up to see Phineas bounding toward them. "How did she do?" he asked Finn as he came closer.

"Very well," Finn responded with a grin. "She's going to be a fine rider."

"Good!" he responded, grabbing Nia and holding her firmly in an embrace close enough for her to notice he had been drinking. "Finn, after you rub down Belle, go on out to the south field and check on how the planting is progressing. Then I want you to look at Thunder's hooves. I think he's losing a shoe." Finn nodded and turned to comply.

"And you, Nia, go back to the house," he commanded. "I've a little job for you to do as well," he added with a wink and a leer. Nia, stifling a sigh, also turned to comply.

Chapter Fourteen

November 25, 1791

Dear Papa, Mama and Mellie,

I cannot believe in just a few weeks it will be Christmas. This Christmas will be very different than my last Christmas here. Then we hardly celebrated at all. But this year we plan to have a very big party, which will also celebrate two major accomplishments. The first is the completion of Phineas' improvements to our home. The house is almost three times as large as it originally was, and is now well decorated with carpeting, furniture, and a set of very attractive whale oil lamps. So our Christmas party will, in part, be a housewarming as well.

Secondly, we will be celebrating, win or lose, the first race for Duke, the quarter horse Phineas has been grooming for Three Ponds Farm's entrance in the St. Catherine Racetrack schedule. Horses and horseracing are all the rage among the nabobs of Natchez. Even I have become quite an accomplished horsewoman. I cherish my early morning rides on Belle, my faithful, trusty steed.

How is little Benjy? Is he walking yet? How is Abby's health? Is she hoping for a little girl this time? You must be excited at the thought of becoming the grandparents of two children by the end of this year. Please give my love to Abby and her growing family, and ask her to write to me when she has time. And Mellie, please write to me as well. You must have grown to be quite the young lady by now.

I have become very busy lately. Our piano-forte arrived a little over a month ago. I warned Phineas about my lack of skill as a musician, but I do not think he believed me until I played for him the first time! But all is being remedied. Mr. McDermott comes to give me a lesson once a week. Right now we are concentrating on Christmas carols, as I will be expected to play at our party.

I have also become a member of the ladies' traveling backgammon group, which meets every Wednesday afternoon. Next week we will be meeting here at Three Ponds. Our group comprises eight women, so four games are played for the first match. Then winners play winners, until one woman becomes the ultimate winner for the session. The prize is hosting the next session at her home! So, as you can see, I have become quite accomplished at backgammon.

Finally, Phineas has commissioned portraits of each of us to be hung over our new parlor mantel. This means I must endure a three-hour sitting with Mr. Nash every Friday afternoon. I cannot move even my little finger for three hours: Mr. Nash allows only a fifteen minute break at the half-point of each session. But both of our portraits are coming along very well.

Thank you for your last letter: I cherish hearing news of home, so please write me again as soon as possible. I wish you all a very happy Christmas and many blessings in the new year of 1792.

Your loving and devoted daughter and sister,

Nia

Nia searched the new rosewood desk for the sealing wax, which Phineas seemed to put in a different place every time he used it. The desk was an accompaniment to the carved rosewood suite, lavishly upholstered in a crimson brocade, that now graced their parlor.

Finding the wax in a bottom drawer, she sealed her letter and prepared for another busy afternoon. She needed to confirm with Maggie the menu for the next day's backgammon luncheon and then double-check it with Hetty, who was still unable to accept her capability in dealing with any household responsibility.

The weekly backgammon game had become an important social ritual; Hetty stressed the absolute necessity of Nia's maintaining good standing with the members of the group, all of whom were the wives or widows of some of the most distinguished members of Natchez society. Its grand dame, Mrs. Fanny Merrill, was an eighty-year-old dowager whose husband had made a fortune in the cane trade. Her grandson, a banker, handled most of the biggest financial deals in the area. Phineas counted on Nia to help him establish strong social ties with Fanny, who could influence any individual's standing within the Natchez social structure.

But it was difficult. Fanny dominated the group's choice of conversational topics, which consisted largely of criticism of any female member of Natchez society not present at the backgammon game. She found it necessary to inform the group of such misdoings as Mrs. Hendricks having worn a terribly inappropriate hat at last Sunday's Episcopalian church service, to which Mrs. Corbett had not shown up at all, or Sally Grant's having served spirits at a midweek luncheon, when it wasn't even 2:00 in the afternoon.

Nia found these conversations exceedingly boring, particularly because she did not know many of the women being castigated. The only interesting thing she could recall Fanny ever saying was that Rachel Jackson was a divorced woman. "And to think," Fanny had huffed, "Rachel is the daughter of John Donelson, a founding father of the city of Nashville. Why, the family has been one of the most well-known and respected in Natchez."

"Her parents must be mortified," interjected Hepzibah Morgan, one of Fanny's dearest friends.

"I should think so," replied Fanny. "And to take up with that Jackson character! Why, the man is no more than a tradesman!" The sounds of "Oh, dear," "My word!" and the commonly heard "Tsk, tsk, tsk," filled the room.

The other women in the group were, for the most part, nice enough, but none of them was under forty years old. Nia felt she had very little in common with any of them. She had never really enjoyed parlor games. She found backgammon boring and would have loved to be included instead in one of Phineas' occasional poker games. He always came home from a night spent gambling at Kings Tavern with tales, probably somewhat edited for her behalf, of the raucous time he had enjoyed. Of course, joining him at the Tavern for an evening's fun was never going to happen.

Now that her letter home was written, her next task was to practice piano for the two hours before Mr. McDermott would come for her lesson. She had a great deal of work to do before she would be capable of playing well enough for the Christmas party. Her fingers seemed too short and stubby to ever allow her to become even a fair pianist, but Phineas insisted she be ready to entertain the group with at least a few carols that evening. He seemed to need to show her off to his new society friends, but she sometimes wondered whether this need was a substitute for his not yet having a bonny baby boy—a son and heir—to exhibit. She too longed for a child. But every month found her wanting and still waiting.

The bright spot of her day was her ride on Belle. She and the mare had developed a relationship rivaling any she'd had with another human. Belle was responsive to all her commands, sometimes reacting so rapidly Nia wondered if the horse could actually read her mind. She and Belle had spent many hours exploring the property in all its beauty and variety, from its cliffs of sandy loess, to its deep pine and live oak forests, to its mysterious swamps with the ubiquitous Spanish moss draping every cypress tree.

She and Phineas had finally gotten the chance to ride out to the property's third pond, which really seemed more like a lake to her. There they were able to view the graceful swoops of cormorants, great blue herons and egrets hunting for their meals. When Phineas had pointed out a mink with three of her cubs sunning herself on the rocky shore, Nia regretted the mink collar she had requested for a new jacket Maggie was fashioning for her. "A mink collar, you say?" he had asked, then laughed, somewhat derisively she thought, when she shared that thought with him. They had spent the rest of the afternoon fishing the pond's waters and had brought home several brown trout for Sara to prepare that evening.

Often on her morning rides she encountered herds of deer that bolted immediately upon sensing her arrival. Their white tails bobbing up and down as they escaped into the forest soon became all she could see of them amidst the dense green foliage. Phineas had invited her several times to join his next hunting party, but did not seem particularly disappointed when she had declined.

During her riding lessons she had been careful to maintain her distance from Finn, both physically and verbally. She made it clear from the very start that teaching her to ride was his job and not a social occasion. He had seemed a bit confused at her new attitude, but comported himself well and did an excellent job of showing her everything she needed to know to become a competent rider. All in all, Nia felt she was becoming more comfortable at playing the part she had chosen for her life: the wife of a successful man and the mistress of what was soon to be an elegant estate.

"Ah, Nia, you look stunning! Turn around so I can check the bustle." Nia did more than turn around: laughing, she pirouetted three times before stopping to allow Maggie to complete her adjustments. Maggie had truly outdone herself with this dress, a dazzling white Swiss muslin with short sleeves, trimmed at the waist with a wide band of black velvet. A straw hat, beribboned with black bows and sporting two white magnolias, was set at a jaunty angle on her head, and shirred white gloves reaching just above her elbows completed the effect. "You will be the belle of the race!"

This was to be a very exciting day: Duke's first turn at the St. Catherine racetrack. Preparing Duke had become a group project: Finn trained, Leville groomed, Phineas supervised, and Nia provided moral support, cheering them on during fair afternoons at the makeshift straightaway Phineas had ordered staked out. They had spent the evening at Springfield Plantation, just north of Natchez, as the guests of Thomas Green, a magistrate of the Mississippi Territory, which saved them the rigors of having to travel a long distance before attending the race. Two o'clock found Phineas and Nia standing near the starting gate, examining the competition Duke would face. Although she was no experienced judge of horseflesh, Nia thought Duke looked far superior to the others: more lively, stronger, and, if a horse could be said to be smart, smarter and more aware.

"Hallo there, Campbell," came a loud voice. Nia turned to see a tall, thin man, probably not yet thirty, whose most distinguishing features were a shock of bright red hair and deep, penetrating blue eyes. With him was perhaps the most beautiful woman Nia had ever seen. Her pale skin was dramatically set off by lustrously dark hair and eyes, and she would have looked as dignified as a portrait of an ancient Roman noblewoman were it not for the dimples that appeared every time she smiled.

"Hallo, Jackson," answered Phineas. Introductions were made, and Nia learned that Andrew Jackson was the proprietor of the local trading post. He and his wife, Rachel, had been recently wed at Springfield Plantation, with Magistrate Green officiating. *Ah,* thought Nia, *so this is Rachel Jackson.* She was thrilled at the thought of actually meeting the woman who had been the major topic of the previous week's backgammon game.

"So," Phineas continued, "have you a horse in this race?"

"Why, yes. That sorrel standing right next to the bay with the three white stockings," Jackson answered. Finn was just beginning to mount Duke. Nia raised her hand to wave to him, but then, conjecturing that he was probably concentrating too much on the race to notice her, quickly lowered it.

"Fine looking animal," Phineas commented. "Did you find him in Nashville?"

"New Orleans. And you? Do you have a horse entered?"

"The bay you just mentioned. From New Orleans as well," Phineas answered, beaming with obvious pride.

"Mighty fine animals to be had from New Orleans," Jackson asserted. "One almost need not go to Nashville to find good racers."

Phineas nodded in agreement. "Tell me, Jackson, is your horse fast?"

"Very. Would you care to make a small wager?" Jackson asked, his blue eyes twinkling in anticipation.

"Don't mind if I do."

While the men huddled to discuss the terms of their wager, Nia had a chance to speak with the infamous Rachel Jackson. Since they had both spent time at Springfield Plantation, they discussed the stylishness and beauty of that mansion and all its accoutrements. Nia could not help wondering about the scandal surrounding Rachel. Having never before met a divorced woman, she rather thought that, should she ever meet such a person, the woman would have a decidedly red cast to her skin and tiny nubs of horns protruding from her head.

But here, in the flesh, stood this captivating object of scandal and gossip who seemed to be a perfectly nice person. Although Nia was curious, Rachel's divorce was a topic that could not be mentioned in polite conversation.

"Well, ladies, are you ready?" Phineas asked, taking Nia's arm. Spectators were already beginning to gather along the quarter mile track, actually just a packed dirt road, which would provide the venue for the race. Phineas wanted to secure a good place on the raised owners' pavilion, which was located approximately three quarters of the way down the track. This vantage point would give him the opportunity to assess the skills of both his horse and his rider as well as provide a good view of the finish.

They had been at their position for only a few minutes before a young boy, crouching in the center of the road with his right hand shading his eyes, shouted "They's lined up!" Moments later the shot was fired: the race was on!

All spectators squinted and craned their necks to face southward, where the line of horses, tiny at first, was quickly becoming a larger, thundering mass. Shouts of "Run, Diablo!" "Ginger! Ginger!" and "Come on, Hercules!" filled the air. Nia, caught up in the excitement and losing any sense of propriety, began screaming "Duke! Duke!" at the top of her lungs. Phineas' body seemed cast in stone, with only his head turning northward in tiny increments as the pack of horses, enveloped in a cloud of dust, came closer and closer.

Soon the pack was near enough that those in the lead could be identified through the dust. "A bay! It's a bay!" shouted Phineas. But Nia knew, even before Phineas did, that Duke was in the lead. Even though he was flattened against the horse's neck with only his right arm, whip in hand, rising and falling against the horse's haunches, Nia could recognize Finn's form.

"Duke! Duke!" she continued, more hoarsely now. At this point all the spectators in the pavilion could clearly see the leading mounts, and first among them was Duke. Nia's excitement reached heights unknown to her.

Then everything changed.

Duke took a misstep, stumbled, and fell, toppling the two horses immediately behind him. A loud gasp, breathed in unison, came from the crowd. "Finn," Nia exclaimed, her body, lurching toward the track, held back only by Phineas' firm grasp on her shoulder.

"I'll take the ladies away from the track," Jackson told Phineas, who, nodding his agreement, rushed toward his horse and rider. By this time the race was completed, and not one person seemed to be paying attention to the palomino that actually won. Finding his coachman among the crowd, Jackson quickly made arrangements to have Nia taken back to Three Ponds Farm, and as the buckboard drove away, Nia shuddered, then dissolved in tears, at the ominous sound of three shots being fired.

"Dear Lord, no," cried Maggie once Nia had relayed her sad story. "Do you think Duke is dead?"

"I don't know," responded a tearful Nia. "Those three shots. I've spent the whole ride back here wondering what they mean."

"And Finn? Is he all right?"

"I don't know that either. Mr. Jackson's coachman took Rachel and me away from the track so rapidly there was no time for questions." Nia took a sip of the strong tea laced with brandy which Maggie had prepared to rejuvenate her. But it would take much more than fortified tea to help her overcome her fear and sense of loss.

"Well," pronounced Hetty. "We'll just have to wait until Phineas comes home. My guess is that will not be until tomorrow some time. It's very late. We should all get some sleep."

For once Nia agreed with Hetty. No further words any of them could say would lessen the anxiety she felt right now. She doubted she could sleep, but the thought of burrowing under a soft quilt was very comforting.

Her desire to be alone caused her to turn down Maggie's offer to help her undress. In the dim lamp light of the bedroom she shared with Phineas, she dropped her now-soiled and crumpled white gown to the floor and, dressed only in her shift, searched the chest at the foot of their bed for the soft velvet robe Phineas had bought her in New Orleans. She hoped the feel of something soft and luxurious would help distance her, if only for a while, from the events of the day.

The noise of angry shouting woke her. Her first thought was surprise that she had been able to sleep at all, but she soon realized the room was dark, the oil lamp having burned out. She must have been sleeping for at least two or three hours. Looking toward the window, she saw darkness there as well, but could discern a bit of light, probably from an open fire, flickering in the distance near the slave quarters.

Flinging herself out of bed, she dashed to the window where, by the light of a small fire, she could see a mass of dark bodies gathered closely together, all still and silent. Suddenly the door was thrust open and Phineas, carrying a torch, burst into the room.

"Get dressed, Nia," he shouted. "You need to come outside." Phineas could, even at his most pleasant times, be an intimidating man, but this night he actually looked terrifying. His bloodshot eyes were those of a madman, and the scowl on his face reminded her of nothing more than a wolf baring its teeth.

"Phineas, what in God's name..."

"It was Leville—the bastard son of a bitch. It was his fault."

"Leville?" Nia questioned. *Sara's son*, she thought. *Leville of the radiant smile. Leville, who was always polite and eager to help.* "But what could...?"

"He trimmed the hoof too short and the nail couldn't hold. Duke threw the shoe. Now Duke is dead—and two other horses, as well. That bastard Leville cost me dearly today, and I'm about to take it out of his hide!"

"You don't mean to beat him?"

"No! Not me. That will be Finn's job. He's at fault too. He was supposed to watch Leville, to train him. Now get dressed! You need to come outside."

"Why?" Nia asked. "Why must I...?"

"You are the mistress of this house. The time may come when I'm not here and you will need to be the one to administer punishment! The slaves need to see you as an authority as well," he shouted, grabbing her arm and pulling her toward the door.

"Never! I could never," she cried, pulling away from him as hard as she could. "Please do not do this. Leville is a good boy—it was an accident. Have mercy!"

"Mercy?" he cried. "Don't be a fool! Think, Woman! There are three of us here, twenty of them. We must be strong and united. They must always understand their place. Do you wish for an insurrection? It's happened elsewhere. Women have been defiled, even killed! Is that what you want? "

"No, of course not. But please, Phineas, don't make me watch this." She realized by this point that nothing she could do or say would stop him from carrying out the punishment.

"Be a fool then!" he shouted, pushing her away. "I've work to do yet this night! But next time, I'm warning you, next time you will do as I say!" With that he rushed out.

Nia ran to the window. The fire was already much larger than it had been when she had first seen it. By its light she could clearly see the slaves gathered together standing perfectly still, holding their children close, all eyes cast downward. She gasped when she saw the slim body of Leville, stripped to the waist and tied to the post erected about half way between the house and the slave quarters. She had passed that post nearly every day since she had come to Three Ponds Farm, but had never before considered its purpose.

She caught sight of Finn leaning against a tree, his left arm in a sling. So, he had been hurt in the accident. He looked in pain, dejected. She hoped at least some of that pain and dejection was caused by his horror at the part he was to play in the evil action to be carried out.

Then Phineas strode into the scene and, facing the gathered slaves, began spouting angry words like some demented preacher at his pulpit. Nia could not bear the thought of listening to his lecture or witnessing even one moment of this abomination. Throwing herself onto the bed, she covered her head with her pillow and quilt and choked out a flood of tears.

Chapter Fifteen

December 25, 1792
Dear Papa, Mama and Mellie,
Happy Christmas to you. We are enjoying a fine Christmas here a

December 25, 1792
Dear Papa, Mama and Mellie,
Happy Christmas to you. I hope you are all well. We here at Three Ponds are celebrating

December 25, 1792
Dear Papa, Mama and Mellie,
Happy Christmas. On this joyous day of Christ's birth

Nia crushed a third sheet of her fine ivory-colored linen paper and threw it to the floor. She had awakened early to write a Christmas letter to her family, but nothing she could write would express the feelings she had this day. She was not enjoying Christmas. There was no celebration. She could think of nothing to be joyous about.

She had just dismissed Sara, telling her she was not hungry and required no breakfast, and then sent her back to the slave quarters to spend Christmas with her family. She had tried the day after the whipping to express to Sara her sorrow at what had occurred, but Sara, her dark eyes misting with tears, had whispered "Massa Campbell know what's best."

But "Massa Campbell" certainly did not know what was best. He had commanded Finn to administer the ultimate punishment—thirty-nine lashes—allowed by Mississippi territorial law. Leville would be scarred and would suffer the effects of the beating for the rest of his life, and for what? For a horse?

No. Not for a horse. To satisfy the anger and pride of a cruel and evil man. To meet the goals of a cruel and evil system. And she had allowed herself to benefit from that system.

Part of her punishment for daring to challenge Phineas had been his canceling their party and then leaving her alone for Christmas. Surely he knew that being alone on the holiday would cause her to miss her family and their traditional Pennsylvania Christmas: the Christmas Eve Ball, the house festively decorated with vases of holly and bay, and a feast that included oysters, mincemeat pie, and brandied peaches. He had departed on Christmas Eve for an extended trip to New Orleans to purchase a replacement for Duke and had even taken Hetty with him, ostensibly so she could visit an old friend who was not feeling well. But Hetty had never mentioned any old friend in New Orleans, or for that matter, any friends at all.

At least Maggie had been left "to tend to her needs," although Nia certainly appreciated Maggie more for her pleasant company than for her service. Finn was charged to protect Three Ponds, but Nia was certain that he realized he was still being punished as well. Finn would have enjoyed nothing more than being allowed to travel to New Orleans to participate in the selection of a new racehorse. Phineas even darkly hinted at the possibility of hiring a new trainer to replace him, leaving to Finn only such tasks as mucking the stables and supervising field workers.

She and Phineas had lived together in near stony silence since the day of the race, a silence not broken until the day before he left. Summoning her into the parlor, he had demanded she sit down, then lectured her at length on the necessity of "mending wrongful thinking and actions." He quoted the Bible, "Slaves are to be submissive to their own masters," and "That servant who knew his master's will but did not act accordingly will receive a severe beating," to justify his actions.

"Search your soul, Eugenia," he had reproved her, "and think of where ye've gone wrong. Ye've disobeyed me, breaking God's law." He had threatened her with divorce, threatened to cast her out of the house without a penny. To ruin her name, and leave her without any recourse. She believed he could, and would, do all that, and was not at all surprised he had not bothered to search his Bible to see what it said about the evils of divorce.

The threat of divorce was real and daunting. She did not have the resources and family standing of Rachel Jackson. She could return, in disgrace, to her family, where her mother would never cease criticizing her for her foolishness and refusal to take good advice. She would be seen as a fallen woman who had, by her own doing, forfeited her place in polite society.

In her darkest moments she wondered how much laudanum would constitute a fatal dose. But these thoughts were fleeting. She did not know whether she resisted that fatal dose because of her fear of death, her occasional ray of hope, or simply her refusal to give Phineas any satisfaction. She did want to live. The problem was that she did not know how to make her life livable.

A knock on her door was followed by a welcome voice. "Nia?"

"Maggie, come in please. Happy Christmas to you." Nia folded the remainder of her stationery and placed it neatly in one of the cubbyholes of her secretary. No letter to her family would be written this day.

"Happy Christmas to you as well," Maggie responded. "You have a visitor. Would you like me to help you dress?"

"Whoever would be visiting me today?" she asked.

"Mr. Finn. He would like to speak to you."

This surprised Nia. Of course, she knew Finn was on the property. But they had avoided each other since the day of the race. Part of this was circumstance: as disgraced members of the household, she had been commanded to stay indoors while he had been kept busy from dawn until late at night completing various, and generally odious, tasks. But part of their avoidance was intentional. Nia, thinking of Finn's part in the whipping, could hardly bear to see him. She imagined that he, knowing how she felt about that night, was probably not eager to see her either.

"Shall I ask Mr. Finn to wait?"

"No," Nia said, and Maggie turned back toward the door. "No, wait," she then reconsidered. She thought she should at least find out what Finn wanted. Perhaps a situation on the plantation needed her attention. "Ask him what he wants. And then please come back to let me know."

The moment Maggie left, Nia reached for her hand mirror. She did not like what she saw. Her skin tone was sallow. Her eyes were swollen from intermittent crying. Her hair was dull and limp: it dearly needed a washing. Still, it was too late to change her mind.

Maggie soon returned with a message from Finn. "Mr. Finn wants to take you riding. He says Belle is getting peckish from lack of exercise. He would like you to be ready within the hour."

"Hmmph!" Nia snorted. Another man giving her orders. Still, Belle's welfare was important. The poor horse had been woefully neglected in the past couple of weeks. And in a way, Belle's care was her responsibility. Hadn't Phineas demanded she take a greater interest in the workings of the plantation, frequently reminding her that she was mistress of Three Ponds Farm and needed to take her responsibility more seriously?

Besides, it was a beautiful day for a ride, with a clear blue sky punctuated by cottony white clouds calling her out of her confinement. She certainly needed the exercise, if only to maintain her own good health. Despite all these reasons, which she was starting to believe were both compelling and valid, a part of her still wanted to tell Maggie to send him packing.

Finally, her decision was made. "Tell Mr. Finn that he is to return for me in two hours," she said. "Oh," she added, "and tell him not to be late."

Chapter Sixteen

"I see many sheep and just a few lambs. Can you see the three lambs side by side?" Nia questioned, pointing upward and slightly to the right.

"No. Look harder. Everyone sees sheep when they look at clouds," Finn insisted, taking a last bite from a drumstick. Finn had had the foresight to bring potato pies and the drumsticks from the goose they had eaten the previous evening, with thick slices of sponge cake as a sweet.

Nia shrugged, then turned her full attention to the task at hand. "Very well then," she began, "an alligator—over there. See him? Next to those... sheep!" *This man can certainly eat,* she thought. When he had unpacked the carpetbag containing their luncheon, she had thought he'd brought enough food to feed an army. She had nibbled only on a potato pie and some cake, and yet the mass of food was nearly gone.

Finn laughed. He and Nia, reclining quite comfortably against two ancient cypress stumps, gazed at a sky piled with mounds of billowy clouds sun-kissed at their feathery tips. At a distance they could see a wide expanse of clear azure sky dotted with wisps of pure white. "You still see sheep."

"Look over there then," Nia pointed. "Far away. Tiny white islands in a sea of blue."

"That is a bit better," he conceded. "But you could still try harder."

"Then you try," she demanded. "See if you can do better. What is it you see in the clouds?"

Nia could hardly believe she was spending Christmas afternoon with Finn, reclining in a grassy field, searching for images in clouds. She fondly remembered long afternoons playing this same game with Abby and Mellie when they were children, but thought she was long past such childish amusements. Somehow, playing this game with Finn did not seem childish at all.

When she had told him she felt ready to attempt a more ambitious ride, Finn had suggested they go to Rocky Springs, a site he had spoken of frequently. While riding on the Trace, Nia was once again awed by its majesty and mystery and, once they finally arrived there, was no less awed by the site itself. The springs, hidden deep within the dense forest, tumbled over a wide, flat rock into a pea green pond far below. The air was cool and dry—far different from the oppressive heat and humidity she was beginning to consider normal—and the meal was a welcome surprise after their long ride. The forest setting, the waterfall, the weather, the picnic all brought back memories of Pennsylvania.

Several hours earlier, she would not have believed she could be able to find any pleasure in this day. She had been enjoying their ride on the Trace when they encountered a slave coffle, most likely on its way to the Washington Road slave market in Natchez. The coffle had appeared at a particularly narrow section of the road, and Finn suggested they dismount and wait in a small cleared area to let it pass.

Nia counted nine men, nearly naked and barefooted, shackled at the neck and ankle and chained closely together in line. The men, who looked emaciated, were too dispirited to look up as they passed. Even more distressing to Nia was the buckboard that carried the slave drivers along with three women and four very young children, one of whom was feeding at his mother's breast. Finn and the slave drivers shared greetings as the buckboard passed, but Nia could not stand to look at those men, much less speak to them.

Finn waited until the wagon was out of sight to speak to Nia, who was noticeably upset. "I know this disturbs you, Nia," he had started, "but slavery exists all over the world, and always has."

"Do you support it?" she had challenged.

"No, but..."

"But you are a part of it," she accused angrily. "You beat Leville!" *There*, she thought, *I've said it*. It felt good to let him know why she had been avoiding him for weeks, why, for several days, she had been sickened at the very sight of him. The memory of that terrible night was never far from her thoughts.

"Nia," he said, almost too silently for her to hear, "Leville was going to get beaten that night, whether I held the whip or not. Pa would have done it. And in his anger, Pa would have beaten him to death. I've seen him do that before."

"That's no excuse for..."

"At least Sara and Leander have their son," he continued. "There is some, although little, I know, good in that."

Nia's tears came hard and fast, and Finn waited several minutes before he first touched her shoulder, then drew her close to him. She resisted only slightly, then fell against his chest, crying on his shoulder with the same intensity and abandon she would display when she was a little girl crying on her father's shoulder. "But it is so hard..." she sobbed, once she regained the ability to speak.

"I know. This is a hard, hard land," he responded, "and a hard time. Hard in every way one can imagine. Just surviving this time and this place is almost impossible."

"Mississippi is a terrible place." Finn did not respond to this statement, but waited, still holding her close, for her to regain her composure. Eventually, shaking her head with a shudder, she pulled away from him.

"Do you want to return to Three Ponds?" he asked.

"No," she responded, reaching for Belle's reins. "Going back will not change anything. We should continue the ride." They rode quietly for almost an hour before Nia, breaking her silence, asked about the flowers she saw dotting the grassy boundaries of the path. Not only was the sight of any wildflower unusual this time in December, but these plants had no apparent leaves and both the stems and the bell-shaped, nodding petals were white.

"Those are Indian-pipe," he answered. "Would you like to stop and see them more closely?"

By this time she was eager to remove her aching posterior from the saddle and stretch her stiff legs. Squatting somewhat less gracefully than her norm, she bent to examine the flowers. "They're waxy," she said, "and the stems are so strange. You can almost see through them."

"They're translucent," he said, surprising her at the extent of his vocabulary. "They grow off rotting plants. You don't want to pick..."

But it was too late. Nia had already picked several of the blooms and was looking back and forth between the flowers in her hand and Finn's face. "They're turning black," she said, confused and disappointed.

"They do that," he explained. "They turn black once you pick them."

"How unusual." She tossed them back onto the grass. *But perhaps not very unusual,* she thought, *like so many things here that seem beautiful, but upon further examination..."*

"Unusual," he agreed, "and my mother's favorite flower."

Nia was taken aback by this response. Finn had never mentioned his mother; Nia had more or less assumed she was dead. And disclosing any information about his background was highly unusual for him. "Your mother. Do you see her often?" she asked.

"Rarely." he said. "We should remount. We've still about a half hour's ride to get to the spring."

Nia had thought this was all the information she was going to get from this taciturn man. But the mention of his mother seemed to transform Finn. During the next half hour, with only minor urging from her, he spoke about his life as a child and young man. Nia was surprised to learn that his mother, Raven Sam, still lived in a small Indian compound north of town. Phineas had sent Raven back to her own people when Finn was only five years old.

"Were you able to visit her when you were a child?" she asked.

"Not very often," he responded.

"Then Phineas raised you?"

"I saw little of him until I was older. Sara was very young then. She was, in many ways, a mother to me." Nia was dumbfounded at the complexity of the relationships between the inhabitants of the plantation. Here was Finn, born of a Scots father and an Indian mother, and raised by a black woman. This put a very different, and very confusing, perspective on his beating of Leville. In a sense, Leville was Finn's younger brother. She feared she would never be able to understand the underlying motivations that led to the actions of the people she now lived among.

Finn further explained that when he was ten years old his father had sent him to New Orleans to study with a defrocked Jesuit priest who ran a small school for boys in an abandoned convent. Rations were limited, punishments were common, and all the boys were expected to work many hours a day in the extensive vegetable gardens and cane fields that had once comprised the convent's grounds. But it was during the three years he spent there that he learned to read, write and keep a ledger book, which accounted, Nia surmised, for his extensive vocabulary. It was there, too, that he developed a distinct dislike and distrust of Christianity and any of its representatives.

He spoke a little of the Natchez Indians and, a bit shyly, disclosed that he was a member of Natchez nobility through his grandparents. "My grandfather, had he lived, would have become the Great Sun, the supreme ruler of our people," he informed her.

"Your grandfather was a nobleman?" she asked.

"No, a commoner," he replied. "My grandmother was noble. In Natchez tradition, nobility is passed through the mother, not the father. My grandmother was to be the next Sun Mother."

Now Nia was completely confused: nobility passed through the maternal line? This was never done in any European country she knew of. But Finn assured her it was a common practice among Indians, which made Nia wonder why they were called savages. Determining nobility through maternal lines sounded very civilized to her. "But what happened?" she asked.

"Terrible times. The Natchez Indians became angry with the French for taking their land. They attacked Fort Rosalie, captured the fort and killed more than two hundred people. Only a few got away."

"My Lord," exclaimed Nia, "how horrible."

"Yes. And then the next year the French and our enemies the Choctaw united to take back the fort and destroy our villages. They killed the Natchez warriors and sold their women and children into slavery. My grandmother was one of the few who escaped."

Nia was once again mystified by the contrasts between brutality and civility she found here. But then, were things so different in Philadelphia? Many on both sides had died under cruel and inhuman circumstances during the war with England, and it was most likely that the early settlers in the North had treated the native Indians as harshly as they had been treated here. She had never considered the Indians as the victims of injustice before.

"There," Finn pointed to the sky. "A rabbit. He's hiding behind that bush. Do you see him?" Nia stared at the area Finn pointed to, but could not discern any rabbit in the clouds. Finn tried again, leaning over her to point to another area of the sky. "And there. A warrior falling to the ground. Do you see him? His legs are bent as he falls backwards. See how he thrusts his bow up into the air?"

"Yes, I think I do see him," she said, bending forward to see, her body touching his, her face close to his. From this distance she could feel his heat, smell his scent. Was it salty? No, tangy would describe it better. He smelled of woods and streams. Of smoke and animals. Of desire.

Later she would not remember who was first to run fingers across the other's face, the other's body. Who initiated the first kiss. Who was the first to begin undressing the other. She did remember that Finn insisted on seeing her naked, on slowly investigating every inch of her, first with his eyes, then with his hands and lips. This was something Phineas had never done. Coupling with her husband had always been done quickly, under covers, while she remained modestly attired in her shift.

Finn's lovemaking was passionate, intense, exciting. At first his kisses and caresses teased her, taunted her, only hinting at the fire he was about to ignite. When her suspense and desire for more became unbearable, he brought her passion to heights she had never before experienced and kept her soaring to ever more delectable levels of ecstasy.

But there was also a sweetness to his lovemaking that Nia had never before experienced, as though the world and everything in it had paused, waiting for them to quench their thirst for each other. Nothing in life mattered more than their being together.

As she lay in his arms, casually tracing the strawberry shape of a wine-colored birthmark on his upper chest, just above his heart, she thought she should feel shame at what she had just done. She had been unfaithful to her husband. She had broken her wedding vows. Perhaps the shame would come later, but for now she felt at peace, refreshed, happy to be alive.

"What are you laughing about?" Finn asked, running his fingers gently up and down her thigh.

"Oh, nothing," she answered, laughing even more heartily at the remembrance of something Maggie had told her over a year ago: *It depends on the boy. Or the man.*

Maggie had been right.

Chapter Seventeen

"How is the wee mother today?" Nia had become used to being wakened to these words on the rare mornings when her husband was present in their home.

"Fine," she responded, rubbing her eyes and forcibly swallowing the bile rising into her throat. She checked to be sure her chamber pot was near. Her morning sickness had, for the most part, abated, but she never could be certain it would not return to plague her yet again.

"And the bairn? How is me boy?" he asked, gently patting the extended girth of her stomach.

"Active. Jumping most of the night."

"Good. Good," he smiled.

Nia certainly did not see the baby's tendency toward late night gymnastics in the same positive light as did her husband. "Phineas," she reminded him once again, "it could very well be a girl."

"'Tis true. But then we'll just hope for a boy for the next one, or the one after that. It'll happen, Lassie. Never you fear."

Just how many children does this man want me to bear? she thought. At this point she considered giving birth to one child more than enough effort on her part. But at least once she had made known to Phineas that she was in the family way, his anger and frustration with her had been transformed into delight. He immediately told Hetty to arrange a separate bedroom for Nia which would later become the baby's, and eventually the children's nursery, and to allow her to decorate it in any style she wished, whatever the expense. He ordered Leander to build a sturdy cradle of black walnut and Maggie to embellish its hood with yards of fine white lace. Hetty was commissioned to knit the bed coverings that would keep Phineas' son warm.

In the first months of her pregnancy, Phineas and Nia had resumed their active social life with the Natchez nabobs, attending and hosting parties and socials and once again making regular appearances at the

St. Catherine races. Phineas had insisted their socializing was crucial to making sure his boy "would find his proper place in the world." He had reluctantly begun declining invitations only once the fuller skirts and expansions Maggie had sewn into Nia's clothing were not enough to hide the fact that she was expecting a child.

"Ah, Nia, me darlin'," Phineas continued, taking her hand in his. "Ye've made me a happy man. Do ye ever imagine who the bairn will resemble? Are ye hopin' our boy will have your honey-colored hair or be a true red-headed Scotsman like his papa? I've been hopin'..." But Phineas ceased speaking immediately once he saw Nia's complexion turn gray as she began reaching for her chamber pot. Handing it quickly to her, he rose and headed toward the door saying "Hold steady, me darlin'. I'll be sendin' Maggie to ye directly!"

Nia, already a veteran of morning sickness, did not need Maggie's help to see her through another fit of vomiting. But Maggie's presence was always comforting, even though Nia had not been able to share with her the question that constantly troubled her mind and kept her tossing in bed even on nights when the baby was peaceful:

Whose baby is this?

When she considered the question mathematically, she assured herself that it was Phineas' child. After all, she and her husband had had relations many times in the months leading up to her pregnancy, even during the time when his anger was at its peak. The fact that he would hardly speak to her had not stopped him from regularly reaching for her in bed. Those couplings had been brief and silent, leaving her feeling empty and alone.

She had been intimate with Finn only the one time, despite his desire to continue their relationship. Although her thoughts had returned to that day at Rocky Springs many times and she had twice dreamed of being with him, she had steadfastly forced herself to refuse all his entreaties. He had begged her to run away with him to New Orleans or even as far north as Nashville, if that was her preference. But she did not wish to be a kept woman for the rest of her life.

One day, in what seemed to be a fit of desperation, he had even offered to marry her. "I love you," he had told her, "and I believe you love me. You should never have married my father. You are not happy with him, and you never will be."

"But I *am* married," she sighed. "I cannot be married to two men."

"The white man's laws—his formalities and regulations—do not need to stop us. We can cross the river into Indian territory and get married there." But she knew this would be dangerous—Phineas was too proud a man to let her go—he would search until he found them. And even if he did release her from her marriage vows, she knew that despite her feelings for Finn she could never adjust to the life of an Indian squaw.

Finn had been particularly compelling in his entreaties when he visited her the day he learned she was expecting a child. "Could it be mine?" he had asked. She assured him the child was not his and prayed she was telling the truth. But she had to wonder: after all, her many couplings with her husband had not previously resulted in a pregnancy, even though she knew Phineas had fathered many children already. Was it possible that, in some cases, a particular man was unable to impregnate a particular woman? She wished for some way to find the key to the question that she so desperately needed answered. She was confused—confused and pregnant—a combination that would allow neither tranquility during the day nor peaceful sleep at night.

The bedroom door opened a crack and a welcome face appeared. "Do you need me, Nia?" asked Maggie.

"No," Nia replied, handing her the chamber pot. "I've managed. But please do come in anyway."

Maggie had come prepared with a cool, wet cloth to wipe her mistress' face and a biscuit to settle her stomach. "Did you get any sleep?"

"A little," Nia answered. "I honestly do not know how women keep on doing this."

"Ah," Maggie laughed, "we'd none of us be here if they didn't. Me own mother had eight. Eight that lived." The look on Nia's face obviously caused Maggie to regret her last words. "But you'll do fine," she quickly added. "Flora will do well by you. I hear she's brought many a healthy baby into this world."

Nia had felt reassured when Phineas had procured the services of Flora, the slave of a neighboring plantation owner, whose midwifery skills were renowned in the area. But right now she wished to move her conversation with Maggie away from her pregnancy, a subject that had dominated her thought practically every minute of the last eight months. "Have you gotten any word from Jacques?" she asked.

"Oh, yes," Maggie beamed. Nia repressed any envy she felt at the smile on Maggie's face and the sparkle that lit up her dark, almost black, eyes. "A friend who was on his way to Nashville brought me a letter. Jacques is in New Orleans now, but will return to Natchez early next year. And Nia, I believe he will ask for my hand in marriage! Do you think Mr. Campbell will allow Jacques to buy out my indenture?"

The hope that this was possible infused Maggie with a radiance Nia was loathe to destroy. "I believe he will," she responded, though she certainly could not be sure Phineas would agree to such a request. Maggie had proven to be an exceptional servant who was well worth her price of indenture as well as her keep, and Nia knew her husband was a man who always watched out for the best possible profit in any situation.

"Can you speak to Mr. Campbell for me?" Maggie pleaded.

"I will certainly try."

Nia's promise gave rise to the most exuberant hug Maggie had ever given her, even despite Nia's advanced pregnancy. "Oops, I almost spilled this," Maggie laughed, nodding toward the chamber pot she still held in her hand. "I'll be getting' rid o' this directly." With that she literally skipped out of the room, throwing Nia a kiss on her way out.

I'll miss her, Nia thought as she contemplated life on the plantation without Maggie. Perhaps Jacques would be willing to wait for his bride until her indenture was completed, or even to settle down in Natchez or on one of the plantations. That seemed unlikely: she had met several trappers since she had come to Mississippi, and they seemed to be an independent, free-wheeling lot, unwilling to become any more civilized than they needed to be. Perhaps that was what Maggie found so attractive in the man.

Whatever the case, she promised herself to do everything she could to convince Phineas to give Maggie her freedom. She hoped the birth of the child would extend his benevolence toward her and cause him to agree, as he had the past few months, to her every whim and desire. At least she could try. Maggie had become her best friend, and it seemed only fair that one of them should find happiness in her marriage.

Nia's labor pains started at approximately 4:30 in the morning. She tried to bear them silently, hoping to hold off calling for help until at least the early morning light. But by 5:00 she could wait no longer. A long scream, loud enough to wake the whole household, emerged from within the depths of her body, despite her efforts to suppress it.

"Ma'am, is it time?" Sara asked, peeking through the door she cracked opened. Sara had been sleeping every night on a pallet just outside Nia's bedroom door for the past two weeks. "Do I send Leander for Flora?"

"Yes, yes!" gasped Nia.

Before her next scream reached its full crescendo, Sara returned to the bedroom holding a pan of steaming water. "Flora be here soon, Ma'am," she assured her, pulling from her apron pocket a cool cloth to place on Nia's forehead. "I sent Leander on horseback. You gonna be all right."

"Mr. Campbell?"

"Not home yet, Ma'am. But we be sendin' someone to find him and ah'm sure he be heah raht soon."

Nia was not surprised her husband was away from home. He had spent very few nights on the plantation once she had shared with him the news of her pregnancy. He said he had business in Natchez and beyond, but she was quite certain that much of the "business" was related to the cessation of intimacy between them once she became with child. Still, she would not be disappointed if he failed to be with her for the birth; in fact, she wished that would be so.

Soon the very female business of birthing was underway. Maggie, quite disheveled after being awakened from a deep sleep but with a glow of anticipation in her eyes, came rushing in to help. She and Sara assisted Nia out of bed and positioned her on the birthing chair that would support her during labor. Gallons of hot water and plenty of clean white linens were carted into the room by Eleanora, who had been summoned from the slave quarters. Hetty, whose presence had not been requested by Nia but who had been wakened by the commotion, wrung her hands and paced in one corner of the room, sporadically giving orders that were for the most part ignored by the other women.

Flora, still in her nighttime shift with a robe thrown over her shoulders, her mobcap askew, arrived within a half hour. She quickly administered the twenty drops of laudanum that in a very short time changed Nia's ear-shattering screams into long moans and whimpers. Upon examining Nia, Flora assured her and the other women present that labor was proceeding well. "You gonna be all right, Ma'am," she said, holding Nia's hand in a firm grasp. "You young and strong. De baby be along any time now." Nia nodded and smiled through her pain which, in a strange way, seemed to hover in a place above her body.

At some point in the hazy fog that had overtaken her mind, she heard a chorus of female voices crying "Push! Push!" and then soon felt a rush of wind hitting her stomach as the painful pressure in her lower body was relieved. A hearty howl soon drowned out the sound of the communal female sigh of relief.

"She be beautiful, Ma'am," announced Flora while Sara and Maggie helped her to her feet and assisted her back to bed. *She*, Nia heard. *A baby girl. Phineas will not be pleased.* Within minutes Flora was by her side, holding a closely wrapped bundle and placing it gently into Nia's outstretched arms as the other women huddled together, waiting to see the child they had just helped bring into the world.

Nia, holding the squirming bundle close to her chest, beheld her daughter's face. It was beautiful, beautiful beyond belief, with a slight tint of bronze in her full cheeks, a mass of dark, straight hair, and solemn black eyes that gazed directly into her own. Slowly unwrapping the covers, Nia discovered a delicate, well-proportioned body, ten fingers, ten toes, and a tiny strawberry-shaped port wine birthmark just below her left shoulder-blade.

The baby was beautiful, and perfect in every way.

Phineas would not be pleased. He would absolutely, positively, undoubtedly not be pleased.

Chapter Eighteen

"'Well,' said the ant, 'you sang all summer, and now you will have to dance all winter.' The End!" With this Nia displayed the picture for Lydia to see. "Do you remember what the moral of this story is, darling?"

"That you have to work to eat?"

"Yes, very good!" Nia beamed at her daughter and smoothed an already smooth section of Lydia's straight, almost black hair. At five years old, Lydia's flashing black eyes gave testament to both her intelligence and her curiosity and her tall, lithe body was suited to the physical activities she loved. She was equally adept at sounding out the words in the primers Nia had discovered in an old chest as she was at galloping one of the work horses over the open fields of their property.

"But we don't work," responded Lydia, looking up at her mother through the deep dark eyes that always reminded Nia of the depths of a well. "Sara and Leander and them work. But we don't."

Nia was once again amazed at her daughter's instinct for observation and insight. She wondered if this would be a good time to share with Lydia her own opinions about "the peculiar institution," as she used to hear the Natchez nabobs call it. But she didn't dare. Her daughter needed to learn to be a part of this system if she was destined to live her life in it.

"We all have different work to do," Nia replied. "Some people have to work in the fields or in the house. Other people, like Papa, work away from home. And your work is to be a good girl and learn to do things like reading." She saw what appeared to be a look of skepticism on Lydia's face, then wondered whether a five-year-old would be capable of such an adult emotion. "This is all God's plan," she added, practically gagging on the words.

"Can you read me another story?" Lydia asked. Nia had read her daughter every story in *Aesop's Fables* dozens of times, but Lydia never seemed to get enough of them.

"No, dear, it is almost time for bed."

"Oh, please. Just one more!"

Nia could seldom resist her daughter's pleas. Those deep, dark eyes. "All right then. But only one more. Would you like the one about the country mouse and the town mouse?"

"Oh, yes!"

Nia turned to the well-worn page in the book she had been given as a child by her own Grandmother Lydia Meier, her daughter's namesake. Nia would never forget Phineas' response when he had first laid eyes on the baby. He had arrived home the day after Lydia had been born, and had burst into the bedroom while Sara had just begun giving her a bath. Ignoring his wife in his haste to see the baby, he rushed to Sara's side and looked closely into the basin where Sara's strong hands were gently dribbling water over Lydia's dark hair.

"A little girl," Nia offered.

"Yes," he answered, "I can see that." Looking even more closely at the baby, he then turned to Nia, who could see confusion in his face. Then, looking back into the basin, he pointed at the strawberry-shaped mark high on her chest. "Sara, what is this?" he asked.

"A birthmark, Massa," she answered. "Sometime dey go 'way when de baby grow up."

"Have you... have you thought of any names for our daughter?" Nia quickly interjected, hoping the wavering of her voice did not reveal the fear that gripped her heart.

Phineas looked once more at the baby, then once again, long and hard, at Nia. Finally, "Name the wench anything you want!" he sneered, storming out of the bedroom and then out of the house, to which he did not return for three days. Nia realized immediately that her husband was aware of what she herself already knew: that Lydia was her daughter, but his granddaughter.

Over the past five years he had never uttered the words, either to her or, she suspected, to anyone else, that would brand her as an unfaithful wife. Nia believed his pride would not allow him to do that. But the knowledge of her betrayal hung in the air and affected every aspect of their life together. Though they shared the same house during the rare times when he was there, he spoke to her only when it was absolutely necessary. And he made her pay dearly, and in many different ways, for her transgression.

The first payment was made at Maggie's expense. As bad luck would have it, Jacques LeBeau had returned to Three Ponds Farm only five days after Lydia's birth. Marching forthrightly to the front door, he had asked

Phineas for a short audience, and Phineas, who probably knew nothing about LeBeau's interest in Maggie, invited him in. But Maggie, wringing her hands and pacing back and forth as she waited on the long front porch, did not have to wait long for her master's response.

After only a few minutes, Jacques dashed out the front door onto the porch, followed by an obviously enraged Phineas brandishing a pistol. "Stay off my property," he shouted. Seeing Maggie, he grabbed her by the arm and pulled her tightly to him. "And stay away from this woman! She is my property too!"

Jacques, despite the weapon pointed directly at him, had called out to Maggie, swearing that he would return to make her his wife on the day her indenture was completed. Maggie had called out to Jacques as well, promising she would wait for him, as Phineas pulled her into the house. But by the end of the day Phineas had forced Maggie to become his property in a way that had not been stated on the contract. By the time the remaining three years of the indenture was up, Maggie was the mother of Phineas' two-year-old son and eight-month-old daughter.

The morning after Jacques' ill-fated visit, Phineas, declaring that Nia no longer needed the services of a lady's maid, had made the vegetable garden Maggie's responsibility. Even worse, claiming that the two women would have no need for further contact, he had forbidden them to speak to each other. Now the only time Nia saw Maggie was when she caught sight of her friend slouching between the vegetable garden and the shack that had been built for her and their children. Seeing Maggie so disheveled and obviously completely dispirited never ceased to cause Nia spasms of pain and guilt.

"'Do you not get weary of living in a hole?' said the town mouse," Nia read. "'You cannot prefer rocks and woods to the excitement you will find in the town. A mouse does not live forever. Come to town with me, and I will show you a better life.'"

Every time she read this particular fable to Lydia, Nia thought of herself as a very unwilling country mouse. Although Phineas had made many trips to Nashville, New Orleans, and even Baltimore in the past five years, he had never permitted her to leave the plantation, not even for a visit to Natchez or Rocky Springs, which was becoming a booming little town on its own.

Nia would never have believed she could miss the endless whist games with the dowagers who comprised Hetty's social circle: the cucumber sandwiches, the sweet tea, the petits fours. The endless gossip about other women in the community—whose child was not doing well, whose husband was suspected of having an affair, who may have succumbed to the sin of excessive drinking—all with an affectation of concern for the unfortunate woman being discussed.

She had even begun to again enjoy accompanying her husband to the races once the horrid memory of Duke's demise and the following evening's horrors had begun to fade. But all these amusements were now missing from her life.

Phineas' business travels had brought him success and the plantation now boasted over three times its earlier acreage and almost a hundred slaves. But the enhancement of the mansion and its gardens had been abruptly halted once Lydia had been born. Some rooms on the first floor remained unfinished, their furnishings beginning to look shabby and outdated. A crystal chandelier in the parlor was missing its glass globes, making it unusable, and the piano-forte had gone untuned for years. The second floor was even worse, with draperies still in boxes and walls left unpainted.

But what did it matter? No one had been invited to Three Ponds Farm since Lydia's birth. Nia believed Phineas still belonged to the St. Catherine race club, but he never invited her to attend any of the races. Nia surmised that, if he wished to maintain his standing with the other Natchez planters, he was most likely socializing in Natchez, Rocky Springs or beyond. Of course, her piano instructor had been dismissed, and while her husband's portrait had been prominently hung over the fireplace mantel, hers remained unfinished in the back of a bedroom wardrobe. The only escape Nia had from the house was an occasional ride on one of the work horses or a solitary practice session on the shooting range which, though much deteriorated, was still usable.

All the servants, whether slave or indentured, had obviously become aware of her diminished status in the household: none of them paid any particular attention to her requests. Hetty was now, in every way, the true mistress of Three Ponds Farm, and everyone who lived there realized it. Any suggestion Nia made about household affairs, no matter how minor or necessary, was sure to be countermanded by Hetty.

Nia often felt she was a prisoner of war stranded in hostile territory. During the first two years after her daughter's birth she had written several times to her family in Pennsylvania, giving the letters to Hetty with the request that they be posted. But she never knew whether that had actually happened. She had not received any communication from them, leaving her to wonder whether they had never received her letters or had, themselves, abandoned her to her fate. She wished for the former, but in her darkest hours felt that she perhaps deserved abandonment.

"I like the country!" Lydia piped in. "I like the chickens!"

"Of course you do," Nia responded. "We both like the country," she lied. She now hated this god-forsaken country with its swamps filled with some of the strangest and most noxious examples of flora and fauna known to creation. Alligators. Wild boars. Venomous snakes and spiders. Poison mushrooms. Mosquitoes the size of hummingbirds. Seeming to forget her reasons for leaving Philadelphia, she remembered her life there as a near paradise of refinement and joy.

And poor Lydia. Much to Nia's distress, the child had never been allowed to leave the confines of Three Ponds Farm and knew nothing else. What would become of her? Nia prayed that some day Phineas would realize how bright and lively Lydia was, and that any remaining humanity residing in his heart would persuade him to provide for her education and advancement. But at times she wondered whether her husband actually had any remaining humanity: she'd seen little if any indication of that since the day Lydia had been born. Still, the child was blameless in every way and deserved more than the meager life available to her.

Often, Nia dreamed of escape—of grabbing her daughter and little else and making their way to the Trace and, if need be, all the way up to Nashville, or even back home. But she had no one here, no trusted friend, to help her, and doubted she and her daughter could survive even a short trip up a road full of gangs of villains and murderers. If only Finn were here.

At the time, she had not believed the contrived story Phineas had told her only two weeks after Lydia had been born: that Finn had been ambushed and murdered while riding to Nashville on the Trace. Phineas, with what appeared to be a shoddy theatrical performance of grief, had shown her a bloodied vest that did look a great deal like the fringed buckskin Finn often wore. As Phineas provided more details about the gruesome ambush scene, he seemed to be watching her closely, looking carefully for her reaction.

She was convinced her husband was trying to torture her or perhaps to trap her into some reaction that would seal her guilt. She forced herself to react in a subdued manner that she hoped reflected the appropriate level of sorrow at the death of her husband's son who, supposedly, she hardly knew.

But Finn hadn't returned to the plantation in these five years. She had received no word from him, had overheard no whispered gossip, had never again heard his name mentioned at Three Ponds Farm. It was as if Finn had never existed. If he was not actually dead, he was certainly dead to her.

Sometimes she relived that conversation with Phineas over and over. Did anything Phineas say suggest he was hinting at something even more vile—that Finn was indeed dead, and that he had something to do with it? Would a man actually kill his own son?

But why not? Why was she so scandalized by this thought? Wasn't she about to commit the same crime?

Phineas' obvious hatred had not diminished his desire for her. Within just six months of Lydia's birth, Nia was shocked and dismayed to learn she and her husband were indeed capable of producing a child after all. When the pregnancy ended in miscarriage in less than a month, even before she had notified Phineas of the coming blessed event, she had been more relieved than saddened.

Now she again found herself with child. She despaired. How could she bring another child into this household? Her relationship with her husband had become intolerable. His physical abuse of her had begun slowly, with only an occasional off-handed shove or push that, she hoped, had been unintended. Then one day, when she had made some minor request the gist of which she had by now forgotten, he had slapped her face so hard that she carried the bruise on her cheek for over a week.

But the actual beatings had not begun until the day she overtly defied him. He had sent his new overseer, Jack Colbert, to summon the slaves to witness another lashing. Lashings had become a frequent occurrence at Three Ponds, one that was occasioned by almost any small mistake a slave would make. As always, Nia fled to her bedroom to avoid any sight or sound of the atrocity that was to take place. This day was judgment day for Prissy, a young house slave who had been accused of stealing a spoon.

"But who accused her?" Nia had asked Phineas as she saw him in the hallway that separated their bedrooms. She did not believe that Prissy, who was terrified of even her own shadow, was capable of such a crime.

"'Tis none of your business, Woman," he had responded. "Do ye question my judgment?" His laughter expressed his derision of such a notion. "What d' ye know of running a farm?"

"Nothing, it appears. But I do know that an accusation is not the same thing as a finding of guilt."

"Oh, we shall find the lass guilty all right! It won't take but a few lashes before she'll be confessing. They always do!" he responded, turning away from her toward the staircase.

"But that is unjust!" She had heard this bizarre comment about determining guilt through torture before, and had always found it senseless and repugnant. "Of course she would confess, whether she had done the crime or not. Can you not see how evil…"

But Phineas had not given her the chance to finish her sentence. Pushing her back into her room and slamming the door behind him, he had forced her onto her knees beside her bed, then pushed her body forward onto the mattress, straddling her with such force that she could scarcely breathe. She could hear him muttering under his breath, but could make out only the words "Jezebel" and "Whore of Babylon." The next thing she heard was the sound of his loosening his belt, then snapping it in the air once, twice, three times before applying it to her. Her mother's beatings had been nothing like this. The pain was unbearable, but not more so than the terror she felt at being completely helpless against his rage and his power.

Perhaps even worse, after the beating he had demanded she witness Prissy's punishment. He had made this demand many times before, but had always relented. This time he was impervious to her pleas. "You wish to see justice?" he had screamed into her face. "'The wicked reap what they sow'—remember that! Prissy shall get her just reward, and from now on, so shall you. You are my wife. You live here under my roof. You will do what I say in all things," he spit out, "or pay the price for your disobedience. 'Tis the responsibility of the mistress of the house to participate in the correction of the workers, and to correct them herself, if need be. You will no longer shirk that responsibility."

So she had stood beside her husband, who held her hand hard enough to send shooting pains all the way up to her shoulder, and watched as Prissy was reduced from a pleasant young girl with bright eyes and a wide, friendly smile to a mass of tattered flesh, blood pooling at her bare feet. Of course Prissy confessed to the crime—as early as the third lash—but Phineas had demanded an extra twenty lashes for punishment. The spoon was later found wedged in a space between the slats of a kitchen drawer.

No, Nia could not bear to bring another soul into this world. Once she was certain she was pregnant, she persuaded Hetty to send for Flora on the pretext of having difficulty with her monthly menses. Convincing the midwife to help her was not easy, but Nia was able to bribe her into coming to the planting shed later this evening.

"'Living this way may be good for those who like it,' replied the country mouse, 'but I would rather have my barley bread in peace and safety than your dainty food eaten with fear and trembling.' The End."

"Just one more?" begged Lydia. But this time her mother would not be persuaded.

"Up to bed with you, right now," she insisted, watching her child climb slowly up the stairs. "I will be up in just a minute to hear your prayers."

The prayers of a child must wend their way directly to God, she thought. But she knew that no prayer she could possibly say this night would make up for the wrong she was about to set in motion.

Chapter Nineteen

Nia wrapped the old shawl around her shoulders more tightly. It felt cool in the planting shed, but perhaps her purpose for being here in the middle of the night was the real cause of her chill.

Flora was late. Nia rose once more from the bench on which she sat and walked to the tiny window that opened onto the path Flora would be taking from the Gordons' farm. Perhaps Flora was not coming. Perhaps something had happened—maybe she had been discovered leaving the slave quarters without permission. What if she had been compelled to confess to the purpose of her leaving? Nia forced herself to stop speculating on what the outcome of such a situation would be.

Suddenly she saw a blurred motion far down the path she had already scrutinized many times. Yes, it was a figure, getting closer. A woman wrapped in a shawl much like her own, her covered head shaking from side to side. As the figure came to the planting shed door, Nia opened it quickly. "Did you have any problems getting here?" she asked.

"No, Ma'am. You sho you wanna do dis?"

"Yes," Nia answered, sounding much more convinced than she actually felt.

"You got da ring?"

"Yes, here it is," Nia responded, reaching into her skirt pocket to remove a small silver ring Phineas had given her on their first anniversary. Phineas would never realize it was missing; he paid no attention these days to what she wore or how she looked. She handed it to Flora.

"Sho is purty," the woman responded. "You really sho?" Nia nodded. "Den heah," Flo said, reaching into her own pocket to take out two folded paper packets. Opening the first, she showed the contents to Nia, saying "Dis one be tansy. Two tablespoon." Nia looked carefully at the small mound of dried leaves and nodded solemnly. "And dis one heah be pennyroyal. T'ree tablespoon. Boil bot' togedah in a quart o' water."

"Yes," nodded Nia. "I can do that. How much should I drink?"

"One cupful ever' fo' hour. Startin' tomorrow mornin'. Drink it hot."

"For how long?"

"Long as it take. Mebbe t'ree, fo' day."

"And then?"

"Den you be rid o' wat you don' want. But be careful, Ma'am. You gonna prob'ly be sickin' up some."

"Vomiting?" Nia asked, receiving a nodding affirmation from Flora. This would not be a problem. She had vomited nearly every morning for the past three weeks.

"An' shakes," Flora continued. "You mebbe gonna get de shakes. An' mebbe you see t'ings."

"See things? What kind of things?"

"Ah don' know. Mebbe ha'nts. Could be anyt'ing. You see t'ings, you stop."

Ghosts? Thought Nia. *I could be seeing ghosts?* She considered how powerful these small mounds of dry leaves must be.

"You be careful now, Ma'am," Flora said, heading toward the door. "You nevah see me tonight."

"Yes, of course," Nia responded gravely, knowing that this evening's meeting was as dangerous to herself as it was to Flora.

"You sick again?" Hetty asked sharply. Nia had just returned from her third visit that morning to the outhouse.

"Just a little bit," she responded. But Hetty would have had to be almost blind to not notice Nia's disheveled hair and sunken eyes, as well as the greenish gray tint of her skin.

"Might you be..." Hetty began. "What did Flora say?"

"No, I'm not," Nia responded to Hetty's unfinished question. "It must just be influenza. I'm going back to bed. No need for anyone else to get sick. Would you ask Prissy to come get my chamber pot again?"

Vomiting. Painful cramps. Dizziness. Nia reflected that ridding oneself of a pregnancy was even more difficult than enduring one. But she hoped all these symptoms meant the vile brew she had been drinking was doing its job.

Staggering back to her room, she practically tumbled into the bed and pulled the three coverlets she had removed from the linen chest up to her chin. It was a hot September day, but her body shook with chills. Closing her eyes, she prayed this would soon be over.

She heard them before she saw them. A tapping noise, just barely audible. She thought it must be mice in the walls—there were certainly plenty of them in the mansion. But these taps were coming from up high, near the ceiling. She had never heard mice in that area.

The taps became pecks, and looking up she saw what appeared to be the tip of a tiny black arrow popping in and out along the molding just above her bed. Soon she saw several more, then even more, and within seconds the whole ceiling seemed full of them, forming tiny crevices along the whole molding, their pecking sound soon becoming a cacophony. She sat up quickly, then retreated back under the covers when she sensed something flying swiftly past her, just missing her head. That was when the cawing began.

Within seconds the whole room whirled with their motion. The combined noise of cawing and the flapping of hundreds of wings was thunderous. Peeking out from beneath the covers, she saw masses of them, their black feathers shining in the filtered light. Crows! Dozens, maybe hundreds of them, circling the air above her head, some diving toward her before swerving back upward toward the ceiling. Grasping her pillow in both hands, she began swinging wildly at them, never hitting one but at least keeping most of them at bay.

She heard pounding at the door and her name being called, then felt a force grabbing her arms and shaking her soundly. Terrified, she fought, but was far too weak to counter her attacker. She felt a slap on her cheek, then another.

"Nia! Nia! Wake up!" Lurching out of the dream-like state that held her it its grasp, she opened her eyes to see the face of Hetty, her steel gray eyes and thin-lipped mouth wide open in alarm, with an equally wide-eyed Prissy visible just over her shoulder.

"I... I saw crows. Where are they? Did you see them?" she asked, looking warily around the room.

"A dream. It must have been a dream," Hetty responded, releasing Nia's arms and stepping backward. "You scared us half to death!"

"I... I'm sorry. You're right," Nia conceded, seeing no evidence of any crow attack. "I must have been dreaming."

"Do you want me to send for someone? Doctor Rodriguez? Flora?"

"No, no," Nia answered. "I feel better now. I believe I just need more sleep."

"Very well then," Hetty answered, looking somewhat skeptically at Nia. "I can't stay with you any longer; I have work to do. Prissy, you stand outside Missus Nia's door in case she needs something."

With that they were both gone, and Nia tried to make sense of what had happened. Had she experienced the hallucinations Flora had warned her about? It had seemed so real. She could see, hear and feel those birds. Perhaps she should stop taking the brew, as Flora had advised. But she was already two days into the process, and the hallucination might have been an indication that the medicine was working.

Next time I'll remember, she thought, deciding to complete the treatment. *I'll just remind myself I'm dreaming.*

"Mama, these are for you."

"Oh, how pretty," Nia responded, reaching for the somewhat crumpled bouquet in her daughter's hands. "Look," she added, holding it out and pointing to a bloom. This spiny pink one is a bull thistle. And this big yellow one is a sunflower." Lydia craned her neck forward to examine the individual flowers more closely. "And these tiny white ones are yarrow. Here," she said, rubbing the leaves between her fingers. "Smell." Lydia, bending even closer, breathed in deeply.

"It smells sweet," she said.

"Yes, my darling, but no sweeter than you," Nia said, pulling her daughter close. "You are so sweet to bring Mama wildflowers. Are you ready to go back to the house?"

Nia had had a comparatively peaceful morning, having gotten sick only once upon first awakening. Hoping to alleviate the burning cramps that tore at her midsection day and night, she had taken Lydia for a walk to their favorite place, a meadow only fifteen minutes from the house. The cool, crisp morning air and the gentle breeze that floated the scent of fall wildflowers around them had revived her physically and mentally. She was confident she was close to being finished with the treatment which, she told herself over and over, was painful but necessary.

"Can I go for a horse ride when we get back?" asked Lydia.

"Of course. We'll ask Sam to saddle Candy when we get back."

"Let's go now!" Lydia said, taking her mother's hand and comically attempting to pull her up. "Do I have to have a saddle?"

That must be the Indian in her Nia thought, looking lovingly at her daughter. Lydia was so full of life, so attuned to the natural world around her. She was physically adept, and had a depth of feeling rare in a child so young. Her father would have been proud of her.

"Let's see what Sam says." Sam, the new stable boy, was only recently purchased to replace Leville, who had never fully recovered from the lashing he had received years earlier. Nia had begged Phineas not to sell Leville for the sake of Sara and Leander, if for no other reason, but her pleas were in vain. Phineas, stating that the boy was no longer useful to him, had sold him at auction.

Nia could never determine whether her husband did these things out of meanness or spite, or simply because he was part of a system that considered a slave no more than a horse, a wagon, or a piece of furniture: something that could be sold or destroyed when it no longer served its purpose. She wondered whether, had he been raised in a different situation, he would have realized how truly evil his actions were, but she realized she would never know the answer.

She had no sooner entrusted her daughter to the capable hands of Sam than a cramp threatened to double her over, right there at the stable. She considered waiting until later that day to take the next dose of her potion, but decided she wanted to be through with the whole process. Sneaking warily into the kitchen, she removed the jar of fluid from its hiding place in a back closet and, measuring out a cup, heated it on the constantly burning hearth. Grimacing at its hideous taste and smell, she swallowed the concoction quickly, then headed upstairs to her room.

Sitting on the rocker she had used while nursing Lydia, she picked up the needlework she had been working. But cramps and nausea made it too difficult to concentrate on the complicated cross-stitch pattern. Grateful once again that the long velvet drapes in her room had been installed before Phineas had discontinued rejuvenation of the mansion, she closed them and, grabbing a pillow, hugged it tightly to her stomach.

Later on she would remember the shooting pains becoming increasingly stronger as she rocked and groaned on the bed. *It must be happening,* she thought, forcing herself to remain silent through her suffering. Fearing she could no longer stop herself from screaming and that Hetty would hear her and, rushing into the room, observe what was happening, she forced herself out of bed and managed with great effort to push a small storage trunk against the door. Staggering into her bed and groaning softly into her pillow, she surrendered herself to the pain and once again tried to convince herself that she was doing the right thing.

She must have dozed off, since she could not clearly remember when the pounding had begun. But it was deafening. And the howling! It sounded like a chorus from Hell.

As she opened her eyes, she saw the room, its walls now swirling with fiery slashes of color, red, yellow and orange, dripping to the floor. And the pounding, which became even louder, was coming from behind the door.

Soon the door was shaking—whatever evil lay outside was forcing its way in. As the door rattled and shook, she saw a wicked darkness behind it—a blackness that defied any thought of light—and glimpsed the hideous face of the monster that was forcing its way in.

The face was red, its black lips set in an evil scowl. Spurts of red and putrid green filth spewed from its eyes and mouth. Its red hair was coarse and matted into plaits that swirled like snakes upon its head. The devil! It was the devil! Come to take her to Hell!

Summoning the last of her strength, she reached toward the nightstand and pulled open the drawer. In the dark she felt for the butt of her pistol then struggled to pull it out, managing to cock and point it with both hands just as the door burst open and the monster plunged into the room. The sound of the shot, magnified in the confines of the small room, deafened her as she felt a burst of warm, sticky liquid spatter her face, arms and hands. Holding her hand up to her face, she recognized the color and consistency of blood. She forced herself to look at a figure that lay on the floor beside her bed. She recognized something—the new tooled leather boots he had bought during his last trip to New Orleans.

The last thing she heard before passing out was Hetty's scream, followed by the words "My God! What have you done!"

Part II—Lydia—1807

Chapter One

Give me, O God, a mild, a peaceable, a meek, and a humble spirit, that remembering my infirmities, I may bear with those of others. Give me, O God, a mild, a peaceable, a meek, and a humble spirit, that remembering my infirmities, I may bear with those of others. Give me, O God, a mild, a peaceable, a meek, and a humble spirit, that remembering my infirmities, I may bear with those of others. As Lydia dipped her quill for what seemed to be the thousandth time, she heard the quick rapping of a cane against the door, followed by the sound of the door opening. *Madame Girard,* she thought, releasing a sigh.

"Are you nearly finished, child?" Madame asked, hobbling over to Lydia's desk. Adjusting the voluminous skirts of her black crepe gown and raising a monocle to her left eye, she squinted at Lydia's work.

"Forty-eight done, Madame. Two more left to write."

"Finish quickly, or you shall miss dinner once again," the old woman advised, pulling the room's second chair up to the desk where Lydia, bent to her task, continued writing. Lydia realized she would be better able to complete her assignment if Madame simply left, but she said nothing. She was hungry this evening.

"I hope you take those words to heart," Madame said. "The words of Hannah More should provide an example to you, particularly since you are leaving the Academy well before matriculating."

"Yes, Madame," answered Lydia as she continued writing. At this point her cramped hand made her handwriting more of a scribble than anything, but having been assigned this punishment many times previously, she knew Madame Girard would not take the time to closely examine her penmanship.

"You do not need to leave, you know," Madame continued. "You are certainly one of our more intelligent students. What we teach you here is meant to prepare you for life as a wife, mother, and mistress of a home. If you would simply apply yourself and subjugate your rebellious spirit... "

"Done," Lydia announced, completing the last word with a flourish and handing the pages to her teacher. "May I go to dinner now?"

"Very well," Madame sighed, giving only a cursory glance at her student's work. "But mark my word, child. You still have very much to learn."

"Yes, Madame. Thank you, Madame," Lydia responded icily, rising from her chair and turning toward the door. *Only two more days*, she thought, *and I shall be free of this woman.* At nearly fifteen years of age, Lydia, tall and lithe like her father, did not fit the mold of the typical student of the Chambers Female Academy. Her long, straight, raven-black hair, dark piercing eyes, and honey-colored skin stood out among a class of mostly blue-eyed, curly-haired blondes with peaches-and-cream complexions.

But she hadn't seemed to fit in well at any of the "situations" her Aunt Hetty had found for her. Lydia had received her first introduction to the rudiments of reading and mathematics at Miss Hill's Primary School for Young Ladies in Rocky Springs. There she had spent mornings studying with the other five girls in residence and afternoons weeding the school's gardens and cleaning its chicken coops. But Miss Hill could not abide Lydia's tendency to regularly wander off the property, and several sessions with the paddle had not resolved the issue. Aunt Hetty was faced with the problem of finding another place for her niece.

Lydia was next sent to board at Sacred Heart Convent in New Orleans with the Ursaline sisters, whose curriculum stressed religious studies and deportment. This situation was even less successful, as Lydia not only seemed incapable of conducting herself with proper ladylike decorum, she also had the audacity to question even the most basic tenets of religious faith.

The Chambers Female Academy had been her home for the last five years. She liked this situation no more than her previous two, but being so far from home, she realized she had no alternative but to persevere. The previous Christmas, the only time she had been allowed to return to visit Three Ponds Farm since she had been sent to the Academy, she had begged her aunt to release her from her studies. Hetty, perhaps worn down by her niece's nagging pleas, had promised that, if she could manage to survive the Academy without being expelled, she could return home once she turned fifteen. This would happen in two days.

Even after five years at the Academy, she felt out of place. Althea Middlemas, her best and probably only friend there, often urged her to use her eccentricity to advantage. "You are *très belle*," she would say, "an *exotique!*" Althea's favorite course at the Academy was French. Lydia did not have a favorite course. She hated cooking as much as writing, etiquette as much as religion, and needlework most of all. French knots. Seed stitches. Bullion knots. Who could possibly care about such things?

Dancing could have become a favorite course: she actually enjoyed the free movements of the contredance and the allemande, although the tightly patterned steps of the minuet were much less to her liking. Her main objection to dancing class, however, was that, as the tallest girl in the fourth form, she was frequently required to play the male role. This meant she was, once again, *required* to do something that other girls found disagreeable.

She waited impatiently until Madame, her cane tapping at every step, left the room: not doing so would have broken an etiquette rule that would have had her copying Hanna More edicts once again. Perhaps she hated etiquette class most of all, not that Aunt Hetty would allow her to break many of those rules once she returned home. There she would be expected to exercise the rules she had learned in her years at boarding school in every aspect of her daily life.

Rushing to the dining hall, she was pleased to see that Althea had saved a place for her at the senior girls' table. The hall, its paneled walls adorned with portraits of the various headmistresses who had kept the Academy running for almost forty years, was occupied by the other thirty-five girls currently in residence. They sat at four long tables, conversing in lowered voices with the girls sitting on wooden benches adjacent to or across from them. Loud conversations were not allowed.

"What is dinner tonight?" Lydia asked Althea as she pulled up her skirt and stepped over the bench to take her seat to the right of her friend.

"*Ragoût de lapin*," Althea answered.

"Rabbit stew again?" Rabbit stew was also a staple at Three Ponds Farm, but Sara was a much better cook than the *chef de cuisine* at the school.

"It sounds better if you say it in French," insisted Althea. Lydia smiled, but did not agree. "May I introduce Polly?" Althea continued, gesturing toward a rather stout girl with long brown braids, a girl Lydia had never seen before. "Polly recently arrived here from New Orleans."

"*Enchanté*," Polly said. "Althea tells me you are leaving the school."

"Yes," Lydia answered, trying to suppress the broad smile Polly's comment had initiated. Although she couldn't quite comprehend why, she knew Althea's feelings would be hurt if she expressed her happiness at leaving. Althea would see it as a rejection of their friendship. "I leave in two days."

"You must be very happy to be going back to your papa and mama," Polly responded with a smile. But the look of alarm on Althea's face must have let Polly know immediately that she had committed a *faux pas*.

Lydia, who had quickly hunched over to begin shoving spoonfulls of stew into her mouth, did not answer. An uncomfortable minute passed before Althea, cautiously looking at Lydia and then back to Polly, responded. "Lydia lost her parents years ago to yellow fever. She is an orphan."

"Oh, I am so sorry," Polly said, looking crestfallen. "*C'est dommage!* I did not mean to..."

"Don't be sorry," Lydia interrupted. "I was only five years old; I hardly remember them. I have my Aunt Hetty. She raised me."

Lydia truly did not remember her parents, or at least the parents her aunt had often spoken of. Hetty spoke mostly of Lydia's papa who, her aunt said, was a tall, handsome, kind-hearted man who was successful in business and adored his daughter. When Lydia would ask about her mama, Aunt Hetty gave little response, simply saying that her mother was a small, quiet woman, a Northerner who had never really adjusted to Southern life, and who had been the first to contract the fever. Her papa, while taking care of his ailing wife, had then also succumbed to the dreaded disease.

Yet Lydia had other memories: of plucking flowers in the field, riding horses, listening to stories about grasshoppers and mice. She also carried in her heart terrible memories: of darkness, loud sounds in the middle of the night, screams. Aunt Hetty told her those last memories were only dreams, and that she should best forget them.

"Well, I hope you have a safe trip," chirped Polly. "I am sure your friends here will miss you."

Lydia nodded and smiled at Polly, but in her mind she was already on the schooner sailing back to Three Ponds Farm.

Chapter II

"I believe God hath given us a more temperate day today; think ye not, Lydia?"

Lydia forced herself to nod and smile at Mrs. Hunt, the chaperone Madame Girard had arranged for her trip on the Schooner *Aphrodite*. But she hardly agreed; today seemed as unbearably hot and humid as yesterday, and the day before that, and the day before that. Although Lydia had attired herself in the lightest cotton frock she owned, by 9:00 in the morning she was already drenched in sweat, her damp hair hanging lankly over her shoulders.

She wondered how Mrs. Hunt could so cheerfully bear the heat dressed as she was in her customary heavy serge gown, bib apron, and bonnet, or even how she survived a wardrobe comprising only drab brown gowns and starched white aprons and bonnets. How could she remain placidly composed, even through many everlastingly long days at sea? Of course, Martha Hunt was old—twenty-seven, she had told Lydia. She was traveling to New Orleans to join her husband, the Reverend Israel Hunt, who was attempting to establish a Quaker meetinghouse on the outskirts of the city. Apparently no one there had any interest in what he had to say about the evils of slavery.

Lydia was not surprised that Reverend Hunt was having difficulty. Once, after listening to yet another of Mrs. Hunt's diatribes against keeping slaves, Lydia had tried to explain to the woman how important slavery was to the Southern economy and culture. How it was an ancient institution, a necessity in a rural society. How it was heartily endorsed by the most revered of sources, the Holy Bible, and thus was the will of God. Because her arguments had had no effect whatsoever, Lydia, reverting to her boarding school etiquette lessons, decided to simply smile and nod whenever Mrs. Hunt brought up the subject.

"Ye wouldst be better off if ye kept yourself busy, dearest Lydia," Mrs. Hunt suggested. "Idle hands are the devil's workshop. I have a charming pattern of a rose in full bloom. Would ye care to join me in embroidering some hand towels?" Mrs. Hunt had tried unsuccessfully to interest Lydia in taking up needlework during their journey. But Lydia had so hated needlework class at the Academy that even the boredom of this trip was not enough to make her pick up an embroidery frame.

She thought of the thrill she had felt two weeks earlier while stepping off the Baltimore Harbor dock onto the smooth, glistening decks of the schooner. In the distance she could see the sails of double masts billowing in the heady winds; soon her schooner would be joining them.

Captain Noren himself had guided her on a tour of the luxurious accommodations the ship offered passengers: the commodious dining hall with its mahogany chairs and tables, the wide upper deck where passengers could enjoy the breeze on sunny days, the cabin which, although she shared it with Mrs. Hunt, actually provided her more personal space than she'd had in the Academy's dormitory.

But the trip had been dull. For other than a few blustery hours several days earlier, the sea had been calm. Compared to Baltimore, the towns where they had docked to take on supplies and accommodate embarking and disembarking passengers had been nothing more than backwater villages. She had found no passenger who interested her enough to engage in anything but the most trivial social amenities. The previous evening she had even declined Mrs. Hunt's invitation to walk a bit around St. Augustine, having no interest in seeing yet another Spanish mission, particularly in the company of a woman who spoke only of sin, prayer, and redemption.

"Perhaps tomorrow," she said to Mrs. Hunt, brushing the back of her hand against her forehead as she began to rise from her chair. "I fear I must return to our cabin. Another fainting spell ..." But before she could finish her excuse, she caught a very welcome sight: Captain Noren entering the dining hall accompanied by two young men.

"Oh," Lydia said, quickly retaking her seat. "I suddenly feel much better. I must have caught a bit of a breeze." She chose to ignore the look of disapproval Mrs. Hunt flashed her way as Captain Noren headed directly to their table.

"Mrs. Hunt, Miss Campbell, may I introduce Messrs. Nigel Masters and Harry Russell?" asked Captain Noren with a short bow. "They will be joining us for part of our journey." Messrs. Masters and Russell bowed slightly to Lydia's broad smile and Mrs. Hunt's curt nod. Lydia realized her chaperone saw this encounter as a challenge to the responsibility she had undertaken.

"Only part of our journey? How long will you be with us?" Lydia asked, wishing she had spent a few minutes longer on this morning's toilette. Masters was handsome enough, with a full, friendly face, hazel eyes, strawberry blonde hair and a matching mustache. His morning dress was the gentleman's standard pea green single-breasted coat with drab britches and Hessian boots. But Russell had theatrical good looks and flair, with chestnut curls, a clean-shaven, square chin, strikingly blue eyes and a wicked smile. He was quite the dandy in his Prussian blue coat and scarlet waistcoat, coupled with tight fawn pantaloons and half boots.

"Only a few days," responded Russell. "We're disembarking in Cayo Hueso. We have some business there."

"Cayo Hueso?"

"Yes," added Masters. "It is the last of a series of beautiful islands extending west from the tip of the peninsula. It's been a Spanish port since the sixteenth century." Lydia smiled and nodded toward Masters at the information—more than she needed just then—although it pained her to take her gaze away from Russell's icy blue eyes.

"Perhaps we will have some time to walk about the island when we land there. The town is charming—quite exotic. What do you say, Captain?" asked Russell.

"Yes, we will be there overnight," Captain Noren responded. Then, after a quick glance at the sour look of disapproval on Mrs. Hunt's face, he quickly added, "But the gentlemen wanted to see the binnacle, did you not?" Turning toward Lydia, he informed her that Mr. Masters had a keen interest in compasses and log-glasses.

"Why, yes," responded Masters brightly. With that, the gentlemen took their leave. Lydia would have been deeply disappointed by their quick departure were it not for the mischievous smile Harry Russell cast her way as he closed the dining hall door behind them.

It began slowly. Lydia could not see but could hear waves, some rumbling, some lapping, but each sounding distinctly on the shore. The cobalt sky turned ochre, then a deep rose, just before a shimmer of color leading to a halo of yellow appeared on the horizon. Three palms which had appeared a faded black began to take on definition and color.

For a moment the ocean seemed unwilling to surrender its grasp on the throbbing globe that, in its effort to break free, appeared as a living thing. The globe hovered for a moment, but when it finally escaped, it forcefully shot upward. A flock of seagulls, then a few pelicans appeared, each bird searching the waves for its breakfast. The sky was awash in robin's egg blue with just a few wisps of clouds skimming the horizon.

"It is like a miracle," sighed Lydia.

"Yes. And it happens every day. The sunset on Cayo Hueso is even more spectacular. I know no other place where both a beautiful sunrise and a glorious sunset can be seen every day."

"I must go," Lydia said, rising from the blanket Harry had been thoughtful enough to bring as she brushed off the few grains of sand stubbornly clinging to her skirt. "Mrs. Hunt will awaken very soon."

Harry, rising quickly and taking her hand, held it to his lips for just a moment before releasing it. "May I visit you in Natchez?" he asked.

Yes! Yes! Lydia thought. But she reminded herself she was no longer a schoolgirl who had the luxury of saying whatever came to mind. A young woman had to be more calculating, more elusive, in her dealings with a young man.

"Why, Mr. Russell," she replied, practicing her most coquettish smile, "Natchez is a lovely place to visit in late spring when the bougainvillea are in bloom. I am certain you would enjoy a visit."

Chapter III

The flatboat rounded the final bend of her voyage. From this distance Lydia could see buildings, perhaps forty of them, crowded together on the low bank jutting out into the river; the town had grown measurably since the last time she had been home, almost three years earlier. From her vantage point on the deck she could see a great number of wagons, buggies, and pedestrians busily traversing Silver Street. She was not surprised; even in Baltimore she had heard Natchez acclaimed as a vibrant, flourishing town, a good place to do business.

Above the lowest row of buildings a ragged line of trees bordered what must be a newly constructed road: in the cleared spaces between trees Lydia could see swiftly moving wagons tilting upward or downward in what looked to be a treacherous angle. If Natchez-Under-the-Hill had morphed into such a bustling center of commerce, she could scarcely imagine the changes she would see in the city proper.

Mr. Stuart, the overseer Aunt Hetty had hired several years earlier, was waiting on the dock to meet her. Lydia remembered him from her previous trip home as a taciturn man, which suited her well. She had a great deal to observe and to think about on her trip back to Three Ponds Farm.

Central to her thought was the role she was to play there. At almost sixteen she had not yet reached her majority, but she was aware that the plantation had belonged to her parents, not to her aunt. Of course, Aunt Hetty had made Three Ponds a great success, expanding the number of acres as well as the number of slaves on the property. But she herself was the heiress. Would Aunt Hetty see her as such, relinquishing at least some of the authority she held over Three Ponds' matters? Lydia doubted she would, at least not without a struggle.

Once the wagon conquered the challenge of the steep road and pulled into town, Lydia was delighted to see how much Natchez had grown. Magnificent new mansions, most sporting carefully tended gardens, appeared on every street. New businesses, including a general store and a haberdashery, had sprung up on Canal Street. A beautiful new church graced Jefferson Street. As the wagon made its way on Washington Street toward the entrance to the Trace it was stalled by a large number of wagons and buggies. "What is happening here?" asked Lydia.

"Slave sale, Ma'am. Forks of the Road market."

"Might we stop there for a moment?" Lydia asked. If she was going to take a part in the management of the property that was rightfully hers, she needed to see to business immediately.

"Miss Hetty mightn't take a likin' to that," Mr. Stuart answered. "The Trace ain't a safe place fer a lady after dark. Ain't really a safe place fer anyone after dark. We'd best be gettin' back to the farm now if'n we wanta make it back before the sun sets."

"Very well, then," responded Lydia. "Carry on," she continued in the most authoritative tone of voice she could muster. She found the opportunity to give orders to a grown man intoxicating.

But very soon she saw the wisdom in Mr. Stuart's advice. In bright daylight the Trace was as enchanting as she remembered it. At its entrance on the outskirts of Natchez, centuries of travelers had worn the trail into a wide crevice almost ten feet deep. Bluffs on either side were highly vegetated with grasses, wildflowers, and the sprouting shoots of trees, interspersed with bare areas of the sandy loess common in the area. Beams of sunlight dappled the trail floor where the canopy of branches opened to the sky. While Lydia felt nestled in a natural fairyland, she realized how threatening the place could be once the sun set.

Fortunately, they arrived at Three Ponds Farm just before sunset. In the hazy near-evening light Lydia saw little change in the mansion other than a bit more shabbiness than she had noticed during her last trip. But great changes had been wrought on the rest of the property. The slave quarters were at least three times as large as they had been during her last visit. Several outbuildings had been added. Even the perimeter had changed; where before she could view forest beyond the fields, now only tilled fields could be seen all the way to the horizon. Aunt Hetty had been busy.

"Here ya be, Ma'am," said Mr. Stuart as he pulled up to the front entrance of the house. "Welcome home."

As Lydia grabbed her rucksack and climbed out of the wagon she decided the purchase of a buggy and the training of a coachman might be two of the first items of business she needed to address.

Opening the front door, she stepped into the parlor. "Aunt Hetty?" she called, but received no reply. Lydia noticed that nothing had changed in the room since her last visit: the old-fashioned sofa, chairs and carpeting were still there, still immaculately clean, but faded and somewhat worn. Her father's portrait hanging above the fireplace mantle was still the only decorative item in the room. As a child Lydia had often wondered why no portrait of her mother accompanied her father's picture, but she had never had the nerve to ask. Her aunt always seemed to become upset any time Lydia asked a question about her mother.

"Aunt Hetty, are you here?" she called up the staircase, noticing how the railing's finial wobbled loosely in her hand. "Aunt Hetty?"

Hearing the creak of a door, she looked up toward the room where her aunt's face appeared in the doorframe. "I'm here, Child. I am working on books. You may begin moving your things upstairs to your room. It is the same one you have always had. I have asked Sara to keep your dinner warm." With that the door closed.

Lydia hadn't expected much more of a welcome than she received, but this lackluster greeting only intensified her desire to effect some seriously needed changes. Although she had not been the most social member of her class at the boarding school, she had during her time there had the opportunity to visit the homes of several of her classmates, where she learned what was expected of a great house. For example, why didn't Three Ponds Farm have a footman? She knew Aunt Hetty had procured a great number of slaves in the past few years: why had none of them been trained for this position?

"Miss Lydia! Welcome home." Lydia turned toward the first genuinely welcoming voice she had heard since returning to Mississippi.

"Sara," she cried, accepting the warm hug offered her. Sara had certainly aged over the past few years. She had always been slim, but now her frame was almost skeletal and her shoulders bent forward far more than they had during Lydia's last visit. The hair at her temples was now fully white and patches of gray dotted her wiry black curls.

"Lemme hep' you wit' dem bags," she continued, picking up two of the satchels Mr. Stuart had left on the landing. "Then we gonna get you sumpin' to eat. Ah made yo' fav'rit dinnah—ham an' co'npone, wit' apple crisp fo' dessert."

By 10:00 the next morning the air was already sultry. The day would be typical of late winter Mississippi—warm, humid, a preview of what spring would bring and summer would intensify. Lydia had gathered early-blooming sprigs of hawthorn and aster to place on her parents' graves. The small graveyard had frequently drawn her to its serenity even as a child, particularly at times when she had a great deal on her mind. Today her eyes were riveted on the inscriptions: R.I.P Phineas Stuart Campbell 1745-1797; R.I.P. Eugenia Meier Campbell 1776-1797. She considered how little she remembered of her parents, whose bodies had lain in this peaceful space for over ten years.

She was grateful to her Aunt Hetty for keeping this place, at least, beautifully tended. The grass was manicured and the low picket fence surrounding the graveyard was painted a brilliant white. She had not seen her aunt, who had complained of having to work on "her books" until late the previous evening, until this morning at breakfast, where she was surprised at how much the woman had aged over the past three years. Her hair, pulled into a tight bun, was now entirely gray, and she now walked with the aid of a walnut cane that sported a bright brass tip and handle, which seemed an uncharacteristically decorative choice for her.

Their reunion had been all business. Hetty had followed a short summary of the plantation's history over the past three years by introducing Lydia to Tussy, who was to be her new ladies' maid. Tussy, who seemed to be about her own age, struck Lydia as being somewhat childish and perhaps not particularly bright.

The one item of business that lifted Lydia's spirits considerably was Hetty's mention of the Natchez social season, which was already well underway. "You have already missed a number of major balls," Hetty had told her, "but there are still several upcoming. You will need to prepare yourself for those." Preparation meant new ball gowns, new dance slippers, new jewelry. Lydia could hardly wait to begin.

Her aunt had instructed Maggie, her mother's seamstress, to meet with her later in the day. Lydia hoped the woman's skills were not outdated or, if so, that it would not be difficult to bring her up to date. It was obvious to Lydia that her aunt was eager to see her married off, a prospect she found equally attractive. At least they agreed on one major goal for the future.

"Miss Lydia?" Lydia turned to see Maggie standing at the graveyard's gate. "Miss Hetty said I would find you here." Lydia, gesturing her in, noticed one thing that had remained the same. Maggie, whom she had seen only in passing during her last trip, had not changed a bit. The woman's porcelain skin and black curls and the occasional flicker in her dark eyes seemed to suggest a sprightliness that her quiet demeanor did not match.

Maggie informed Lydia that Miss Hetty, expecting her imminent arrival, had ordered a number of fabrics sent from New Orleans and Nashville: Maggie hoped Lydia would be available that afternoon to make her selections and choose some patterns. Lydia was ready, even at that very moment, to begin. But as they walked together to the graveyard's gate and Lydia reached for the latch, she turned toward Maggie. "You were my mother's seamstress," she said.

"Yes, Ma'am, for many years."

"I hardly remember her."

"She was a wonderful woman," responded Maggie. "Beautiful and kind. And she loved you very much."

Lydia's eyes misted. She hoped Maggie was not telling her only what she wished to hear, but the actual truth. But her memories of her mother were few and faded with time. "You must have been here when she died."

"Well, no. No, Ma'am," Maggie stammered. "I... I had been sent with Miss Hetty on a trip to New Orleans to purchase some curtain fabric. The... the yellow fever came on very fast. They were... your parents were gone by the time I came back."

"Oh," Lydia replied. She hadn't heard earlier about the trip to New Orleans. But then, she hadn't known to ask. "Well," she continued with a smile, "let us get started. Aunt Hetty tells me we have a great deal of work to do."

"Ouch! Tussy, you are trying my patience! Can you not fix my hair without pulling it out from the roots!"

"Yes'm. Sorry Ma'am. But yo' say yo' want dis sweep up."

Lydia fumed in disgust. "Yes, I want it *upswept*. But you don't have to torture me to make that happen!" Tussy had turned out to be quite unsuccessful as a lady's maid. Not only was the girl incompetent, she had a tendency to be surly. Lydia was sorely tempted to "slap her into kingdom come," as her aunt described it, but earlier slaps had not produced any desired effect.

Lydia had to admit that part of her frustration with Tussy had to do with her own nervousness. She was preparing for her fourth ball of the season, and it was a particularly important one that was being held at the most elegant plantation in Mount Locust. The unwed daughters of all the important families in the Natchez area would be present.

She had experienced great success at the three balls she had already attended, having filled her dance card every dance. Louisa Ferguson, her new "dearest friend," ascribed her success to being new to the season—men always enjoyed novelty.

Although she had attracted a number of admirers, she had not yet acquired a true beau, and the season was nearing an end. Was her family not wealthy enough? Her home not acceptable? Her orphan's status a hindrance? The last should have worked in her favor. After all, she was the only heir to her property, and most young men would consider the absence of a watchful papa a benefit.

"Dere yo' be, Miss," Tussy said, tilting a hand mirror to allow Lydia to examine the back of her head in the large mirror on her dresser. Lydia liked what she saw. Tussy had done a beautiful job of forming one fat braid of Lydia's dark tresses into an attractive crown atop her head. She had used the diamond-tipped hair pins Lydia had found in her mother's jewelry box to add sparkle to the coiffeur.

"Ah! C'est vrai! Il faut souffrir pour être belle!" Lydia exclaimed.

"Huh?"

"Oh, it's French. 'One must suffer to be beautiful.' Madame Girard used to tell us that at the Academy." Lydia had begun practicing her French at home after noticing that the most genteel of the other girls casually dropped French sayings into their conversation. Who would have known that Madame Girard had, at least once, given her advice she could use?

"Well, yo' sho' gonna be bootiful dis night," Tussy responded. "Yo' decide on de dress yet?"

Lydia took one last look at the dresses spread out on the large feather bed that was now hers. It had taken some doing, but Lydia had finally persuaded Aunt Hetty to allow her to move into her parents' old bedroom. After all, her parents weren't using it—but that was certainly not the argument she used. Instead she convinced Hetty she needed more space to prepare for her most important occupation—completing a successful season—than the little warren of a room which had served her as a child. The same explanation was also successful in convincing Hetty to relinquish her mother's jewelry box.

"The lavender organdie." Although the rose-colored muslin and the canary yellow taffeta were equally beautiful, the organdie, with its flounced sleeves and deep décolletage, was definitely what she needed this evening. To get past Aunt Hetty and out of the house she would need to fasten her wide cream-colored satin sash, meant to drape diagonally from her shoulder to her hip, in a manner clever enough to hide the dress's daring neckline. The sash could be removed in the buggy on the way to Mount Locust.

"De pin? Yo' gonna wear dis?" asked Tussy, pointing to the brooch Lydia had carefully placed on top of the dresser.

"Yes, if you can find enough space on the bodice to attach it," Lydia said with a laugh. She had chosen the fabric for the dress with her mother's amethyst brooch in mind. The large stone, set in gold and surrounded by tiny seed pearls, was her favorite among the items in her mother's jewelry collection. Lydia wondered whether she had ever, as a child, seen her mother wearing it: if she had, perhaps that was the reason she found this particular piece of jewelry so lovely.

A knock on the door, followed by Sara's "Jerome see de buggy comin' down de road," was Lydia's signal to finish her toilette and go downstairs. Jerome was the footman Aunt Hetty had grudgingly purchased. Lydia had been successful in persuading her aunt that a footman was absolutely necessary for answering the door when neighbors' buggies appeared to take her to balls or, hopefully, when young men came to call. But after two failed attempts to train field slaves for the position of footman, Lydia and Aunt Hetty had found Jerome at Forks in the Road. A tall, light-skinned man from Jamaica, Jerome had the presence and the dignity to serve as footman at even the most elegant plantation in the area.

Once Tussy helped fasten her sash to provide modest coverage, Lydia dashed out the door to the staircase. Seeing her aunt waiting at the foot of the stairs, she muttered a quick "I must run. Cannot be late!"

"But your sash. That is not the way you wear it. You need to drape..." Hetty began. But Lydia was too swift. Before Hetty could complete her sentence, Lydia was flying out the door that Jerome, a conspiratorial smile on his face, conveniently held open for her.

"Why, Elmer," Lydia said, "you are a *wonderful* dancer!" Lydia had been tempted to agree with Elmer Stryker when he described himself as quite deficient on the dance floor—after all, he had already stepped on her toes three times, and their waltz was not even half over. If it were not socially unacceptable, she would have also mentioned that his hands were sweaty and his breath smelled of barbecued pork. But Elmer was the only heir to Live Oaks mansion, where this ball was being held; it would not do to insult this possible beau.

Oh, she thought, *to be a man.* Men were able to eat barbecued pork at parties and balls, free of the tight corsets that allowed women who attended such parties only the tiniest morsels of food. This evening's dinner had looked and smelled delicious. Although she only sampled the food, the stays on her corset that were necessary to keep the dress's low neckline decently in place were pressing deep, painful welts into her torso. But she needed to suffer through her pain and hunger a while longer.

Despite the distasteful thought of marriage to Elmer, becoming the mistress of Live Oaks would certainly have its charms. Mount Locust was much closer to Natchez than Three Ponds, which would allow her greater opportunity to enjoy everything the city had to offer. The grounds were large and beautifully landscaped, and the mansion itself was resplendent with its high ceilings, exquisite furnishings and imported crystal chandeliers. For this ball, the last of the season, every surface in the entrance hall had been decorated with sweet-smelling bayberry candles and fragrant blooms, while trumpet vines, their orange blossoms hanging in clusters, entwined the railings of the circular double staircase.

The ballroom encompassed the entire third floor. If she looked up she could see, far into the distance, stars twinkling through the long, narrow windowpanes which adorned the vaulted ceiling. Six musicians played on a platform decorated with swags of southern magnolia, and during the short breaks between sets a pianist softly played serenades at the mansion's magnificent grand piano.

Finally, the set was over and Elmer, taking her hand, ushered her back to the upholstered bench she had been sharing earlier with Louisa. Before he could request the pleasure of sitting beside her, Lydia, feigning great thirst, asked him to fetch her a glass of tea. The young man jaunted off on his quest, quite cheerily, she thought.

"Shall I?" asked Louisa, giving Lydia two light taps on the shoulder with her peacock feather fan.

"Yes, please do," answered Lydia, patting the seat next to hers, which Louisa quickly took.

"So, you do not relish more time with Mr. Stryker?" Lydia's rolled eyes gave her friend all the response she needed. "Perhaps you are not giving the young man enough of a chance," Louisa cautioned, waving her gloved hand at the immensity of the room that surrounded them.

"It is tempting," Lydia answered, stroking a crystal vase holding a dozen red roses on the table beside her. She was thinking of some gracious way to let her friend know that, although her own family's fortune was a pittance compared to that of Louisa's, she hoped she would not have to settle for a clumsy oaf with sweaty hands and bad breath.

Before she could give any further response, a servant approached and, with a slight curtsey, told her a gentleman was waiting in the library and wished to see her. "The gen'lman say he met yo' on yo' trip from Baltimore."

Harry Russell! Lydia practically sprung from her seat. *Perhaps salvation from Elmer was at hand!*

"You are not going to see him, are you?" asked Louise. "Is that proper? It sounds as if he was not invited to the ball."

"He is an old family friend I hadn't seen for years until we met once again on the flatboat," Lydia lied awkwardly. "His name is Harry Russell."

"But what about Elmer?" Louisa, raising one eyebrow, asked. "Isn't he bringing you a glass of tea?"

"You drink it," Lydia answered, pinching her cheeks and biting her lips as she followed the servant downstairs to the library.

Only a few candles had been lit, so the room was quite dim; obviously, her hosts did not imagine anyone would care to read that evening. As she entered the room, she saw only his back as he bent over a heavy volume set on a lectern. But as he turned, his strawberry blonde hair and matching mustache made her catch her breath.

"Why, Mr., Mr..." she stumbled. *What was the name of Harry's friend?*

"Masters."

"Yes, Mr. Masters, of course," she said, wondering if she sounded as flustered as she felt.

"Please, call me Nigel." He blurted out a flurry of words so rapidly that Lydia was unable to respond. He had thought of nothing but her since their meeting on the schooner. She had haunted his dreams, distracted him from his work. He had been in Natchez for almost a week, and had wanted to see her, to speak with her, but had not summoned the courage to do so until today. He was leaving almost immediately for Nashville; in fact, the flatboat awaited him as they spoke. But he would be back in a month. Could he visit her at her home when he returned? He would be immeasurably honored if she would allow him to walk with her when he came.

Lydia, caught off guard, could only nod. But that seemed enough for him. Nigel Masters smiled broadly, then turned and strode briskly toward the door. "In a month, then," he promised, turning once again to face her and bowing deeply. With that, he was off.

Lydia spent several minutes in silent thought. *What a strange encounter. What a strange man.* Well, she had a whole month to consider the best way to discourage him without being overly cruel. As she opened the door to enter the hall, partiers in couples or small groups, all chatting merrily, were descending the long, curved staircase. *The ball must be over,* she thought. Nigel Masters had provided a truly unusual conclusion to the evening's festivities.

"Ah, there you are," said Louisa, grabbing Lydia's elbow from behind. "Our carriage is ready. What did Mr. Russell want? Is he a possible beau?"

As soon as the Stryker footman handed them into their seat and the driver, with a quick flick of his whip, trotted the beautiful matched bays down the drive, Louisa took Lydia's hands tightly into her own. Lydia smiled, thinking how much fun it would be to tell her friend about the encounter with the very strange Mr. Masters. The story would certainly amuse her. "Actually," she said, "it was not Mr. Russell. It was his friend, Mr. Nigel Masters. We spoke about..."

But before she could say another word, Louisa broke in. "How exciting for you! Just imagine! A *tête-à-tête* with Nigel Masters!"

"Do you know him?"

"Not personally," Louisa answered. "But everyone knows who he is."

The confused look on Lydia's faced was met by a look of shocked surprise on Louisa's. "Lydia," she continued, "surely you've heard of the Masters family. Nigel is the son of Douglas Masters. Nigel's daddy owns the biggest bank in Nashville."

Chapter IV

The wedding was held at the Masters' mansion in Nashville. Although the groom's parents had initially objected to the union based on the bride's inferior social standing, Nigel was, after all, their third son, the youngest of their five children. The Masters had plenty of other children upon which to build their aspirations.

Lydia had had no intention of accepting Nigel's proposal of marriage, which he had offered almost immediately upon his arrival at Three Ponds Farm. Were it not for his answer to the only question Lydia had for him, she probably would never have become Mrs. Nigel Masters. After about a half hour of engaging in idle banter on the porch swing Lydia, feigning only the most casual interest, asked if he had recently seen the friend who had accompanied him on their flatboat journey.

"Harry? Harry Russell?" Nigel asked.

"Yes, of course, Harry. That was his name."

"I saw him just last week at the Nashville races. He was there with his fiancé."

"Fiancé?" Lydia had almost choked on the word. "Has he recently become engaged?"

"Oh, no," responded Nigel. "They've been engaged for over a year. I suppose Agatha finally became tired of waiting." Within minutes after Nigel had offered this information he had bumbled out his proposal, withdrawing from his breeches' pocket a stunning marquis cut ruby ring set among four equally stunning diamonds. Lydia, inwardly fuming about the perfidy of men, looked longingly at the ring, then not particularly longingly at the man, then again at the ring. Although her lips said, "Yes, I accept," her thoughts were more on the order of, *Might as well.*

Although the Masters family mansion was immense and lavishly decorated in a style Lydia knew was costly, she thought it was overdone and dated. Every chair sported a curlicued back and a seat cushion embroidered with a cross stitch floral pattern; every surface was garnished with its starched crocheted doily. The Oriental carpeting, prized for its intricate patterning and variety of colors, seemed garish to Lydia. Gertrude, Nigel's mother, had a penchant for hair art—dozens of samples of this craft appeared as wall hangings and table decorations. When her mother-in-law requested several cuttings of her hair to create a new masterpiece, Lydia knew she was being honored. But she could not help being repelled by this particular method of artistic expression, which, although popular, had always seemed grotesque to her.

She and Nigel had begun their marriage ensconced in the small bedroom that had been his since he had been a boy. It was here that Lydia discovered her husband's greatest talent. Even as early as the night of their wedding, Nigel had been able to bring her body to levels of ecstasy she could never have imagined. His lips very quickly discovered every inch of her body that thrilled to being kissed. His hands were a marvel of dexterity, petting where she wanted to be petted, caressing where she needed to be caressed, restraining and compelling her in ways she had never imagined she would desire.

And his manhood—as a child, she'd had occasional opportunities to observe farm animals mating. Nigel's private member reminded her of Aunt Hetty's prize bull, Diablo. If romping in bed with Nigel was what she had always heard derogatorily referred to as "the wifely duty," then she was more than happy to be Nigel's dutiful wife.

But a dutiful daughter-in-law? That was not to be. From the very beginning of her residence in Natchez, her life with Gertrude Masters came with even more restrictions than she had borne with Aunt Hetty. Her mother-in-law was set on determining what she ate, what she wore, how and with whom she spent time. And although the confounded woman obviously considered her authority over everyone and everything within her home to be absolute, Lydia was unable to convince her husband that this was a problem.

Lydia had never noticed before her wedding how frequently Nigel began sentences with the phrases "Mama always says..." or "Mama believes that ..." She would never have imagined how annoyed she would become on hearing those phrases. Still, she could not complain about her life. She spent her days browsing the delightful shops the city of Nashville had to offer or performing the requisite social visiting at other women's homes. And she was surprised to discover how much she enjoyed reading, especially romances like *The Coquette* by A Lady of Massachusetts and *Sense and Sensibility* written by A Lady, an author who was rumored to be part of the British aristocracy.

Of course, she kept her taste in literature a secret from her mother-in-law, who believed the Holy Bible was the only book appropriate for a young woman to read. Lydia hid her romances under her bedding. One late afternoon, as she returned from an unusually boring session of Patience with several of Gertrude's friends, she found her cache of forbidden reading missing.

"What are you looking for under the bedding?" asked Nigel, appearing at the door to their bedroom.

"Oh, nothing."

"Nothing?" he asked.

"Well, just a book."

"Something you took from the library?" he wondered. Lydia wanted to laugh. The Masters' library contained only ponderous histories, business ledgers, religious and political treatises, and philosophical works. She'd found nothing there to her liking.

"No, not from the library. If you must know, it was just a simple novel, something to help pass the time."

"And you keep such things under the bedding?" he laughed, arching his left eyebrow in the manner she had first found amusing, then annoying, then infuriating. "How strange!"

"Well, your mother..."

"Lydia, please, do not ruin this evening by another complaint about my mother. I hardly believe she would enter our room and take a book from you."

"No, but Eliza would." Eliza was the upstairs housemaid, and Lydia had learned very early that she was certainly capable of doing such a thing. One evening when Lydia, feeling bored in the house, had gone for a half hour walk, Gertrude had questioned her about it the following morning. Afterwards, Lydia remembered seeing Eliza walking down the stairs into the parlor as she had re-entered the house. On another tedious day, Lydia had sampled a small amount of brandy from her father-in-law's liquor cabinet and foolishly left the glass on a table, where Eliza had discovered it. Naturally, that transgression had also been reported. Eliza was devoted to her mistress and enjoyed nothing more than being her spy. Incidents like these often made Lydia feel like a prisoner in the Masters' household: this was a far cry from what she had expected upon becoming a married woman.

"Well, if Mama believes that you should not be reading such a book, perhaps you should consider the possibility that she is correct," continued Nigel. "After all, she acts in your best interest."

"I rather doubt that," mumbled Lydia under her breath.

"Lydia, my dear, you are being obstinate again," Nigel replied. "You really must learn how to behave. I believe my beautiful wife needs a bit of chastisement." With that he grabbed her arm and pushed her onto the bed, pressing his body against hers as he pinioned her arms above her head. Lydia struggled to resist him, but accompanied her resistance with a throaty laugh. She knew this evening's "wifely duty" would be rather rough.

She tingled with anticipation.

Chapter Five

"Now, now, Junior, don't cry." Lydia wiped a tear from her son's eye, then checked her faun-colored kidskin glove for any sign of grime. Children could be so dirty. "Mommy will be back before you even know it." She nodded to Florence to signal that it was time to return the boy to the nursery, choosing to ignore the disapproving look she often saw on the nursemaid's face. She would complain to Gertrude about the insolence of the woman if she believed it would do any good. But Gertrude seldom, if ever, paid any attention to anything she said.

"De boy jes gettin' ovah his fevah, Ma'am," Florence told her. "Dat be why he so teary-eye."

"Thank you for that information," Lydia huffed. "Now take him back. Isn't it time for his nap?" Lydia watched as Florence shuffled Nigel Junior out of the room. She knew everyone in the household was critical of her mothering skills, or more precisely, of her lack thereof. But she did not see herself as differing greatly from some other mothers she knew; after all, raising children was primarily the job of nursemaids.

Still, she did not seem to share even an iota of the mild interest other mothers seemed to have for their offspring. Perhaps it would have been different if she had given birth to a girl. She could pamper a little girl, dress her in pretty little smocks with bright ribbons instead of in the plain white nursing clothing most children wore, and put colorful bows and flowers in her hair.

But for now she could not spend any time worrying about her lack of maternal feeling: the coach awaited her. She was headed once more for Natchez, but this trip would be different. She would not be traveling down the Mississippi River on a flatboat, but on one of the new steamboats that had revolutionized river journeys. Steamboats were not only much larger and luxurious than flatboats, they had the added advantage of being capable of traveling upstream, eliminating the need to make the difficult and dangerous trek north on the Trace.

The invention of the steamboat had been instrumental in convincing Nigel of the wisdom of developing Three Ponds Farm. Steamboat travel had revolutionized the cotton industry, making transport much less expensive. Her property now grew mostly cotton, making the Farm a far more profitable enterprise than it had been when she married.

Nigel had little interest in farming, and although his position at his father's bank was quite menial, he had neither the aspiration nor the talent to advance beyond whatever familial advantage he had there. But like his wife, Nigel was very interested in money. He had allowed Lydia the freedom to travel south several times to oversee Three Ponds Farms' development. While there, she had arranged the purchase of property and slaves and had supervised construction of the buildings needed to warehouse tons of baled cotton as well as two hundred additional workers.

Although the amount of responsibility she had been given to improve the property's income made her feel quite giddy at times, her real interest was in improving the mansion herself. She had enlarged it by more than half, adding more bedrooms and a library, filling these rooms and the rest of the house with precious furniture and adornments imported from France and England.

But even more important than the improvement of the physical appearance of Three Ponds Farm was the change she was able to effect in the tone of life there. A severe case of gout had rendered Aunt Hetty incapable of resisting Lydia's intervention: the old biddy was confined to her bedroom for a good part of every day. Such amusements as horse racing, dancing, gambling and the drinking of spirits, which had been strictly forbidden by her aunt, had been reinstated at Three Ponds Farm, making it a haven for young men and women who sought the kind of social interactions they could not find at many of the other great houses. Lydia was not only an accomplished hostess, but also a welcome guest at nearly every mansion in the territory.

Nigel's one objection to her leaving for Natchez at this time was the threat of war with Great Britain. "Don't you think you should stay in Nashville?" he had asked. "The legislature has asked President Madison to declare war against England."

"Oh, pshaw!" Lydia scoffed as she held up two of her ball gowns, looking from one to the other to decide whether to pack the apricot organdie or the crimson taffeta. "It will never come to that."

"And when did you become an expert in matters of war?" he asked.

She packed the taffeta into her trunk, carefully folding the voluminous skirts to prevent wrinkling. "If war should come to the Mississippi Territory, Andrew's men would put a quick end to it," she assured him. Of all her social conquests, she considered her friendship with General Andrew and Rachel Jackson the most brilliant. Jackson was a shrewd and clever businessman who had been happy to share his expertise in land speculation and slave trading with her: his advice had been integral to the success of her own plantation. Rachel Jackson at forty-five years old was still considered one of the most beautiful women in Natchez. Lydia had spent many pleasant evenings at the Hermitage, the Jacksons' magnificent estate, where she'd had the opportunity of meeting and befriending many of the most illustrious members of Natchez society.

"Ah, dear Nigel, as you well know, I am expert in a great many things," she teased. "But now I must go; the steamboat will not wait for my arrival. Behave yourself while I am gone," she said, brushing his cheek with a quick kiss.

"And you as well. Be a good girl," he answered, smacking her derriere soundly. Lydia paused and considered whether she had time for a hasty romp with her husband before her departure, but a quick look at the grandfather clock he had given her for their last anniversary told her she did not. With a soft sigh she gathered her gloves from the night stand and headed out the door.

Chapter Six

"Why Señor Gonzales, you've wakened early this morning." Lydia smiled at the handsome young man who stood beside her patiently waiting for an invitation. It was a beautiful morning to be sitting on the second floor deck of a magnificent steamboat rolling down the Mississippi. The great river's waters were calm, and a breeze from the west freshened the air. "Won't you join me for tea?"

"Gracias, Señora," he said, slipping into the chair across from hers with the smooth, silken movements that had so attracted her the previous evening. "Did you waken early this morning to see the sunrise?"

Lydia told him she had. She wanted to enjoy every moment of this trip. Although most women would shrink at the idea of traveling alone, Lydia treasured the sense of freedom solitary travel gave her.

The flatboat trip from Nashville to Memphis had been uneventful and rather tedious; she'd traveled on flatboats enough times in the past few years to expect only discomfort and boredom. But her first glimpse of the *Tennessee Maiden* dominating the Memphis harbor had filled her with awe. The two-tiered paddle steamer, glistening in the sun like an immense, white frosted cake, beckoned her to come aboard. Once settled in her private cabin, with mirror-lined walls that sparked decorating ideas for her bedroom at Three Ponds, she could hardly wait for the captain to blow the whistle to signal the beginning of their journey.

She had met Ignatius Gonzales the previous evening as she dined in the ship's magnificent grand salon. She was in the process of admiring the room's gilded ceiling when she lowered her gaze and saw something at least as admirable: the deep-set brown eyes and languid smile of Señor Gonzales. Although Spain had reluctantly given up its claim to the southern part of the Mississippi Territory fourteen years earlier, many Spaniards still kept major holdings there. Ignatius' father was a cattleman: his ranch had been raising longhorn Iberian cattle in the area since the mid-sixteenth century.

Something about Señor Gonzales reminded her of her pet tomcat, Liberty. Those smoothly graceful, somewhat stealthy movements were countered by a visage that was alert and watchful. Gonzales and Liberty shared a demeanor that was generally languid and luxurious—both seemed to want nothing more than to be petted and coddled. Even Gonzales' mustache was reminiscent of Liberty's whiskers.

But Liberty became a completely different animal when he pounced upon a mouse. Then he was pitiless, relishing tearing the poor creature to bits, tossing the bits into the air, rolling his body over his meal before settling down to devour it. Lydia could not help wondering what Gonzales' pounce might be like.

Flashing the toothy smile that had so charmed her the evening before, he asked if she'd had a comfortable evening. "Very much so," she responded to his question. "And you? Did you sleep well?" She wondered how old he was. She thought he might be about eighteen—two years younger than herself—and two years older than the saucy little harlot Nigel had taken for his mistress. Nigel had no idea that she knew about Emmaline Glover, the daughter of an itinerant salesman. He would be shocked to know that she had once had their footman, Rufus, drive her to the outskirts of Natchez and stop at the cottage Nigel had purchased for his *rendezvous* with Emmaline. Knowing how easily Rufus could be bribed, she had then asked him to drive the carriage around town for a half hour or so.

She did not have to wait long. Carefully hidden behind a large mountain laurel bush, Lydia soon watched the strumpet, dressed casually in a floral printed cotton frock and bearing on her arm a large basket, come out to pick magnolias from one of the large trees adorning the property. Emmaline was known throughout the city as a beauty: she was a flaxen blonde with cornflower blue eyes and a complexion the color of fine cream. Short and slim with a waiflike quality to her, Emmaline's appearance was the absolute antithesis of her own.

At first she had been furious about her husband's affair. She wanted to order Rufus to take her to Nigel's office at the bank where she could chastise him for the scoundrel he was. But upon reflection, she reconsidered. She determined to get her revenge, but at a time of her choosing.

"Yes. The rocking of the boat is quite—how do you say in English?—trankil?" offered Gonzales.

"Tranquil? Yes, it can be quite tranquil," she responded with a sly smile, her eyes sparking with mischief. "But sometimes the rocking can be quite stormy, uncontrolled, you might say."

"So tonight may be very different?" he asked. His tilted head and one raised eyebrow suggested to Lydia that Señor Gonzales was trying very hard to determine whether any hidden meaning lay behind her words.

"Yes, it could very well be," she answered. "It could be quite different tonight." She knew she could change the direction this conversation was taking with just a word, just a look. But the old saying, "What is sauce for the goose is sauce for the gander," came to mind. Wouldn't the opposite—that sauce for the gander was sauce for the goose—be just as true?

"Were you aware, Señor Gonzales," she asked with a throaty laugh, gently placing her hand on his wrist, "that our cabins are adjacent to each other?"

Chapter Seven

"Ahhhhh," Lydia yawned, stretching in the luxurious bedding she had purchased for her four poster bed. Nothing was more enjoyable than waking late on a summer morning at Three Ponds, particularly when the evening's activities had been so enjoyable.

Pulling herself out of bed, she drew the velvet curtains and gazed lovingly at the panorama before her. At long last and after much effort, everything at Three Ponds satisfied her. Even though they were still far smaller than they would be years from now, the six live oaks lining the new brick walkway commanded her view. She counted twenty large waxy flowers showing against the silvery gray leaves of the bigleaf magnolias, and the crepe myrtles were just beginning to break out in masses of fuchsia blooms. The color and detail of the formal gardens scattered throughout the front yard captured her attention. Finally, she surveyed the fields of cotton and other income plants stretching to the horizon. It was hers—all hers!

Of course, by law the property belonged to Nigel. But for the past two years, he had resided for the most part in Nashville while she had spent most of her time at Three Ponds. This arrangement suited them both; it seemed the less they saw of each other, the better they got along.

The mansion itself now suited her as well. She had replaced the parlor suite, its crimson upholstery worn and faded with time, with a baroque-style settee, loveseat and four armchairs upholstered in peacock blue damask. Dainty pedestal tables and a handsome writing desk in matching hand-carved rosewood balanced the furnishings, while an ornate bombe with an intricate bas-relief of a rural Chinese village provided a touch of the exotic.

Her favorite room was the library, where tall French mirrors had been hung over the mantels and crystal chandeliers glimmered against the sedate mahogany shelves. An enormous harp set in one corner added even more elegance to the room. Lydia was determined to learn to play it one day.

She climbed back into bed to reminisce about the previous night but was interrupted by three sharp knocks. "Ma'am, Ma'am, may I enter?" came the rather frantic voice of her ladies' maid Queenie. Queenie's mother had been brought to Natchez from Jamaica and had been purchased at the Forks of the Road market; her daughter had inherited both her beauty and poise. Queenie added a sense of graciousness to any social gathering at which she served, and she seemed truly devoted to her mistress. She and her man Auguste had already added a robust baby boy to Lydia's holdings.

But right now a tone of distress had replaced Queenie's normally melodious voice. "Enter," Lydia commanded, and soon beheld an obviously flustered Queenie in her midst.

"Ma'am, Massa be heah," Queenie exclaimed.

Lydia laughed at Queenie's mistake. "Now, Queenie. Even though you must always refer to Señor Gonzales with the greatest respect, he is not the master of Three Ponds Farm and should never be addressed in that manner." Queenie had been recently promoted from field worker to ladies' maid, and Lydia rather enjoyed tutoring her in the ways of a great house; the girl was a quick study.

"No, Ma'am, not de Señor. Massa Nigel be heah."

"Nigel? Nigel here?" Lydia cried with even greater distress than she'd heard in Queenie's voice. "And Señor Gonzales," she choked out. "Is he..."

"He be gone. He leave early dis mo'nin'."

"Thank God," Lydia uttered under her breath. "Queenie, hurry! Open my armoire and take out one of my nightgowns." Queenie rushed to the wardrobe and opening it, pulled out a black bit of silk and lace trimmed with fur.

"No, no, not that one." Lydia tried to tone down the scream she wanted to hurl Queenie's way. "The cotton one—yes—the one with the little pink roses. Bring it to me!" Lydia just managed to smooth the gown over her naked hips and legs before the door opened and an obviously excited Nigel burst into the room.

"Darling!" he cried, rushing to embrace his wife as Queenie silently slunk out the door.

"Nigel! What a wonderful surprise," she managed in a breathy tone before he practically smothered her with kisses. "I wasn't expecting..." she finally managed to say before he interrupted.

"It's war!" he said. "War!"

"What war?" she asked, perplexed.

"With the British! I told you we would go to war!"

For once Nigel had been correct in his prediction. She had never believed that disagreements with the British would cause President Madison to actually declare war. Nigel's excitement and delight in the thought of war with the British confused her; but then, men enjoyed some very strange things. She wondered if the fool was planning to enlist and was about to ask him if that were the case when he presented her with what was even more alarming news.

"This war will bring many opportunities," he said, smiling broadly, "and Papa plans to take advantage of those opportunities. He is opening a bank office in New Orleans, and he's sent me to begin preparations."

"You will be managing the new office?" she asked. This was a surprise. Nigel had never attained any advancement at the bank, even though it was owned and operated by his father. As a young man, he had begun working there as a cashier and had hoped to rise to the position of head cashier, but that had never happened. Later, when an opening in the loan department had arisen, Nigel had applied for that position and had been delighted when his father had awarded him the promotion.

However, when irregularities in some of the loans which Nigel had handled began to appear, due, Nigel insisted, to misunderstandings caused by his lack of experience, he had been demoted to a rather menial assignment in the accounting department. Still, Lydia had not given up hope that her husband would one day come into his own.

"No, assistant manager at first. But once Papa sees my worth in this position, surely he will make me manager."

Nigel's daddy has already made a good assessment of his son's worth she thought, realizing her husband was not destined to become a bank manager. Nigel had been a disappointment to her in so many ways. But she was even more discouraged to know that he was equally disappointing to his parents, who seemed to see him as the least intelligent, energetic, and ambitious of their brood. Although Nigel and his family connections had served her own purposes quite well through the years, she would never attain the elevated status among the Nashville society which she so desired connected to a spouse who was seen as the family dunderhead. *Oh well,* she thought, *someone has to be last.* If she'd only met one of his older brothers first...

"I've already taken steps to find suitable accommodations for myself in New Orleans and to move our family to Natchez," he continued.

"Our family?" she blurted out before realizing how ridiculous that question was. Now she was really alarmed.

"Of course our family!" he laughed.

Damnation!!! she thought, restraining herself from actually saying the word. *Adios, Iggy,* was her second thought. Their affair had been dangerous enough when her husband lived in Nashville; continuing it could be disastrous once Nigel moved to New Orleans, close enough to make short unannounced trips. Besides, Natchez society relished in spreading New Orleans gossip; it was one of their favorite occupations.

I shall have to find a nursemaid was Lydia's next thought. When Lucy had been born, Lydia had hoped giving birth to a daughter would give rise to the maternal feelings many women proclaimed. But those hopes had not materialized, which was a shame. Lucy was a bonny little sprite, with features incorporating the best qualities of both her parents. Her chestnut hair color, hazel eyes and parchment-toned complexion were a complete balance between the appearances of both her mother and father. As far as disposition was concerned, she had inherited Lydia's vivacity and drive, tempered by Nigel's easy-going nature.

But Lydia had soon learned that a baby girl was just as much trouble as a baby boy, and she happily handed her infant daughter to the nursemaid at every opportunity. Perhaps when the child was older...

"We need to celebrate!" proposed Nigel, grabbing her hand. "To the gazebo!"

Nigel had a penchant for taking his wife to the gazebo for lovemaking. Normally Lydia would not have minded; she thoroughly enjoyed the decadence of their outdoor romps. And after all, making love was the one activity in which her husband truly excelled; were she to compare the two, she would have to admit that both his stamina and the quality of his technique exceeded Iggy's.

But the sun was bright; she would never be able to hide the evidence on her body left by Iggy's ardent lovemaking. Nigel would certainly notice some bruising and some very telltale marks on her neck and shoulders, even if they made love in the semi-darkness of her bedroom. She desperately thought of a way to distract him.

But how? What would distract Nigel until later in the day, possibly until the evening? He would certainly not wish to see any of the improvements she had made in the house or on the property, having never taken any real interest in Three Ponds Farm. Gossip would not distract him; they shared no friends and few acquaintances in the Natchez area. She could suggest breakfast, but it was quite obvious that he hungered for something other than food.

From the way he was fondling her she knew that the only thing that could possibly distract him was another woman.

"I can't. Not now, my darling," she cried as he began to tug at the neckline of her nightgown. An idea was beginning to take shape. "I am in so much distress!"

"What could distress you, now that I am here?" he asked. She would have laughed out loud were the circumstances not fraught with danger.

"My earrings!"

"Your earrings?" Nigel looked thoroughly confused.

"Yes, the pearl earrings. The ones you gave me for our second anniversary. To me, they have always been a special symbol of our love." Lydia brushed the tears forming in her eyes, some of which were quite genuine, with the sleeve of her nightgown. She was not sure where she was heading with this fabrication, but knew now that she had begun to lie, she needed to continue to do so convincingly.

"Very well, your earrings. What about the earrings distresses you?" he asked, quite impatiently, Lydia thought. Her mind raced.

"They were stolen!"

"Oh, is that all?" Nigel asked with a sigh. "Perhaps they've only been misplaced. And if so, I can buy you another pair," he offered, brushing at her tears with his thumb.

"But I am almost certain they were stolen by my new lady's maid—you saw her—Queenie. She is the only one who had the opportunity."

"Well, then," he said, shaking his head, "take that up with Reginald. Isn't disciplining the slaves the job of the overseer? They have ways of making slaves confess."

"But Queenie is stubborn—perhaps because her mother came from Jamaica—Jamaican slaves are so often uppity and need to be put in their place. In fact, Papa sold Queenie's mother soon after she was born. And besides, the overseer is busy in some of the distant fields with the harvest." Lydia knew the cotton would not be harvested for another two months, but she relied on her husband's complete ignorance about cotton farming to cover her lie. "Queenie will hide the earrings where we will never find them, and they mean so much to me."

"Queenie. The mulatto who was with you when I came into the bedroom?" he asked, beginning to show some interest.

"Yes. And darling, if you are going to be at Three Ponds more frequently, you will need to have the slaves understand that *you* are the authority here. I will be so grateful when you'll be able to take that loathsome responsibility from me." One look at Nigel's face told her that appealing to both his pride and his lecherous nature was having the desired effect. "Hurry, Nigel. Sara can summon Queenie for you."

"And bring her back here?" he asked. "Will you want to question her?"

"No," she responded. "You must be in charge. Take her to the planting shed," she suggested, realizing no one would be there at this hour. Besides, she had installed a comfortable divan in the shed to accommodate late summer trysts with Iggy when her bedroom was too hot for comfort.

I will make it up to Queenie she thought as Nigel, brushing her cheek with a quick kiss, hurried to do her bidding. Perhaps a small gift—some piece of jewelry she herself no longer wore. And a gift for Auguste as well. She would ask Maggie if any fabric was left from this year's slave outfitting—Auguste would most likely appreciate a second work shirt.

But her guilt was only momentary. *What am I thinking?* she asked herself. After all, the slaves were her property. She could do anything she wished with them.

Reginald had frequently told her that she treated her slaves too leniently. "If'n you be too kind, Ma'am," he had warned her more than once, "dey might gonna revolt."

"Oh," she had responded, "our slaves would never revolt."

"It happened in Virginee a little whiles back," he continued. "Dem slaves kilt dere masters whiles dey slep. Kilt de chillen, too! 'Twas turrible."

Reginald had frequently warned Lydia about the Bible classes Maggie taught on Sunday mornings, saying that slaves had no need of instruction beyond learning how to work hard and to obey. The class Maggie had held on a Sunday during the previous month, when she had allowed Queenie and Auguste to jump the broomstick, was especially offensive to him.

"Now dem two tink dey's really married, 'jes like white fo'ks," he complained. "No good kin come o' dat. And how 'bout dat Queenie's man Auguste. She like to call him 'husband,'" he smirked. "An' Auguste be bad as dey come. Uppity from de start. He on'y been here a few months befo' he see de whippin' post up close a number o' times."

Lydia hadn't wanted to believe Reginald, particularly when he spoke of slave revolts. She truly could not believe that could happen at Three Ponds. But then, Reginald had a great deal of experience as an overseer. And she had to admit that there was a bit of sassiness in Queenie's behavior.

Sassiness. Lydia feared, for just one moment, that Queenie's sassiness could be a danger. Queenie knew about Iggy. *Might she tell Nigel?* But then, Lydia reflected, Queenie was smart—too smart to speak of something her mistress would surely deny. Any slave in that situation would be branded a liar. Queenie, Lydia was certain, would realize that informing Nigel about her activities would only lead to more punishment for her and a certain demotion back to field worker. Or the outcome could be considerably worse.

Lydia snuggled back into the comfort of her feather mattress and was soon fast asleep.

As expected, Nigel did not return to her until later that evening. He admitted that despite his best efforts, he had been unable to convince Queenie to confess.

"Oh, darling, never mind," Lydia soothed, doubting those efforts were particularly distasteful to him. "Sara found the earrings lying on the lace mat covering the piano-forte. I must have left them there the last time I practiced. The lace and the pearls are the same color—they were hard to see."

"The poor girl!" Nigel said. "Perhaps I should..."

"Never mind," purred Lydia. "Come to me. I have missed you all day."

"But the girl..."

"Don't worry about Queenie. As I told you, she is quite stubborn and probably needed some correction. Now, blow out that candle and come to me."

As Nigel complied with her command, Lydia was pleased to notice that the room had become too dark to see anything clearly. Her ruse had been a success.

"Oh dear, I cannot see you," she laughed, reaching out to him with triumph and some relief. "Come here so I can touch you. Tell me, darling, where would you like to be touched first?

Chapter Eight

Lydia was exhausted. Thank God she was almost home. But what a week it had been!

Parties! Balls! Parades! The war was over, and all of Natchez had gathered to celebrate the return of Andrew Jackson and his troops.

She had spent the whole week lodged at various plantations and mansions within and on the outskirts of Natchez. Luckily she'd had the foresight to order enough fabric to have Maggie make numerous ball gowns before the blockade had halted all import of foreign goods. None of the pretty young women who had come of age during the war could even hope to hold a candle to her; her dance cards had proven that.

The parade celebrating Jackson's victory at the Battle of New Orleans had been the perfect finale to a perfect week. How the crowds had cheered as the troops marched smartly down the streets of Natchez! The officers, marching first, looked dashing in their white breeches, long blue jackets with short matching capes trimmed with red or white fringe, and black top hats. They were followed by legions of ragtag soldiers, some of them Indian or half breed, who had been an integral part of the fighting force.

And Andrew! Marching with his men, graciously waving and smiling to the adoring crowds. Lydia was almost certain he had recognized her among the masses: the smile he sent her way seemed to signify acknowledgement.

Later that evening at his victory ball she first heard the sobriquet his troops had given him: Old Hickory. His command against the redcoats had combined the elements of prudence, brilliance and daring. Natchez residents viewed the past three years as a second war of independence, and their new favorite son had been instrumental in the victory. Already they predicted further advancement, perhaps in politics, for Jackson. Lydia, however, hoped Andrew's future would not take him out of Natchez: evenings at the Hermitage were much too enjoyable to come to an end.

As her carriage reached the outskirts of Three Ponds, she wondered whether Nigel had returned during the week she was gone. The letter she had received from him told of the final two weeks of the war, when the fighting near the port of New Orleans was furious. At times it was feared the British would prevail. But now New Orleans, like Natchez, basked in the glory of a victory won.

Nigel wrote that he would soon visit Three Ponds, but that his intention was to continue living in New Orleans. Now that the Treaty of Ghent had been signed, the banking business in the city would surely flourish, as would his own career. He closed by saying that with the war was over, he was making arrangements to move their children to Natchez. Nigel and Lydia had both agreed that Junior and Lucy would be safer with their grandparents in Nashville during the war's duration, but now the war was over, Lydia knew she had no viable reason to object to having her children live with her. *Time to find a new nursemaid*, she thought.

The carriage arrived at Three Ponds Farm at sunset. Lydia thrilled at the stunning effect the bright white columns and façade made standing against the brilliance of the sky. This evening's sunset displayed a canary yellow horizon that melded into a bright flamingo pink, gradually fading into first a violet, then an azure sky dotted intermittently with tufts of feathery white clouds.

She waved at a small group of slaves standing before the front lawn's white picket fence. She imagined they were waiting to welcome her back, although this was quite peculiar. Perhaps Reginald had given them the opportunity to celebrate the end of the war; that might account for their not being in their quarters at this time of the evening.

But as soon as the carriage stopped and Lydia's feet hit the ground, Sara rushed up to her. "Dey's sumpin' strange goin' on in deah," she said, a worried look adding more than the usual number of wrinkles to her brow. "Dey a strange man inside. Miss Hetty tole me go 'way."

"A strange man?" Lydia asked.

"Yes," she said, nodding.

"He look like maybe he be Injun," Leander added, looking every bit as worried as his wife. "Miz Maggie in deah too. Dey been some loud talk goin' on."

"Well, thank you," Lydia told them. "I will go see what this is all about," she added in a voice ringing with much more confidence than she actually felt. "Y'all can just wait right here."

As she entered the parlor, the first thing she noticed was Hetty bent double in an arm chair, her shoulders shaking as she cried into a handkerchief. The past few years had not been kind to Hetty, whose faded, wrinkled skin, scant white hair and bleary eyes made her appear even older than her years. But now she seemed to be only a shell of the person Lydia had left behind one week earlier.

Behind Hetty, hands firmly braced on the back of the arm chair, stood Maggie, her visage bearing a grim look that Lydia had never seen before. Standing next to Maggie was an unfamiliar man, most likely a half-breed, dressed in buckskin similar to what she had seen on many of the soldiers marching in the parade just the day before.

"Does this man need a place to stay?" she asked Maggie. Many of the plantation owners from New Orleans to Natchez had opened their barns and other outbuildings to Jackson's troops as they made their way back home. Before leaving for Natchez, Lydia herself had instructed Reginald to provide such shelter for any returning troops who stopped at Three Ponds and asked for a night's lodging.

But getting no response other than a strange look that passed between Maggie and the stranger, she added in a louder, more authoritative voice, "Maggie, please escort this gentleman to the barn and ask Reginald to make some arrangements for him there."

"Tell her," Maggie demanded, turning to Hetty, who looked up at Lydia with swollen eyes, then slowly shook her head "No."

"Tell her, Hetty," said the stranger in a soft, kind voice. "She needs to know."

Lydia stood speechless. Who was this stranger who had the gall to be standing in her parlor, calling Hetty by her first name? But finally Hetty, sitting up and straightening her shoulders, looked Lydia squarely in the eye. "This man is your father."

With eyes the size of the saucers in the china cabinet and her jaw dropping nearly to her chin, Lydia turned to stare at the stranger. "But he... but he's a..."

"There's more," Maggie interrupted. "Tell her, Hetty."

Hetty sniffed, then wiped her nose with her handkerchief. She waited at least a full minute before answering. "Your mother is still alive," she finally said, her voice croaking harshly.

Lydia, her knees nearly buckling, collapsed into the nearest arm chair. "My mother? But my mother died years ago..."

"And the rest?" interrupted Maggie. "You need to tell her the rest, Hetty. Get this travesty of the past you invented over with."

Hetty looked up to Maggie, then to the stranger as though she were begging for relief. But neither appeared willing to show any pity to the old woman. Finally, the Hetty that Lydia had learned to know seemed to emerge for just a moment. Looking defiantly at Lydia with what appeared to be consummate hatred, Hetty spit out her last words.

"You have a sister."

Part III—Ada—1815

Chapter One

Quóniam
Tu solus Sanctus,
Tu solus Dóminus,
Tu solus Altíssimus,
Iesu Christe.

The heavenly sound wafting to the rafters of the chapel would surely be mistaken by any stranger for the voices of angels glorifying God. But no stranger would ever be given entrance to this austere, yet beautiful, chapel: after all, the Ursaline Sisters of New Orleans were a monastic order.

Ada's voice stood out among the others for its sincerity and pure expression of joy. Singing this passage of the *Gloria*, its triumphant affirmations punctuating every line, always brought her to the threshold of an almost trancelike ecstasy. *Yes, Jesus*, she fervently thought, *You alone are the Holy One, the Lord, the Most High.* Jesus Christ was her master, her savior, her very life. And soon, in just two weeks, she would be his bride.

And to think. If it had not been for Jesus, if it had not been for the Ursaline sisters, she would not know the joy and the privilege of devoting her life to the glory of God. Sister Marie Justine, her Mother Superior, had told her the story many times, of how sixteen years earlier, as a tiny infant of indeterminate parentage, she had been left in a woven basket on the stairway of the convent. She had been taken to the first floor orphanage and was tenderly cared for there until she became old enough to begin her education as a student boarder at the convent. Even as a young child, she had dreamed of becoming a nun. Based on her piety and charitable nature, she was welcomed into the candidacy by the sisters who had been her family her whole life.

Soon, very soon, she would enter into her final vows and become Sister Marie Dominique. She would be allowed to wear the habit of the Ursalines: the pure white wimple worn over a black tunic, the white-lined black veil. She would be given a rope cincture, new rosary beads and a cross, the only adornment, a holy and blessed adornment, she would need for the rest of her life.

She would continue the work she had been assigned since she was twelve years old—teaching the younger girls reading and writing, domestic arts and the love of God. Sister Justine had recognized her skills and her vocation from that early age, and had allowed her to become a novice teacher in the same classroom in which she'd been a student for seven years. Ada loved teaching and loved the children, whose parentage covered almost the whole spectrum of the area's inhabitants. The Ursaline Convent's school welcomed the children of poor whites, free blacks, and Indians.

"Ite. Missa est," chanted Pere Andre.

"Deo grátias," she responded. *Could the mass really be over? Already?* But this was certainly not the first time she had lost track of time during daily mass; Sister Justine had often told her that life could stand still when in the presence of the Almighty. The fact that this happened so frequently to Ada was further evidence of her vocation to the sisterhood.

She collected her prayer book and rosary and, genuflecting deeply, exited the pew. As she was about to pass through the arched doorway of the chapel on her way to breakfast, Sister Marie Angelique, the convent's second in command, grasped the hem of her sleeve and, bending close, whispered in her ear. "Mother Superior wishes to see you."

"Now?" Ada asked. It was unusual for Sister Justine to hold conferences before breakfast.

"Yes, dear," Angelique answered. "Right now. Please come with me."

Ada was surprised to see two strangers in the convent's office. One was a middle-aged woman whose jet black hair was just beginning to gray at the temples. While her weathered complexion and rough clothing identified her as a member of the working class, her deep, dark eyes sparkled with what seemed an inherent sprightliness. The man who accompanied her was tall and thin, and his black hair, bronze complexion, and fringed buckskin jacket and boots identified him as being at least part Indian.

"Come in, Ada," Sister Justine said with her characteristic warmth, but tempered with an uncharacteristic reserve. "Here are two people who have come to meet you. They have something very important to tell you. Please meet Mr. Finn Campbell."

Ada managed a weak smile at the man who, rising from his chair with a kind but determined look, nodded at her.

"And this is Miss Margaret Connally," she continued.

"Your mother called me Maggie," the woman said, smiling broadly as she rose to take Ada's hand firmly in both of her own.

"My mother?" Ada questioned, looking piercingly into the stranger's eyes. "You knew my mother?"

"Yes, dear. I knew your mother," she said, pulling a handkerchief out of a pocket of her full skirt. "I *know* your mother," she continued, now dabbing the handkerchief at emerging tears. "Ada, your mother is still alive."

"But...but?" Ada sputtered, looking toward Sister Justine. "I was told I was an orphan."

"Yes, dear," said Sister Justine. "You came to us an infant, only a few days old. Your father was dead, and your mother was unable to care for you." Ada peered closely at Sister Justine, looking more confused than upset. "Under the circumstances," the nun continued, "it was unlikely that your mother would ever be able to care for you. The person who brought you to us asked that you be told you were an orphan, and it seemed the best course of action to follow at the time."

"The person who brought me to you?"

"Yes, a relative. Your aunt, I believe."

"My mother," Ada whispered, almost to herself. *And my aunt,* she thought. She wondered what kind of mother or aunt could treat an infant the way she had been treated: abandoning her, almost from birth. The thought of having a mother, a living mother, as well as an aunt she had never known, was unimaginable, a concept as foreign as a flying dog or a speaking fish. Finally, turning to Maggie, she asked, "Was my mother very ill?"

"Your mother..." Maggie began, looking to Sister Justine, who nodded solemnly. "Yes, your mother was ill." Maggie paused and brushed away tears before continuing. "Ada, for the past seventeen years your mother has been living in the Charity Hospital, here in New Orleans."

The Charity Hospital! It was only a short distance from the convent. As a child, she had frequently passed the hospital while running errands for the sisters. And in all that time, she'd not known her mother was there, living a life separate from her own. "Dear God," Ada whispered, "If my mother is so near, why was I never permitted to see her?"

"Your mother has been a prisoner there!" Finn interrupted, with a great deal of heat. "She was sent to the insane ward of the hospital before you were born." Ada clutched at her heart as she collapsed into the chair Finn had had the presence to move behind her.

"But she is not insane," he insisted, passion straining his voice. "Maggie and I have been to see her. Your mother has been cruelly mistreated."

Ada felt that in the past few minutes she had entered a new world, a world she never knew existed. Had she been living in a dream her whole life? "It is possible to have her released from the asylum," Finn continued. "You are her next of kin. Only you can legally force her release."

"Next of kin," Ada repeated, nodding her head in wonder and confusion. She had never thought of herself of having physical kinship with any other person in the world outside of the convent. The Ursaline sisters were her family.

"Well," Maggie corrected, "there is your sister, Lydia. She is your mother's kin as well." A quick look at Ada's face must have caused Maggie to wonder if she had said too much, too soon. But she quickly continued. "We've already spoken to Lydia, but she refuses to help. She willna' even go to see your mother."

"My sister!" This was more information than Ada, who looked helplessly toward Sister Justine, could bear. She had a sister, one who was unwilling to help a mother who was in need.

"Please leave us now," Sister Justine said, not unkindly, to Finn and Maggie. "As you can see, Ada is in considerable distress. She needs some time to reflect on this information, to come to understand what you have told her today, and to pray for guidance. Will you be in New Orleans for very long?"

"As long as we need to be," answered Finn, reaching out to a tearful Maggie. "Come, Maggie. Mother Superior, when may we return to the convent?"

"I will send for you once Ada has decided how to respond to your visit and your request. Sister Angelique, please escort Mr. Campbell and Miss Connally to the front door." As Ada watched them leave, Sister Justine went to her and, kneeling before her, took both of her trembling hands into her own. "Child, let us pray for guidance. I fear there is much more you need to know."

After nearly an hour in communal prayer, Ada was willing to listen Sister Justine deliver the shocking details of her family history. That her mother, in a fit of rage or lunacy, or perhaps in her own defense, had shot her father. That her father had died instantly, and her mother had been taken to the asylum. That she, Ada, had been born in the asylum, and had been brought to the convent by her father's sister, Hetty Campbell.

"And what of my sister? Did Miss Connally say her name was Lydia?" Ada asked.

"I know little about your sister. She was a child herself, five or six years old, I believe, when you came to us. I imagine that she has been raised by your aunt," Sister Justine answered.

"And you knew all this time. You never told me."

"Ada, you were an infant when you came here. As you grew into childhood, would you have wanted to know any of this? Could you at that age have understood?"

"No. But I have not been a child for many years. "

"Yes. This is true. You grew into the lovely, prayerful young woman you are. But in all that time, we never heard from your aunt again, or from any other member of your family. And once you told me your most fervent wish was to join us—was there any point in telling you the sad story of your family? It seemed better that you did not know."

Ada looked with new eyes at the woman whom she had always considered almost a mother to her.

"Ada," Sister Justine continued, tears coming to her own eyes, "not telling you was my decision. I made it with your best interests in mind. I may have made a mistake, but if so, it was made with good and loving intentions."

For several minutes Ada said nothing. Finally, rising from her chair, she said "Mother Superior, may I be excused?"

She fled to the chapel that had always been her refuge in times of trouble or distress. There was so much she needed to know, and so much she now wished she did not know. *Why, God?* she prayed, *Why must I learn of this now, when my hopes and wishes are about to be fulfilled, and I am so close to entering the sisterhood? Why have I been lied to for so long? Who are these people—a family I've never known—who seem so troubled and so full of sin? Who is my sister, and why is she unwilling to help our mother?*

"God, what do you want of me?" she finally called out, her voice reverberating in the silence of the small, dark room. "Now, when I am so close to my fulfilling my desire, is this a sign that I am not to become a nun?"

How could she leave the convent? It was the only life she had ever known, the Father, the Son, and the Holy Ghost her true family. In prayer she had shared her dreams and fears with them alone; they had never abandoned her when she had called out to them.

This could not be said of the real family, the very human family which she now knew she had been born into, who had been willing to give her up before even coming to know her. And they seemed troubled, truly troubled, and full of sin. All her life she had been warned to avoid the near occasion of sin, lest she fall into its evil trap. Would association with this family lead her, as well, into perdition?

She thought about her work with the convent's children. How could she give that up? Her work had given her a sense of accomplishment along with the satisfaction of being needed. The peace of convent life had kept her away from the chaos of the outside world, giving her great joy. Of course, joy in the monastic life was not the experience of all of the sisters. Sister Marie Jeanette was subject to frequent bursts of anger, and Sister Louisa often spent days alone in her room, refusing to leave it for meals or even for devotions. And Sister Marie Agnes, who was known to harm herself when she was distressed: she was certainly a troubled soul. Would her own future at St. Ursula's eventually mirror the path their lives had taken?

Perhaps receiving this startling information now, when she was so close to achieving her goal of sisterhood, was actually a calling from God, who might very well want her to reach out to this troubled family, to help them find their way to Him. And now that she knew they existed—her aunt, her sister, her mother—how could she turn away without at least meeting them? Could she live the rest of her life knowing she had a mother, but never actually coming to know her?

Ada reflected that Sister Justine, the woman who had been closer to a mother than anyone else in her life, would be disappointed if she left St. Ursula's. But she was now very disappointed in Sister Justine, who had kept information from her and had even lied doing it. Did Sister not have the confidence in her to trust that she was capable of deciding the path her own life should take? Could she ever forgive Sister Justine for not letting her know that other paths were available to her?

Dusk turned to twilight and then to night. Ada, still alone, climbed the two steps leading up to the altar and gazed prayerfully at the crucifix hung above it. After lighting the votive candles under the crucifix, she returned to her pew and, kneeling in the flickering light, prayed once more.

She prayed for strength to Saint Ursula, the virgin martyr who was the patron saint of the order of Ursaline sisters. She prayed for wisdom to Saint Ada, her own patron saint, a French abbess known for her piety and good counsel. Finally she prayed to Jesus, her bridegroom-to-be, whom she wished to serve for the rest of her life. To Him she prayed for love and understanding.

She spent the remainder of the night on her knees in the chapel, but once morning came she believed her prayers had been answered. Even before matins, Ada requested a conference with Sister Justine, who immediately ushered her into the office. Ada felt pity for the woman, whose bloodshot eyes, stooped shoulders and downcast demeanor told her that, like herself, Sister Justine had spent a very difficult night. But Ada had decided on the direction she would take, and was determined to see it through.

"Please send for Mr. Campbell and Miss Connally," she requested, refusing to respond to the questioning look Sister Justine gave her. "May I return to my room until they arrive?"

"Of course," answered Sister Justine. Within an hour Ada was summoned to the convent office, where Finn stood ramrod straight, his coonskin cap in his hands, while Maggie, nearly shredding the lace handkerchief she twisted between her fingers, stood beside him.

"I must leave St. Ursala's," she told them. "I wish to see my mother."

"Will you return?" Sister Justine inquired, but her question was answered by only a silent shrug. "Do what you must, my child," the nun finally responded, as tears began to trickle down her cheeks. "Know that we love you, that we will pray for you every day, and that you will always be welcome here. Go with God."

Ada fervently hoped that was exactly what she was about to do.

Chapter Two

"**A**re you absolutely certain, Miss Campbell, that this is the course of action you wish to pursue?" Dr. Turner, who was the chief administrator of Charity Hospital, fingered his goatee and slowly shook his head in dissent as he stared icily at Ada. "Your mother is very ill. Are you certain you have the ability and the experience to manage her care?"

At that moment Ada was not certain she had the ability to manage anything whatsoever. Traveling to Canal Street by buggy from the boarding house where she, Maggie and Finn had spent the previous three days, she had felt like a wee mouse set loose in a den of bobcats. So many buildings! So many horses! So many people! So much noise!

Even her new appellation, "Miss Campbell," seemed somewhat ominous to her. She had never been given a last name in the sixteen years she had spent in the convent. When called by this new name, she wanted to look for the actual person being addressed. But even more discomfiting, she found a last name seemed to bring with it responsibilities and entanglements. It signified belonging to a family, and she was discovering that a family could complicate life in ways she had never imagined.

Maggie had brought her a very demure gown and a bonnet to wear to the hospital, but Ada felt almost naked without the heavy black habit and veil she had worn as a postulant. Her long, strawberry blonde hair could not be contained by the bonnet—try as she might, she could not keep all of her curls modestly tucked into its rim. And while Maggie assured her the lavender floral print on her gown suited her alabaster complexion and brought out the green tints in her hazel eyes, she felt confused. She'd never participated in these kinds of conversations before: the sisters at the convent had never discussed such things as ways to enhance one's eye color or complexion.

All in all, Ada felt far too conspicuous: strangers were looking at her, and she was definitely not used to such scrutiny.

Upon seeing the new building which housed Charity Hospital, Ada almost lost her resolution. An imposing structure of neo-classical design with an entrance flanked by Doric columns, the building was dominated by huge windows: eight double hung windows on the first floor, with nine casement windows, each topped by a fan light, on the second. Ada was accustomed to the convent, where the atmosphere was private, silent, enclosed, and somber. Were it not for the support of Finn and Maggie, she would never have had the courage to enter.

"These kinds of patients should be handled by professionals in the medical field," Dr. Turner insisted. "A woman like yourself, with no medical training, cannot possibly know how to handle the melancholia and the homicidal and suicidal tendencies of a lunatic."

"You been handling Ada's mother for over sixteen years," interjected Finn. "It don't seem to me you done her much good." Ada was fortunate she had not been with Finn and Maggie when they had first gone to see Nia. They had found her chained to her bed, her arms folded across her chest and tied tightly behind her by straps contained in the long sleeves of a white canvass strait waistcoat.

The spattering of dry vomit on the waistcoat gave proof to Nia's having spent a long time confined in this manner. Staring into space, Nia had rocked back and forth as far as the chains would allow. Neither Finn nor Maggie had expected Nia to recognize them, but she would not even look up when they tried to speak to her. It was as if she neither saw nor heard them.

"Miss Campbell, you do not understand the intricacies of dealing with the insane," Dr. Turner continued, ignoring Finn's comment altogether. "You do realize your mother has a history of violence, do you not? She was responsible for the murder of your father."

"Mrs. Campbell has never been charged with any murder," interrupted Finn. "There is no legal reason to keep her here."

"Well, no," admitted Turner. "Her admission was based on information we received from ..." he spent a moment shuffling some papers, "from a Miss Hetty Campbell. So, you are correct. Miss Ada Campbell, as Mrs. Campbell's next of kin, has the authority to demand her release. But she is taking a great risk at doing so. Mrs. Campbell may still pose a danger to others, especially her own family."

Ada had been horrified when Maggie had told her the circumstances that brought about her mother's confinement.

Her mother ... a murderess. A woman who had killed her husband. And, Ada reflected with a sudden shock, the woman who had killed her father.

Were it not for Maggie's depiction of Nia as a kind and loving woman who, as the result of sore treatment, had sunken into a deep depression from which she could not emerge, Ada might have returned immediately to the Ursulines. Maggie had assured Ada that, with the proper care, the true Nia would emerge from the shell of a woman who was imprisoned in the Charity Hospital.

"I recommend that Mrs. Campbell stay here," continued Dr. Turner. "At Charity Hospital we use methods and procedures which have been proven effective."

"What methods and procedures might those be?" asked Maggie sharply. "Just in case we need to use them once we take Mrs. Campbell home," she added, with a wickedly sly wink at Ada.

Dr. Turner harrumphed his annoyance, but answered Maggie's question. "Well, the strait waistcoat, of course, is suitable when the patient needs restraint, for example, if she is in danger of injuring herself or another person. This treatment can be administered for days at a time. And occasional bloodletting—to balance the bodily fluids—is frequently needed." Dr. Turner seemed not to notice the shiver that overtook Ada's body upon hearing this.

"We also use cold baths to pacify patients who have become too excited," he continued. "Submersion in cold water for long periods of time lessens the heated nature of the patients' emotions, causing them to become more easily handled. You must agree that such procedures, which I can assure you reflect the epitome of modern medical practice, should be performed only by trained medical staff."

"I wish to attempt a different method of treatment," announced Ada in a voice much bolder than either Finn or Maggie had previously heard from her. She was horrified at the extreme measures to which her mother had been subjected. No person deserved to be treated so cruelly.

"And what would that be?" asked Dr. Turner. "Surely you are not aware of any method of treatment more modern and effective than what I have described."

Ada suddenly realized what her mother needed. Fortunately, it was a treatment which she, herself, could provide. "No, it is not modern at all. In fact, it is the oldest, but most effective, method of treatment that exists."

"And what," sneered Dr. Turner, "might that be?"

"Love."

Chapter Three

Ada had always enjoyed walking in the small walled garden of the convent, where plantings of bush palmetto, rosebay rhododendron, and mountain laurel offered not only beauty but also glorious scents. At the conclusion of her walk she would sit on the stone bench placed before the statue of St. Ursula, contemplating the meaning of the saint's life and how it related to her.

Ursula's crown and scepter referenced her royal ancestry, while her demure expression, eyes closed and only the hint of a sweet smile, signified her modesty and piety. Her floor-length cape sheltered several children, identifying Ursula as the patron saint of both students and teachers. Finally, the flowering plants surrounding the statue bloomed in tints of vibrant red: cardinal bellflowers and trumpet honeysuckle predominated, while three magnificent rose bushes provided abundant blooms throughout the summer. The red roses were a symbol of the saint's status as a martyr.

The beauty of the convent garden lay in its order, its minutely planned arrangement. The garden paralleled Ada's life in the convent: both were quiet, peaceful, and predictable, with every day like every other.

But nothing could differ more from the convent garden than the wild, natural beauty bordering the postal road, on which their small group traveled. On this road a flowering eastern redbud, its blossoms a globe of magenta, or a vibrant red maple would suddenly appear among the masses of green vegetation. A swarm of viceroy or swallowtail butterflies might cross their path, their numbers so great they blocked visibility. Once, as Ada peered out the window of the buggy, she spied two bald eagles in flight; another day's delight might be seeing the white breasts and black-tipped feathers of a flock of white ibis gliding above or hearing the shrill *kee kee kee* of a multitude of migrating passenger pigeons.

By the second day of their trip, she had stopped counting the number of white-tailed deer and raccoons she saw, but still thrilled at the sight of an occasional lone alligator sliding through a veil of Spanish moss into one of the swamps visible from the road, or of a black bear, watchfully following their progress while chewing a branch. Evenings might offer the sight of a pair of Carolina parakeets, perching on a branch, intertwined so closely their jade-colored plumage and yellow and rust-colored markings were not enough to distinguish one bird from the other. The postal road seemed a reflection of her new life, in which everything was fresh, exciting, and overwhelming in its novelty.

In much the same way, her current companions differed greatly from those she'd lived with for sixteen years. True, in the convent one could hear an occasional angry outburst or muffled weeping emanating from behind a closed cell door. But for the most part, the Ursulines shared a life of serene, pious, dedicated service, working toward a noble common cause, the education of children. Any overt dissonance or disparity was quickly and quietly resolved.

Her traveling companions, on the other hand, differed so much from herself and from each other that they could almost have all been members of different species.

Her mother. The very idea that she had a mother was difficult to assimilate. Of course, Mother Superior had been central to her entire life, but the thought that the woman sitting across from her, an actual person who had given her birth, seemed foreign and abnormal.

She had met her mother the day after their interview with Dr. Turner, when she, Maggie and Finn had, by arrangement, come to remove Nia from the hospital. An orderly had led a thin, pale woman, dressed in a shapeless black gown, into the parlor in which they waited. Nia's body twitched almost ceaselessly, and her eyes remained steadily focused on the floor. It wasn't until days later, when Ada had loudly exclaimed over some remarkable example of flora or fauna she noticed out of the buggy's window, that Nia, obviously startled, had quickly looked up, giving Ada the opportunity to notice the beauty of her mother's striking sapphire eyes.

While they traveled, Nia had twirled swatches of her honey colored hair, already streaked with gray, in her fingers, and had picked at and bitten her already bleeding fingernails. She had not yet uttered a word; Ada wondered if her mother's illness and the harsh treatment she had endured in the asylum had robbed her for all time of the possibility of speech.

In contrast, *Magpie*, Ada thought, *could be a suitable nickname for Maggie*; the woman chattered constantly. Before they were even into the second day of their journey, Ada had learned a great deal about her. She had emigrated from Ireland as an indentured servant, and had remained at Three Ponds Farm when her indenture was completed. She had raised her three sons, Michael, Timothy, and Aidan, on the Farm, and had seen all three boys leave to pursue different occupations: Mike as a blacksmith, Timmy as a cobbler, and Aidan, "The saints be praised!" as a priest. Maggie had not mentioned a husband; Ada thought she must be a widow, perhaps recently widowed, who was not yet able to speak of her loss.

It had taken Ada longer to learn anything about Finn, who spent all day on the driver's seat while the women sat inside the buggy. He had stopped infrequently, and only for a few minutes at each stop, to give the women a chance to devour a quick meal or stretch their legs a bit in the forest. The first night they had lodged in a stand, one of the hastily built cabins constructed along the road to accommodate travelers. But finding it filthy, loud and crowded with suspicious-looking characters, neither Maggie nor Ada had objected when Finn suggested they spend the remainder of their nights camping.

Ada found camping to be the best part of the trip. Finn had constructed a small teepee from three stout branches he had found lying in the forest and a couple of large deerskins he had brought with him. Finn's skill as a hunter had given the travelers the opportunity to enjoy fresh meat, a pair of mallards on one evening and some cottontail rabbits on another. Maggie was expert at finding edible greens in the forest and mushrooms along the swamps. But best of all, camping gave Ada the opportunity to get to know Finn.

Speaking to him had been difficult at first. The only man she had ever really spoken to during her time in the convent was Pere Andre, and almost all their conversations had been held in the confessional. But Finn had first drawn her into conversation by telling stories about her mother—how she had been born in Pennsylvania, had traveled to Natchez on a flatboat, and had become the mistress of a plantation. It wasn't long before Ada began to thoroughly enjoy sitting around the crackling fire, serenaded by a symphony of full-throated frogs and the occasional hooting of an owl, while Finn entranced her with stories about his life.

"I grew up at Three Ponds Farm," he told her, "though it wasn't called that way back then, and it wasn't so grand. My mother was a Natchez Indian of royal birth, and she went back to her people when I was a boy."

Ada was intrigued. "And you didn't go with her?" she asked.

"No," Finn responded, clearing his throat. "My father lived at the farm, and he wanted me to stay there. I always loved horses, and was good with 'em. I wound up bein' his wrangler. Stayed there until I was about twenty."

"What made you leave?" Ada asked.

"Well…" Finn began. He cleared his throat again, coughed a few times, and after a short pause, continued. "Maybe because I was a young man, lookin' for adventure. I traveled the Trace north and wound up livin' for a couple years with a tribe of Creeks near the Tennessee River. But they were fightin' the whites the whole time I was with them. The whites' major general, Andrew Jackson, was winnin' all the battles—it was pretty clear which way the wind was blowin'. When the Creeks signed a treaty and I heard Jackson was headed south to fight the British, I joined up with him."

"Wasn't it hard to join the people you had been fighting?" Ada asked.

"Not so hard. My father was white, so it didn't seem to matter so much what side I was fightin' on. Truth is, around that time something in me just made me want to fight more than anything. And in New Orleans it felt good to be on the winnin' side. A man could learn a lot from General Jackson. We were outnumbered and itchin' to get the fight over with once we saw them redcoats comin' through the bushes. But Jackson made us wait. He told us 'Don't fire 'til you see the whites of their eyes.' Smart man, Andrew Jackson. It worked. We won that battle. And it ended the war. "

"I know about that battle," responded Ada. "We prayed for the soldiers all night. General Jackson came to St. Ursula's the next day to thank us for our prayers." *And here I am*, she thought, *miles away from the convent, with a man who fought in that battle.* Ada considered that, for the first time, she was involved in real life with all its dangers, surprises and delights.

By the sixth day of their journey, Ada felt as though she had been traveling on the back seat of a bouncing buckboard wagon for her entire life. Her posterior, which had ached mightily the first few days of travel, now felt numb, and she was able to feel each individual vertebra in her back. While the game Finn caught and the greens Maggie gathered had supplied sustenance for their small group, she had begun to miss the sumptuous meals Sister Marie Francine had prepared in the convent three times a day. And although the territory they were traversing was beautiful, she was beginning to become tired of the color green.

Still, life outside the convent was a never-ending marvel. The last few days had been revelatory for her: the beauty of the convent garden was just a tiny mirror image of the panoply of nature she had experienced. The people she had come to know on this trip, even though their number was small and one of them had not uttered a word during the whole time, had opened her eyes to the variety of human nature and human experience:

Maggie: so open and amicable. So willing to share her life story. In just a few days, Ada had become closer to this woman than she had become to anyone she had known at St. Ursula's. But Maggie treated her with a deference she found confusing. She refused Ada's offer to collect firewood or help with preparing dinner. Ada wondered if this was the result of Maggie's status as an indentured servant.

"I don't know much about the role of an indentured servant," Ada told her after Maggie had again refused her offer of help with the cooking. "In the convent we all shared the work. But you are not my servant. I wish you would accept my help."

"Oh!" Maggie's high-pitched laughter sent some flycatchers bolting out of the upper limbs of a river birch. "I ha'nt been indentured for a great many years. 'Tis just that I like serving you—you remind me so of your mama when she was young."

"Really?" Ada was surprised at how pleased she was to hear this.

"Yes. She was always a lady, just like yourself. She was kind—we were more like friends than like mistress and servant. It was a pleasure to work for her. Not at all like your Aunt Hetty or your sister."

This conversation was taking an exciting direction. Ada felt she was finally going to learn a great deal more about her family. "Of course, your sister Lydia had it rough growin' up without a mama and all," Maggie continued. "There were reasons behind her meanness, although..." Here Maggie paused to think a bit, "you didn't have a mama, and you turned out all right. But Hetty—I'm pretty sure Hetty was born into this world mean as a wild boar. 'Twas just her nature."

"And my papa?" Ada asked, hoping to direct the conversation toward the person who remained the most mysterious of her relations. "What was he like?"

"Oh look." Maggie pointed to an opening in the dense foliage. "Here comes Finn, and it looks like he's got a goose for tonight's dinner. Tend the fire if you've got a hankerin' to help, m'dear. I need to pluck the bird."

Finn: an adventurer. A person who had a diverse and exciting assortment of life experiences. And a man. Ada had never, in her sixteen years, had this much exposure to the nature of the male—his speech, his ideas, his actions—so different from hers, or from those of anyone she had ever known. *Are all men like Finn?* she wondered, although she did not yet have any clear idea of what, exactly, was the nature of even this particular man.

In some ways, he seemed to be two men. She knew he had killed men during the war and seemed to have come away from that experience without any guilt or sorrow whatsoever. Perhaps that was just the way men reacted to war, but it was something she would never be able to understand. She had seen his power while he chopped wood or helped pull the buckboard through a particularly swampy area, and had heard him cuss profusely when one of the buckboard's wheels had been damaged on a stump hidden in the path. But he always apologized to the ladies whenever such lapses occurred, always treating them with deference and respect. He was gentle in all his dealings with Nia, and Ada had even seen him give Maggie a tender kiss on the cheek one evening.

Finn could be a true raconteur at the campfire, entertaining Maggie and her with stories about river boats and hunting trips. But other evenings he chose to spend alone, either in the tent or wandering in the woods, and seemed to want nothing to do with any of them. She knew he was both Indian and white and wondered if the ambivalence in his nature was caused by that heritage. Everyone she knew referred to Indians as savages—perhaps that was where his rude and somewhat violent behavior came from. But then, she knew that many white men, and women as well, could be rude and violent.

Thinking about Finn's and Maggie's family backgrounds made her more interested in learning about her own heritage. She now knew something of her mother, although she did not feel she actually *knew* her. But she knew she'd also had a father.

"If you lived on Three Ponds Farm, you must have known my father," she began one evening after Finn finished telling a long and very funny story about his attempt to capture a bull that had escaped from its enclosure. "Can you tell me..."

"It's getting late," Finn interrupted, rather sharply, Ada thought. "We have a lot of miles to cover tomorrow." With that he stood and began stamping out the last embers of their campfire. "You better get some sleep."

Her mother: a true mystery. Ada knew there was a person inside that silent shell, a person whose care she felt committed to no matter how long her recovery would take. Already Ada had seen improvement in her mother's condition. Nia's body no longer trembled continuously, and her fingers no longer bled. Although Nia spent most of her time either peering out the buggy window or looking down onto her lap, Ada had on several occasions caught sight of her mother peeking at her, perhaps studying her face. But whenever Ada had responded with a smile, Nia had immediately resumed her downward glance.

Despite some improvement, her mother obviously was not yet capable of initiating any real contact with her. Ada wished she'd had an opportunity to know her much earlier and feared her physical and mental health were too far destroyed to ever allow that to happen. But she continued to pray that a day would come when whatever barriers stood between them would crumble.

On the ninth morning of their journey, as they were breaking camp, Finn made the announcement Ada had been waiting for—they would reach the Natchez area that day.

"Will we be staying at Three Ponds Farm?" Ada asked, pouring water fetched from a nearby stream onto what remained of the morning's fire.

"No. We'll be in a little place nearby," Finn answered.

Ada was disappointed. She had been looking forward to seeing the family home and, more importantly, to meeting her sister. Lydia still remained a complete unknown. There were many things about her family that, perhaps because they were disgraceful or even sinister, Maggie and Finn were not willing to share. She already knew her mother had killed her father, which was alarming enough, and wondered if it could have been an accident, although no one had suggested that possibility. It was very difficult to think of her quiet, timid mother as a murderess. But something had to account for Finn's, and particularly Maggie's, frequent silences or attempts to divert her attention whenever she touched on subjects that seemed to be forbidden to her.

Would meeting Lydia be the key to opening the door to her family's history? Ada could not know it was not Lydia, but someone else, who held the key. Phineas Campbell—though dead—was the bond that tied them all together in ways she could not possibly have imagined.

Ada, Maggie and Finn arrived at their new home, a two-room rustic log cabin on three acres of forested land, later that afternoon. The cabin needed a great deal of work: Finn started patching mortar and fixing the door almost immediately upon their arrival, and as soon as Maggie fashioned two brooms out of fallen branches and twigs, she and Ada began sweeping out piles of accumulated brush and dirt from the cabin floor. Ada hoped their work would discourage the numerous mice and the family of raccoons already settled there from trying to continue their residency.

By the time they had eaten the swamp rabbit Finn had killed for their dinner and doused the campfire, they were all more than ready to settle in for the night. The cabin contained no furniture, but the fireplace was in good working condition, and as a heavy rain began falling, Ada was grateful they were not spending this night in the tent. Before she could complete even half of the litany that was her customary evening prayer, she was fast asleep.

At daybreak, Ada was wakened by a gentle knock on the door. Her companions still slept, and Ada wondered whether she should wake Finn. But summoning her courage, she rose and, upon opening the door just a slit, breathed in an incredibly sweet smell.

"Good Morning," chirped a friendly female voice. "Have thou had thy breakfast as yet?"

Ada saw before her a woman holding a large pan, which accounted for the heavenly smell. The woman, short, plump, and dressed in a plain brown chambray skirt, a knitted shawl and a bonnet, had a broad smile that animated her blue eyes and ruddy cheeks. "My name is Lucretia Bennett," the woman continued, "and I am thy nearest neighbor. Do thou like apple pandowdy?"

The sound of voices, or perhaps the rich apple smell, had awakened the others. Ada could sense the tense alertness of Finn, who had suddenly appeared beside her. But Maggie was the first to speak. "Let the woman in," she said. "She's just bein' neighborly."

Ada soon learned that Lucretia and her husband, Bartholomew, lived in a wooded area less than a half mile from their cabin. Bartholomew, while hunting, had noticed their buggy passing by. Lucretia seemed a bit embarrassed to admit he had followed their buggy and watched them move their belongings into the cabin, but explained that thieves and other criminals were always a danger in this region; he was simply being cautious. She was so delighted to have new neighbors that she had risen before dawn to prepare this welcoming breakfast.

As there was no furniture in the cabin, they all retreated to the previous evening's campsite, where Finn had fashioned tree stumps into stools and one large tree trunk into a bench. Soon there was a fire, coffee, and pleasant conversation.

The Bennetts were the parents of six children, four sons and two daughters. Lucretia's husband worked as a blacksmith and general handyman, and she assured Finn that Bartholomew would be happy to help with any repairs needed on their cabin.

"Thou should know," Lucretia said, suddenly becoming quite serious, "before we get to know each other better, that Bartholomew and I are Friends."

Ada was confused. Wasn't it expected that a husband and wife be friends? Or was the woman requesting their friendship? If so, she had a strange way of doing so. "Well, of course," she responded, "I hope as neighbors we do become friends."

"No, no," Lucretia corrected. "We are members of the Society of Friends. Some people call us Quakers."

"I've heard of the Quakers," interposed Maggie. "They're a religious group. When I was a child in County Cork, we had some Quakers living near us."

"Some folks hereabouts do not want us," Lucretia continued. "The Friends strongly oppose slavery, which we believe is an evil abomination. Our beliefs have caused much persecution against us in the Mississippi Territory and everywhere else, especially in the South." Lucretia looked with some concern at the faces of those who surrounded her as all three quickly glanced toward each other in a questioning manner.

"I don't see a problem," Finn finally responded with a laugh. "Not a one of us has ever owned a slave." Lucretia could not have known that she had come to visit three of the area's inhabitants—a former indentured servant, a prospective Catholic nun, and a half-breed—who would be among the most unlikely individuals in the whole territory to strongly support slavery.

Only Maggie knew that the fourth among them, the silent soul sitting alone in a copse apart from the others—most likely opposed slavery more strongly than any of the others.

"Very well then," chirped Lucretia, once again beaming. "Thou must come to visit. If thou would like to attend a Meeting some time, we do try to come together at least twice a week. Sister Sarah is in charge of the children. The poor dear is very old and has almost lost both hearing and eyesight, but she does try very hard."

Sudden smiles animated both Ada's and Maggie's faces: neither could know the other was thinking the same thing. *Children. I wonder if Quakers teach their children the same way I taught Bible School. I wonder if Sister Sarah could use some help.*

"And if thou do come," Lucretia continued, looking toward Nia sitting by herself, half hidden by vegetation, "please bring the lady with thee. She may enjoy the singing."

Chapter Four

Lydia knelt in the small flat area she had stamped out between the two graves, carelessly pulling some of the carpet of weeds that covered them. The tiny cemetery was in disarray, its picket fence demolished in some areas by scavenging animals, the graves and Lydia almost hidden from view by overgrown shrubs and grasses. Three stately live oaks surrounding the plot were almost completely draped in Spanish moss, which at least, Lydia thought, gave the cemetery the eerie, haunted aspect suitable to its purpose.

She scrutinized the weathered wooden grave markers, their black lettering almost indecipherable: *R.I.P. Phineas Stuart Campbell 1752-1797; R.I.P. Eugenia Meier Campbell 1776-1797.* At each of her infrequent visits home during the time she was imprisoned in various boarding schools, Aunt Hetty would insist on their customary visit to the cemetery. There Lydia and her aunt would kneel to pray for the souls of her parents, Lydia never suspecting that only one body was buried at the gravesite.

All those nightmares she'd endured as a child: loud noises, screams, blood. They weren't nightmares: they were memories. Hetty had lied—about her mother's death, about her father. This graveyard, her family graveyard, was fraudulent in every way. Even the one body it contained had no relation to her. Her real father was the halfbreed she'd met just days earlier. No wonder her hair was so straight, her eyes so black, her complexion so dark. She looked nothing like Ada, the girl who she had been told was her sister.

Her father: a halfbreed. There were some women among the Natchez nabobs who would truly enjoy knowing that: they could destroy her standing in society. Of course, the Colberts were all part Indian, and they were accepted to a certain extent. But they were all businessmen, not planters. Plantation owners were a step above.

She turned when she heard rustling sounds coming from the heavy brush behind her. "Here she be, Ma'am," said Rufus as he motioned to the other four men to place the plain pine box, the coffin, on the ground.

Two other men carrying shovels came forward. "Where does you want her, Ma'am?"

She looked at her father's grave, *No, at Phineas' grave,* she reminded herself, and considered whether she should put Aunt Hetty's body, *No, Hetty's body—we never were related* she remembered, to its left. She contemplated for a moment the startling realization that the "family graveyard" she had visited since she was a child contained no one to whom she was actually related.

She had found Hetty that morning, dead in her bed, an empty glass on the nightstand beside her. Hetty was old and had been ill for years. Still, Lydia had to wonder what had been in that glass: plain water? Something else? *What does it matter?* she thought. *She's dead. Dead and unmourned.*

"Did you want me to gather de other slaves," Rufus asked, "so's we can pray?"

Pray, Lydia thought. *When was the last time I prayed? Do I even remember how?* She thought again of her sister—the sister she'd just met—the sister she never knew she had. *Didn't Maggie say she was a nun? Ada would know how to pray—maybe I should send for her.*

Lydia took one more look, a long, hard look, at the coffin. Then she looked at Rufus. "No. No prayers are needed. Bury her in that grave to the right of my father," she said.

"Where yo mama lay buried?" he asked in horror.

"Yes," she insisted. "To the right of my father's grave."

Rufus was visibly frightened. "Sorry, Ma'am, but dat ain't right. Ain't you afeared o' ha'nts?"

"No," she answered. "Do as I tell you. It's not the ghosts I'm afraid of. It's the living you've got to watch out for." With this she turned away from the graveyard and started walking away.

The slaves pitched the tips of their shovels into the sandy soil.

Lydia had no sooner entered the house when Queenie had bad news to deliver. "Ma'am," she began, "Miz Underwood cain't stay wit de chillen any mo' today. She suddenly gone sick."

"Oh, dear. Not another megrim," Lydia responded, beginning to develop a headache herself. Miss Underwood did a good job as the children's governess, but was susceptible to the strange headaches that made her nauseous and caused intolerance of light and noise. The only cure was several hours of quiet in a dark room.

"What are the children expected to be doing right now?" she asked. Miss Underwood believed in strict scheduling for children. Lydia's time for seeing her children generally ran from 10:00 to 11:00 in the morning, a time that suited her well. It was now nearing dusk; if she were well, Miss Underwood would be with them in the nursery.

"A'most dey bed time, I tink," Queenie told her. "Dey already et dey suppah."

"Oh, very good," Lydia responded. "Can you prepare the children for bed?"

"Yes'm, but Miz Underwood always read dem a story befo' bed."

"Can't you..." Lydia began, then realized how ludicrous the question she was about to ask would have been. *My mind is really disordered right now,* she thought. Of course Queenie could not read the children a story. "Can they not go to bed one night without a story?" she asked.

"Yes'm. But Miz Lucy gonna cry fo a whole hour witout her story. She be real partial to de readin'."

"Very well," Lydia said with a deep sigh as she gathered her skirts for the trip upstairs. The day had been frustrating enough without this added annoyance. Although she had never read to her children, she imagined doing so would not take long, perhaps only a few minutes. She could soon be back downstairs, where a glass of sherry, or perhaps two or three, would help soften the edges of this very rough day.

When she entered it, she realized she had almost forgotten how charming the nursery was; she was there so seldom. The entire room, including its floor-length white lace curtains and the netting over the four-poster crib, was pure white, which contrasted beautifully with the dark floors and rosewood furniture. A matching rosewood child-sized table with two tiny chairs was set with three dainty place settings of fine bone china, and the mantle was decorated with a variety of porcelain dolls beautifully dressed in elaborate costumes. The children, already wearing their white night dresses, sat cross-legged before the Chippendale rocker, patiently waiting for their story.

"Mama?" Lucy said with surprise. One thing Lydia could say about her husband was that he fathered beautiful children. Junior, at five years old, and three-year-old Lucy, with their curly blonde locks and blue eyes, resembled the paintings of cherubs that decorated ceilings in the Renaissance cathedrals Lydia had seen in the travel and art books that decorated her society friends' end tables. "Where is Miz Unnerwood?" the child asked.

"Ah," she answered, tousling Junior's hair as he pulled just slightly away from her, "Miss Underwood is not feeling well tonight. Mama will read you a story. Would you like that?"

"Yes! Yes!" they responded together, their sweet voices filling the room.

"Very well, then. What story would you like me to read?" she asked, thinking that, perhaps, she might on occasion take over this task from Miss Underwood. She was surprised to find she was beginning to enjoy herself.

"Tonight is my turn," asserted Junior. "We take turns choosing the story, and tonight is my turn to choose." With that he got up and, with a solemnity uncommon in a five-year-old boy, began looking through the collection of children's books on the bureau. Finally he chose one, and handing it to his mother, flopped back down onto the floor.

"Oh, my," Lydia said. "This is a big book, and it has many stories. Which one would you like me to read?"

"'The Cat and the Mice,'" requested Lucy. "I like that one best."

She really is a pretty girl, thought Lydia. *She'll start attracting beaus in just a few more years.*

"But it is my turn," insisted Junior. "I get to choose."

He certainly looks like his father, Lydia mused. *But I wish his father had a bit more of his son's tenacity.* Junior seemed to know what he wanted and how to acquire it. "I think Junior is right," she said, smiling at Lucy, who, nodding, accepted her mother's decision with her own smile.

This is much easier than I thought it would be, thought Lydia, impressed at how well-behaved her children were and thinking she might increase Miss Underwood's wages. The woman was obviously doing a fine job.

"So, Junior, what story will you hear this evening?" she asked.

"'The Country Mouse and the Town Mouse.' That one is my favorite."

"Very well," Lydia said, checking the index for the proper page. "Ah, here it is. 'The Country Mouse and the Town Mouse,'" she began. "'Once upon a time, a country mouse had a friend who lived in the city. He invited his friend to visit him at his home. Though he was plain... plain and rough and frugal, he opened...opened... his larder...his larder of barley and nuts...'"

"Mama," said Lucy, "why did you stop?"

"Mama," said Junior, "why are you crying?"

Chapter Five

"'Blessed are the poor in spirit, for theirs is the kingdom of heaven. Blessed are those who mourn, for they shall be comforted. Blessed are the meek, for they shall inherit the earth,'" Ada read.

"What do meek mean?" asked Saul, looking up at Ada with dark, soulful eyes.

"Why, it means humble, lowly, patient," explained Ada. "It means you are not proud."

"I wanna be proud," Saul responded. "I don'wanna be humble."

"But that is not what Jesus says," Ada insisted. "He says that those who are meek will inherit the earth."

"When?" Saul asked. Ada knew he was being impudent. At fourteen, Saul was the oldest of the children she taught at the Bennetts' Sunday school. He was smart, with a clever mind capable of seeing the truth behind the platitudes. *Why shouldn't a fourteen-year-old boy admire strength and pride over meekness?* she wondered. "Because it will get him killed," would be Lucretia's answer. And Lucretia would be right.

In the months since she had left the convent, Ada had been exposed to the true horror of the institution called slavery. Of course, during her earlier life she had known slavery existed, but had never imagined the cruelty and depravity that that lay at the base of the whole system. She had seen slaves beaten for no reason, had even seen two slaves hung in the town square. And their crime? They were runaways—runaways from a system that demeaned and impaired them, a system that never should have existed in the first place.

Basing their actions on the fear of insurrection, plantation owners and overseers were now being particularly strident in the treatment of their slaves. Slave rebellions had recently been repelled in Virginia and South Carolina, and the massive New Orleans insurrection of 1811 was still a frightening memory in most planters' minds. Lately, there had been much talk of possible trouble brewing in Natchez, based only on rumors, but alarming to the white population nonetheless. Any trace of resistance from a slave, be it a word or even a look that suggested a hint of obstinacy, was dealt with harshly.

To Ada, the Bennett farm was a haven of light amidst the darkness. Based on their previous experiences teaching Bible studies, she and Maggie had been solicited to teach Sunday school classes to the children of the adults who attended the Bennetts' twice weekly Meetings. This gave Bartholomew and Lucretia more time to address the needs of their adult congregation. Maggie was responsible for the younger children and Ada for those who were older. Their classes comprised the four youngest Bennetts and the offspring of other Friends living in the area, as well as the children of free blacks and of a very few slaves.

Sunday mornings at the Bennett homestead placed Ada in a world apart from the rest of the Natchez area. At the Bennetts' home all were seen as equal in God's eyes. But Ada knew once Sunday services were done, those in attendance would have to leave this haven and deal as best they could with the outside world and all its brutality.

"We must trust in Jesus," she answered Saul, knowing the boy would not settle for that answer. "He will show us the way." These words seemed far less reassuring here than they had been in the convent. As much as Ada wanted to let Saul know she understood his desires and frustrations, she knew Lucretia was right; doing so would only expose the boy to grave danger.

Seeing the adults leaving the Bennetts' large cabin, Ada knew it was time to end the day's class. As always, the hours she spent with the children had flown by. Once the Meeting was over, the congregation would share a bounteous dinner brought by all who had the wherewithal to contribute to the meal. Sniffing the air, Ada tried to guess what dinner would be: probably grilled pork, she decided, based on the pungent smell wafting from the fire pit.

The Friends' service, being so different from church services in the convent, seemed very peculiar to Ada. For one thing, it was held in the Bennetts' parlor, a very plain setting compared to the adornment of the Ursuline chapel. There were no crosses or statues of saints, no candles or incense, no priest dressed in splendid vestments, and although all attendees participated in singing, no organ or choir leading them.

Most remarkably, women were allowed, even encouraged, to preach the gospel. Before Ada and Maggie had been asked to take over the responsibility of Sunday school, they had been invited to attend several Meetings. At her first Meeting experience, Ada noticed that all members of the congregation were encouraged to speak during the service. But most surprisingly, Lucretia, and not Bartholomew, was the designated preacher for that day. She spoke on holiness, or Christian perfection, which was the ability to rid oneself of sin by following Jesus' model of loving God and all humanity. No confession, no penance, was required. Lucretia's words were powerful. Ada could not wholly accept what she had preached, but the sermon gave her a great deal to think about.

She led the children in reciting *The Lord's Prayer*, a form of worship shared by Catholics and Friends, then dismissed them. Chattering gaily to each other, they raced to claim seats at the sturdy wooden tables set up for the feast. "Are you ready for supper?" Maggie asked her, as they watched the antics of Maggie's class of youngsters making their serpentine way toward the tables. One little boy had segued to a small pond in search of frogs while an even littler girl was wandering toward the meadow, most likely in search of wildflowers.

"Yes," Ada laughed, "but you had better collect your charges! They seem to be escaping." As Maggie hurried to round up her flock, Ada headed toward the glorious red maple to which Finn had laid claim. On their first Sunday visit to the Bennetts he had set a bench for himself and Nia under this maple; from there they could watch Maggie and Ada teaching the children. Nia always sat silently, her only motion an occasional move to push aside the veil from her prim spoon bonnet.

Ada was grateful for the solicitous care Finn took of her mother. He would spend the entire Sunday morning sitting next to Nia, speaking softly despite her inability or unwillingness to respond. Sometimes Finn would lead Nia and Ada on short walks around the property, pointing out a particularly showy patch of wildflowers or a pair of great blue herons flying overhead. His patience and perseverance were remarkable to Ada, and highly commendable.

Ada often wondered whether it was lack of competence or of desire that caused her mother's muteness, and whether a remedy would ever be found. She sensed her mother had a great deal to say to her, but wondered if she would ever have the opportunity to hear any of it. "Mama," she said, smiling at Finn as she took her mother's hand into both of her own. "Would you like to come to supper now?" Nia was always compliant, immediately responding to any request made of her. But today she remained seated, staring at her daughter with what appeared to be confusion.

"Mama," Ada repeated, "it is time for supper. Are you not hungry today? Or shall I bring something to you?" Nia, her eyebrows pinched in a manner that seemed to indicate speculation, continued to scrutinize her daughter's face. Ada turned to Finn, who shrugged his shoulders and whispered "No" as he shook his head from side to side.

"Mama?" Ada questioned, responding to the inquisitive look she had never before seen in her mother's eyes. "Are you feeling well? Is anything the matter?"

"Lydia?" Nia asked. For the first time in her life, Ada was able to see the beauty of her mother's smile.

"Hyagh," Ada shouted, lightly flicking the reins over Misty's rump. Despite his assertion that she was headed on a fool's errand, once Finn realized Ada was determined to go to Three Ponds Farm, he had volunteered to take her.

"No," she had responded, "I need to go alone."

"She will not speak to you," he insisted.

"She is my sister," Ada added, somewhat heatedly. "Eugenia is our mother. Lydia is the only one who can help her." Reluctantly, Finn had agreed to give Ada a lesson on how to drive a buckboard as well as directions to Three Ponds Farm.

Ada had been thrilled to hear her mother speak her first word after months of silence. She hoped the breakthrough for which she had passionately prayed had actually occurred. And Nia had continued to speak, but "Lydia" was the only word she would utter throughout that day and into the next two.

Sometimes Nia whispered "Lydia" under her breath, as though she were praying. Often her daughter's name became a question, and she would look longingly at Ada, repeating "Lydia?" over and over, then dissolving in tears when the question could not be answered to her satisfaction. Occasionally she would shout the name in anger.

Ada was convinced that seeing Lydia would be the key to their mother's recuperation, possibly to her very survival. Finn and Maggie had held her back from going to Three Ponds Farm, from meeting her sister, for far too long already. She should have insisted they take her sooner, but they had both agreed that Lydia was not yet ready for a visit from any of them.

Now things were different. Ada feared that if Nia did not see her older daughter soon, she would sink once again into silence. Once she knew how important she was to their mother's future life, how could Lydia refuse?

Chapter Six

"What do you want, Queenie? Can you not stop that infernal knocking?"

"Ma'am, dey's a lady heah. She say she gotta talk to you."

"Oh, pshaw!" Lydia responded, pushing the ruffled satin sleep shade from her eyes. "Can't you send her away? Tell her to come back tomorrow. What time is it anyway?"

"She already in de house, Ma'am. I don' t'ink she gonna go nowheah 'til she see you. It's 'bout one o'clock, Ma'am."

"Do you want me to go?" slurred her sleeping companion, rolling toward her.

"No. I'll go down," she answered, thinking that Queenie deserved a slap for allowing someone into the house without her permission. Grabbing her best silk robe from the floor where she had dropped it the night before, she quickly wrapped it around her naked body and headed out the bedroom door.

Even from the staircase landing, Lydia knew exactly who the person pacing her parlor floor must be. The strands of honey blonde curls escaping from beneath her black bonnet and the unfashionable cut of her sedate black gown gave her away. *So,* she thought, *this is the sister.* She was tempted to turn around and go back to her bedroom, but then rethought that course of action. *It had to happen some time,* she considered. *I might as well meet her on my own ground.*

Lydia, wanting time to assess the young woman waiting in her parlor, took each step down the massive circular stairway in a deliberative, leisurely manner. *She could be pretty,* she thought, assessing the upturned face of the young woman who watched her closely, *if she did something with her hair and got rid of those hideous* vêtements. *That hat alone! I could help her..."* The last thought shocked her—was she, at her age, assuming the role of big sister? How ridiculous!

She is beautiful, thought Ada as she watched Lydia make her way down the stairs. *How can I convince her to help us?*

"You must be Ada," Lydia began. "What brings you to Three Ponds Farm?" Lydia scrutinized Ada for any signs of undue interest in her surroundings. Any girl who grew up in a convent must be nearly overwhelmed by the luxury of a home like Three Ponds. Would Ada be jealous? Enough to attempt to lay claim to part of the property? Lydia made a note to herself to alert Nigel to the fact that he might need to set up a conference with one of his lawyers.

"Lydia," began Ada, "dear Sister Lydia, I have longed to meet you since I first learned about you."

Lydia, sharing no similar feelings, chose not to respond to that comment. Instead, she reverted to customary social intercourse, always a good refuge when faced with an awkward situation. "Would you care to sit down?" she asked in a very impassioned manner. "Shall I ask Queenie to bring you some tea?"

Ada accepted the seat but declined the tea. There was something very intimidating about her sister Lydia; Ada wanted to approach the purpose of her visit before courage deserted her. "I am here to speak to you about our mother," she began, then waited almost a full minute for a response. Receiving nothing but a noncommittal look from Lydia, she continued. "There has been a breakthrough in her ability to speak, but I believe you are the only one who can help her improve even more."

"Really?" Lydia responded coolly. "She cannot speak?"

"Well, not until recently. I think you can help her."

"You do know our mother is a murderer—and insane," Lydia responded. "Perhaps her guilt causes her silence, or she may not wish to remember the evil she has done and has tried to push her crimes out of her mind. She likely belongs back in the asylum you so foolishly released her from, if not in prison."

Ada was taken aback at the directness of her sister's response. "Dear Lydia," she pleaded, fighting back tears, "you would not feel that way if you but met her. She is gentle, loving, a lost spirit who needs our help. She particularly needs *your* help, and you may be the only one who *can* help her. I beg you to do so."

Where was any help from my mother as I grew up in boarding schools? thought Lydia as she glared at her sister. *How dare this woman ask for my help now?*

Ada continued with a bit more confidence, believing her sister's hesitation to respond suggested sympathy, or at least interest, in the mission of her visit. "She spoke her first word several days ago. To me, it seemed like a miracle. And the word she spoke was 'Lydia.' Since then, she has uttered your name, and only your name, many times."

Lydia, startled by this information, remembered the strange, conflicted feelings she had experienced while reading to Junior and Lucy. She knew those feelings were tied to remembrance of her mother. But how could she forget the loss she had experienced believing her mother had died of fever, or the hot anger she'd felt once she had learned the truth.

"Liddy, darling, are you coming back up?" Both women were startled at the sound of the deep male voice coming from the second floor landing. Ada looked up to see a dark-haired, mustachioed man wearing a night shirt open almost to the waist. The sight of black chest hair disturbed her in ways she could not understand.

Still, she was not going to let this deter her from her mission. "Good Morning, Mr. Masters," she called out as she, wishing to look at something besides the inadequately dressed gentleman, began closely examining her hands, which were carefully folded in her lap. The sudden, loud guffaw emanating from the gentleman and the giddy giggle from her sister caused her to look up once more.

"Ada," Lydia began once she regained her composure. "I would like to introduce my friend, Señor Gonzales. An old family acquaintance." *What was I thinking?* she mused, any nascent kindness toward her mother leaving her mind immediately.

"Very pleased to meet you," said Gonzales with a toothy smile. "Liddy, perhaps the young lady would like to join us in..."

"Iggy!" Lydia exclaimed in what sounded like shock, although his intended suggestion caused her to giggle even more. "You debauched reprobate! Go back to bed. I'll be back up there soon." The look she saw on her sister's face made it difficult for her to restrain the laughter bubbling within her.

Ada was not quite sure what she had witnessed, but knew what was going on in this house was not acceptable behavior. In the convent she had been taught to "avoid the near occasion of sin," and her sister's behavior was clearly sinful. "I must go," she said, quickly rising from her seat.

"So! Shocked, are you?" Lydia challenged. Ada was surprised to see fury and hatred in her sister's eyes.

"I am sorry, but I cannot stay in a house where..."

"Where what? Where a woman would have the iniquity to lay with a man who is not her husband?" Now Lydia's voice was even louder and certainly more piercing. Ada, beginning to head toward the door, was stopped cold by her sister's next words. "Then you had better abandon that evil mother of ours."

"Mama? Abandon Mama?"

"Yes, unfortunately for both of us, we do share the same mother. But not the same father." Ada, wide-eyed and almost comically open-mouthed, looked at her sister as though Lydia had suddenly grown another head.

"Phineas Campbell was *your* father. Finn," Lydia said, acid dripping from every word, "is mine. Let me see, that would make Finn, well, imagine that, your brother!"

"Finn is your father? And my brother?"

"Yes. Your brother. Phineas Campbell fathered Finn as well as you, and probably about one out of every ten slaves on this property. Is that enough sin for you, Sister?"

"I... I don't know what to say. I can't believe..."

"Believe it, Sister," Lydia sneered. "And if you do not know what to say, just listen. Perhaps you should also know that you and Maggie, our old indentured servant who seems to have become your friend and benefactor, are also related in a manner of speaking. Her sons are your brothers through your father. But, fortunately, they're not my relatives!" She followed this with an almost fiendish chortle. "There is plenty more 'family history' I can share with you, should you be interested. My, my, you don't look well at all. Use that fainting couch against that wall," she taunted, pointing, "should you need it." But Ada was already hastening toward the door.

"Yes. Run away, Sister," Lydia shouted to Ada's retreating back. "Run away from the real world. Run all the way back to that convent where you belong."

Ada wasn't more than a mile from Three Ponds Farm before the heavens opened up, drenching her in a summer thunderstorm. Within minutes a smell much like that of rotting mushrooms began to nauseate her; whether it came from the forest's dense vegetation or from the heavy serge of her habit she could not tell. Pulling Misty's reins sharply to the right with a loud "Whoa!" she stopped to take cover beneath the limbs of an immense sycamore.

Bending over the side of the wagon, she spewed out what seemed like the entire contents of the last three meals she had eaten. But the sharp taste of bile told her she was not actually vomiting food, but rather the enormity of the information she had just received. Her mother, an adulteress. Her father, a lascivious rogue. Four half brothers, or perhaps even more, she never knew she had, all most likely born in sin.

Both Finn and Maggie knew her family's sordid saga, but neither had the fortitude or the righteousness to tell her about the lives they lived. Did they believe she would never learn about her family's misdeeds? Did they accept such conduct as normal? She wished she had never left the convent, had never met this passel of sinners. If only a company of angels could transport her back to St. Ursula's right this minute, she would pray for that very miracle. Would God answer such a prayer?

She had been certain God had sent her here for a reason. Her years in the convent had taught her that nothing happens without the will of God. But what was His will? Did He wish her to return to the cabin, perhaps to help her family see the error in the lives they'd lived? Or was this entire journey a terrible mistake?

One thing was certain: she could not face them now. But where else could she go? Suddenly, she knew. Turning an obviously reluctant Misty back into the storm, she headed toward the one place where she both wished to go and knew she would be welcome.

"Now, now, dear, please do not cry any more. Do thou wish another cup of tea?"

Shaking her head in the negative, Ada looked up into the deep brown eyes of her benefactor. "But it is all so terrible! My family. All my life I wished I had a family. And now I do—all of them vile sinners. I wish I had never left the convent."

Lucretia, pulling her chair closer to Ada, gently placed an arm around her shoulders. "I am certain God sent thee here for a purpose," she said, "perhaps to help them. But even if that is not the case, what would Jesus have thee do? Judge them?"

"No, no," Ada sniffled, "of course not."

"And think not so much of the history thou learned from thy sister today, but of the people thou has gotten to know. Thy mother. Thy brother Finn. Thy friend Margaret. Has thou not found them to be good, righteous people?"

"Yes, but..."

"Ada, thou has come from a life which sheltered you from the evils of this world. But those evils do exist, particularly here, where we live. The debauchery of slavery affects all behavior; this is a belief all Friends share. A man owns another man, a woman, a child. He believes they are possessions, and that he may do whatever he wishes with them. Believing this, he feels justified in mistreating them, and often mistreats his wife and his children as well, since he also sees these as his possessions. The evil caused by the institution of slavery surpasses all understanding."

"I know you are right," answered Ada, trying to rub away the last vestige of tears from her eyes. "But I can do nothing to change all this. I am useless. At least in the convent I can do some good. I need to return there."

"Perhaps," Lucretia replied sadly, "perhaps thou are right." Then tilting her head to one side, she reached out to Ada and, with one hand placed under the girl's chin, lifted her head so they looked at each other eye-to-eye. "But before thou make thy decision, Child, please spend the night here with us. I have something to show thee."

Chapter Seven

"**M**iss Ada! Miss Ada! Wake up. It is time." Ada wakened to the sound of this urgent plea, accompanied by the sensation of her shoulder being shaken soundly. "Miss Ada, they will soon be here."

Opening her eyes, Ada saw the lovely face of Fanny, the Bennetts' eldest daughter. A tall, willowy girl of fourteen, Fanny always struck Ada as a serene, gentle young lady mature beyond her years. But Fanny's demeanor was anything but serene right now.

"Who? Who will be here?" Ada asked, rising up on one elbow from her pallet.

"Come with me. Mama will explain."

Holding one finger against her mouth in a warning for silence, Fanny, tip-toeing silently around the inert bodies of sleeping children, led Ada to the front door. As she opened it, Ada saw a gray misty darkness signaling the coming transition between night and morning, with a pink glow on the horizon promising an imminent sunrise.

Taking Ada's hand, Fanny led her through Lucretia's vegetable garden and past the chicken coop toward the barn. Instead of entering the barn, however, they walked around it, finally stopping at the raised entrance to the root cellar. As Fanny lifted the slanted roof of the cellar, Ada was surprised to see light flickering through the opening.

"Watch thy head," Fanny warned as she carefully led Ada down the four steps leading to the cellar floor. Knowing the excellence of Lucretia's housekeeping skills, Ada was not surprised to find an immaculately clean room, paneled in wooden slats, and well stocked with barrels and shelves full of glass jars containing brightly colored preserves arranged carefully by kind.

She was surprised, however, when Fanny, walking up to one of the shelves and placing her hand behind it, was able to shift it away from the wall just far enough to allow a person to squeeze behind it. Had Ada not been warned to be silent, she would have asked the girl what kind of marvelous contrivance allowed such a thing. Instead, she followed Fanny into a dirt-walled room just large enough to hold several pallets, a small table holding a candle that provided very little light, and two chairs.

"Thank thee, Child," came Lucretia's voice from a shadowy corner of the room. "Hasten thou back to the house before the children find thee missing."

Mystified, Ada watched Fanny silently slink out the entrance and Lucretia, just as silently, push the wall closed and latch it securely. "Now we wait," she said, signaling silence with the same gesture her daughter had used only minutes earlier. "It will not be long."

Although their wait was no more than thirty minutes, to Ada it seemed much longer. She had so many questions. What was going on here? Surely something secret, if not sinister. Had she misjudged Bartholomew and Lucretia? They seemed to be upright, virtuous people. But then, all those she had come to know since she left the convent were, she had learned to her disappointment, not the persons she had believed them to be. Could this be true of the Bennetts as well?

Three sharp knocks on the closed panel door startled her, but fortunately she was able to stifle the scream that had nearly escaped her throat. She heard a gruff voice utter the words "The cargo is here" through the door and watched as Lucretia hurried to open it.

"Thank thee," she whispered to the man with the gruff voice as two shadowy figures entered the tiny room. "Go with God." With that she closed the door and addressed the two young black men who had entered. "Welcome," she said. "Thou will be safe here. Thou will find food in that knapsack in the corner. Try to sleep. The shepherd shall come at sunset to lead thee to the next station."

With that, taking Ada's hand, she quickly led her out of the tiny room. Ada had just enough time to glance back at the men, both of whom looked exhausted and nearly emaciated, already rummaging through the knapsack for food. "God bless you," they said in unison as Lucretia closed the secret panel and, with her fingers, lightly scattered the dirt on the floor leading to the opening.

"Lucretia, what..." Ada began as they reached the stairs leading out of the root cellar.

"Shhh," she warned. "I shall explain later. We musn't wake anyone. We must stop by the coop. If any of the children are awake when we come to the house, tell them we went to get eggs."

Ada saw the beginning of a shimmering yellow crescent rising on the horizon. Soon the sun would burst free and a new day would begin. It would be cooler in the cellar than outside, but the air there would still be heavy with humidity. She tried to remember if she had seen a jug of water available for them.

She determined to hold the myriad questions swirling in her mind until Lucretia felt ready to speak of this morning's proceedings. She knew she had witnessed something illegal, something that posed a danger to every person involved. Following Lucretia's example, she helped collect eggs, and by the time they entered the cabin to find the remaining Bennett children stretching and yawning as they wakened from their sleep, she was able to act as though this morning had been as ordinary as any other.

"Ada, would thou care to spend some time knitting with me? We could sit under the shade of the old sycamore on Millers Creek, where it will be cooler." Ada, realizing this would be Lucretia's opportunity to explain the morning's activities, quickly grabbed the baby's cap she had been fashioning and followed Lucretia out the door.

After a few minutes of silent walking they reached the creek and, sitting on the bench Bartholomew had carved years earlier from the trunk of a fallen oak, they began to knit. To Ada's knowledge, Lucretia had not returned to the root cellar during the entire day. Ada burned to learn the meaning of what she had experienced earlier. But knowing that Lucretia would explain things only in her own good time, she forced herself to sit silently and tried, despite the throng of questions cluttering her mind, to determine whether the next stitch was to be a knit or a purl.

"Ada," Lucretia finally began, "thou knows the Friends believe slavery to be an abomination and a grave sin against humanity." Ada nodded. Surely Lucretia realized by now that she herself shared their feelings.

"While some of our company believe that slavery will, in the course of time, fall on its own," Lucretia continued, "many Friends believe we cannot stand idly by as this evil continues. We have taken it upon ourselves to help free as many slaves as we possibly can."

"But how can this happen?" Ada finally asked, perplexed. "Those young men cannot stay in your root cellar forever."

"No. But many of us have joined forces to provide safe places for runaway slaves to hide as they make their way north. Our home is one of those places."

Ada was flabbergasted. She had never imagined that Lucretia and Bartholomew could be involved in such an undertaking, or even that such an undertaking could exist. "But will they not be caught once they reach the North? Even in free states runaway slaves must be returned to their masters."

"This is why we must find places for them all the way to British North America, where they can live as free men and women."

Ada considered the enormity of such an enterprise. Traveling to British North America, even without the necessity of having to hide during the day, took months. A great many safe places would be required, which meant that a great many people must be involved. "Is this not dangerous?" she asked.

"Very dangerous, particularly for the slaves. They face severe punishment if caught and returned to their masters. Many are hung as a warning to others."

"And for those who help them escape?" Ada asked, seeing Lucretia in a new light. She knew her friend had a good heart; she was not aware it was the heart of a lion.

"According to the Fugitive Slave Act, anyone who helps a slave escape can be fined. In some cases, they can be imprisoned. This is why we must be so careful. Even the children, other than Fanny, cannot know. Any careless word could put us all in danger—and the people we are trying to help would be in the most danger of all."

"I shall be very careful," Ada assured her. "I promise never to utter a word about what I saw today."

"I thank thee for that. But it is my hope that thou may wish to do much more than keep silence. Will thou consider joining our cause?"

"My, my, what pretty ladies we have here," said the man as he reined his skittering stallion closer to their buckboard. "What a beautiful day you have for a drive."

"A beautiful day indeed," replied Ada. "Please do not come too close. My horse is easily spooked." Ada, feeling guilty at slandering the gentle Misty with a lie, vowed to give her an extra ration of oats and an apple when they returned to the cabin.

"Please allow me to introduce myself. Jeremy Reynolds, at your service," the man said smartly, tipping his hat. "Would you ladies like an escort? The Trace is a dangerous place, even in broad daylight. How far are you going?" Ada wondered whether she should fear this man. He seemed harmless, and quite the dandy, with his shiny riding boots and scarlet waistcoat. And his horse was a treasure.

"Not far," Fanny answered, giving him a broad smile. "We are visiting friends who live just off the next path." Ada, hoping to follow Fanny's example, tried to relax. Fanny was a trained expert in this type of subterfuge, and handled the pressure of a situation as dangerous as this as calmly as most women would handle an afternoon tea with an old friend. Of course, the .45 caliber flintlock hiding under her skirt and the knowledge that her father was traveling less than a quarter mile behind them helped. "But you are welcome to join us, if you would like." Ada admired the way the girl could drop her "thees" and "thous" when needed.

The three travelers continued their repartee until fifteen minutes later when Ada noticed a path veering away toward the left. At a signal from

Fanny, Ada reined Misty in and they came to a stop. "This is where we depart the Trace," said Ada. "It has been a pleasure speaking with you, Mr. Reynolds."

"It has been a pleasure speaking with you as well, Miss Brown," the stranger said, tipping his hat as he bowed slightly toward Ada. "You certainly have a lovely niece. Miss Sally, I do hope I run into you some time in Natchez."

"Perhaps that shall happen," Fanny responded with an encouraging smile as Ada turned Misty down the path to the left. They took that path a quarter of a mile before stopping in a small clearing of trees. Within just a few minutes Bartholomew, riding his mare Beulah, appeared.

"Is he gone, Papa?" asked Fanny.

"Yes. I followed him riding north for a quarter of a mile. Are thou both all right?"

"Yes," answered Ada. "Your daughter knew exactly what to do. I imagine Mr. Reynolds will spend quite a bit of time walking Silver Street hoping to get another glimpse of 'Miss Sally.'"

"And you have no reason to believe the man suspected anything?" Bartholomew asked.

"No, Papa. We have nothing to fear from this man."

"Very well, then," Bartholomew replied. "Let us give ourselves and our passengers a chance to stretch their legs before we return to the Trace. But only for a few minutes' time—this interlude has put us behind our schedule." With that, he pulled aside the tarp covering the bed of the buckboard, allowing the man and woman who had been hiding under a blanket the opportunity to see some sunlight this beautiful day.

The Bennetts had soon realized having added Ada to their company could improve the efficiency of their endeavor. The opportunity of using Fanny and Ada to move their cargo up the Trace during the day, instead of exclusively at night, shortened the traveling time for their charges, thus lessening the chance they might be caught *en route*. Of course, it made Fanny's and Ada's participation more dangerous. But Fanny was already a seasoned veteran of their work, and Ada, to both the Bennetts' and her own surprise, was quite adept at learning the ways of subterfuge.

Ada had, at first, questioned the propriety of what the Bennetts were doing. Helping slaves escape was clearly against the law. "Whose law?" Lucretia had asked when Ada had brought legality into their discussion that afternoon under the old sycamore tree.

"Why, the law of the land," Ada had answered. "Even Northerners accept slavery as legal in some parts of the country."

"And God's law?" Lucretia had responded. "Dost thou believe God desires people to enslave and mistreat others?"

"No. But slavery appears in the Bible," Ada countered, using the argument she had heard many times over.

"Yes, slavery was the practice during the time of both the Old and New Testament. But dost thou see in the Bible any words by which Jesus praises that evil practice?"

It hadn't taken long for Ada to agree with Lucretia; after all, she was only articulating concerns that had troubled Ada for some time. From the time Ada was a child, she had wondered why God would want some of His people to be owned by others. It was easy for her to believe He did not.

But other elements of the whole enterprise still concerned her. "Are you not concerned about Fanny's safety?" she had asked.

"Of course. Every day. But Fanny is a grown woman. She learned what we were doing by accident, and once she realized the purpose of our endeavor, she begged us to allow her to help. She is as passionate about our work as we are."

Ada had further reservations when she learned that a rifle would be brought on her expeditions with Fanny. "Are not the Friends pacifists?" she asked.

"Yes, we truly are," answered Lucretia. "Thankfully, we have never needed to use a weapon against another person, and we pray to God we never shall."

"But if the need arises?" Ada insisted. She needed to know what, exactly, she would be expected to do if such an unthinkable situation should occur.

"We hope the only way we would ever need to use a weapon against another person is as a deterrent. Should otherwise be the case, we trust that God will show us what to do."

It all came down to trust: trust in God, and trust in the Bennetts. Ada chose to trust both.

Ada had found peace and purpose with the Bennetts. But, as she expected, it was only a matter of time before staying with them would force her to search deep within herself for her ability to forgive.

"Ada, is it not true thou wished for a family thy whole life?" Lucretia had asked one morning during the second week of her residence in the Bennett household. They had spent the past two hours mixing and kneading two dozen loaves of bread, and were soon to begin taking the unbaked loaves outside to the brick oven.

"Yes, that is so," Ada answered. She began kneading the dough she was working far more vigorously than before. She had suspected this topic would come up one day, and had a good idea of the direction their conversation would take. Lucretia's arguments were always stated gently and thoughtfully, and they were always highly persuasive.

"And yet thy mother and brother live but a mile away, and thou hast not visited them in these past two weeks."

"You know the reason for this," Ada answered, finally giving the loaf on which she was working one more sharp thump before dropping it into a greased pan. Wiping her brow with the hem of her apron, she placed another pan on the rack.

"And did they not teach thee the importance of forgiveness in thy convent?" Lucretia asked.

Ada was ready with a response. "Yes, Lucretia, they did. And they also taught me to avoid the near occasion of sin. My mother and brother, and certainly my sister, are sinners. I must avoid them lest I fall into their sinful ways."

Lucretia's hearty laughter filled the room. "Dear, dear Ada. Thou does not truly believe that. It would be against thy very nature to suddenly turn to deadly sin. And it appears your family, or at least your mother and brother, have reformed; did Jesus not love sinners who repent?"

"Yes, Lucretia," she answered with a sigh. *Lucretia*, she thought, *would have made an excellent Mother Superior.*

"Your mother and brother have certainly suffered greatly in life. And they have sinned. But did Jesus 'avoid the near occasion of sin,' as you say? Did He not go among tax collectors, lepers and women of the night?"

Tarnation! Ada thought. *Is this woman always right?* Deep within her heart, Ada knew Lucretia's advice was correct. Although she was greatly distressed at her family's sordid history, she had missed them during the previous two weeks. She had grown to love them, and to find much to admire. Her mother was gentle, fragile, and loving. Maggie was unceasingly loyal and true. And Finn. She saw him as strong, capable, and steadfast. "Very well," Ada finally capitulated, "I shall arrange to see them some time next week."

"Next week? Why not today?" asked Lucretia, lifting a heavy rack of loaves to take to the oven. "We are finished here, and are expecting no cargo for the next couple of days. Thou could leave immediately, if thou so wished."

"I don't know whether I can..."

"Of course thou can. Never put off until tomorrow what thou can do today."

"Yes, but I..."

"Strike while the iron is hot."

"I understand. But..."

"Make hay while the sun shines. Does thou need any other applicable sayings to help thee decide to leave directly? Please do so. This rack is getting heavy, and these loaves must soon go into the oven."

"You win once again," Ada said, laughing as she untied her apron. "I will go saddle Belle."

Chapter Eight

"Damnation!"

"What is the matter?" Nigel asked, lifting his body on one elbow from the feather mattress and rubbing the sleep out of his eyes.

"This button! It came off again." A pouting Lydia displayed the ornately detailed silver button which had just fallen from the sleeve of her favorite silk jacket, which she had been planning to wear later that day. "Queenie can be truly useless at times," she complained. Lydia's frustration with the running of the household had begun the day Maggie had left Three Ponds Farm. She could not imagine why Maggie had wished to join the band of miscreants living in the dilapidated cabin just three miles away. She'd had to enlist Queenie to perform small sewing tasks, but found her not up to her expectations.

"Find another seamstress," Nigel suggested, turning away from his wife and snuggling back into his pillow. "You can afford it."

"I still cannot believe Maggie left me," whined Lydia. "She was here for so many years. You would think the woman would have some loyalty after all that time."

"Lydia," Nigel responded, turning to face her. "She was an indentured servant, and her indenture was completed years ago. I'm surprised she didn't leave earlier. It is not as though she were family."

Family, Lydia thought bitterly. *What would I know of family?* It was one thing for Nigel to speak of family—he had grown up with the man who had actually fathered him and a mother who had raised him. What did she have? An insane mother and a sister who wanted to be a nun. But a halfbreed father—that revelation was, quite possibly, the worst. Lydia prayed every day that her husband, as well as her friends within the Natchez elites, would never learn the truth of her parentage. What a scandal that would be!

When she had learned that Finn Campbell, and not Phineas Campbell, was her father, she had lost many nights' sleep worrying that Ada, or perhaps Finn, would threaten her with blackmail. After all, she and Nigel were wealthy, and everything at Three Ponds Farm was designed to display that fact. Besides, Ada, as Phineas' legitimate daughter, could legally claim part ownership of the property—or perhaps all of it, since Lydia herself was only Phineas' stepdaughter—a fact she certainly did not wish her Natchez friends and acquaintances to know.

But as months passed and she did not see or hear anything further from Finn or Ada, her sleep improved. She was pleased, but could not understand why they seemed to have no interest in pursuing any claim on her property. Had their situations been reversed, she would certainly have looked for legal redress: but if they wanted to be fools, who was she to object?

"Nigel," she continued, "Maggie did other things. She helped Sarah in the kitchen and took care of Junior and Lucy when their nurse was ill. And I now have no one to handle the slaves' Sunday service."

"Perhaps getting rid of the service would be a good thing," Nigel suggested. In the wake of insurrections taking place in the territory and rumors that a small group of slaves were planning a rebellion in Natchez, many of the local planters had ceased holding Sunday services for their slaves. They believed providing any form of education for a slave, even a religious service, was dangerous; after all, slaves were not put on God's earth to think, but to work. Others argued that learning about the word of God would benefit anyone and could teach the slaves to better understand their place in life.

In the past, Lydia herself had occasionally considered discontinuing the Sunday service at Three Ponds. Maggie often seemed to concentrate too much on passages such as "The meek shall inherit the earth" and not nearly enough on such verses as "Slaves, obey your masters with fear and trembling." Lydia had shared her concerns with Nigel during his visit. It was time to make a decision.

"Stop the services then, at least for the time being," he advised, abandoning his pillow and sitting up. "That might be the best thing to do, particularly if the rumors about insurrection have any merit. I've already spoken to Reginald about stepping up his discipline. Everyone knows the best way to handle any thought of rebellion is to keep the slaves working hard and make sure they are always fearful of the overseer. And I've asked him to look for two or three good men who know their way with a musket to help out. They'll keep you safe while I'm away."

As though you *would be able to keep anyone safe*, Lydia thought. She had never perceived her husband as the stalwart, heroic type of man. Often she felt she possessed a great deal more gumption than he did. Still, she had to admit he possessed some very good qualities. He cut a fine figure for a gentleman in his late thirties. While many of her friends' husbands were balding and had already become quite portly, Nigel was still trim and fit, with a fine head of sandy-colored hair just beginning to gray slightly at the temples. He was very generous as well; he was not the kind of husband who complained that his wife owned too many hats or too fine a carriage, or that the plantation could do just as well with fewer household slaves.

He was also good with the children—he was perhaps a better father than she was a mother. He had spent considerable time in selecting an excellent boarding school in Nashville for Junior and had made this trip to Three Ponds specifically to escort his son there. Lydia had persuaded him to take Lucy with them to Nashville for an extended visit with her grandparents. Iggy had told her he would be in Natchez within the month, and her daughter, even at five years old, was becoming increasingly curious.

"So do not be concerned, my darling," Nigel soothed. "I've assured your safety once I'm gone. But while I am still here..." he continued, patting the mattress beside him.

Lydia smiled. Nigel had not lost the one quality she most appreciated in her husband. He was still a stallion in the bedchamber.

Ada, arms akimbo as she pressed her fists against her aching back, looked with pride at the three bushels of apples she'd picked this morning, which represented considerable effort. She had certainly had plenty of work to do at the convent. "Cleanliness is next to godliness" was Mother Superior's favorite adage, and keeping a building which was as old and large as St. Ursula's spotless required effort from every sister capable of helping. But other than clipping blooms and pulling weeds in the tiny convent garden, she had never had the experience of doing real yardwork. She now enjoyed it, particularly during those mornings when the temperature was less than ninety degrees and there was the chance of catching an occasional refreshing breeze.

She attempted to lift one of the bushels, but immediately reconsidered. It was too heavy for her to even move, much less lift, so she decided to ask her brother Finn for help. *Her brother.* She loved saying those words to herself. *Her mother.* Another delightful thought. She looked forward to the day when thinking of the words *her sister* would give her something other than pain.

Her brother and Maggie had really shown their mettle last week. Ada's time in the convent had not prepared her for deceit and secrecy, and she had hated lying to Finn and Maggie, even if it was for a good reason. But she'd been doing just that for weeks and could hardly bear the guilt her actions were causing her.

It was after dark when Finn had discovered her in the barn saddling Belle. "Where are you going so late?" he'd asked.

"Oh, I thought it would be a good night for a ride," she had lied, knowing full well how ludicrously false this answer had sounded. "The full moon drew me out of bed. I could not sleep."

It would have been impossible for anyone to misinterpret the look of skepticism on his face. Finally, with a small smile, he spoke. "You're a terrible liar, Ada. Not surprising, considering where you were brought up. And this is the second time this week I've seen you leaving late at night. Last time you were gone before I could stop you."

Feeling her face flush, Ada was certain that even in the darkness of the barn Finn could tell she was blushing. "Brother," she assured him, "I am not doing anything shameful. But I must leave, and it must be now."

"I would never believe you capable of acting shamefully," he responded, "but it's too dangerous for you to be out alone this time at night. No, no," he insisted, responding to the vigorous way she was shaking her head. "You call me Brother. As your brother, I cannot let you go alone." With this he opened the gate to the stall of his favorite paint, Chief.

"There is no time for you to bridle and saddle...," Ada began as she mounted Belle. But Finn had already pulled himself up onto Chief's back.

"You forget my lineage," he said with a laugh. "Let's go. I'll follow you."

Finn did not seem surprised to learn they were headed to the Bennetts'. Bartholomew, who came out of the cabin to take their horses, looked askance at Finn, then back to Ada. "I am sorry," she said, "He would not let me come alone."

"Does he know?" Bartholomew asked.

"No, not yet. But I am certain there will not be a problem once he does." Ada was not as certain as the confidence in her voice suggested. She knew Finn hated slavery and often compared the injustices done to slaves to those done to Indians. But this did not necessarily mean he was ready to take an active part in righting a terrible injustice.

"Then hurry," Bartholomew exhorted as he began leading the horses to a cleared hiding place behind the house. "You are already late. Take our cargo to Swamp Station."

Finn followed Ada to the root cellar behind the Bennetts' barn. "Wait here," she said as she opened the slanted door leading to the cellar. In just a few minutes she returned, carrying a knapsack and followed by a young man and woman. Their tattered clothing, the fear in their eyes, and the lash marks beginning to scab on the young man's back and shoulders identified them as runaway slaves.

"This way," Ada whispered, walking toward the dense forest to a narrow opening which would have been almost impossible to discern by anyone who did not already know of its existence. They stepped onto a line of trod-upon undergrowth too inconspicuous to be called a path. "It's four miles away. Are you well enough to walk that far?" she asked.

"Yes'm," the young man said. "We can do that."

Hoping to reach the station before first light, Ada held the group to as rapid a pace as possible for travelers who needed to crouch for most of the route. Finn, who had not spoken a word since they had arrived at the Bennetts', was helpful in holding back some of the lowest branches that had grown over the narrow path. At times Ada, raising a hand, would halt the group to listen for unwelcome noises or to assure herself they were still traveling in the right direction.

They arrived at an open swampy area just as light was beginning to appear on the horizon. After giving them only a few moments to stretch out the aches in their backs and shoulders, Ada led her charges through the shallower waters of the swamp to an area of higher ground densely forested with pond cypress.

"Here it is," she said. Though she stamped only lightly on the ground, the sound was loud enough to disturb a flock of egrets nesting on the other side of the small island; their flutter of wings and harsh cawing startled the whole group. "O Lordy!" cried the young woman while Finn reached behind his back for the pistol he always kept snugly beneath his belt. But the sight of the birds flying over the swamp was enough to release some of the tension they all felt. Ada stifled her laughter while the young man could not stop himself from letting out a loud guffaw.

"Shhhh," she warned, although she couldn't stop smiling. She had successfully brought two more souls just a bit farther on their path to the Promised Land. Bending to brush the moss covering a wooden plank door that led to a small man-made cave carefully supported by wooden beams, she ushered them into their next station.

"You'll be safe here," she told them, placing the knapsack on the dirt floor. "Someone will be here tonight to take you to your next station."

"Ma'am, Dorrie here and I thank you..." began the young man.

"No names," Ada insisted. "Just be safe, and go with God."

"Steady, Belle. Steady." Ada patted the mare as she carefully combed tangles out of her mane. "There, that's a good girl," she said.

"Good girl," repeated Nia, who was sitting on the bench Finn had placed for her in the stable. Ada was always pleased to hear any words at all issue from her mother's mouth. Even when those words made little sense in the context of a conversation, the fact that her mother was beginning to communicate was a blessing. And Nia was beginning to lose the haunted look she'd had since leaving the asylum. She had gained some weight and color was returning to her cheeks. Ada could now see vestiges of the beauty her mother had once possessed.

"Yes, Mother," she replied. "Belle is a good girl."

"Ada too. Good girl." Ada had been thrilled the first time her mother had called her by her name. She was quite certain Nia did not recognize her as a daughter, but was sure that, with time, this would change.

"Well, thank you," she responded to the compliment. Ada, stepping outside to the yellow rose bush she had planted months earlier, picked the largest, showiest of the blooms. She brought it into the stable and, with a flourish, handed it to her mother.

"Well, thank you," said Nia, again echoing her daughter's earlier words.

It's a beginning, Ada thought. *With time and God's blessing, we'll soon be sharing long conversations.*

Once Finn and Maggie had fully understood what the Bennetts were doing, both had agreed to help with their rescue work. Finn helped Ada lead runaway slaves to various stations along the way to freedom, while Maggie provided food and clothing for the escapees. Right now Maggie was at the oven, removing another dozen loaves of soda bread to be taken to the Bennetts.

The three of them had decided from the beginning that their cabin would not become a station. Nia's presence, and her tendency to repeat words and phrases she had heard them use, could very well put them all in jeopardy. Finn and Maggie had learned a new terminology from Bartholomew and used it exclusively any time they needed to converse about their activities. The runaway slaves were "cargo," and their own role was to become "shepherds." British North America, the preferred destination for most of the escapees, was the "Promised Land," but their cargo would become relatively more safe once they had crossed the "River Jordan," more commonly known as the Ohio River. Using this illicit terminology often felt to Ada as though they were playing a children's game, but all three knew what they were doing was deadly serious.

Patting the smooth surface of what had been Belle's tangled mane, Ada turned to her mother. "Would you like to go inside now and have some tea?" she asked.

"Have some tea," Nia answered. The smile on her mother's face told Ada her answer was meant to be an affirmative.

That evening, Finn and Ada could again be found in the stable saddling their horses. "Here 'tis," Maggie said cheerfully, handing Finn a heavy knapsack. "Six loaves o' soda bread and three jars o' spuds 'n cabbage, with just a wee bit o' brisket to give it some flavor, as well as some warm shawls in case it cools down tonight. You two take care now."

Ada promised they would.

Chapter Nine

"**M**iz Lydia, Miz Lydia, dey's someone knockin' at de do.'"

"Queenie?" she asked, trying to rub the sleep out of her eyes. "What time is it?"

"It be a bit befo' midnight, Ma'am. But dis ain't Queenie. Dis be Tussy."

Lydia, with a deep sigh, rolled herself out of bed, wishing the tiny hammers pounding inside her head would cease for at least as long as it would take to deal with this disturbance. *Too much wine and rich food,* she thought. She'd spent the last week celebrating the winter season in Natchez. A ball at the Elliots'. Dinner at the Stantons'. Tea at the Jacksons'. Another ball at the Hunts', this one particularly festive, with mistletoe hanging from every chandelier and every tabletop tree sporting red, white, and blue decorations in honor of Mississippi's entrance into the union as its twentieth state. It was a time for celebration: all at the party were certain statehood would bring even greater prosperity to Natchez.

"Come in," she called, pushing herself into a sitting position. *This had better be important, or someone's going to be sorry,* she fumed. "Where is Queenie?" she asked a befuddled-looking Tussy.

"Queenie be wit' her chillen," Tussy answered. "Her boys got some fever."

"Well," Lydia responded, "then that's where she belongs. I certainly don't need to be around sick people right now. But is *that* what you woke me for? Surely that information could have waited until morning." Lydia was reminded of why she'd replaced Tussy with Queenie as her lady's maid. She'd felt that although Tussy meant well, the poor child was rather feeble-minded. Besides, Queenie possessed her own sense of style. She'd often given Lydia good advice about which gloves to wear with which ball gown or what hat would look best with a particular jacket. And Queenie would never have dared waken her for such a minor problem.

"No, Ma'am. Dey's a man at de do'. He need to speak wit' you."

"What man is calling at this time of night?"

"He be Sheriff Hardy, Ma'am."

"Oh for goodness sake, Tussy," Lydia muttered. "Why didn't you tell me that in the first place? Go tell the sheriff I will be downstairs in just a few minutes."

Lydia shuffled along the floor searching for the robe she'd dropped just an hour earlier. Slipping into its comforting silkiness, she lit the single candle on her dressing table and spent another couple of minutes fingering her hair into place and pinching her cheeks. Realizing nothing could be done about the dark circles under her watery eyes, she quickly left her bedroom to meet the sheriff.

"Sorry to disturb you, Miz Masters," he said, tipping his hat. "But we got some trouble."

"Would you care to sit down? Can I have someone get you something to drink?" *He's rather attractive*, she thought, *if you like a man with his scruffy, rugged looks.*

"No, Ma'am. I gotta git to all the plantations in the next couple hours. There's been some bad business in Natchez. We heard tell a bunch of slaves was plannin' a rebellion, and we got word of a meetin' bein' held in a shack down near the dock. We caught a few of 'em—some of 'em have already started confessin' and givin' the others up—but some got away. We don't think the ones that got away are gonna cause any trouble—they're just tryin' to find places to hide. But you never know what desperate darkies will do."

"Oh, my," said Lydia, fanning her face with her hand. "What should I do?"

"Well, Ma'am, I'm guessin' since your girl got you up that Mr. Masters ain't here. They're probably not gonna get this far out from town, but you oughta send for your overseer and tell him to watch out for anythin' suspicious."

"I will," Lydia promised. "I'll send someone to him immediately." She saw Sheriff Hardy out the door, then considered calling Queenie—no, she remembered, it would have to be Tussy—to fetch Reginald. Tussy would take forever to find him, and she herself would have to wait up to speak to the overseer. But the hammering in her head had reached staccato proportions, and it would be morning in just a few hours. Hadn't the sheriff said the runaways were unlikely to get this far? Deciding she could wait until morning to speak to Reginald, she staggered up the stairs to where her feather bed awaited her.

Plink! Plink! Lydia rose suddenly, wondering if she had actually heard those sounds.

Plink! Plink! Plink! There it came again. *Could it be hail?* she wondered. She had experienced hailstorms only two or three times in her life, but those times had been memorable for the destruction they had caused to buildings and vegetation. *Could it hurt the cotton crop?* she worried. By early December most of the crop was usually harvested, but this year a late spring had caused a delay in the planting season.

Plink! Plink! Lydia pulled herself out of bed once more, cursing this night for its never-ending interruptions. Raising the window, she saw nothing but a rose-colored haze in the east foretelling an imminent sunrise and felt nothing but a gentle breeze typical of early December.

"Lydia! Lydia!" whispered a voice which, though somewhat familiar, was not immediately recognizable. "Sister!"

Ada! What could Ada want from me? Lydia wondered as she looked at the clock on her bureau. *It's not even six o'clock in the morning!*

"Lydia! Sister! Please, let me in!"

"Very well," she called down, "I'll ring someone to..."

"No, please! Ring no one. Go to the door yourself."

Damn her! Lydia thought as she once again found her robe and once again headed toward the stairs. She hadn't seen Ada in months and had hoped not to see her for a much longer time. But Ada had sounded frantic. Perhaps something had happened to their mother? Lydia could not imagine Ada would be foolish enough to believe that even something as dramatic as Nia's death would be reason for a pre-dawn visit.

Although Lydia opened the front door only slightly, there was enough room to give Ada an opportunity to push herself in. *Well*, Lydia thought, *I suppose I will have to listen to what she has to say.*

"Let me light the gas lamps," she offered, being somewhat moved by the panic in her sister's eyes. "Please sit down."

"No. No lights. Lydia, you must help us. You are the only one who can."

"Help whom?"

"Do you know a slave rebellion was being planned for tonight?"

"Yes," Lydia answered, now alarmed. "Sheriff Hardy came to tell me. Are the rebels coming here? Did you come to warn me?" she asked, cursing herself for not rousing Reginald when she'd had the chance.

"Well, no—not to warn you. And yes. One rebel. One rebel is here."

"My God!" Lydia exclaimed. "Wait here! I have a pistol in my dresser drawer."

"No! No!" cried Ada. "The rebel is Rufus."

"Rufus? Queenie's Rufus?" Lydia quickly turned toward the stairs. "I always knew he was dangerous! I'll get my weapon."

"We are in no danger from Rufus," Ada said, grabbing her sister by the elbow. "I brought him here."

Lydia gasped. "Here? You brought him here? What in God's name were you thinking!"

"Lydia, we need to hide him at Three Ponds. There is no other place to go." Ada could not hide Rufus at the Bennetts' for fear one of the captured slaves may have known their home was a station for runaway slaves. She feared that hiding place might already have been compromised.

"But why here?" Lydia was astounded. "He was part of this rebellion, and now you want to hide him? Have you considered the danger you've brought us?" Lydia was certain her sister had lost her mind.

"Rufus is no danger to us. And if they catch him, they will hang him."

"That would serve him right! To think, he lived beneath my roof and all that time he was plotting against me!"

"If they identify him, they will arrest Queenie and hang her too." Tears were beginning to well in Ada's eyes.

"Don't be a fool, Ada. Just because Rufus is Queenie's man..."

"Queenie's husband. They are husband and wife."

"Oh, how little you understand!" Lydia snorted. "Just because they jumped the broom..."

"Queenie was involved in the conspiracy as well," Ada interrupted. "One of the captured slaves is sure to tell. They will hang her too."

With this Lydia crumpled into a chair. She was about to lose two young slaves, a great financial blow. But she was surprised at how disappointed she was in Queenie's actions—she could not believe the girl would betray her in this way.

"Well, then, I suppose Queenie too deserves..."

"Deserves to die?" Ada cried. "Because she wishes to be free?"

"She is a slave. That is her ordained lot in life!"

"Lydia," Ada said solemnly, "Queenie is just as much my sister as you are."

"Oh, pshaw! What are you saying? She is no more your sister than is the queen of England!"

"You and I have the same mother. Queenie and I had the same father."

Lydia laughed at the outrageous thought. "Now you are speaking idiocy. If you believe that makes her your sister, then a good number of the slaves on this property are also your relations, and some of them could be mine!" Amazed at her sister's naiveté, Lydia wondered how, even though Ada grew up in a convent, she knew absolutely nothing about the way things worked in the real world.

"I claim kinship to every person, black or white, who had the same father or mother. And since you mention it, I am aunt and you are step-aunt to Queenie's children. What is to become of them?"

"Aunts? To a bunch of pickaninnies? You have truly lost your mind. Neither you nor I have any legal relationship to any slave. Queenie's children will grow up here, not as my relatives, but as my property. Other slaves will raise her children, I imagine."

"Without a mother and father. The same way we grew up."

"Well, yes," Lydia responded after a short pause. She had often wondered if she herself would have been a better mother if she'd been raised by hers. Still, what Ada was asking was outrageous. Slavery was a longstanding tradition that was vital for the economic welfare of the South. All her friends accepted it as a necessary institution. Was it her fault some were destined to be slaves and some masters? "But even the Bible accepts slavery," she continued, using an argument she believed Ada, with her background, could not refute. "Why, Paul says..."

"Lydia, we have no time for religious or philosophical arguments." Ada was surprised at the level of stridency she heard in her own voice. "The sheriff and his men will be here soon. If they find Rufus and Queenie, they will hang them. Do you want their blood on your hands for the rest of your life?"

"Ada, I..."

"We have very little time. I beg you. Show me a place to hide Rufus. Show me now!"

Chapter Ten

Lydia flinched at the sound of a sharp knock at the door.

"Courage, Sister," Ada admonished. Lydia wondered how her sister the nun could appear so relaxed. She herself had never doubted her own courage, had always, even as a child, felt in control of almost any situation she encountered. Of course, she had never been in such a peculiar situation before.

"Should ah ansah de do'?" asked a confused-looking Tussy, who had never seen her mistress up this early, arrayed in a housedress and having tea in the library with a young woman who, if Tussy was not mistaken, was wearing another of her mistress' housedresses.

"Yes, Tussy, please do." Within a minute Tussy, followed closely by Sheriff Hardy, entered the library.

"Why, Sheriff," Lydia purred, "do you bring more news of the rebellion? Have you caught the culprits?"

"Yes, I do have news, but I fear it is not very good," he answered, casting a quick glance at Ada.

"Oh dear, you must tell us. But first, let me introduce my sister Ada, who is visiting for a short while."

The sheriff nodded a "Pleased to meet you, Ma'am," and Ada, being careful not to move too quickly, smiled. Lydia had thought to dress her sister to appear as a house guest instead of a traveler who had arrived only that morning. Since Ada was quite a bit smaller, Lydia had to gather the extra fabric of one of her own housedresses behind her sister. Her armchair's sturdily upholstered back was the only thing keeping the dress from slipping off Ada's slender shoulders.

"Well, Ma'am, we've got most of 'em, but not all. We're trackin' the slave who seems to be their leader. We don't know his name yet, but he's a big man, very dark, kinda rough lookin'. We got a young boy who saw him run out the back door of the shack where the meetin' was held. Any of your slaves missin'?"

"Why, no. I had my overseer check last night. And I can't think of any who would fit that description." Usually lying came quite easily to Lydia, but the fear that the sheriff would run across Reginald and find out she was not telling the truth was daunting. She hoped her fear was not apparent in her response.

"Well, then, I better be on my way," the sheriff said. "Do you want me to check your property on the way out?"

"How very kind of you to offer," Lydia said, favoring him with her most charming smile. "But Mr. Masters has hired extra men to guard the property in his absence, and I am certain my overseer has this whole terrible situation under control. Please do not detain yourself further. You have some very urgent and important work to do." With this she rose and led him to the front door.

"Is he gone?" asked Ada as an anxious Lydia returned to the library only moments later.

"Yes, thank God."

"I can see you are quite an expert at prevarication," remarked Ada with a sly smile.

Lydia wondered whether the tone of her sister's voice and the look on her face suggested the comment was not meant as an insult. Could her sister, the prospective nun, be treating with levity what certainly would be seen in the convent as sinful behavior? And in such dire circumstances as they found themselves at the moment? "You, too, seem quite capable of deception," she responded with the same light tone, curious about how Ada would react. "Did they teach you that in the convent?"

"No, not that I can remember," Ada riposted, trying to determine the significance of the arch in her sister's eyebrows. "Perhaps I was ill the day they covered that topic." She wondered how Lydia would respond.

"Hmmm," hummed Lydia, arching her eyebrows even more as, tilting her head to the left, she gave her sister her most piercing look. "And it seems you are quite capable of criminal behavior as well." Lydia shook her head with a muttered tsk, tsk, tsk. "You do know you have broken the law. You could be arrested, fined, even imprisoned."

"And you as well. It appears we are partners in this crime," Ada answered, shaking her head slowly back and forth.

Lydia was surprised at her sister's clever responses, which did not at all fit her own concept of any conversation she could possibly have with a nun. The thrust and parry of their dialogue displayed a witticism Lydia would never have expected from her sister. There was more to this young woman than she had expected. "You appear to be a bad influence on me," she responded. "Not what one would have expected, considering your upbringing."

Still, Lydia thought, *Ada needs to be put in her place.* The child was woefully ignorant of the behavior required in this society, and she needed to learn quickly how things were done outside the convent. Flaunting Mississippi's legal, and even social conventions, was a dangerous game. Raising her delicate cup to her lips, Lydia took a sip of tea and then, with a grimace, rang the small hand bell on the tea table. Soon Tussy appeared. "Pour this out," she commanded harshly, "and refresh the teapot immediately. This tea is cold!"

"Yes, Ma'am," Tussy answered.

"And do not dawdle if you know what's good for you," she continued, tapping a closed fan she had picked up from the end table against her open left hand. As Tussy hurried out of the room, Lydia turned to Ada and, using her most haughty voice, instructed her sister. "Do you see? This is how a slave is to be treated. They are meant to serve us."

"Sister, we are all meant to serve a higher power," Ada responded, "and treating another in such a manner is not service to God."

"But you cannot compare a slave to a white man or woman. Their inferiority..."

"The Negro's inferiority is a false assumption," Ada interrupted. "Free Negroes in the North hold jobs and own businesses like anyone else. Even in the South some are free, and they live their lives much as we do." Ada had learned a great deal from the Bennetts.

Lydia opened her mouth to respond, but Ada cut her off. "We have no more time for discussion. No matter your unfortunate feelings on the propriety and morality of slavery, you are now an accomplice in the so-called crime of helping a slave escape. You need to help me secure safe passage for Rufus and Queenie, at least for your own sake, if not for any other reason. We have no time to waste."

"I have not agreed to go so far as to..."

"And passage for their children as well."

"You certainly have gotten yourself and many others into a passel of trouble. What in God's name were you thinking?" Lydia demanded of Rufus as Ada brought him to the back door.

"Sorry, Ma'am," he said, shaking his bowed head.

"You ought to be ashamed of yourself for..."

Ada interrupted her. "We have no time for a lecture. We need to hide Rufus and to inform Queenie about what is happening. You and I will need to make plans for tonight."

"Well, I cannot imagine where to hide him. The barn and slave quarters are very busy right now: someone would be bound to see him there. I suppose I shall have to put him in..."

"No. Do not tell me. The less I know the better. This is our most strict policy. We tell others only what they need to know."

"We?" Lydia was astonished. Her sister was part of a conspiracy! "There are others? Who are they?" But one look at Ada's face told Lydia her sister would not answer that question. "Then you have done this before," she said, shaking her head in disgust.

"Yes. And God willing, I will do it again."

"Then you are a fool. Please understand. I do not support your misguided cause. You pulled me into this, but never again involve me in any of your foolishness."

"I never shall. But we have no more time for this discussion. You need to hide Rufus."

"Very well. Go to the library and stay there until I return. Rufus, come with me."

Ada paced the library floor in wonderment at the strange turn this latest undertaking had taken. That she'd had to involve her sister in a slave rescue was unthinkable. She hoped she had made the right decision in bringing Rufus to Three Ponds Farm; but then, what other option had she?

When Lydia returned twenty minutes later, both sisters feared they would be facing a long, agonizing wait for darkness to come. Lydia, settling into a wicker rocker, picked up the frame of needlepoint she'd been working—a pastoral scene of a swan resting within the safety of a cattail marsh—and tried to concentrate on her needlepoint. Ada wandered toward the library shelves and spent some time browsing for an interesting volume to help relieve her tension. But neither her sister's collection of romances nor her brother-in-law's multitude of accounting tracts could capture her interest.

Nearly an hour of prickly silence broken only by an occasional sigh ensued. At times, Lydia would straighten her back a bit and open her lips as though wishing to speak, but thinking better of it, would quickly sit back and return to her needlepoint. Ada twice cleared her throat as if to say something, but coughed instead.

Later, neither sister would remember who had been the first to break the silence, but once it was broken, a veritable deluge of communication ensued. Their first attempt at conversation quite naturally concerned the subject of slavery, with Lydia continuing to defend its necessity while Ada decried its immorality. Eventually both realized their disagreement could not be reconciled, and continuing this discussion would only add more tension to what was going to be a very disquieting day.

"Lydia," Ada ventured, seeking a topic that would not lead to more contention, "Maggie tells me you have two children."

"Why yes, a boy and a girl," Lydia responded, pointing to the silhouettes of her children displayed in ornate frames on the bureau. "Harry Junior and our darling little Lucy."

"I would love to meet them one day."

"Oh, perhaps. They are currently visiting their grandparents in Nashville," Lydia responded.

"You must miss them terribly," Ada replied.

"Yes, terribly," Lydia said, hoping her sister would not detect any falsehood in her voice. Still, there had been that day when she'd read from *Aesop's Fables* to the children. Since then she'd felt a greater tenderness toward her offspring than she'd previously felt. Some days she actually did miss them, if only for a little while.

"I miss the children in the convent," Ada added.

"There are children in the convent? Are they learning to become nuns?"

"Well, perhaps some will. Many of the children are orphans, and others have been sent there because their parents are unable to care for them. Some come only during the day to receive instruction."

"Oh, the children of indigents. Or beggars."

"Some are the children of slaves or of free Negroes."

"Oh my! You don't teach them to read..." Lydia was aghast. She wondered what other strange ideas the convent was fostering.

"No, but we teach them skills to help them make their way in this world. And of course, we teach them about the love of Jesus. When our mother was mistress of this plantation, she held regular Sunday classes for the slave children, and many of their parents attended as well. Did you know that?"

"Let us not speak of her," Lydia said haughtily. "That woman has done unspeakable things."

"'That woman?'" responded Ada. "That woman is our mother. I know you do not wish to know her, but she is not the evil person you believe her to be. She is kind, gentle. She misses you very much. As I told you before, the first word I ever heard from her lips was your name. And though she speaks very little, she still speaks mostly of you. Although we will never know what led her to do what she did, I must believe she was more sinned against than sinner."

Lydia, with a disdainful "hmph," returned to her needlework, and another half hour of silence ensued. But her finely tuned social graces eventually triumphed over her desire to ignore her visitor. "Are you hungry?" she asked. "Sara made a lemon syllabub yesterday, and I imagine there is some left."

"Syllabub," Ada answered. "That is my favorite sweet."

"Mine as well," responded Lydia, who was surprised they shared a fondness for a favorite dessert, although Ada mentioned later she had never experienced the wine-spiked version of the parfait. As the day wore on and their conversation continued, they found they shared other similarities. They certainly shared the same acerbic sense of humor, as evidenced by their banter earlier in the day. They were both passionate, although their passions had taken them in very different directions. They were avid readers, though their taste in reading material could not have been more different.

Over the course of the long afternoon, Ada began to appreciate her sister's ambition and intelligence. She began to recognize Lydia's strength and determination in being not just the mistress, but the person most responsible for the success of Three Ponds Farm. Very few women would have been able to take on such a daunting responsibility and handle it so well.

Lydia, during this time, began to look into her sister's heart and found a genuine goodness she'd never discerned in any other person. Ada seemed to possess none of the competitive jealousy or the acquisitiveness she recognized in her own character. And Ada was brave; Lydia could not imagine placing herself in danger for a stranger, and a slave at that. Although she saw no merit in the cause of abolition, she had to admire a person who would sacrifice so much for her convictions.

She did consider Ada naïve and desperately lacking in sophistication, but was surprised to find this deficiency refreshing in its way. She had never before met anyone quite like her sister.

By early evening, barriers had broken down sufficiently to allow them to speak of some of the disappointments and sorrows they had experienced. Each acknowledged a lack of confidence she was unwilling to show the world. Both felt that, in some ways, their understanding of life and its possibilities had been limited by the circumstances of their childhoods. Most telling, they sensed something very important had been missing in their lives. As late afternoon turned to evening, each wondered privately if what was missed was the mother she had hardly known.

With the approaching darkness came a gentle rain. "Will the rain postpone your plans?" Lydia asked. She was surprised to find she wished this were the case; they could then have more time to spend together.

"No, not at all. There is too much danger in waiting." Ada's response was accompanied by a crack of thunder that made both sisters flinch. As she peeked for perhaps the twentieth time behind the parlor's heavy drapes, Ada noticed that, as often happened in December, the evening's gentle shower was quickly becoming a downpour. Then, squinting into the distance, she noticed something else. "It is time," she said. "Please get Rufus."

"But how can you tell that..." Lydia began to ask, then retracted her question. "Oh, never mind. I do not need to know."

"You can tell me where you hid him," Ada informed her, smiling at her sister's acquiescence to the Bennetts' rules.

"In Nigel's bedroom, inside his wardrobe." Ada's grin was the last thing Lydia had imagined she would see this evening, but it caused her to grin as well. "If I had hidden him anywhere else on the property or in the house he could have been found," she explained. "But how Nigel would have hated it if he knew!" This comment, despite the intensity of their concerns, occasioned a quick laugh from both sisters.

As Lydia hastened up the stairs to her husband's bedroom, she considered that, had things been different, she might have grown up loving her sister. There was so much she wished to know about her, so much she wanted to share about herself. She would have been surprised to know Ada was thinking the same thing.

Feeling very much the co-conspirator, Lydia looked carefully along the upstairs hallway before ushering Rufus down the stairway. They found Ada waiting at the open back door. Ada peered closely into the darkness before sending Rufus out toward the flicker of a single lantern's light swinging slowly in the distance, then prepared to head out the door herself. But she was taken aback by a near flash of lightning.

"Wait!" Lydia exclaimed. "You cannot go out in such a storm dressed like that. You need something to keep you dry."

"No. I must go now," Ada began, but Lydia was already rushing upstairs to her bedroom. She returned with a long hooded cape of crimson velvet trimmed with a mink collar. "I can't take this," she said. "It will be ruined by the rain."

"What does that matter?" Lydia replied, draping the cape around Ada's shoulders.

As she stepped out into the storm, Ada turned to her sister. "Thank you for..." she began. But before Ada could finish the sentence, Lydia embraced her, holding her in her arms as though she never wished to let go. Ada responded with a kiss on her sister's cheek.

As Lydia watched Ada disappear into the darkness, she whispered "Go with God," hoping the God she had forsaken so many years earlier would not choose to ignore her prayer this night.

Chapter Eleven

Ada's back disappeared into the storm. A bolt of lightning, more powerful than any so far that evening, provided one last view of her body turning toward the roadway, but for only an instant. Once the flash dissipated, Lydia could see nothing but darkness.

She spent the next few minutes wringing her hands as she paced the library floor. Hoping to take her mind off the dangerous proceedings happening outside, she grabbed the copy of *The Coquette* that had so interested her just hours earlier. She'd been immersed in the heroine's story, and was about to learn if Eliza would succumb to the charms of the rogue Sanford. But after reading a paragraph three times without comprehending anything it contained, she threw the book against the wall with a loud "Damnation," taking a bit of small comfort in the resounding thump the volume made as it hit the floor.

She thought about the time she'd spent with her sister. She was unable to understand what motivated Ada's dangerous actions. This made her sister a mystery, but a fascinating one. And what about their mother? And her father? Had she been foolish in not wanting to get to know either of them? Could she, in learning more about them, learn more about herself?

Thinking of a fourth person, one to whom she was not actually related, she turned to look at the portrait of Phineas Campbell prominently displayed over the mantel. He looked imperious, dressed in his tartan, standing with one foot placed before the other and holding a fancifully carved walking stick. Tufts of red hair could be seen escaping his Balmoral, and his eyes, a clear, icy blue, were fixed steadily forward. He too was a mystery. She'd thought so little about him, remembered almost nothing about him from her childhood, but sensed that, in some way, he was central to the dissolution of her family. She had hardly noticed the portrait for the last twenty years and had not thought of the man it portrayed during the same time. Should tonight's adventure succeed, she vowed to learn more about her family and about the history she and Ada shared.

The staccato of three sharp peals of thunder brought her to the door. Opening it, she saw the downpour had turned into a deluge and was now accompanied by a furious, twisting wind that almost took her breath away. She heard another thunderous sound, this time much closer, but it was not accompanied by any flash of lightning. Could it be something else? Stepping out the door, she heard that sound once again, but this time recognized it as not thunder, but gunfire.

Without stopping to take any covering or even to change the velvet house slippers on her feet, she rushed out the door and ran toward where she believed she had heard that horrifying sound. Guided only by the occasional bolt of lightning, her progress was further impeded by debris being furiously cast about by the wind and by deep ruts the rain had already furrowed into the sandy soil. She stumbled several times, finally falling into a small pool of water created by the storm.

"God help me!" she cried into the darkness. Struggling to get to her knees and realizing she had not been injured in the fall, she attempted to get her bearings. In the distance she could see a shadowy structure that must be the barn but not much else. A sudden flash of lightning was bright enough to reassure her she was very close to the roadway. Neither a wagon nor the sign of any person was visible, but what she saw was much more alarming: a small crimson pile by the side of the road.

Crawling through the mud toward that pile, she saw what she had most feared to see: the body of her sister, lying still on the ground.

Chapter Twelve

"Ada! Ada!" screamed Lydia, falling to her knees to embrace the still body lying before her. Feeling in the darkness for her sister's shoulders, she shook them gently, then a bit more forcefully as she repeatedly called her name. She received no response.

The downpour had already turned the long velvet robe into a heavy sodden mass, making it difficult for Lydia to turn her sister's body toward her. With much effort, she finally managed to pull Ada's torso up onto her own thighs where, embracing her, she gently slapped her cheeks while calling her name over and over. Again, there was no response.

A flash of lightning afforded Lydia a terrifying sight—her sister's face, pale beyond belief, with trickles of blood commingling with the streams of rainwater running down her forehead. "God help me," she prayed, pulling Ada's body closer and reaching through the opening of the robe to feel for a heartbeat. She thought she felt a faint beating, though it was difficult to tell whether that sign of life was genuine or only a reflection of her own desire. She knew she needed to take Ada back to the mansion as soon as possible but could not conceive of a way to move her. She hadn't the heart or the energy to think about what would follow next.

"Mizz Lydia," sounded a voice over her shoulder. Startled, she turned to see Tussy standing over her, looking almost as stricken as she herself felt. "Is dat Mizz Ada? Do she be alive?"

"I don't know," Lydia cried. "I only know I need to get her back to the house."

"How can ah he'p?"

Lydia tried to focus her mind on a possible course of action. Reginald could help, but could he be trusted to keep a secret? After all, what she and Ada had done was a crime, one that virtually none of her friends or acquaintances would defend. Still, she decided she had no choice. "Can you find Master Reginald?" she asked.

"Massa Reginald gone off wit' de sheriff and dem othah men lookin' fo' dat runaway slave. Dem othah men he hired gone off wit' him too."

"Oh my God," Lydia cried in desperation. "Then we have to find some way move her ourselves, but..."

"Leander and some o' de othah boys be heah," Tussy interrupted. "Dey kin he'p."

"No, Tussy, I don't think..." Lydia began. But she soon realized she had no choice. She and Tussy could not possibly move Ada themselves without causing her further harm—if, *Please God*, she prayed silently—Ada was still alive. Involving the other slaves was her only hope of saving her sister's life. "Run, Tussy," she cried. "Get Leander. Go now!"

As Tussy disappeared into the darkness, Lydia embraced her sister once more, holding her close while repeatedly whispering "Please God, please God, let her live." But she had very little hope. Why should God answer her prayers, when she'd done so much that would certainly have displeased him? Although Tussy and Leander arrived in only minutes, those minutes crept by painfully slowly for Lydia.

"Heah," sounded Leander's voice in the darkness. "We need to put Mizz Ada on 'dis," he said, placing an old wooden ironing board on the ground next to Ada. Soon Leander and Tussy were gently lifting her inert body just enough to glide it onto the board. Balancing their burden as gently as possible, they ran as rapidly as they could on the sandy soil shifting beneath their feet in the rivulets of water created by the storm. Lydia prayed the sound she had heard as Ada's body touched the board was a groan and not merely the wind rushing through the trees.

Sara was waiting for them as they angled the makeshift stretcher through the open door into the parlor. She had already placed a pan of hot water, a bottle of alcohol and a roll of gauze on the tea table. "Put her on the fainting couch," Lydia told Leander. Once that was done, she knelt before her sister and reached her hand under the robe, feeling her chest for any sign of life. "I think I feel a heartbeat!" she exclaimed to Sara. "But I fear she was shot in the head."

A quick examination revealed that although Ada had only a deep wound on her forehead, probably suffered during her fall, she had actually been shot and was bleeding copiously from a wound located just below her left shoulder, dangerously close to her heart. Sara used some of the gauze to clean the wound, and Lydia rejoiced when she heard a feeble moan as Sara poured alcohol over it. Ada was alive! But for how long?

"Ah kin pack dis wit' dressin'," Sara said, expertly shredding the remaining gauze into lint and gently pressing it onto the wound. "But dey's shot in deah, an' ah cain't get dat out wit'out hurtin' her even mo'. Mizz Ada need a doctor."

Lydia considered her options. The nearest doctor was miles away. Looking at Ada's pale skin and shallow breathing, she realized her sister would most likely not survive the wait. Suddenly one possibility, perhaps the only possibility, of saving Ada's life came to mind. The Bennetts.

"Lucretia Bennett! She can help! Leander, hurry! Take a horse from the stable and ..." But before she could complete her sentence, Leander was already halfway out the door.

Part Four—Lydia—1882

Chapter One

"Triple skunk!"

"Again?"

"Peg the board. You'll see ah got well ovah one hunnert twenty-one."

"Never mind, Tussy. I trust you."

"Play again?"

"No. I can't. Miss Robertson will be here soon."

"Mizz Robberson?"

"Yes. The lady from the newspaper. *The Boston Herald,* I believe she said."

"De one who gonna interview you?"

"Yes, that's the one. I suppose that's why you've already beaten me twice today. My mind wasn't on the game."

"You say dat yestiddy, too," Tussy laughed. "An' you wasn't havin' no fancy interview dat day. You jus' don wanna say ah's bettah at cribbage den you."

"Very well, then. You *are* better at cribbage than I am. Tomorrow we'll play piquet instead." At this they both laughed. "Put the board away, will you? I'll go start the tea."

They began the task, more arduous for Lydia than for Tussy, of rising from their chairs. Lydia, grabbing her favorite cane, the slender ebony topped with a gold-plated finial, used both hands to push herself to her feet, while Tussy, the younger of the two, was still able to rise using just one hand on the back of her chair to steady herself. Tussy would have been happy to help Lydia to her feet were she not certain her stubborn friend would resent the offer.

Both women were dressed in their standard morning outfit: long, dark brown skirts, slightly flared at the bottom, topped by simple long-sleeved white blouses with high fitted collars. Neither sported adornment of any kind. Both had white hair, but Tussy's short curls were sprinkled with touches of gray and black while Lydia's hair, long, straight, and piled into a trim bun on top of her head, was as white as the snow on the sidewalk of their Philadelphia home on this bright February day.

"Wat time she say she gonna be heah?"

"She said 11:00," Lydia answered, glancing at the grandfather clock standing in the far corner of the parlor. "She should be here in half an hour or so."

"Wat you two gonna talk 'bout?"

"The Movement, of course."

"Well den, you jus' sit yo'sef down in de parlor an wait fo' her to get heah. Ah can start de tea."

"Thank you, dear." Lydia watched fondly as Tussy, still as slim as she was as a girl and quite spry for a woman nearing eighty, carefully placed the cribbage board on the oak buffet and headed toward the kitchen door of the apartment they had shared for over twenty years. The apartment was small, with room in the parlor for not much more than a small horsehair sofa and a worn, but still comfortable, armchair. Their dining room was even smaller and could seat, at most, only four, and those four rather intimately, while the two bedrooms were hardly larger than pantries. But the apartment still met their needs after all these years.

It seemed to Lydia she had been sitting on the sofa for only minutes before she heard the knocker. "Ah'll get it," Tussy called, entering the parlor from the kitchen door.

"Is she early?"

"No. She be a bit late. You got yo'sef a li'l nap while you was waitin'."

Lydia sighed. Her little naps were becoming a regular feature of life: Tussy loved to tease her about them. But what did Tussy expect of a woman who would be ninety in just two weeks?

It had taken the first five years of their coexistence for Lydia to realize how bright Tussy was. When Tussy had been her lady's maid at Three Ponds Farm, Lydia had seen the girl as foolish and slow-witted. But living with her had been a revelation. Lydia had suspected quite early on that Tussy hid her true level of intelligence, but it wasn't until a disagreement they'd had about General Sherman's behavior during the War Between the States that she realized just how clever her roommate really was.

Lydia had stated that Sherman's destructive strategy had been necessary to win the war, but Tussy believed his actions had made life even more difficult for slaves after the war than it had been before. Her statement that Sherman had not followed the Golden Mean had caught Lydia off guard.

"The Golden Mean?" she had asked. "Do you mean Aristotle's Golden Mean?"

"Yes'm," Tussy had responded, dropping her eyes to the floor as she began to twist the dust cloth she was holding between her hands.

"Who told you about Aristotle?"

"Ah read about 'im—in dat book you got sittin' on de top shelf."

"Someone taught you to read?" Lydia was astounded. None of the slaves on Three Ponds Farm had ever been taught to read. Doing so had been against the law.

"Ah taught mahsef'," Tussy responded, now looking into Lydia's eyes with a bit of defiance. "Wat you gonna do 'bout it?"

"Well, nothing. I am just so surprised. Why did you never tell me?"

"Well, massas an' dey mizzes doan cotton to us darkies actin' smart. Dey'd tink we'd be dangerous."

"But Tussy, I wouldn't think that," declaimed Lydia, but the doubtful look on Tussy's face reminded her there had been a time when she definitely would have done so.

"You nevah do know," Tussy responded. "Ah was jes' pertecken mahsef'."

The great advantage to Lydia of this conversation was that after that day she had a person with whom to share her love of philosophy. They spent many evenings discussing Aristotle and Plato, but Tussy's favorite was St. Augustine. "Ah lahk wat Augustine say 'bout de evil of slavery," she declared. "He say dat no man should have dominion ovah no uddah man. Even way back when Augustine lived, he knowed bettah den we knew befo' de war."

And better than many know even now, Lydia had thought. Even though slavery had been abolished in 1865 with the ratification of the Thirteenth Amendment, Lydia knew that many of the men and women she had grown up with still resented the loss of their slaves, or their "property," as slaves had been considered. They would do almost anything to return to the lives they felt had been stolen from them. And of course, for many years she had shared their views. She had known no better.

Knowledge of Tussy's intelligence and rhetorical skills had made Lydia hope Tussy would consider joining her on the very popular abolitionist speaking tours that had provided her income for many years. Even though the abolitionist movement had met its goals, there was still much that needed to be done to help freed slaves; a former slave, and a female no less, who could speak about Plato and Aristotle would certainly draw crowds. Lydia had suggested they seek the services of a good speech coach to help formalize her speech patterns.

Tussy had refused. "First of all," she had said, "Ah ain't doin' no speeches. An' secon' of all, ah ain't changing de way ah speak—it de way mah mama spoke, an' it be good 'nuff fo' me.

That was Tussy: stubborn as a mule. *And she believes I am the stubborn one!* Lydia often thought. Still, they had become close friends.

"Welcome, Miss Robertson," Lydia heard Tussy say in her most amiable voice. "Please do come in. Mrs. Masters is waiting for you in the parlor. May I take your wrap and muff?"

Lydia smiled. Tussy could use the King's English whenever she chose to do so. Just another frustrating, yet endearing trait that made her friend such an interesting person.

"Miss Robertson...Mrs. Masters," Tussy said in introduction. "You ladies settle in while I get you a nice pot of tea."

Miss Robertson was a tall, blonde woman dressed in the height of fashion: a gray serge dress with a tight bodice and a straight skirt flared slightly at the hem. The neck and wrists of her dress were trimmed with black velvet bands overlaid with white lace, and her veiled hat sported a bronze ring encircling a small clutch of pheasant feathers.

"Please sit down," said Lydia, motioning toward the arm chair with a sweeping gesture. Once the required pleasantries were performed (Yes, Mrs. Masters was doing well. Yes, Miss Robertson *had* had a pleasant train trip from Boston. Yes, they were certainly experiencing a cold winter.), Miss Robertson, who asked to be called by her first name, Alice, removed a small writing pad and a freshly sharpened pencil from her bag and immediately set to work.

She first congratulated Lydia on receiving the Lucretia Mott Memorial Award from the American Woman Suffrage Association, which was to be presented at a ceremony in two weeks' time to coincide with Lydia's birthday. Lydia had been active in the group from its inception in 1869.

"The award is quite an honor, Mrs. Masters," gushed Alice.

"I can assure you the award is completely undeserved," Lydia responded with a small laugh.

"My, my, Mrs. Masters, you are certainly being modest. I cannot imagine anyone who could deserve the award more than yourself. After all, you've been involved in the abolition movement, and then the Negro suffrage movement, for the last forty years." Lydia lowered her eyes as a small smile lit up her face. *This young woman really knows how to flatter a person. But forty years? Has it really been that long?*

"And even more remarkably," continued Alice, "I understand from my notes that you were once the mistress of a large plantation in Mississippi. It must have been difficult to be an abolitionist under those circumstances."

"Well, I wasn't an abolitionist then," Lydia responded. "I believed slavery was perfectly acceptable, just like every other plantation owner in the Mississippi Territory. But my mother was an abolitionist, according to her family in Philadelphia."

"Your mother never shared her views with you?"

Lydia didn't quite know how to answer that question. She wasn't sure just how much about her family's unusual history she wished to share with this bright, perky young woman; after all, she would also be sharing that history with the entire *Boston Herald* readership. But after a short period of silence, which she hoped Alice would attribute to her advanced age, she responded.

"My mother was ill for quite a long time while I was a child. I was raised by my aunt. I became interested in the abolition movement first through conversations with my younger sister Ada and later with my mother's sisters, my Aunts Abigail and Emilia, who took me in when I moved to Philadelphia in 1841." *Actually,* Lydia thought, *when I escaped to Philadelphia. If they hadn't been so welcoming, I don't know what would have become of me.*

She had chosen Philadelphia because while going through some old papers of her mother's she had found letters from two aunts she had not known existed. Curious, she sent them a letter at the address written on the envelopes, hoping that after all these years she would be able to find them. She was delighted when they responded, and a lively correspondence over several years had followed.

Both Abigail and Emilia were ardent abolitionists active in Philadelphia: Lydia was surprised to learn her family had a long history of abolitionist beliefs. Her aunts urged her to visit, and Lydia thought that someday she would.

That day came soon after her mother's death, a time when her life felt unfocused and limited. Her children were adults who spent most of their time in Nashville. Ada was in the convent and could be visited only twice a year. And her mother's death seemed to awaken a desire in her to learn more about her maternal ancestry—to meet her aunts and cousins and to see the places where her mother had spent her childhood.

Aunt Abigail and Aunt Emilia were waiting for her at the pier when she disembarked at Penn Landing. The moment she saw them, she thought they would make a great study in contrast. Abigail, tall and slim, was dressed in a black serge gown that featured no hint of decoration at the high neck or wrists. Only a few wisps of hair, more gray than pale blonde and severely parted in the center, could be seen under the wide brim of her black bonnet.

Emilia was as short and stocky as Abigail was tall and slim. While her dress was similarly designed with a high collar and long sleeves, its fabric was a dove gray peau de soie with black buttons and scarlet piping trimming the bodice in a v-shaped pattern. A bowl-shaped straw bonnet decorated with three stunning peacock feathers could not contain the mass of brick red curls falling to her shoulders.

"Welcome to Philadelphia," said Abigail, reaching out to take Lydia's hand. "And please, just call me Abby. We're all adults here."

Emilia seemed unable to control her exuberance—she grasped Lydia in a tight embrace and kissed her cheek, saying "You are the picture image of your mother! God bless her soul. And you can call me Mellie. Everyone does."

They took a hackney carriage to Abby's brick rowhouse on Society Hill. On the short ride to "the Hill," Lydia learned that once Abby's four children had married and moved away and her husband, whom she referred to as "my dearest Benjie," had passed away, Mellie, who had never married, had moved in with her.

It did not take long for Lydia to become impressed by the vast array of abolitionist activities in which they were active, from fund-raising, to lecturing at conferences, to drafting treatises on the need for political and legal action. Within a week her aunts had invited her to attend a meeting of the Female Anti-Slavery Society.

"Do come, dear Lydia," begged Mellie. "We have a meeting at Pennsylvania Hall, and Angela Grimke will be our speaker tonight. She and her sister Sarah are amazing speakers, and I am certain you will learn a great deal from Angela's speech."

"Thank you," Lydia responded, "but I do not feel I belong there."

"Why not?" asked Abby sharply.

"I... legally, I still own slaves."

"All the more reason!" Abby responded.

"Nobody needs to know that," said Mellie. "We will keep your secret. But you will surely benefit by what Miss Grimke has to say."

The meeting hall was filled with women and a smattering of men, all chatting excitedly about the upcoming speech. Lydia's first shock on entering the hall was to learn that the society was integrated, with Negro women and men collegially interspersed among the others. She was also surprised that Negroes served on the governing board of the organization and were responsible for many of its activities.

Miss Grimke's speech was well received, but Lydia was most engaged by a conversation she had with her aunts and several of their friends who gathered at the sisters' home after the presentation. Clara Stewart, perhaps the most outspoken of Abby and Mellie's friends, had some reservations about the speech they had heard.

"I certainly believe in the justice of our cause, but I do have some reservations about what Miss Grimke said this evening." Clara Stewart appeared to Lydia to be the oldest member of the small group, and the quality of her silk gown as well as the size of the ruby ring she noticed as Mrs. Stewart carefully placed her teacup onto its saucer, suggested that she was also the wealthiest. Mellie informed her later that Mr. Stewart owned the largest clothing store on High Street.

"Really, Clara?" asked Abby. "What reservations have you?"

"Well, Miss Grimke referred to her Southern upbringing, so I believe much of what she says is true. But I wonder if some of the examples she used about the cruelties committed against slaves are somewhat exaggerated to make her point."

"What makes you believe she exaggerates?" asked Mellie.

"Well, the beatings and the chains. Mr. Stewart and I were speaking of this very thing before I dressed for the meeting. He, of course, has been a successful businessman for a great many years, and he insists that businessmen must take good care of their property and their workers to be successful. Slaves are considered both property and workers in the South. In order to get the most benefit from their work, slaveholders would need to treat them well."

Several of the other women nodded, and Abby seemed about to speak when Lydia, to her own surprise, charged into the conversation. "I can attest to the truth of what Miss Grimke says," she stated. She spoke to them of the Natchez slave market and of the severe punishment she'd observed her overseers administer at Three Ponds Farm, some of those incidents initiated under her own command, and all of them, she now knew, with no justification. The horror she saw on the women's faces was an indictment, not only of the system, but of all those who had participated in it. For the first time she felt a deep shame that could not be eradicated by assuring herself she was merely a small part of a much larger institution, "the curious institution," as her friends in Natchez chose to call it.

"That must have been horrible for you," soothed Mellie once the other women had left. Placing her arm around her niece, she held her tightly and kissed her cheek. "Having had to observe such terrible things. But take heart. You are here now, where none of those atrocities are allowed. And you can help us change the system. Let me get you another cup of chamomile tea. It will steady your nerves. You were very brave to speak to the other women tonight of what you have seen done."

Abby, who had been silently following their conversation, then entered it. "Mellie, did you notice how carefully the other women listened to Lydia? I honestly think that even Clara Stewart was moved by what our Lydia had to say."

"I believe you are right, Sister. Lydia's little speech was quite a success. Most of the time, moving Mount Ararat would seem more easily done than moving Clara Stewart once she gets an idea stuck in her mind!"

"This is true," agreed Abby. "I remember the time when Clara..."

But Mellie, quite uncharacteristically, interrupted her sister's remembrance. "Abby, I have an idea," she exclaimed, a broad smile lifting her freckled cheeks. "Perhaps we could persuade our dear niece to become a speaker for abolition!"

"What a wonderful idea!" Abby gushed, making Lydia wonder if Abby had actually planned for the conversation to take this turn. "She has a great deal of knowledge about slavery and she speaks so well. What do you think, Lydia?" Abby's smile was warm and inviting.

Lydia's face flushed crimson. "Oh, I don't believe I could possibly do that," she answered.

"Now don't be modest," responded Mellie. "You have a gift, and you could be using it for a great cause."

"Do not push her so hard," scolded Abby. "Give her some time to think about it. I know she will do the right thing."

Lydia did not believe she needed time to think, nor was she the least bit modest. But their suggestion was ludicrous. How could she lecture other women about the evils of slavery when she did not even have enough courage to confess to her aunts that she had been not just an observer, but a willing participant in "the curious institution."

"Were the rest of your mother's family also abolitionists?" asked Alice.

"My mother's family were all strongly against slavery," Lydia responded.

"Were they also involved in the Underground Railroad?"

"Yes. But we didn't call it that then. In fact, we didn't call it anything. We were just a group of people who wanted to right a terrible wrong." And it's a good thing one doesn't need to be an angel to do a good thing, thought Lydia. I would never have qualified.

"How did you get involved in that group?"

"Through my association with some of the people who had befriended my sister: the Bennetts, who were a family of Quakers, and Finn Campbell and his wife." Lydia paused for a moment to consider how best to describe her complicated relationship with Finn, deriding herself for not considering these difficulties before agreeing to the interview. But she quickly decided that, having outlived them all, she could describe her family in whatever manner would most honor their memory.

Lydia's description of her relationship with Finn was the truth, although certainly not the whole truth. She had never developed anything even closely resembling a normal father/daughter relationship with him, but she did develop a deep respect for him, particularly when she observed his loyalty to her mother. Finn had remained faithful to Nia, supporting her and assisting Maggie in her care until Nia passed away eight years almost to the day after the night Ada had been shot.

While Nia's health had improved over time, she had never regained full use of her senses and needed constant assistance and companionship. Occasionally she would experience a very good day when she was able to communicate, if only in short sentences. Lydia cherished those days. But Lydia would have had to be blind not to notice that Finn and Maggie loved each other. When, six months after Nia's death, Finn had invited Lydia to their wedding, she was delighted for them.

They had married in a Natchez/Cherokee compound located several miles up the Trace. Finn explained to Lydia that the Natchez had lost their homeland almost a hundred years earlier after being defeated in their war with the French; most of those who survived had been sold into slavery in the Caribbean. The few who remained had assimilated with other tribes: the Chickasaw, the Creek and the Cherokee. The wedding ceremony would include elements of both Natchez and Cherokee culture.

As they traveled up the Trace to the compound, Finn told Lydia she would be meeting his mother, whose formal title was Sun Mother. It took Lydia only a few moments to realize that in meeting Finn's mother, she would be meeting her grandmother! Another relative she had never known. Finn explained that Natchez nobility was passed down through the mother—had the Natchez survived, Finn, as his mother's only son, would have become the Great Sun, supreme ruler of the tribe. My heavens, she thought, I am an Indian princess. Will my life forever be filled with surprises? Still, this surprise was much more pleasant than many of the others she'd had to face.

The compound, comprising only a few teepees and mud huts, was located in a wooded area a mile west of the Trace. Finn's mother's home, set on a small mound several hundred feet away from the rest of the buildings, stood out from the rest. It was a circular building constructed of mud walls covered with woven cane mats and topped by a thatched roof that rose to a point at its center.

Finn, Maggie and Lydia found his mother busily working over an open fire, roasting venison and turkey for the wedding feast. She was short and slight, with long black braids extending almost to her waist that showed no hint of gray. "Osiyo," she said in greeting to her granddaughter and the woman who was soon to be her daughter-in-law. She indicated they were to call her "Ama," her Cherokee name, which Finn explained meant "water" and referred to her love of rivers and streams. She spoke no English, but the sparkle her wide smile brought to her eyes made them know they were welcome.

The wedding was held that evening in the center of the compound where a sacred fire had been lit. Finn and Maggie appeared, both resplendent in white, he in a long tunic over buckskin trousers and she in a dress decorated with bands of fringe topped with an intricate pattern of tiny shells. Each was wrapped in a blue blanket. After the officiating priestess, a woman who looked even older than Ama, blessed the couple, she removed their blue blankets and wrapped them together in a white blanket, symbolizing their entrance into a new life together.

The couple exchanged gifts. Finn gave Maggie a venison ham, affirming his vow to provide for their family, while Maggie's gift to Finn of an ear of corn signified her pledge to run their household prudently. Finally, they drank from a maize-colored vase beautifully decorated with a sepia image of a hummingbird approaching a branch. It was cunningly crafted with two openings so the couple could drink together. Lydia was surprised to see them, after drinking, throw the handsome vase to the ground, breaking it into many pieces. But she was told this act would seal the couple's vows.

What followed was an evening of feasting and dancing, with all guests enjoying themselves so fully that no one noticed the couple slipping away. The next morning, when Lydia rose from her pallet in Ama's home, she could not remember how she *got there. But she did remember wondering during the previous evening why anyone would refer to these people as savages.*

"And your husband and children," said Alice, thumbing through her notes. "I understand you had a son and a daughter. Did they share your views about the Movement?"

"Hardly," responded Lydia. "Their attitude toward slavery was consistent with the culture they'd grown up in, much as mine was."

"Even later, after the war? Did they accept your views then?"

Lydia paused for a moment to compose her response. "My husband lost his life in 1854 when the steamboat Munroe sank only ten miles from Natchez, and my son died at the Battle of Vicksburg while serving as a colonel in the Confederate cavalry. My daughter..." Lydia paused. Taking a handkerchief from her pocket, she wiped her eyes.

"Do you wish to stop the interview?" asked Alice. "You look distressed."

"No, I can continue. My daughter has, to my knowledge, never changed her mind about slavery."

"Do you ever discuss the abolitionist movement with her?" Even now, Lydia could not restrain the emotion that overcame her whenever she thought about the last time she had seen Lucy. "No," she answered. "I am afraid we are estranged."

As Lydia had disembarked from the steamship Island City, she was most surprised at how little Natchez had changed since she had last seen it twenty-five years earlier. She knew that the city, having surrendered to Union forces early in the war, had not suffered any major battles, although it experienced a short fleet bombardment when some fool, probably drunk, had fired on Union ships from the shore. Even King's Tavern remained, and it was there she was able to hire a buckboard and driver to take her to Three Ponds Farm.

Lydia spent much of her time on the buckboard wondering what kind of reception she would experience. Although she had never been charged with any crime under the Fugitive Slave Act, she had known the rumors circulating in the community about her abolitionist activities could turn to legal action being taken against her. When she had left Mississippi for Pennsylvania, she left the plantation in the hands of Lucy and her husband Harold, who moved in with their young son.

Philadelphia would become her haven.

While in Philadelphia, Lydia wrote sporadically to her daughter and sent gifts to her grandson, Lucy's only child, at Christmas, but seldom received any response. She wasn't really surprised at Lucy's reluctance to have much to do with her. After all, Lydia had become somewhat of a pariah in the Natchez community, which caused her daughter to be ostracized by much of Natchez society. Besides, Lydia knew she had not been a good mother to either of her children: her relationship with Junior was practically nonexistent as well. Lydia threw herself into her work in the Movement, and was gratified to see it flourish.

Once the war started, mail communication between the North and South was sporadic at best, and none of the letters she sent to Lucy were ever answered or returned. Lydia worried about Junior and Lucy, but knew she was only one of the many mothers who were unable to communicate with their children during that time. When the war ended and steamboat travel down the Mississippi was reinstituted, she had immediately booked passage to Natchez on the Island City, wondering the whole trip who and what she would encounter at Three Ponds Farm.

From the moment the buckboard turned into the once magnificent drive leading to the mansion, Lydia realized all was not well. Fence posts were broken or missing, with some slats lying on the ground. The garden was a mass of weeds, and the lawn had grown into a prairie of bluestem and switchgrass. Fingers of moss crept up the once-pristinely white building, and several shutters hung precipitously from their hinges.

Lydia saw no activity in the slave quarters, where many of the buildings lay in ruins or were entirely missing, and the fields beyond showed no sign of having been cultivated. The stable, or the half of it still standing, held no horses, no dog barked to signal their arrival, and not even one chicken could be seen running in the yard.

"Do you want me to wait, Ma'am?" asked her driver, his apprehension about the surroundings seeming to mirror her own. "You sure someone lives here?"

"Yes, please wait. I will go up to the door."

Lydia walked up the staircase, almost twisting an ankle on a loose step. When she got to the door she knocked, waited, knocked again. Finally she heard a voice.

"Who deah?"

Lydia was taken aback. Never had a visitor to Three Ponds Farm been treated so rudely. Thinking her daughter must have moved, leaving the vacant house open to squatters, she almost turned to leave. But she had come so far.

"Who deah ah say! Ah got me a pistol heah. Ansah me or go 'way!" Although the voice sounded familiar, she could not quite place it.

"This is Mrs. Masters," she said hopefully. "I used to live here. I am looking for my daughter."

Lydia heard at least three locks click before the door opened, revealing a tall black woman whom she could almost, but not quite, recognize.

"Mizz Lydia! Come on in."

"Tussy?" Lydia asked, stepping into an entryway that looked as neglected as the outside of the building.

"Yes'm. Ah's still heah. Din't leave de place after de wah ended lahk dem udder rapscallions."

"Are you the only one here?" Lydia asked.

"No, Ma'am. Mizz Lucy be heah too. She be a bit under de weather..."

Lydia sighed with relief. Her daughter was alive. "She's not well?" she asked.

"Well, Ma'am, no, she ain't well. Maybe you kin he'p..."

"Tussy! Who is it?" came a garbled cry from upstairs.

"Mizz Lucy, come on down. You gonna be raht suprize at who all is heah."

Lydia and Tussy listened to the commotion of Lucy stomping onto the landing and muttering all the way down the stairs. Lydia looked up to see her daughter dressed in an old flannel robe, its floral pattern nearly worn away from long use and many washings. Lucy's long chestnut hair had lost its sheen and was tangled in disarray, and her posture, previously honed to perfection at boarding school, was no more than a slouch.

As Lucy reached the first floor, Lydia rose to watch the look in her daughter's bloodshot eyes turn from mild curiosity to confusion to anger. "Mama!" the woman finally cried in recognition. "What in tarnation are you doing here?"

"Lucy, I..." Lydia began, taking a step toward her and reaching her arms out for an embrace. But the fire she saw in Lucy's hazel eyes caused her to step away. "I've been so worried about you and your family," she began.

"Worried? You worried? Isn't it a bit late for that?"

"Darling, it's never too late when family..."

"Family! What family? I have no family. My Harold—dead! My boy—gone too. I begged Harry Junior not to leave, told him he was too young, but he wouldn't listen. Both died in the war. A war over what? Your dirty slaves that you love so much?"

Lydia realized her daughter's reaction was no less than she deserved. But she still hoped to salvage their relationship, if only to some small extent. "Lucy, I'm sorry I've distressed you. Please allow me to... "

"I hold you responsible—you and all the other damned abolitionist scum! You killed my man and my boy! May you all rot in hell!"

Tussy, rushing toward her mistress, reached out to her. "Now, now. Mizz Lucy, dat be yo mama," she said. "Yo maybe bin drinkin' awready dis mo'nin? But it be so long since you seen her. You oughta at least heah what she have to say." Lucy pushed her away so violently that Tussy fell, hard, to the floor.

"Lucy," Lydia cried in horror, rushing to help Tussy to her feet.

"Get out! Get out of my house," Lucy screamed. "And take that tramp with you. She's worthless to me—I can't even afford to feed her. Get out now!"

Lydia and Tussy left. Upon their return to Natchez, Lydia rented a room at King's Tavern for herself and found a black family who would take Tussy in for the night. Lydia returned to Three Ponds Farm the next day, but her reception was no different. She stayed in Natchez for the next six days, returning to the farm every day but garnering nothing from her efforts. When she returned the seventh day, Lucy was gone, leaving the plantation deserted. Lydia realized any further effort would be futile.

She asked the driver to take her to the home where Tussy was staying, wishing to know if the woman had any plans for the future. "Ah don' know, Ma'am," Tussy told her. Ah don' think ah kin go back to de plantation, even if Mizz Lucy

*come back. But don' you worry 'bout me. Ah'll git by some way." Lydia heard no
confidence in her voice.*

*"Come with me," she said impulsively. Later, she realized she had acted not
on impulse, but on prescience.*

"Come wit you wheah?"

"To Philadelphia."

*Tussy's eyebrows spiked skyward. "Oh, Ma'am, ah couldn't do dat. Me? Live
up No'th? Ah done lived mah whole life heah."*

But in the end, Lydia booked passage for two on the steamboat to Philadelphia.

"This is a most remarkable story," Alice said. "Did your support of
abolition develop over time, or was there any one person or situation
which caused you to change your mind?"

"Over time. But one person, Ada, and one night, opened the door to
this change," Lydia said, smiling.

"Ada," Alice said, flipping through her notes, "she would be your..."

"My sister."

"And is Ada still involved in the Movement?"

"Ada passed away many years ago. But she was involved in it until the
day she died."

"And the night to which you referred?"

Lydia paused to collect her thoughts. Finally, she began. "Ada became
involved in rescuing runaway slaves through the Bennetts, the Quaker
family I mentioned earlier. I knew nothing of the Movement or her
involvement in it until the day she came to our plantation in desperation.
She needed to find a place to hide a slave who had gotten involved in
planning an insurrection. He was hoping to escape with his wife and their
children, who were our property." Lydia shuddered at the thought that she
had ever considered any person as nothing more than a possession. That
slavery had ever existed, and that she had profited from that institution,
was a disgrace she could never escape.

"And you agreed to do so?"

"Well, not immediately. But the fugitive slave catchers were right
behind them: I suppose that at the time I did not wish the trouble of
having slaves caught on my property. Nor did I wish to have anyone learn
my sister was an abolitionist."

"So you helped."

"Yes. I felt trapped, but it seemed helping them was the only thing I
could do to save my reputation. I found a place for Rufus to hide and lied
to the sheriff when he came to the house."

"Which made you complicit in the act."

"True. I hoped the whole miserable situation would be over as soon as the sheriff left. But something terrible happened." With this Lydia removed the embroidered handkerchief tucked into the sleeve of her gown.

"Please, Mrs. Masters, take all the time you need," Alice offered as Lydia, her eyes cast downward and her head shaking slowly from side to side, dabbed at the tears beginning to collect in the corners of her eyes.

"No, no. I can continue." She paused once more to collect her thoughts. "There was a terrible storm that night, but we were able to just barely hear the Bennetts' wagon arrive through the sounds of thunder and falling rain. Ada rushed to the door, and I stopped her long enough to give her one of my cloaks. She was gone only a few minutes before I heard another sound: the sound of gunfire."

"Oh my!" Alice, writing furiously, responded.

"I rushed out into the storm to search for Ada. Were it not for a bolt of lightning picking up the red color of the cloak, I probably would not have been able to find her."

"But you did find her."

"Yes. Lying on the ground. She had been shot."

Alice's eyes, which had been riveted on her notebook, suddenly shot up to Lydia's face. "So the death of your sister..."

"Oh, no," Lydia responded with a smile. "Ada did not die that night. If she had, I do not think I would ever have seen the light. I would have missed the greatest opportunity of my life."

"The opportunity of becoming active in the abolitionist movement?"

"Well, yes, but much more. I would have missed the opportunity of getting to know my sister."

"I fear I must take her back with me," said Lucretia Bennett.

"Is it safe to move her?" Lydia asked.

"No, it is not. It would be far better to be able to keep her here. But nothing is safe tonight. The sheriff has already come to our house once, and I am certain he will come again tomorrow. We need to hide her. I have a safe place at my home, and there I can give her the help she needs."

Lydia faced a dilemma. Lucretia Bennett's nursing skill had impressed her, and although Ada had not regained consciousness, her color had improved and she was breathing more easily. Mrs. Bennett's compassion and concern were obvious; Lydia was convinced Ada would receive excellent care at the Bennett's compound. Still, Lydia worried that the buckboard ride on washed-out trails would be dangerously rough. And for reasons she could not fully understand, she felt an almost overwhelming desire to keep her sister near.

"Thou must decide soon, Mrs. Masters," Lucretia urged. "If I am to take Ada home with me, I should do so in time to get her to my home before sunrise."

"Very well," Lydia responded reluctantly. Immediately Lucretia, assisted by her daughter Fanny and son Israel, who had accompanied her to Three Ponds, carefully transferred Ada' inert body to the makeshift pallet and whisked her out the door and into the night.

"Don' you worry, Ma'am," soothed Tussy, bringing Lydia a cup of hot tea. "Miz Ada gonna be all raht."

Lydia prayed that would be the case.

Lydia saddled her own mount and set out for the Bennett compound the next morning just after sunrise. The heavy rains had subsided, leaving the air cool and crisp. Were she traveling for any other reason than the one that brought her out so early, she would have relished this morning's relief from the last few weeks of oppressive heat and humidity and enjoyed the sounds of birdsong reverberating through the woods.

She was met at the Bennetts' front door by the same young woman who had accompanied her mother the previous evening. "Thou are very welcome here," Fanny said. "Thy sister is doing well."

"Thank God," responded Lydia. "May I see her?"

As Fanny led her to a room toward the back of the cabin, Lydia could not help but notice the simplicity of the furnishings and the rough whitewashed walls. No pictures hung on the walls. No knickknacks decorated the tables. But somehow, the lack of decoration imparted a sense of tranquility to the dwelling.

"Ah, thou art here already," smiled Lucretia as Lydia entered the back room. "As thou can see, thy sister is sleeping peacefully."

"She hasn't awakened?" asked Lydia.

"She has, but for just a moment," Lucretia responded. "Ada opened her eyes and favored us with a small smile. I gave her another dose of laudanum just an hour ago—I expect she will sleep for quite a while. Thou art welcome to stay with her as long as thou wish."

Lucretia explained to Lydia that she and her children had first taken Ada to a secret room in a separate building of the compound. This turned out to be a necessary precaution, as the sheriff and some of his men had come in the middle of the night to search the entire cabin and its surroundings. The men had wakened and questioned all the children, but most knew nothing about Ada's presence on the property, and those who did know had already had a great deal of experience in prevarication for the sake of abolition.

"Do you think Ada will recover fully from her injuries?"

"Ah, that is too early to tell. We must trust in God's will."

Lydia was about to respond when a faint knock at the door interrupted their conversation. Lucretia opened the door, revealing a slight woman, dressed in a flowered housecoat and wearing a white mobcap that barely concealed her long gray curls, holding a pan of steaming water. "Fanny told me you needed this," *said the woman as she stepped into the room. Something in her voice set Lydia's spine tingling.*

"I thank thee," said Lucretia, turning and gesturing toward Lydia. "My dear Nia, this is..."

But Nia was already looking closely at her daughter, her look of confusion quickly blossoming into a smile. "Lydia?" she said. "My Lydia?"

Later that day Lydia, alone with Lucretia, shared her wonder at being recognized so quickly by her mother. "Did she know I was here?" she asked.

"I cannot imagine who could have told her," Lucretia responded.

"Then how was it possible that she recognized me? My mother has not seen me since I was five years old."

"Ah, Lydia, it is not a bit surprising to me. What is true for lambs and calves and even baby chicks must surely be true for those who have been made in the likeness of God." Lucretia smiled at the confusion on Lydia's face. "Lydia," she continued, her smile becoming even broader, "a mother always knows her own."

Sighing, Alice returned to her notes. Lydia wondered whether the sigh was the result of relief at learning of Ada's survival or disappointment because her article would have had more impact had Ada died. But Lydia continued her story.

"Lucretia Bennett, our Quaker neighbor, saved Ada's life that night, and together we nursed her back to life. Ada was seriously injured, and her convalescence was long and painful, but it was during those weeks of her recovery that, little by little, I began to understand her passion for the Movement. And later, when our mother joined us to live on the plantation, I saw in both of them what I had been seeking all my life."

"And what had you been seeking, Mrs. Masters?"

"Oh, I do not quite know how to describe it. Peace, perhaps. The kind of peace I observed in Ada and in our mother, and in Lucretia Bennett as well. Perhaps some new, useful direction in my life. Or maybe I was merely looking for the happiness that comes from discovering the right thing to do and beginning to do it."

Alice nodded as she scratched quick notes into her notebook. "Do you know what became of the slaves you helped that night?" she asked, referencing her notes once more.

"Rufus and Queenie and their family?" Lydia offered. "We never found out. We certainly hoped they managed to escape to British North America—what they now call Canada. We never learned who shot Ada and never had any legal action taken against us. For weeks we all waited with great apprehension for the arrival of the sheriff, but he never came."

"Did you and your sister then begin working together to help free the slaves?"

"Yes, eventually. We worked together until our mother died. After her death we both continued our work toward abolition, but separately. Once Mama passed, Ada chose to pursue a path she had dreamed about for most of her life— becoming a nun."

They stood, hands loosely clasped before them, eyes cast down at the fresh grave set several yards distant from the false grave Lydia had for many years believed held her mother's body. The tiny cemetery was ablaze this early autumn day, the leaves of the red maples, brilliant in the bright sunlight, contrasting sharply with the deep, leathery green of the southern magnolias. Ada picked what remained of their cup-shaped blossoms, their brilliant white contrasting sharply with the shrubs' green color, and gently placed the bouquet on the newly carved granite headstone.

"You won't change your mind?" asked Lydia, placing an arm around her sister's slim waist.

"About returning to the Ursulines? No."

"But you can do so much good here."

"I can do much good there as well—teaching the children. Someday everyone will understand what a cruel abomination slavery is, and the children will need the knowledge and skills I teach them to take their place in the new world they will be entering as free men and women."

Lydia tilted her head to one side and tried, with little hope of succeeding, to see if her most ingratiating smile, which had worked so well on so many others, would work on her sister. "But Finn and Maggie must leave next week, and I will be here all alone!" The small local band of Natchez and Cherokee had been notified that under the terms of the Indian Removal Act they would soon be moved from their compound to Indian Territory west of the Mississippi River. Finn, whose half-white ancestry had exempted him from the law, had chosen to accompany Ama, and Maggie, as a faithful wife and daughter-in-law, would be moving with them. Lydia had sadly resigned herself to the thought that she might never see them again.

"Now, Lydia. You are the most resourceful, independent person I know. You will be fine! Besides, Lucretia and Bartholomew will need you more than ever. You will be so busy you will not even know I am gone."

"That could never happen," insisted Lydia, thinking how unlikely this conversation would have been only a few years earlier. She would certainly miss Ada, but was pleased her sister would finally achieve the goal she'd chosen long before. "Lucretia did a beautiful job yesterday, did she not?" she said, realizing there really was nothing more she could, or should, say to persuade Ada to stay.

"Yes. The simplicity of the service would have suited Mama." The funeral, following Quaker custom, had begun with silent meditation. After a short time, Lucretia invited all in attendance to continue meditating, but to feel free to

contribute a memory, a reading, a prayer or a song at any point they chose. Tussy had been the first to respond, leading the small group in a slow, soulful chorus of "Amazing Grace." Ama, encouraged by Ada, had played a short funerary tattoo on a small deerskin drum, while Finn accompanied her on a gourd rattle, its soft patter sounding much like an early spring rain.

At the end of the ceremony, Lucretia recited the twenty-third psalm, speaking its first words, "The Lord is my shepherd," so softly that all present needed to strain to hear her voice. But as she read, her voice rose in both tone and conviction, and by the time she reached the psalm's final passage, "I will dwell in the house of the Lord forever," all present were most certainly filled with confidence that Nia must, even now, be sitting at the feet of her Lord.

"I wish we would have had greater opportunity to get to know Mama," Lydia said.

"But we did get to know her, if only on those days when she was capable of conversation. We certainly learned about her gentleness, her kindness."

"And her strength," added Lydia. "Did you know she traveled down the Mississippi River on a flatboat when she was only a girl of sixteen?"

"No!"

"She spoke of the beauty of the water and the shore, and of the creatures she observed on its banks and in the air. The alligators impressed her the most, since she had never seen such a strange animal in Philadelphia. She must have been very brave to embark on so long a journey alone."

"She may have been escaping," suggested Ada with a smile. "Did she ever speak to you of her papa?"

"No. Never."

"She told me a funny story once when she was having an exceptionally good day and we were able to speak together for nearly an hour. Apparently, she did not get on very well with our grandmother."

"Is that so? Perhaps that explains the mother-daughter conflicts that seem to plague our family," Lydia grinned.

"Perhaps. On the day she spoke about, Mama had sneaked away to go swimming, wearing only her shift, with some of the boys in the neighborhood. When her mother found out, she insisted our grandfather give her a sound beating."

"So, it appears Grandmother was a great deal like Hetty Campbell: strict and pitiless. Poor Mama!"

"But Mama convinced her father to play out a little subterfuge they had developed, in which he soundly beat the mattress while she screamed in counterfeit pain."

"So Mama was a rebel," Lydia laughed. "Good for her!"

"And rather accomplished at deception as well."

Lydia laughed even harder. Ada's story had given her even more insight into Nia's personality. Together, she and Ada were discovering more and more about the woman who had given birth to them.

"Did Ada ever become a nun?" asked Alice.

"Yes. She became Sister Marie Dominique. I was allowed to attend her Perpetual Profession of Vows, but after that could see her only twice a year. The Ursulines are a cloistered order, as you probably know, so their contact with the outside world is limited. But I know she was happy there."

"Well," Alice said, smiling as she finished the note she was writing with a flourish and closed her notebook. "Thank you for sharing all your experiences with me. Yours is certainly an amazing story."

"I cannot see how it is amazing," Lydia responded, genuinely confused.

"Why, Mrs. Masters, going from being the mistress of a cotton plantation to one of the most famous abolitionists of the century! I cannot think of any other woman I have interviewed, or any other person, actually, who was able to change the course of her life so entirely." Lydia wondered whether this young woman's flattery was truly genuine or merely a result of her training in journalism. But she did sense sincere admiration in the way Alice was observing her. "To what do you attribute your remarkable transformation?"

Lydia had never considered herself worthy of high praise. She knew that, in her life, she had been vain.

She had been selfish.

She had been deceitful.

She had been cruel.

And yet, there was some truth to Alice's comment. She had made a significant transformation in her life, had become, in many ways, a different person. This transformation had certainly begun when she'd first seen her sister lying in the rain and felt a loss deeper and more powerful than any she'd previously experienced. But it hadn't happened immediately. Getting to know Maggie, Finn, and Ama had helped. These three people, an immigrant indentured servant, a half-breed, and a Natchez squaw, had found a way to make a life together.

The Bennetts, and later her aunts in Philadelphia, had certainly made an impression as well. Here were people who had the courage and passion to jeopardize everything they had to help others reach their promised land.

And of course, there was Ada. During her sister's long convalescence and beyond, Lydia and Ada had spent a great deal of time debating the issue that so separated them. With time, Lydia had begun to see the wisdom and the truth in Ada's arguments, as well as the passion and the courage her sister expressed. Before long, they were speaking less about abolition and more about themselves: the experiences which had made them who they were, their triumphs, their disappointments, their hopes for the future. Before either of them could realize what was happening, they had become sisters in every sense of the word.

But there was one other person at the center of all their lives whose quiet, gentle presence had done more to turn this disparate group of individuals into a family. She was the only person who could have accomplished this. Suddenly the answer to Alice's question was evident. Why, she had known it all along!

"It is not so remarkable," she said, smiling broadly. "And, in some ways, it was not really a transformation at all. I already possessed everything I required to become the person I wished and needed to become."

"How so?" asked Alice.

"Is it not obvious?" asked Lydia. "I only needed to realize, to my astonishment and joy, that I am truly my mother's daughter."

About the Author

Thirty-eight years of teaching English and a great interest in history led Rebecca Thaddeus to the conviction that she could write historical fiction. Her first novel, *One Amber Bead*, was set during World War II, while *My Mother's Daughter* is set in early 19th Century Mississippi. Rebecca lives on a century-old farm in northern Michigan and is currently working on her third novel.

You can find Rebecca Thaddeus on Facebook, or visit her blog at oneamberblog.blogspot.com. You can also search for her books on the Plain View Press website: http://plainviewpress.net or on Amazon.com.

Acknowledgements

No writer writes alone. This page gives me the opportunity to thank all those whose knowledge or support contributed to the creation of *My Mother's Daughter*.

Family comes first: Thank you Thad Stolarek for being my ever-faithful computer guru and Becky Maholland for being my most dedicated cheerleader. Thanks to Becky's family, Mike, Isaac, Ada and Emilia, for bringing love and joy into my life, to Chris Ebey, for coming back into my life, and to Nancy Kaszyca, for being my forever friend.

Thank you to my faithful writers' group, whose input helped direct the path my story would take: Kelly Thompson, Carole Jones, Julia Reges and Elaine McCullough. And thank you to my Book Club, who helped me take My Mother's Daughter from draft to book form: Jeanette Fleury, Alice Bandstra, Maryanne Heidemann, Peggy Peterson, Michelle Christner, Barb Ross, and Susan Fogarty.

Thank you to the staff at the Judge George W. Armstrong Library, whose extraordinary knowledge and willingness to help made my research much more meaningful, and to Mimi Miller and Joan M. McLemore, who added more to my understanding of life in 19th Century Mississippi. Also, thank you to the staff at the Natchez Trace who helped me appreciate the magic and the mystery of that amazing thoroughfare, and to Dane Johnson for providing architectural background information. Thank you, Mary Loesch, for sharing your black walnut expertise, and Tirzah Price, for your sound advice.

Thank you to all the writers whose work has thrilled, delighted, provoked, saddened, informed, and enlightened me, and a special thank you to Pam Knight for her expertise and her support of *My Mother's Daughter*.

CPSIA information can be obtained
at www.ICGtesting.com
Printed in the USA
BVHW091939011118
531828BV00001B/1/P